OCEANSIDE PUBLIC LIBRARY
3 1232 00195 0072

Books by ROBERT SILVERBERG

Valentine Pontifex
Lord of Darkness
World of a Thousand Colors
Majipoor Chronicles
Lord Valentine's Castle
Dying Inside
The Book of Skulls
The Stochastic Man
Nightwings
Shadrach in the Furnace

Books Edited by ROBERT SILVERBERG
WITH MARTIN H. GREENBERG

The Arbor House Treasury of Science Fiction Masterpieces
The Arbor House Treasury of Modern Science Fiction
The Arbor House Treasury of Great Science Fiction Short Novels

Other Books Edited by MARTIN H. GREENBERG

The Arbor House Celebrity Book of the Greatest Stories Ever Told
(with Charles G. Waugh)
The Arbor House Treasury of Great Western Stories
(with Bill Pronzini)
The Arbor House Celebrity Book of Horror Stories
(with Charles G. Waugh)
Tomorrow, Inc.—SF Stories about Big Business
Run to Starlight: Sports through Science Fiction

The
Fantasy
Hall of Fame

The Fantasy Hall of Fame

Compiled by ROBERT SILVERBERG
and MARTIN H. GREENBERG

ARBOR HOUSE
New York

Library of Congress Catalogue Card Number: 83-48721

ISBN: 0-87795-521-2

Manufactured in the United States of America

10 9 8 7 6 5 4 3 2 1

This book is printed on acid free paper. The paper in this book meets the guidelines for permanence and durability of the Committee on Production Guidelines for Book Longevity of the Council on Library Resources.

Contents

Introduction

THE PHENOMENON of the science fiction convention—a gathering of readers and writers for the mutual exchange of ideas and general social amusement—goes back nearly fifty years. Originally they were small-scale events held in obscure meeting rooms, but currently the annual World Science Fiction Convention is a major happening with six or seven thousand attendees, and most of the best-known writers are present and remarkably accessible to their readers. It is at the World Science Fiction Convention that the Hugo award has been presented each year since 1953, honoring the best stories of the year as determined by vote of the convention's members.

When the writers of science fiction founded their own professional organization, the Science Fiction Writers of America, in 1965, a second award structure developed: the annual Nebula award, chosen by vote of the writers themselves and presented at a formal meeting that has taken on many of the aspects of a full-scale convention, though it is limited only to those who are professionally involved with science fiction. When the Science Fiction Writers of America was a few years old, sentiment developed for a kind of retroactive Nebula award to honor great stories that had been published prior to SFWA's founding; and so the members were polled for nominations for a Science Fiction Hall of Fame, to include the best s-f stories of the preNebula period. It was my privilege to edit the volume that contained the winning short stories (*The Science Fiction Hall of Fame,* Volume One, Doubleday & Co., 1970.) A later Hall of Fame volume, edited by Ben Bova, contained the winning stories of novelette and novella length, which had intentionally been excluded from the first book.

And now, following the example of the science fiction world, the readers of fantasy fiction have begun holding their own conventions, presenting their own annual awards, and—inevitably—creating their own Hall of Fame to celebrate the classic stories of that genre.

I would not care to get entangled in any extensive effort to draw definitional boundaries between science fiction and fantasy. I have my own rough idea of the differences between the two fields, which is operationally useful in an abstract sort of way, but I know (and so does everyone else who has tried to draw these distinctions) that even the best definition is likely to break down into illogicality and inconsistency under close examination. The furthest I will venture is to say that science fiction is that branch of fantasy which generally deals in extrapolations of the consequences of technological development, and which attempts to stick fairly rigorously to known or theoretically possible scientific concepts. Fantasy is a much broader field of fiction that is less firmly bound to the tyranny of fact, and for the purposes of any given story is permitted to assume nearly any idea as plausible, though it is desirable for the author to elicit a suspension of disbelief through the plausible development of a basically unlikely notion. Thus I tend to think of stories about spaceships, robots, computers and the like as science fiction, and of stories about vampires, werewolves, angels and such as fantasy. But I can illustrate the impossibility of making any of these definitions stick for long by telling you that I myself recently wrote a story ("Basileus") in which a computer was used to generate angels. Fantasy? Science fiction?

Be that as it may, the readers of fantasy seem to have a

fairly clear idea most of the time of what they consider fantasy to be, and at the annual conventions that they have held since 1975 they have presented the World Fantasy Award—a statuette of the fantasy master H. P. Lovecraft—to recognize the year's outstanding work in their field. These award-winning stories have been collected in a series of anthologies.

And now the members of the World Fantasy Conventions of 1981 and 1982 have voted on a Fantasy Hall of Fame, which, like the corresponding science fiction volume, takes in those masterpieces that were published before the inception of their annual award program. Because of my involvement in developing and creating the Hall of Fame volumes for the Science Fiction Writers of America, I was asked—along with my invaluable and indefatigable collaborator in many anthologies, Martin H. Greenberg—to assemble the book for publication (on Halloween, the traditional time for holding the World Fantasy Convention!). Ballots were distributed asking the convention members to name their favorites, elaborate tabulation processes were performed, and here at last we have, in one volume, the finest stories of all time.

The finest of all time? A presumptuous statement, perhaps—considering that fantasy is perhaps the oldest of all the branches of imaginative literature, that it goes back at least as far as the Gilgamesh legend of Mesopotamia and perhaps back to the tales that were told in the caves of Altamira and Lascaux. But the Cro-Magnon fantasy stories, alas, are not at the moment accessible to us, and for the purposes of this volume we also thought it best to ignore such things as classical mythology, *Grimm's Fairy Tales, A Thousand and One Nights* and such other works which are undeniably masterpieces of fantasy but which were not quite what everyone had in mind for this particular book. What we have, really, is the Hall of Fame of *modern* fantasy, a specialized field of fiction that has certain special delights well known to all its aficionados. It is those aficionados who chose these stories: a panel of hundreds of experts, to whom ghosts and ghouls and things that go bump in the night are just as familiar as computers and robots, and are, perhaps, somewhat more plausible.

—Robert Silverberg
Oakland, California
May 1, 1983

The Masque of the Red Death

by EDGAR ALLAN POE

THE "RED DEATH" has long devastated the country. No pestilence had ever been so fatal, or so hideous. Blood was its Avatar and its seal—the redness and the horror of blood. There were sharp pains, and sudden dizziness, and then profuse bleeding at the pores, with dissolution. The scarlet stains upon the body and especially upon the face of the victim, were the pest ban which shut him out from the aid and from the sympathy of his fellow-men. And the whole seizure, progress, and termination of the disease, were the incidents of half an hour.

But the Prince Prospero was happy and dauntless and sagacious. When his dominions were half depopulated, he summoned to his presence a thousand hale and light-hearted friends from among the knights and dames of his court, and with these retired to the deep seclusion of one of his castellated abbeys. This was an extensive and magnificent structure, the creation of the prince's own eccentric yet august taste. A strong and lofty wall girdled it in. This wall had gates of iron. The courtiers, having entered, brought furnaces and massy hammers and welded the bolts. They resolved to leave means neither of ingress nor egress to the sudden impulses of despair or of frenzy from within. The abbey was amply provisioned. With such precautions the courtiers might bid defiance to contagion. The external world would take care of itself. In the meantime it was folly to grieve, or to think. The prince had provided all the appliances of pleasure. There were buffoons, there were improvisatori, there were ballet-dancers, there were musicians, there was Beauty, there was wine. All these and security were within. Without was the 'Red Death.'

It was toward the close of the fifth or sixth month of his seclusion, and while the pestilence raged most furiously abroad, that the Prince Prospero entertained his thousand friends, at a masked ball of the most unusual magnificence.

It was a voluptuous scene, that masquerade. But first let me tell of the rooms in which it was held. There were seven—an imperial suite. In many palaces, however, such suites form a long and straight vista, while the folding doors slide back nearly to the walls on either hand, so that the view of the whole extent is scarcely impeded. Here the case was very different; as might have been expected from the duke's love of the *bizarre.* The apartments were so irregularly disposed that the vision embraced but little more than one at a time. There was a sharp turn at every twenty or thirty yards, and at each turn a novel effect. To the right and left, in the middle of each wall, a tall and narrow Gothic window looked out upon a closed corridor which pursued the windings of the suite. These windows were of stained glass whose color varied in accordance with the prevailing hue of the decorations of the chamber into which it opened. That at the eastern extremity was hung, for example, in blue—and vividly blue were its windows. The second chamber was purple in its ornaments and tapestries, and here the panes were purple. The third was green throughout, and so were the casements. The fourth was furnished and lighted with orange—the fifth with white—the sixth with violet. The seventh apartment was closely shrouded in black velvet tapestries that hung all over the ceiling and down the walls, falling in heavy folds upon a carpet of the same material and hue. But in the chamber only, the color of the windows failed to correspond with the decorations. The panes here were scarlet—a deep blood color. Now in no one of the seven apartments was there any lamp or candelabrum, amid the profusion of golden ornaments that lay scattered to and fro or depended from the roof. There was no light of any kind emanating from lamp or candle within the suite of chambers. But in the corridors that followed the suite, there stood, opposite to each window, a heavy tripod, bearing a brazier of fire, that projected its rays through the tinted glass and so glaringly illumined the room. And thus were produced a multitude of gaudy and fantastic appearances. But in the western or black chamber the effect of the fire-light that streamed upon the dark hangings through the blood-tinted panes was ghastly in the extreme, and produced so wild a look upon the countenances of those who entered, that there were few of the company bold enough to set foot within its precincts at all.

It was in this apartment, also, that there stood against the western wall, a gigantic clock of ebony. Its pendulum swung to and fro with a dull, heavy, monotonous clang; and when the minute-hand made the circuit of the face, and the hour was to be stricken, there came from the brazen lungs of the clock, a sound which was clear and loud and deep and exceedingly musical, but of so peculiar a note and emphasis that, at each lapse of an hour, the musicians of the orchestra were constrained to pause, momentarily, in their performance, to hearken to the sound; and thus the waltzers perforce ceased their evolutions; and there was a brief disconcert of the whole gay company; and, while the chimes of the clock yet rang, it was observed that the giddiest grew pale, and the more aged and sedate passed their hands over their brows as if in confused revery or meditation. But when the echoes had fully ceased, a light laughter at once pervaded the assembly; the musicians looked at each other and smiled as if at their own nervousness and folly, and made whispering vows, each to the other, that the next chiming of the clock should produce in them no similar emotion; and then, after the lapse of sixty minutes (which embrace three thousand and six hundred seconds of the Time that flies), there came yet another chiming of the clock, and then were the same disconcert and tremulousness and meditation as before.

But, in spite of these things, it was a gay and magnificent revel. The tastes of the duke were peculiar. He had a fine eye for colors and effects. He disregarded the *decora* of mere fashion. His plans were bold and fiery, and his conceptions glowed with barbaric luster. There are some who would have thought him mad. His followers felt that he was not. It was necessary to hear and see and touch him to be *sure* that he was not.

He had directed, in great part, the movable embellishments of the seven chambers, upon occasion of this great *fête;* and it was his own guiding taste which had given character to the masqueraders. Be sure they were grotesque. There were much glare and glitter and piquancy and phantasm—much of what has been since seen in "Hernani." There were arabesque figures with unsuited limbs and appointments. There were delirious fancies such as the madman fashions. There were much of the beautiful, much of the wanton, much of the *bizarre,* something of the terrible, and not a little of that which might have excited disgust. To and fro in the seven chambers there stalked, in fact, a multitude of dreams. And these—the dreams—writhed in and about, taking hue from the rooms, and causing the wild music of the orchestra to seem as the echo of their steps. And, anon, there strikes the ebony clock which stands in the hall of the velvet. And then, for a moment, all is still, and all is silent save the voice of the clock. The dreams are stiff-frozen as they stand. But the echoes of the chime die away—they have endured but an instant—and a light, half-subdued laughter floats after them as they depart. And now again the music swells, and the dreams live, and writhe to and fro more merrily than ever, taking hue from the many-tinted windows through which stream the rays from the tripods. But to the chamber which lies most westwardly of the seven there are now none of the maskers who venture; for the night is waning away; and there flows a ruddier light through the blood-colored panes; and the blackness of the sable drapery appals; and to him whose foot falls upon the sable carpet, there comes from the near clock of ebony a muffled peal more solemnly emphatic than any which reaches *their* ears who indulge in the more remote gaieties of the other apartments.

But these other apartments were densely crowded, and in them beat feverishly the heart of life. And the revel went whirlingly on, until at length there commenced the sounding of midnight upon the clock. And then the music ceased, as I have told; and the evolutions of the waltzers were quieted; and there was an uneasy cessation of all things as before. But now there were twelve strokes to be sounded by the bell of the clock; and thus it happened, perhaps that more of thought crept, with more of time, into the meditations of the thoughtful among those who revelled. And thus, too, it happened, perhaps, that before the last echoes of the last chime had utterly sunk into silence, there were many individuals in the crowd who had found leisure to become aware of the presence of a masked figure which had arrested the attention of no single individual before. And the rumour of this new presence having spread itself whisperingly around, there arose at length from the whole company a buzz, or murmur, expressive of disapprobation and surprise—then, finally, of terror, of horror, and of disgust.

In an assembly of phantasms such as I have painted, it may well be supposed that no ordinary appearance could have excited such sensation. In truth the masquerade license of the night was nearly unlimited; but the figure in question had out-Heroded Herod, and gone beyond the bounds of even the prince's indefinite decorum. There are chords in the hearts of the most reckless which cannot be touched without emotion. Even with the utterly lost, to whom life and death are equally jests, there are matters of which no jest can be made. The whole company, indeed, seemed now deeply to feel that in the costume and bearing of the stranger neither wit nor propriety existed. The figure was tall and gaunt, and shrouded from head to foot in the habiliments of the grave. The mask which concealed the visage was made so nearly to resemble the countenance of a stiffened corpse that the closest scrutiny must have had difficulty in detecting the cheat. And yet all this might have been endured, if not approved, by the mad revellers around. But the mummer had gone so far as to assume the type of the Red Death. His vesture was dabbled in *blood*—and his broad brow, with all the features of the face, was besprinkled with the scarlet horror.

When the eyes of Prince Prospero fell upon this spectral image (which, with a slow and solemn movement, as if more fully to sustain its *rôle,* stalked to and fro among the waltzers) he was seen to be convulsed, in the first moment with a strong shudder either of terror or distaste; but, in the next, his brow reddened with rage.

"Who dares"—he demanded hoarsely of the courtiers who stood near him—"who dares insult us with this blasphemous mockery? Seize him and unmask him—that we may know whom we have to hang, at sunrise, from the battlements!"

It was in the eastern or blue chamber in which stood the Prince Prospero as he uttered these words. They rang throughout the seven rooms loudly and clearly, for the prince was a bold and robust man, and the music had become hushed at the waving of his hand.

It was in the blue room where stood the prince, with a group of pale courtiers by his side. At first, as he spoke, there was a slight rushing movement of this group in the direction of the intruder, who, at the moment, was also near at hand, and now, with deliberate and stately step, made closer approach to the speaker. But from a certain nameless awe with which the mad assumptions of the mummer had inspired the whole party, there were found none who put forth hand to seize him; so that, unimpeded, he passed within a yard of the prince's person; and, while the vast assembly, as if with one impulse, shrank from the centers of the rooms to the walls, he made his way uninterruptedly, but with the same solemn and measured step which had distinguished him from the first, through the blue chamber to the purple—through the purple to the green—through the green to the orange—through this again to the white—and even thence to the violet, ere a decided movement had been made to arrest him. It was then, however, that the Prince Prospero, maddening with rage and the shame of his own momentary cowardice, rushed hurriedly through the six chambers, while none followed him on account of a deadly terror that had seized upon all. He bore aloft a drawn dagger, and had approached, in rapid impetuosity, to within three or four feet of the retreating figure, when the latter, having attained the extremity of the velvet apartment, turned suddenly and confronted his pursuer. There was a sharp cry—and the dagger dropped gleaming upon the sable carpet, upon which, instantly afterward, fell prostrate in death the Prince Prospero. Then, summoning the wild courage of despair, a throng of the revellers at once threw themselves into the black apartment, and, seizing the mummer, whose tall figure stood erect and motionless within the shadow of the ebony clock, grasped in unutterable horror at finding the grave cerements and corpse-like mask, which they handled with so violent a rudeness, untenanted by any tangible form.

And now was acknowledged the presence of the Red Death. He had come like a thief in the night. And one by one dropped the revellers in the blood-bedewed halls of their revel, and died each in the despairing posture of his fall. And the life of the ebony clock went out with that of the last of the gay. And the flames of the tripods expired. And Darkness and Decay and the Red Death held illimitable dominion over all.

An Inhabitant of Carcosa

by AMBROSE BIERCE

For there be divers sorts of death—some wherein the body remaineth; and in some it vanisheth quite away with the spirit. This commonly occurreth only in solitude (such is God's will) and, none seeing the end, we say the man is lost, or gone on a long journey—which indeed he hath; but sometimes it hath happened in sight of many, as abundant testimony showeth. In one kind of death the spirit also dieth, and this it hath been known to do while yet the body was in vigor for many years. Sometimes, as is veritably attested, it dieth with the body, but after a season it raised up again in that place where the body did decay.

PONDERING THESE words of Hali (whom God rest) and questioning their full meaning, as one who, having an intimation, yet doubts if there be not something behind, other than that which he has discerned, I noted not whither I had strayed until a sudden chill wind striking my face revived in me a sense of my surroundings. I observed with astonishment that everything seemed unfamiliar. On every side of me stretched a bleak and desolate expanse of plain, covered with a tall overgrowth of sere grass, which rustled and whistled in the autumn wind with heaven knows what mysterious and disquieting suggestion. Protruded at long intervals above it, stood strangely shaped and somber-colored rocks, which seemed to have an understanding with one another and to exchange looks of uncomfortable significance, as if they had reared their heads to watch the issue of some forseen event. A few blasted trees here and there appeared as leaders in this malevolent conspiracy of silent expectation.

The day, I thought, must be far advanced, though the sun was invisible; and although sensible that the air was raw and chill my consciousness of that fact was rather mental than physical—I had no feeling of discomfort. Over all the dismal landscape a canopy of low, lead-colored clouds hung like a visible curse. In all this here were a menace and a portent—a hint of evil, an intimation of doom. Bird, beast, or insect there was none. The wind sighed in the bare branches of the dead trees and the gray grass bent to whisper its dread secret to the earth; but no other sound nor motion broke the awful response of that dismal place.

I observed in the herbage a number of weather-worn stones, evidently shaped with tools. They were broken, covered with moss and half sunken in the earth. Some lay prostrate, some leaned at various angles, none was vertical. They were obviously headstones of graves, though the graves themselves no longer existed as either mounds or depressions; the years had leveled all. Scattered here and there, more massive blocks showed where some pompous tomb or ambitious monument had once flung its feeble defiance at oblivion. So old seemed these relics, these vestiges of vanity and memorials of affection and piety, so battered and worn and stained—so neglected, deserted, forgotten the place, that I could not help thinking myself the discoverer of the burial-ground of a prehistoric race of men whose very name was long extinct.

Filled with these reflections, I was for some time heedless of the sequence of my own experiences, but soon I thought, "How came I hither?" A moment's reflection seemed to make this all clear and explain at the same time, though in a disquieting way, the singular character with which my fancy invested all that I saw or heard. I was ill. I remembered now that I had been prostrated by a sudden fever, and that my family had told me that in my periods of delirium I had constantly cried out for liberty and air, and had been held in bed to prevent my escape out-of-doors. Now I had eluded the vigilance of my attendants and had wandered hither to—to where? I could not conjecture. Clearly I was at a considerable distance from the city where I dwelt—the ancient and famous city of Carcosa.

No signs of human life were anywhere visible nor audible; no rising smoke, no watchdog's bark, no lowing of cattle, no shouts of children at play—nothing but that dismal burial-place, with its air of mystery and dread, due to my own disordered brain. Was I not becoming again delirious, these beyond human aid? Was it not indeed *all* an illusion of my madness? I called aloud the names of my wives and sons, reached out my hands in search of theirs, even as I walked among the crumbling stones and in the withered grass.

A noise behind me caused me to turn about. A wild animal—a lynx—was approaching. The thought came to me: If I break down here in the desert—if the fever return and I fail, this beast will be at my throat. I sprang toward it, shouting. It trotted tranquilly by within a hand's breadth of me and disappeared behind a rock.

A moment later a man's head appeared to rise out of the ground a short distant away. He was ascending the farther slope of a low hill whose crest was hardly to be distinguished from the general level. His whole figure soon came into view against the background of gray cloud. He was half naked, half clad in skins. His hair was unkempt, his beard long and ragged.

In one hand he carried a bow and arrow; the other held a blazing torch with a long trail of black smoke. He walked slowly and with caution, as if he feared falling into some open grave concealed by the tall grass. This strange apparition surprised but did not alarm, and taking such a course as to intercept him with the familiar salutation, "God keep you."

He gave no heed, nor did he arrest his pace.

"Good stranger," I continued, "I am ill and lost. Direct me, I beseech you, to Carcosa."

The man broke into a barbarous chant in an unknown tongue, passing on and away.

An owl on the branch of a decayed tree hooted dismally and was answered by another in the distance. Looking upward, I saw through a sudden rift in the clouds Aldebaran and the Hyades! In all this there was a hint of night—the lynx, the man with the torch, the owl. Yet I saw—I saw even the stars in absence of darkness. I saw, but was apparently not seen nor heard. Under what awful spell did I exist.

I seated myself at the root of a great tree, seriously to consider what it were best to do. That I was mad I could no longer doubt, yet recognized a ground of doubt in the conviction. Of fever I had no trace. I had, withal, a sense of exhilaration and vigor altogether unknown to me—a feeling of mental and physical exaltation. My senses seemed all alert; I could feel the air as a ponderous substance; I could hear the silence.

A great root of the giant tree whose trunk I leaned as I sat held inclosed in its grasp a slab of stone, a part of which protruded into a recess formed by another root. The stone was thus partly protected from the weather, though greatly decomposed. Its edges were worn round, its corners eaten away, its surface deeply furrowed and scaled. Glittering particles of mica were visible in the earth about it—vestiges of its decomposition. This stone had apparently marked the grave out of which the tree had sprung ages ago. The tree's exacting roots had robbed the grave and made the stone a prisoner.

A sudden wind pushed some dry leaves and twigs from the

uppermost face of the stone; I saw the low-relief letters of an inscription and bent to read it. God in Heaven! *my* name! in full!—the date of *my* birth!—the date of *my* death!

A level shaft of light illuminated the whole side of the tree as I sprang to my feet in terror. The sun was rising in the rosy east. I stood between the tree and his broad red disk—no shadow darkened the trunk!

A chorus of howling wolves saluted the dawn. I saw them sitting on their haunches, singly and in groups, on the summits of irregular mounds and tumuli filling a half of my desert prospect and extending to the horizon. And then I knew that these were ruins of the ancient and famous city of Carcosa.

Such are the facts imparted to the medium Bayrolles by the spirit Hoseib Alar Robardin.

The Sword of Welleran

by LORD DUNSANY

WHERE THE GREAT plain of Tarphet runs up, as the sea in estuaries, among the Cyresian mountains, there stood long since the city of Merimna well-nigh among the shadows of the crags. I have never seen a city in the world so beautiful as Merimna seemed to me when I first dreamed of it. It was a marvel of spires and figures of bronze, and marble fountains, and trophies of fabulous wars, and broad streets given over wholly to the Beautiful. Right through the center of the city there went an avenue fifty strides in width, and along each side of it stood likenesses in bronze of the Kings of all the countries that the people of Merimna had ever known. At the end of that avenue was a colossal chariot with three bronze horses driven by the winged figure of Fame, and behind her in the chariot the huge form of Welleran, Merimna's ancient hero, standing with extended sword. So urgent was the mien and attitude of Fame, and so swift the pose of the horses, that you had sworn that the chariot was instantly upon you, and that its dust already veiled the faces of the Kings. And in the city was a mighty hall wherein were stored the trophies of Merimna's heroes. Sculptured it was and domed, the glory of the art of masons a long while dead, and on the summit of the dome the image of Rollory sat gazing across the Cyresian mountains toward the wide lands beyond, the lands that knew his sword. And beside Rollory, like an old nurse, the figure of Victory sat, hammering into a golden wreath of laurels for his head the crowns of fallen Kings.

Such was Merimna, a city of sculptured Victories and warriors of bronze. Yet in the time of which I write the art of war had been forgotten in Merimna, and the people almost slept. To and fro and up and down they would walk through the marble streets, gazing at memorials of the things achieved by their country's swords in the hands of those that long ago had loved Merimna well. Almost they slept, and dreamed of Welleran, Soorenard, Mommolek, Rollory, Akanax, and young Iraine. Of the lands beyond the mountains that lay all round about them they knew nothing, save that they were the theater of the terrible deeds of Welleran, that he had done with his sword. Long since these lands had fallen back into the possession of the nations that had been scourged by Merimna's armies. Nothing now remained to Merimna's men save their inviolate city and the glory of the remembrance of their ancient fame. At night they would place sentinels far out in the desert, but these always slept at their posts dreaming of Rollory, and three times every night a guard would march around the city clad in purple, bearing lights and singing songs of Welleran. Always the guard went unarmed, but as the sound of their song went echoing across the plain towards the looming mountains, the desert robbers would hear the name of Welleran and steal away to their haunts. Often dawn would come across the plain, shimmering marvellously upon Merimna's spires, abashing all the stars, and find the guard still singing songs of Welleran, and would change the color of their purple robes and pale the lights they bore. But the guard would go back leaving the ramparts safe, and one by one the sentinels in the plain would awake from dreaming of Rollory and shuffle back into the city quite cold. Then something of the menace would pass away from the faces of the Cyresian mountains, that from the north and the west and the south lowered upon Merimna, and clear in the morning the statues and the pillars would arise in the old inviolate city. You would wonder that an unarmed guard and sentinels that slept could defend a city that was stored with all the glories of art, that was rich in gold and bronze, a haughty city that had erst oppressed its neighbors, whose people had forgotten the art of war. Now this is the reason that, though all her other lands had long been taken from her, Merimna's city was safe. A strange thing was believed or feared by the fierce tribes beyond the mountains, and it was credited among them that at certain stations round Merimna's ramparts there still rode Welleran, Soorenard, Mommolek, Rollory, Akanax, and young Iraine. Yet it was close on a hundred years since Iraine, the youngest of Merimna's heroes, fought his last battle with the tribes.

Sometimes indeed there arose among the tribes young men who doubted and said: "How may a man for ever escape death?"

But graver men answered them: "Hear us, ye whose wisdom has discerned so much, and discern for us how a man may escape death when two score horsemen assail him with their swords, all of them sworn to kill him, and all of them sworn upon their country's gods; as often Welleran hath. Or discern for us how two men alone may enter a walled city by night, and bring away from it that city's King, as did Soorenard and Mommolek. Surely men that have escaped so many swords and so many sleety arrows shall escape the years and Time."

And the young men were humbled and became silent. Still, the suspicion grew. And often when the sun set on the Cyresian mountains, men in Merimna discerned the forms of savage tribesmen black against the light, peering towards the city.

All knew in Merimna that the figures round the ramparts were only statues of stone, yet even there a hope lingered among a few that some day their old heroes would come again, for certainly none had ever seen them die. Now it had been the wont of these six warriors of old, as each received his last wound and knew it to be mortal, to ride away to a certain deep ravine and cast his body in, as somewhere I have read great elephants do, hiding their bones away from lesser beasts. It was a ravine steep and narrow even at the ends, a great cleft into which no man could come by any path. There rode Welleran alone, panting hard; and there later rode Soorenard and Mommolek, Mommolek with a mortal wound upon him not to return, but Soorenard was unwounded and rode back alone from leaving his dear friend resting among the mighty bones of Welleran. And there rode Soorenard, when his day was come, with Rollory and Akanax, and Rollory rode in the middle and Soorenard and Akanax on either side. And the long ride was a hard and weary thing for Soorenard and Akanax, for they both had mortal wounds; but the long ride was easy for Rollory, for he was dead. So the bones of these five heroes whitened in an enemy's land, and very still they were, though they had troubled cities, and none knew where they lay saving only Iraine, the young captain, who was but twenty-five when Mommolek, Rollory, Akanax rode away. And among them were strewn their saddles and their bridles, and all the accoutrements of their horses, lest any man should ever find them afterwards and say in some foreign city: "Lo! the bridles or the saddles of Merimna's captains, taken in war," but their beloved trusty horses they turned free.

Forty years afterwards, in the hour of a great victory, his last wound came upon Iraine, and the wound was terrible and would not close. And Iraine was the last of the captains, and rode away alone. It was a long way to the dark ravine, and Iraine feared that he would never come to the resting-place of the old heroes, and he urged his horse on swiftly, and clung to the saddle with his hands. And often as he rode he fell asleep, and dreamed of earlier days, and of the times when he first rode forth to the great wars of Welleran, and of the time when Welleran first spake to him, and of the faces of Welleran's comrades when they led charges in the battle. And ever as he awoke a great longing arose in his soul as it hovered on his body's brink, a longing to lie among the bones of the old heroes. At last when he saw the dark ravine making a scar across the plain, the soul of Iraine slipped out through his great wound and spread its wings, and pain departed from the poor hacked body and, still urging his horse forward, Iraine died. But the old true horse cantered on till suddenly he saw before him the dark ravine and put his fore-feet out on the very edge of it and stopped. Then the body of Iraine came toppling forward over the right shoulder of the horse, and his bones mingle and rest as the years go by with the bones of Merimna's heroes.

Now there was a little boy in Merimna named Rold. I saw him first, I, the dreamer, that sit before my fire asleep, I saw him first as his mother led him through the great hall where stand the trophies of Merimna's heroes. He was five years old, and they stood before the great glass casket wherein lay the sword of Welleran, and his mother said: "The sword of Welleran." And Rold said: "What should a man do with the sword of Welleran?" And his mother answered: "Men look at the sword and remember Welleran." And they went on and stood before the great red cloak of Welleran, and the child said: "Why did Welleran wear this great red cloak?" And his mother answered: "It was the way of Welleran."

When Rold was a little older he stole out of his mother's house quiet in the middle of the night when all the world was still, and Merimna asleep dreaming of Welleran, Soorenard, Mommolek, Rollory, Akanax, and young Iraine. And he went down to the ramparts to hear the purple guard go by singing of Welleran. And the purple guard came by with lights, all singing in the stillness, and dark shapes out in the desert turned and fled. And Rold went back again to his mother's house with a great yearning towards the name of Welleran, such as men feel for very holy things.

And in time Rold grew to know the pathway all round the ramparts, and the six equestrian statues that were there guarding Merimna still. These statues were not like other statues, they were so cunningly wrought of many-colored marbles that none might be quite sure until very close that they were not living men. There was a horse of dappled marble, the horse of Akanax. The horse of Rollory was of alabaster, pure white, his armor was wrought out of a stone that shone, and his horseman's cloak was made of a blue stone, very precious. He looked northward.

But the marble horse of Welleran was pure black, and there sat Welleran upon him looking solemnly westwards. His horse it was whose cold neck Rold most loved to stroke, and it was Welleran whom the watchers at sunset on the mountains the most clearly saw as they peered towards the city. And Rold loved the red nostrils of the great black horse and his rider's jasper cloak.

Now beyond the Cyresians the suspicion grew that Merimna's heroes were dead, and a plan was devised that a man should go by night and come close to the figures upon the ramparts and see whether they were Welleran, Soorenard, Mommolek, Rollory, Akanax, and young Iraine. And all were agreed upon the plan, and many names were mentioned of those who should go, and the plan matured for many years. It was during these years that watchers clustered often at sunset upon the mountains but came no nearer. Finally, a better plan was made, and it was decided that two men who had been by chance condemned to death should be given a pardon if they went down into the plain by night and discovered whether or not Merimna's heroes lived. At first the two prisoners dared not go, but after a while one of them, Seejar, said to his companion, Sajar-Ho: "See now, when the King's axeman smites a man upon the neck that man dies."

And the other said that this was so. Then said Seejar: "And even though Welleran smite a man with his sword no more befalleth him than death."

Then Sajar-Ho thought for a while. Presently he said: "Yet the eye of the King's axeman might err at the moment of his stroke or his arm fail him, and the eye of Welleran hath never erred nor his arm failed. It were better to bide here."

Then said Seejar: "Maybe that Welleran is dead and that some other holds his place upon the ramparts, or even a statue of stone."

But Sajar-Ho made answer: "How can Welleran be dead when he even escaped from two score horsemen with swords that were sworn to slay him, and all sworn upon our country's gods?"

And Seejar said: "This story his father told my grandfather concerning Welleran. On the day that the fight was lost on the plains of Kurlistan he saw a dying horse near to the river, and the horse looked piteously toward the water but could not reach it. And the father of my grandfather saw Welleran go down to the river's brink and bring water from it with his own hand and give it to the horse. Now we are in as sore a plight as was that horse, and as near to death; it may be that Welleran will pity us, while the King's axeman cannot because of the commands of the King."

Then said Sajar-Ho: "Thou wast ever a cunning arguer. Thou broughtest us into this trouble with thy cunning and thy devices, we will see if thou canst bring us out of it. We will go."

So news was brought to the King that the two prisoners would go down to Merimna.

That evening the watchers led them to the mountain's edge, and Seejar and Sajar-Ho went down towards the plain by the way of a deep ravine, and the watchers watched them go. Presently their figures were wholly hid in the dusk. Then night came up, huge and holy, out of waste marshes to the eastwards and low lands and the sea; and the angels that watched over all men through the day closed their great eyes and slept, and the angels that watched over all men through the night awoke and ruffled their deep blue feathers and stood up and watched. But the plain became a thing of mystery filled with fears. So the two spies went down the deep ravine, and coming to the plain sped stealthily across it. Soon they came to the line of sentinels asleep upon the sand, and one stirred in his sleep calling on Rollory, and a great dread seized upon the spies and they whispered "Rollory lives," but they remembered the King's axeman and went on. And next they came to the great bronze statue of Fear, carved by some sculptor of the old glorious years in the attitude of flight towards the mountains, calling to her children as she fled. And the children of Fear were carved in the likeness of the armies of all the trans-Cyresian tribes with their backs toward Merimna, flocking after Fear. And from where he sat on his horse behind the ramparts the sword of Welleran was stretched out over their heads as ever it was wont. And the two spies kneeled down in the sand and kissed the huge bronze feet of the statue of Fear, saying: "Oh Fear, Fear." And as they knelt they saw lights far off along the ramparts coming nearer and nearer, and heard men singing of Welleran. And the purple guard came nearer and went by with their lights, and passed on into the distance round the ramparts still singing of Welleran. And all the while the two spies clung to the foot of the statue, muttering: "O Fear, Fear." But when they could hear the name of Welleran no more they arose and came to the ramparts and climbed over them and came at once upon the figure of Welleran, and they bowed low to the ground, and Seejar said: "Oh Welleran, we came to see whether thou didst yet live." And for a long while they waited with their faces to the earth. At last Seejar looked up toward Welleran's terrible sword, and it was still stretched out pointing to the carved armies that followed after Fear. And Seejar bowed to the ground again and touched the horses's hoof, and it seemed cold to him. And he moved his hand higher and touched the leg of the horse, and it seemed quite cold. At last he touched Welleran's foot, and the armor on it seemed hard and stiff. Then as Welleran moved not and spake not, Seejar climbed up at last and touched his hand, the terrible hand of Welleran, and it was marble. Then Seejar laughed aloud, and he and Sajar-Ho sped down the empty pathway and found Rollory, and he was marble too. Then they climbed down over the ramparts and went back across the plain, walking contemptuously past the figure of Fear, and heard the guard returning round the ramparts for the third time, singing of Welleran; and Seejar said, "Ay, you may sing of Welleran, but Welleran is dead and a doom is on your city."

And they passed on and found the sentinel still restless in the night and calling on Rolloroy. And Sajar-Ho muttered: "Ay, you may call on Rollory, but Rollory is dead and naught can save your city."

And the two spies went back alive to their mountains again, and as they reached them the first ray of sun came up red over the desert behind Merimna and lit Merimna's spires. It was the hour when the purple guard were wont to go back into the city with their tapers pale and their robes a brighter color, when the cold sentinels came shuffling in from dreaming in the desert; it was the hour when the desert robbers hid themselves away going back to their mountain caves, it was the hour when gauze-winged insects are born that only live for a day, it was the hour when men die that are condemned to death, and in this hour a great peril, new and terrible, arose for Merimna and Merimna knew it not.

Then Seejar turning said: "See how red the dawn is and how red the spires of Merimna. They are angry with Merimna in Paradise and they bode its doom."

So the two spies went back and brought the news to their King, and for a few days the Kings of those countries were gathering their armies together; and one evening the armies of four Kings were massed together at the top of the deep ravine, all crouching below the summit waiting for the sun to set. All wore resolute and fearless faces, yet inwardly every man was praying to his gods, unto each one in turn.

Then the sun set, and it was the hour when the bats and the dark creatures are abroad and the lions came down from their lairs, and the desert robbers go into the plains again, and fevers rise up winged and hot out of chill marshes, and it was the hour when safety leaves the thrones of Kings, the hour when dynasties change. But in the desert the purple guard came swinging out of Merimna with their lights to sing of Welleran, and the sentinels lay down to sleep.

Now into Paradise no sorrow may ever come, but may only beat like rain against its crystal walls, yet the souls of Merimna's heroes were half aware of some sorrow far away as some sleeper feels that some one is chilled and cold yet knows not in his sleep that it is he. And they fretted a little in their starry home. Then unseen there drifted earthward across the setting sun the souls of Welleran, Soorenard, Mommolek, Rollory, Akanax, and young Iraine. Already when they reached Merimna's ramparts it was just dark, already the armies of the four Kings had begun to move, jingling, down the deep ravine. But when the six warriors saw their city again, so little changed after so many years, they looked towards her with a longing that was nearer to tears than any that their souls had known before, crying to her:

"O Merimna, our city: Merimna, our walled city.

"How beautiful thou art with all thy spires, Merimna. For thee we left the earth, its kingdom and little flowers, for thee we have come away for awhile from Paradise.

"It is very difficult to draw away from the face of God—it is like a warm fire, it is like dear sleep, it is like a great anthem, yet there is a stillness all about it, a stillness full of lights.

"We have left Paradise for awhile for thee, Merimna.

"Many women have we loved, Merimna, but only one city.

"Behold now all the people dream, all our loved people. How beautiful are dreams! In dreams the dead may live, even the long dead and the very silent. Thy lights are still sunk low, they have all gone out, no sound is in thy streets. Hush! Thou art like a maiden that shutteth up her eyes and is asleep, that draweth her breath softly and is quite still, being at ease and untroubled.

"Behold now the battlements, the old battlements. Do men defend them still as we defended them? They are worn a little, the battlements," and drifting nearer they peered anxiously. "It is not by the hand of man that they are worn, our battlements. Only the years have done it and indomitable Time. Thy battlements are like the girdle of a maiden, a girdle that is round about her. See now the dew upon them, they are like a jewelled girdle.

"Thou art in great danger, Merimna, because thou art so beautiful. Must thou perish tonight because we no more defend thee, because we cry out and none hear us, as the bruised lilies cry out and none have known their voices?"

Thus spake those strong-voiced, battle-ordering captains, calling to their dear city, and their voices came no louder than the whispers of little bats that drift across the twilight in the evening. Then the purple guard came near, going round the ramparts for the first time in the night, and the old warriors called to them, "Merimna is in danger! Already her enemies gather in the darkness." But their voices were never heard because they were only wandering ghosts. And the guard went by and passed unheeding away, still singing of Welleran.

Then said Welleran to his comrades: "Our hands can hold swords no more, our voices cannot be heard, we are stalwart men no longer. We are but dreams, let us go among dreams. Go all of you, and thou too, young Iraine, and trouble the dreams of all the men that sleep, and urge them to take the old swords of their grandsires that hang upon the walls, and to gather at the mouth of the ravine; and I will find a leader and make him take my sword."

Then they passed up over the ramparts and into their dear

city. And the wind blew about, this way and that, as he went, the soul of Welleran who had upon his day withstood the charges of tempestuous armies. And the souls of his comrades, and with them young Iraine, passed up into the city and troubled the dreams of every man who slept, and to every man the souls said in their dreams: "It is hot and still in the city. Go out now into the desert, into the cool under the mountains, but take with thee the old sword that hangs upon the wall for fear of the desert robbers."

And the god of that city sent up a fever over it, and the fever brooded over it and the streets were hot; and all that slept awoke from dreaming that it would be cool and pleasant where the breezes came down the ravine out of the mountains: and they took the old swords that their grandsires had, according to their dreams, for fear of the desert robbers. And in and out of dreams passed the souls of Welleran's comrades, and with them young Iraine, in great haste as the night wore on; and one by one they troubled the dreams of all Merimna's men and caused them to arise and go out armed, all save the purple guard who, heedless of danger, sang of Welleran still, for waking men cannot hear the souls of the dead.

But Welleran drifted over the roofs of the city till he came to the form of Rold lying fast asleep. Now Rold was grown strong and was eighteen years of age, and he was fair of hair and tall like Welleran, and the soul of Welleran hovered over him and went into his dreams as a butterfly flits through trellis-work into a garden of flowers, and the soul of Welleran said to Rold in his dreams: "Thou wouldst go and see again the sword of Welleran, the great curved sword of Welleran. Thou wouldst go and look at it in the night with the moonlight shining upon it."

And the longing of Rold in his dreams to see the sword caused him to walk still sleeping from his mother's house to the hall wherein were the trophies of the heroes. And the soul of Welleran urging the dreams of Rold caused him to pause before the great red cloak, and there the soul said among the dreams: "Thou art cold in the night; fling now a cloak around thee."

And Rold drew round about him the huge red cloak of Welleran. Then Rold's dreams took him to the sword, and the soul said to the dreams: "Thou hast a longing to hold the sword of Welleran: take up the sword in thy hand."

But Rold said: "What should a man do with the sword of Welleran?"

And the soul of the old captain said to the dreams: "It is a good sword to hold: take up the sword of Welleran."

And Rold, still sleeping and speaking aloud, said: "It is not lawful; none may touch the sword."

And Rold turned to go. Then a great and terrible cry arose in the soul of Welleran, all the more bitter for that he could not utter it, and it went round and round his soul finding no utterance, like a cry evoked long since by some murderous deed in some old haunted chamber that whispers through the ages heard by none.

And the soul of Welleran cried out to the dreams of Rold: "Thy knees are tied! Thou art fallen in a marsh! Thou canst not move."

And the dreams of Rold said to him: "Thy knees are tied, thou art fallen in a marsh," and Rold stood still before the sword. Then the soul of the warrior wailed among Rold's dreams, as Rold stood before the sword.

"Welleran is crying for his sword, his wonderful curved sword. Poor Welleran, that once fought for Merimna, is crying for his sword in the night. Thou wouldst not keep Welleran without his beautiful sword when he is dead and cannot come for it, poor Welleran who fought for Merimna."

And Rold broke the glass casket with his hand and took the sword, the great curved sword of Welleran; and the soul of the warrior said among Rold's dreams: "Welleran is waiting in the deep ravine that runs into the mountains, crying for his sword."

And Rold went down through the city and climbed over the ramparts, and walked with his eyes wide open but still sleeping over the desert to the mountains.

Already a great multitude of Merimna's citizens were gathered in the desert before the deep ravine with old swords in their hands, and Rold passed through them as he slept holding the sword of Welleran, and the people cried amazed to one another as he passed: "Rold hath the sword of Welleran!"

And Rold came to the mouth of the ravine, and there the voices of the people woke him. And Rold knew nothing that he had done in his sleep, and looked in amazement at the sword in his hand and said: "What are thou, thou beautiful thing? Lights shimmer in thee, thou art restless. It is the sword of Welleran, the curved sword of Welleran!"

And Rold kissed the hilt of it, and it was salt upon his lips with the battle-sweat of Welleran. And Rold said: "What should a man do with the sword of Welleran?"

And all the people wondered at Rold as he sat there with the sword in his hand muttering, "What should a man do with the sword of Welleran?"

Presently there came to the ears of Rold the noise of a jingling up in the ravine, and all the people, the people who knew naught of war, heard the jingling coming nearer in the night; for the four armies were moving on Merimna and not yet expecting an enemy. And Rold gripped upon the hilt of the great curved sword, and the sword seemed to lift a little. And a new thought came into the hearts of Merimna's people as they gripped their grandsires' swords. Nearer and nearer came the heedless armies of the four Kings, the old ancestral memories began to arise in the minds of Merimna's people in the desert with their swords in their hands sitting behind Rold. And all the sentinels were awake holding their spears, for Rollory had put their dreams to flight, Rollory that once could put to flight armies and now was but a dream struggling with other dreams.

And now the armies had come very near. Suddenly Rold

leaped up, crying: "Welleran! And the sword of Welleran!" And the savage, lusting sword that had thirsted for a hundred years went up with the hand of Rold and swept through a tribesman's ribs. And with the warm blood all about it there came a joy into the curved soul of that mighty sword, like to the joy of a swimmer coming up dripping out of warm seas after living for long in a dry land. When they saw the red cloak and that terrible sword a cry ran through the tribal armies, "Welleran lives!" And there arose the sounds of the exulting of victorious men, and the panting of those that fled, and the sword singing softly to itself as it whirled dripping through the air. And the last that I saw of the battle as it poured into the depth and darkness of the ravine was the sword of Welleran sweeping up and falling, gleaming blue in the moonlight whenever it arose and afterwards gleaming red, and so disappearing into the darkness.

But in the dawn Merimna's men came back, and the sun arising to give new life to the world, shone instead upon the hideous things that the sword of Welleran had done. And Rold said: "O sword, sword! How terrible thou art! Thou art a terrible thing to have come among men. How many eyes shall look upon gardens no more because of thee? How many fields must go empty that might have been fair with cottages, white cottages with children all about them? How many valleys must go desolate that might have nursed warm hamlets, because thou hast slain long since the men that might have built them? I hear the wind crying against thee, thou sword! It comes from the empty valleys. It comes over the bare fields. There are children's voices in it. They were never born. Death brings an end to crying for those that had life once, but these must cry for ever. O sword! sword! why did the gods send thee among men?" And the tears of Rold fell down upon the proud sword but could not wash it clean.

And now the ardor of battle had passed away, the spirits of Merimna's people began to gloom a little, like their leader's, with their fatigue and with the cold of the morning; and they looked at the sword of Welleran in Rold's hand and said: "Not any more, not any more for ever will Welleran now return, for his sword is in the hand of another. Now we know indeed that he is dead. O Welleran, thou wast our sun and moon and all our stars. Now is the sun fallen down and the moon broken, and all the stars are scattered as the diamonds of a necklace that is snapped off one who is slain by violence."

Thus wept the people of Merimna in the hour of their great victory, for men have strange moods, while beside them their old inviolate city slumbered safe. But back from the ramparts and beyond the mountains and over the lands that they had conquered of old, beyond the world and back again to Paradise, went the souls of Welleran, Soorenard, Mommolek, Rollory, Akanax, and young Iraine.

The Women of the Wood

by A. MERRITT

MCKAY SAT on the balcony of the little inn that squatted like a brown gnome among the pines on the eastern shore of the lake.

It was a small and lonely lake high up in the Vosges; and yet, lonely is not just the word with which to tag its spirit; rather was it aloof, withdrawn. The mountains came down on every side, making a great tree-lined bowl that seemed, when McKay first saw it, to be filled with the still wine of peace.

McKay had worn the wings in the world war with honor, flying first with the French and later with his own country's forces. And as a bird loves the trees, so did McKay love them. To him they were not merely trunks and roots, branches and leaves, to him they were personalities. He was acutely aware of differences in character even among the same species—that pine was benevolent and jolly; that one austere and monkish; there stood a swaggering bravo, and there dwelt a sage wrapped in green meditation; that birch was a wanton—the birch near her was virginal, still a-dream.

The war had sapped him, nerve and brain and soul. Through all the years that had passed since then the wound had kept open. But now, as he slid his car down the vast green bowl, he felt its spirit reach out to him; reach out to him and caress and quiet him, promising him healing. He seemed to drift like a falling leaf through the clustered woods; to be cradled by gentle hands of the trees.

He had stopped at the little gnome of an inn, and there he had lingered, day after day, week after week.

The trees had nursed him; soft whisperings of leaves, slow chant of the needled pines, had first deadened, then driven from him the re-echoing clamor of the war and its sorrow. The open wound of his spirit had closed under their green healing; had closed and become scar; and even the scar had been covered and buried, as the scars on Earth's breast are covered and buried beneath the falling leaves of Autumn. The trees had laid green healing hands on his eyes, banishing the pictures of war. He had sucked strength from the green breasts of the hills.

Yet as strength flowed back to him and mind and spirit healed, McKay had grown steadily aware that the place was troubled; that its tranquillity was not perfect; that there was ferment of fear within it.

It was as though the tree had waited until he himself had become whole before they made their own unrest known to him. Now they were trying to tell him something; there was a shrillness as of apprehension, of anger, in the whispering of the leaves, the needled chanting of the pines.

And it was this that had kept McKay at the inn—a definite consciousness of appeal, consciousness of something wrong—something wrong that he was being asked to right. He strained his ears to catch the words in the rustling branches, words that trembled on the brink of his human understanding.

Never did they cross that brink.

Gradually he had orientated himself, had focused himself, so he believed, to the point of the valley's unease.

On all the shores of the lake there were but two dwellings. One was the inn, and around the inn the trees clustered protectively, confiding; friendly. It was as though they had not only accepted it, but had made in part of themselves.

Not so was it of the other habitation. Once it had been the hunting lodge of long dead lords; now it was half ruined, forlorn. It stood across the lake almost exactly opposite the inn and back upon the slope a half mile from the shore. Once there had been fat fields around it and a fair orchard.

The forest had marched down upon them. Here and there in the fields, scattered pines and poplars stood like soldiers guarding some outpost; scouting parties of saplings lurked among the gaunt and broken fruit trees. But the forest had not had its way unchecked; ragged stumps showed where those who dwelt in the old lodge had cut down the invaders, blackened patches of the woodland showed where they had fired the woods.

Here was the conflict he had sensed. Here the green folk of the forest were both menaced and menacing; at war. The lodge was a fortress beleaguered by the woods, a fortress whose garrison sallied forth with axe and torch to take their toll of the besiegers.

Yet McKay sensed the inexorable pressing-in of the forest; he saw it as a green army ever filling the gaps in its enclosing ranks, shooting its seeds into the cleared places, sending its roots out to sap them; and armed always with a crushing patience, a patience drawn from the stone beasts of the eternal hills.

He had the impression of constant regard of watchfulness, as though night and day the forest kept its myriads of eyes upon the lodge; inexorably, not to be swerved from its purpose. He had spoken of this impression to the inn keeper and his wife, and they had looked at him oddly.

"Old Polleau does not love the trees, no," the old man had said. "No, nor do his two sons. They do not love the trees—and very certainly the trees do not love them."

Between the lodge and the shore, marching down to the verge of the lake was a singularly beautiful little coppice of silver birches and firs. The coppice stretched for perhaps a quarter of a mile, was not more than a hundred feet or two in depth, and it was not alone the beauty of its trees but their curious grouping that aroused McKay's interest so vividly. At each end of the coppice were a dozen or more of the glistening needled firs, not clustered but spread out as though in open marching order; at widely spaced intervals along its other two sides paced single firs. The birches, slender and delicate, grew within the guard of these sturdier trees, yet not so thickly as to crowd each other.

To McKay the silver birches were for all the world like some gay caravan of lovely demoiselles under the protection of debonair knights. With that odd other sense of his he saw the birches as delectable damsels, merry and laughing—the pines as lovers, troubadours in their green needled mail. And when the winds blew and the crests of the trees bent under them, it was as though dainty demoiselles picked up fluttering, leafy skirts, bent leafy hoods and danced while the knights of the firs grew closer around them, locked arms with theirs and danced with them to the roaring horns of the winds. At such times he almost heard sweet laughter from the birches, shoutings from the firs.

Of all the trees in that place McKay loved best this little wood; had rowed across and rested in its shade, had dreamed there and, dreaming, had heard again elfin echoes of the sweet laughter; eyes closed, had heard mysterious whisperings and the sound of dancing feet light as falling leaves; had taken dream draught of that gaiety which was the soul of the little wood.

And two days ago he had seen Polleau and his two sons. McKay had been dreaming in the coppice all that afternoon.

As dusk began to fall he had reluctantly arisen and begun the row back to the inn. When he had been a few hundred feet from shore three men had come out from the trees and had stood watching him—three grim, powerful men taller than the average French peasant.

He had called a friendly greeting to them, but they had not answered it; stood there, scowling. Then as he bent over to his oars, one of the sons had raised a hatchet and had driven it savagely into the trunk of a slim birch beside him. He thought he heard a thin wailing cry from the stricken tree, a sigh from all the little wood.

McKay had felt as though the keen edge had bitten into his own flesh.

"Stop that!" he had cried, "Stop it, damn you!"

For answer the son had struck again—and never had McKay seen hate etched so deep as on his face as he struck. Cursing, a killing rage in heart, had swung the boat around, raced back to shore. He had heard the hatchet strike again and again and, close now to shore, had heard a crackling and over it once more the thin, high wailing. He had turned to look.

The birch was tottering, was falling. But as it had fallen he had seen a curious thing. Close beside it grew one of the firs, and, as the smaller tree crashed over, it dropped upon the fir like a fainting maid in the arms of a lover. And as it lay and trembled there, one of the great branches of the fir slipped from under it, whipped out and smote the hatchet wielder a crushing blow upon the head, sending him to earth.

It had been, of course, only the chance blow of a bough, bent by pressure of the fallen tree and then released as that tree slipped down. But there had been such suggestion of conscious action in the branch's recoil, so much of bitter anger in it, so much, in truth, had it been like the vengeful blow of a man that McKay had felt an eerie prickling of his scalp, his heart had missed its beat.

For a moment, Polleau and the standing son had stared at

the sturdy fir with the silvery birch lying on its green breast and folded in, shielded by, its needled boughs as though—again the swift impression came to McKay—as though it were a wounded maid stretched on breast, in arms, of knightly lover. For a long moment father and son had stared.

Then, still wordless but with that same bitter hatred on both their faces, they had stopped and picked up the other and with his arms around the neck of each had borne him limply away.

McKay, sitting on the balcony of the inn that morning, went over and over that scene; realized more and more clearly the human aspect of fallen birch and clasping fir, and the conscious deliberateness of the fir's blow. And during the two days that had elapsed since then, he had felt the unease of the trees increase, their whispering appeal became more urgent.

What were they trying to tell him? What did they want him to do?

Troubled, he stared across the lake, trying to pierce the mists that hung over it and hid the opposite shore. And suddenly it seemed that he heard the coppice calling him, felt it pull the point of his attention toward it irresistibly, as the lodestone swings and holds the compass needle.

The coppice called him, bade him come to it.

Instantly McKay obeyed the command; he arose and walked down to the boat landing; he stepped into his skiff and began to row across the lake. As his oars touched the water his trouble fell from him. In its place flowed peace and a curious exaltation.

The mist was thick upon the lake. There was no breath of wind, yet the mist billowed and drifted, shook and curtained under the touch of unfelt airy hands.

They were alive—the mists; they formed themselves into fantastic palaces past whose opalescent facades he flew; they built themselves into hills and valleys and circled plains whose floors were rippling silk. Tiny rainbows gleamed out among them, and upon the water prismatic patches shone and spread like spilled wine of opals. He had the illusion of vast distances—the hills of mist were real mountains, the valleys between them were not illusory. He was a colossus cleaving through some elfin world. A trout broke, and it was like leviathan leaping from the fathomless deep. Around the arc of its body rainbows interlaced and then dissolved into rain of softly gleaming gems—diamonds in dance with sapphires, flame hearted rubies and pearls with shimmering souls of rose. The fish vanished, diving cleanly without sound; the jewelled bows vanished with it; a tiny irised whirlpool swirled for an instant where trout and flashing arcs had been.

Nowhere was there sound. He let his oars drop and leaned forward, drifting. In the silence, before him and around him, he felt opening the gateways of an unknown world.

And suddenly he heard the sounds of voices, many voices; faint at first and murmurous; louder they became, swiftly; women's voices sweet and lilting and mingled with them the deeper tones of men. Voices that lifted and fell in a wild, gay chanting through whose *joyesse* ran undertones both of sorrow and of rage—as though faery weavers threaded through silk spun of sunbeams somber strands dipped in the black of graves and crimson strands stained in the red of wrathful sunsets.

He drifted on, scarce daring to breathe lest even that faint sound break the elfin song. Closer it rang and clearer; and now he became aware that the speed of his boat was increasing, that it was no longer drifting; that it was as though the little waves on each side were pushing him ahead with soft and noiseless palms. His boat grounded and as it rustled along over the smooth pebbles of the beach the song ceased.

McKay half arose and peered before him. The mists were thicker here but he could see the outlines of the coppice. It was like looking at it through many curtains of fine gauze; its trees seemed shifting, ethereal, unreal. And moving among the trees were figures that threaded the boles and flitted in rhythmic measures like the shadows of leafy boughs swaying to some cadenced wind.

He stepped ashore and made his way slowly toward them. The mists dropped behind him, shutting off all sight of shore.

The rhythmic flittings ceased; there was now no movement as there was now no sound among the trees—yet he felt the little woods abrim with watching life. McKay tried to speak; there was a spell of silence on his mouth.

"You called me. I have come to listen to you—to help you if I can."

The words formed within his mind, but utter them he could not. Over and over he tried, desperately; the words seemed to die before his lips could give them life.

A pillar of mist whirled forward and halted, eddying half an arm length away. And suddenly out of it peered a woman's face, eyes level with his own. A woman's face—yes; but McKay, staring into those strange eyes probing his, knew that face though it seemed it was that of no woman of human breed. They were without pupils, the irises deer-like and of the soft green of deep forest dells; within them sparkled tiny star points of light like motes in a moon beam. The eyes were wide and set far apart beneath a broad, low brow over which was piled braid upon braid of hair of palest gold, braids that seemed spun of shining ashes of gold. Her nose was small and straight, her mouth scarlet and exquisite. The face was oval, tapering to a delicately pointed chin.

Beautiful was that face, but its beauty was an alien one; elfin. For long moments the strange eyes thrust their gaze deep into his. Then out of the mist two slender white arms stole, the hands long, fingers tapering. The tapering fingers touched his ears.

"He shall hear," whispered the red lips.

Immediately from all about him a cry arose; in it was the whispering and rustling of the leaves beneath the breath of the winds, the shrilling of the harp strings of the boughs, the laughter of hidden brooks, the shoutings of waters flinging themselves down to deep and rocky pools—the voices of the woods made articulate.

"He shall hear!" they cried.

The long white fingers rested on his lips, and their touch was cool as bark of birch on cheek after some long upward climb through the forest; cool and subtly sweet.

"He shall speak," whispered the scarlet lips.

"He shall speak!" answered the wood voices again, as though in litany.

"He shall see," whispered the woman and the cool fingers touched his eyes.

"He shall see!" echoed the wood voices.

The mists that had hidden the coppice from McKay wavered, thinned and were gone. In their place was a limpid, translucent, paley green ether, faintly luminous—as though he stood within some clear wan emerald. His feet pressed a golden moss spangled with tiny starry bluets. Fully revealed before him was the woman of the strange eyes and the face of elfin beauty. He dwelt for a moment upon the slender shoulders, the firm small tip-tilted breasts, the willow litheness of her body. From neck to knees a smock covered her, sheer and silken and delicate as though spun of cobwebs; through it her body gleamed as though fire of the young Spring moon ran in her veins.

Beyond her, upon the golden moss were other women like her, many of them; they stared at him with the same wide set green eyes in which danced the clouds of sparkling moonbeams' motes; like her they were crowned with glistening, pallidly golden hair; like hers too were their oval faces with the pointed chins and perilous elfin beauty. Only where she stared at him gravely, measuring him, weighing him—there were those of these her sisters whose eyes were mocking; and those whose eyes called to him with a weirdly tingling allure, their mouths athirst; those whose eyes looked upon him with curiosity alone and those whose great eyes pleaded with him, prayed to him.

Within that pellucid, greenly luminous air McKay was abruptly aware that the trees of the coppice still had a place. Only now they were spectral indeed; they were like white shadows cast athwart a glaucous screen, trunk and bough, twig and leaf they arose around him and they were as though etched in air by phantom craftsmen—thin, unsubstantial; they were ghost trees rooted in another space.

Suddenly he was aware that there were men among the women; men whose eyes were set wide apart as were theirs, as strange and pupilless as were theirs but with irises of brown and blue; men with pointed chins and oval faces, broad shouldered and clad in kirtles of darkest green; swarthy skinned men muscular and strong, with that same little grace of the women—and like them of a beauty alien and elfin.

McKay heard a little wailing cry. He turned. Close beside him lay a girl clasped in the arms of one of the swarthy, green clad men. She lay upon his breast. His eyes were filled with a black flame of wrath, and hers were misted, anguished. For an instant McKay had a glimpse of the birch old Polleau's son had sent crashing down into the boughs of the fir. He saw birch and fir as immaterial outlines around the man and girl. For an instant girl and man and birch and fir seemed one and the same. The scarlet lipped woman touched his shoulder, and the confusion cleared.

"She withers," sighed the woman, and in her voice McKay heard a faint rustling as of mournful leaves. "Now is it not pitiful that she withers—our sister who was so young, so slender and so lovely?"

McKay looked again at the girl. The white skin seemed shrunken; the moon radiance that gleamed through the bodies of the others in hers was dim and pallid; her slim arms hung listlessly; her body drooped. The mouth too was wan and parched, the long and misted green eyes dull. The palely golden hair lusterless, and dry. He looked on slow death—a withering death.

"May the arm that struck her down wither!" the green clad man who held her shouted, and in his voice McKay heard a savage strumming as of winter winds through bleak boughs: "May his heart wither and the sun blast him! May the rain and the waters deny him and the winds scourge him!"

"I thirst," whispered the girl.

There was a stirring among the watching women. One came forward holding a chalice that was like thin leaves turned to green crystal. She paused beside the trunk of one of the spectral trees, reached up and drew down to her a branch. A slim girl with half-frightened, half-resentful eyes glided to her side and threw her arms around the ghostly bole. The woman with the chalice bent the branch and cut it deep with what seemed an arrow-shaped flake of jade. From the wound a faintly opalescent liquid slowly filled the cup. When it was filled the woman beside McKay stepped forward and pressed her own long hands around the bleeding branch. She stepped away and McKay saw that the stream had ceased to flow. She touched the trembling girl and unclasped her arms.

"It is healed," said the woman gently. "And it was your turn little sister. The wound is healed. Soon you will have forgotten."

The woman with the chalice knelt and set it to the wan, dry lips of her who was—withering. She drank of it, thirstily, to the last drop. The misty eyes cleared, they sparkled; the lips that had been so parched and pale grew red, the white body gleamed as though the waning light had been fed with new.

"Sing, sisters," she cried, and shrilly. "Dance for me, sisters!"

Again burst out that chant McKay had heard as he had floated through the mists upon the lake. Now, as then, despite his opened ears, he could distinguish no words, but clearly he understood its mingled themes—the joy of Spring's awakening, rebirth, with the green life streaming singing up through every bough, swelling the buds, burgeoning with tender leaves the branches; the dance of the trees in the scented winds of Spring; the drums of the jubilant rain on leafy hoods; passion of Summer sun pouring its golden flood down upon the trees; the moon passing with stately step and slow and green hands stretching up to her and drawing from her breast milk of silver fire; riot of wild, gay winds with their mad pipings and strummings;—soft interlacing of boughs, the kiss of amorous leaves—all these and more, much more that McKay could not understand since it dealt with hidden, secret things for which man has no images, were in that chanting.

And all these and more were in the measures, the rhythms of the dancing of those strange, green eyed women and brown skinned men; something incredibly ancient yet young as the speeding moment, something of a world before and beyond man.

McKay listened, McKay watched, lost in wonder; his own world more than half forgotten; his mind meshed in web of green sorcery.

The woman beside him touched his arm. She pointed to the girl.

"Yet she withers," she said. "And not all our life, if we poured it through her lips, could save her."

He looked; he saw that the red was draining slowly from the girl's lips, the luminous life tides waning; the eyes that had been so bright were misting and growing dull once more, suddenly a great pity and a great rage shook him. He knelt beside her, took her hands in his.

"Take them away! Take away your hands! They burn me!" she moaned.

"He tries to help you," whispered the green clad man, gently. But he reached over and drew McKay's hands away.

"Not so can you help her," said the woman.

"What can I do?" McKay arose, looked helplessly from one to the other. "What can I do to help?"

The chanting died, the dance stopped. A silence fell and he felt upon him the eyes of all. They were tense—waiting. The woman took his hands. Their touch was cool and sent a strange sweetness sweeping through his veins.

"There are three men yonder," she said. "They hate us. Soon we shall be as she is there—withering. They have sworn it, and as they have sworn so will they do. Unless—"

She paused; and McKay felt the stirrings of a curious unease. The moonbeam dancing motes in her eyes had changed to tiny sparklings of red. In a way, deep down, they terrified him—those red sparklings.

"Three men?"—in his clouded mind was the memory of Polleau and his two strong sons. "Three men," he repeated, stupidly—"But what are three men to you who are so many? What could three men do against those stalwart gallants of yours?"

"No," she shook her head. "No—there is nothing our—men—can do; nothing that we can do. Once, night and day, we were gay. Now we fear—night and day. They mean to destroy us. Our kin have warned us. And our kin cannot help us. Those three are masters of blade and flame. Against blade and flame we are helpless."

"Blade and flame!" echoed the listeners. "Against blade and flame we are helpless."

"Surely will they destroy us," murmured the woman. "We shall wither all of us. Like her there, or burn—unless—"

Suddenly she threw white arms around McKay's neck. She pressed her lithe body close to him. Her scarlet mouth sought and found his lips and clung to them. Through all McKay's body ran swift, sweet flames, green fire of desire. His own arms went round her, crushed her to him.

"You shall not die!" he cried. "No—by God, you shall not!"

She drew back her head, looked deep into his eyes.

"They have sworn to destroy us," she said, "and soon. With blade and flame they will destroy us—these three—unless—"

"Unless?" he asked, fiercely.

"Unless you—slay them first!" she answered.

A cold shock ran through McKay, chilling the green sweet fires of his desire. He dropped his arm from around the woman; thrust her from him. For an instant she trembled before him.

"Slay!" he heard her whisper—and she was gone. The spectral trees wavered; their outlines thickened out of immateriality into substance. The green translucence darkened. He had a swift vertiginous moment as though he swung between two worlds. He closed his eyes. The vertigo passed and he opened them, looked around him.

McKay stood on the lakeward skirts of the little coppice. There were no shadows flitting, no sign of the white women and the swarthy, green clad men. His feet were on green moss; gone was the soft golden carpet with its blue starlets. Birches and firs clustered solidly before him. At his left was a sturdy fir in whose needled arms a broken birch tree lay withering. It was the birch that Polleau's men had so wantonly slashed down. For an instant he saw within the fir and birch the immaterial outlines of the green clad men and the slim girl who withered. For that instant birch and fir and girl and man seemed one and the same. He stepped back, and his hands touched the smooth, cool bark of another birch that rose close at his right.

Upon his hands the touch of that bark was like—was like?—yes, curiously was it like the touch of the long slim hands of the woman of the scarlet lips. But it gave him none of that alien rapture, that pulse of green life her touch had brought. Yet, now as then, the touch steadied him. The outlines of girl and man were gone. He looked upon nothing but a sturdy fir with a withering birch fallen into its branches.

McKay stood there, staring, wondering, like a man who has but half awakened from dream. And suddenly a little wind stirred the leaves of the rounded birch beside him. The leaves murmured, sighed. The wind grew stronger and the leaves whispered.

"Slay!" he heard them whisper—and again: "Slay! Help us! Slay!"

And the whisper was the voice of the woman of the scarlet lips!

Rage, swift and unreasoning, sprang up in McKay. He began to run up through the coppice, up to where he knew was the old lodge in which dwelt Polleau and his sons. And as he ran the wind blew stronger, and louder and louder grew the whisperings of the trees.

"Slay!" they whispered. "Slay them! Save us! Slay!"

"I will slay! I will save you!" McKay, panting, hammer pulse beating in his ears, rushing through the woods heard himself answering that ever louder, ever more insistent command. And in his mind was but one desire—to clutch the throats of Polleau and his sons, to crack their necks; to stand by them then and watch them wither; wither like that slim girl in the arms of the green clad man.

So crying, he came to the edge of the coppice and burst from it out into a flood of sunshine. For a hundred feet he ran, and then he was aware that the whispering command was stilled; that he heard no more than maddening rustling of wrathful leaves. A spell seemed to have been loosed from him; it was as though he had broken through some web of sorcery. McKay stopped, dropped upon the ground, buried his face in the grasses.

He lay there, marshalling his thoughts into some order of sanity. What had he been about to do? To rush berserk upon those three who lived in the old lodge and—kill them! And for what? Because that elfin, scarlet lipped woman whose kisses he still could feel upon his mouth had bade him! Because the whispering trees of the little wood had maddened him with that same command!

And for this he had been about to kill three men!

What were that woman and her sisters and the green clad swarthy gallants of theirs? Illusions of some waking dream—phantoms born of the hypnosis of the swirling mists through which he had rowed and floated across the lake? Such things were not uncommon. McKay knew of those who by watching the shifting clouds could create and dwell for a time with wide open eyes within some similar land of fantasy; knew others who needed but to stare at smoothly falling water to set themselves within a world of waking dream; there were those who could summon dreams by gazing into a ball of crystal, others found their phantoms in saucers of shining ebon ink.

Might not the moving mists have laid those same hypnotic fingers upon his own mind—and his love for the trees the sense of appeal that he had felt so long and his memory of the wanton slaughter of the slim birch have all combined to paint upon his drugged consciousness the phantasms he had beheld?

Then in the flood of sunshine the spell had melted, his consciousness leaped awake?

McKay arose to his feet, shakily enough. He looked back at the coppice. There was no wind now, the leaves were silent, motionless. Again he saw it as the caravan of demoiselles with their marching knights and troubadours. But no longer was it gay. The words of the scarlet lipped woman came back to him—that gaiety had fled and fear had taken its place. Dream phantom or—dryad, whatever she was, half of that at least was truth.

He turned, a palm forming in his mind. Reason with himself as he might, something deep within him stubbornly asserted the reality of his experience. At any rate, he told himself, the little wood was far too beautiful to be despoiled. He would put aside the experience as dream—but he would save the little wood for the essence of beauty that it held in its green cup.

The old lodge was about a quarter of a mile away. A path led up to it through the ragged fields. McKay walked up the path, climbed rickety steps and paused, listening. He heard voices and knocked. The door was flung open and old Polleau stood there, peering at him through half shut, suspicious eyes. One of the sons stood close behind him. They stared at McKay with grim, hostile faces.

He thought he heard a faint, far off despairing whisper from the distant wood. And it was as though the pair in the doorway heard it too, for their gaze shifted from him to the coppice, and he saw hatred flicker swiftly across their grim faces; their gaze swept back to him.

"What do you want?" demanded Polleau, curtly.

"I am a neighbor of yours, stopping at the inn—" began McKay, courteously.

"I know who you are," Polleau interrupted brusquely, "But what is it that you want?"

"I find the air of this place good for me," McKay stifled a rising anger. "I am thinking of staying for a year or more until my health is fully recovered. I would like to buy some of your land and build me a lodge upon it."

"Yes, M'sieu?" there was acid politeness now in the powerful old man's voice. "But is it permitted to ask why you do not remain at the inn? Its fare is excellent and you are well liked there."

"I have desire to be alone," replied McKay. "I do not like people too close to me. I would have my own land, and sleep under my own roof."

"But why come to me?" asked Polleau. "There are many places upon the far side of the lake that you could secure. It is happy there, and this side is not happy, M'sieu. But tell me, what part of my land is it that you desire?"

"That little wood yonder," answered McKay, and pointed to the coppice.

"Ah! I thought so!" whispered Polleau, and between him and his sons passed a look of bitter understanding. He looked at McKay, sombrely.

"That wood is not for sale, M'sieu," he said at last.

"I can afford to pay well for what I want," said McKay. "Name your price."

"It is not for sale," repeated Polleau, stolidly, "at any price."

"Oh, come," laughed McKay, although his heart sank at the finality in that answer. "You have many acres and what is it but a few trees? I can afford to gratify my fancies. I will give you all the worth of your other land for it."

"You have asked what that place that you so desire is, and you have answered that it is but a few trees," said Polleau, slowly, and the tall son behind him laughed, abruptly, maliciously. "But it is more than that, M'sieu— Oh, much more than that. And you know it, else why would you pay such price? Yes, you know it—since you know also that we are ready to destroy it, and you would save it. And who told you all that, M'sieu?" he snarled.

There was such malignance in the face thrust suddenly close to McKay's, teeth barred by uplifted lip, that involuntarily he recoiled.

"But a few trees!" snarled old Polleau. "Then who told him what we mean to do—eh, Pierre?"

Again the son laughed. And at that laughter McKay felt within him resurgence of his own blind hatred as he had fled through the whispering wood. He mastered himself, turned away, there was nothing he could do—now. Polleau halted him.

"M'sieu," he said, "Wait. Enter. There is something I would tell you; something too I would show you. Something, perhaps, that I would ask you."

He stood aside, bowing with a rough courtesy. McKay walked through the doorway. Polleau with his son followed him. He entered a large, dim room whose ceiling was spanned with smoke blackened beams. From these beams hung onion strings and herbs and smoke cured meats. On one side was a wide fireplace. Huddled beside it sat Polleau's other son. He glanced up as they entered and McKay saw that a bandage covered one side of his head, hiding his left eye. McKay recognized him as the one who had cut down the slim birch. The blow of the fir, he reflected with a certain satisfaction, had been no futile one.

Old Polleau strode over to that son.

"Look, M'sieu," he said and lifted the bandage.

McKay with a faint tremor of horror, saw a gaping blackened socket, red rimmed and eyeless.

"Good God, Polleau!" he cried. "But this man needs medical attention. I know something of wounds. Let me go across the lake and bring back my kit. I will attend him."

Old Polleau shook his head, although his grim face for the first time softened. He drew the bandages back in place.

"It heals," he said. "We have some skill in such things. You saw what did it. You watched from your boat as the cursed tree struck him. The eye was crushed and lay upon his cheek. I cut it away. Now he heals. We do not need your aid, M'sieu."

"Yet he ought not have cut the birch," muttered McKay, more to himself than to be heard.

"Why not?" asked old Polleau, fiercely. "Since it hated him."

McKay stared at him. What did this old peasant know? The words strengthened that deep stubborn conviction that what he had seen and heard in the coppice had been actuality—no dream. And still more did Polleau's next words strengthen that conviction.

"M'sieu," he said, "you have come here as ambassador—of a sort. That wood has spoken to you. Well, as ambassador I shall speak to you. Four centuries my people have lived in this place. A century we have owned this land. M'sieu, in all those years there has been no moment that the trees have not hated us—nor we the trees.

"For all those hundred years there have been hatred and battle between us and the forest. My father, M'sieu, was crushed by a tree; my elder brother crippled by another. My father's father, woodsman that he was, was lost in the forest—he came back to us with mind gone, raving of wood women who had bewitched and mocked him, luring him into swamp and fen and tangled thicket, tormenting him. In every generation the trees have taken their toll of us—women as well as men—maiming or killing us."

"Accidents," interrupted McKay. "This is childish, Polleau. You cannot blame the trees."

"In your heart you do not believe so," said Polleau. "Listen, the feud is an ancient one. Centuries ago it began when we were serfs, slaves of the nobles. To cook, to keep us warm in winter, they let us pick up the fagots, the dead branches and twigs that dropped from the trees. But if we cut down a tree to keep us warm, to keep our women and children warm, yes, if we but tore down a branch—they hanged us, or they threw us into dungeons to rot, or whipped us till our backs were red lattices.

"They had their broad fields, the nobles—but we must raise our food in the patches where the trees disdained to grow. And if they did thrust themselves into our poor patches, then, M'sieu, we must let them have their way—or be flogged, or be thrown into the dungeons or be hanged.

"They pressed us in—the trees," the old man's voice grew sharp with fanatic hatred. "They stole our fields and they took the food from the mouths of our children; they dropped their fagots to us like dole to beggars; they tempted us to warmth when the cold struck our bones—and they bore us as fruit a-swing at the end of the foresters' ropes if we yielded to their tempting.

"Yes, M'sieu—we died of cold that they might live! Our children died of hunger that their young might find root space! They despised us—the trees! We died that they might live—and we were men!

"Then, M'sieu, came the Revolution and the freedom. Ah, M'sieu, then we took our toll! Great logs roaring in the winter cold—no more huddling over the alms of fagots. Fields where the trees had been—no more starving of our children that theirs might live. Now the trees were the slaves and we the masters.

"And the trees knew and they hated us!

"But blow for blow, a hundred of their lives for each life of ours—we have returned their hatred. With axe and torch we have fought them—

"The trees!" shrieked Polleau, suddenly, eyes blazing red rage, face writhing, foam at the corners of his mouth and gray hair clutched in rigid hands— "The cursed trees! Armies of the trees creeping—creeping—closer, ever closer—crushing us in! Stealing our fields as they did of old! Building their dungeon round us as they built of old the dungeons of stone! Creeping—creeping! Armies of trees! Legions of trees! The trees! The cursed trees!"

McKay listened, appalled. Here was crimson heart of hate. Madness! But what was at the root of it? Some deep inherited instinct, coming down from forefathers who had hated the forest as the symbol of their masters. Forefathers whose tides of hatred had overflowed to the green life on which the nobles had laid their *tabu*—as one neglected child will hate the favorite on whom love and gifts are lavished. In such warped minds the crushing fall of a tree, the maiming sweep of a branch, might well appear as deliberate, the natural growth of the forest seem the implacable advance of an enemy.

And yet—the blow of the fir as the cut birch fell *had* been deliberate! and there *had* been those women of the wood—

"Patience," the standing son touched the old man's shoulder. "Patience! Soon we strike our blow."

Some of the frenzy died out of Polleau's face.

"Though we cut down a hundred," he whispered, "By the hundred they return! But one of us, when they strike—he does not return. No! They have numbers and they have—time. We are now but three, and we have little time. They watch us as we go through the forest, alert to trip, to strike, to crush!

"But M'sieu," he turned blood shot eyes to McKay. "We strike our blow, even as Pierre had said. We strike at the coppice that you so desire. We strike there because it is the very heart of the forest. There the secret life of the forest runs at full tide. We know—and you know! Something that, destroyed, will take the heart out of the forest—will make it know us for its masters."

"The women!" the standing son's eyes glittered, "I have seen the women there! The fair women with the shining skins who invite—and mock and vanish before hands can seize them."

"The fair women who peer into our windows in the night—and mock us!" muttered the eyeless son.

"They shall mock no more!" shouted Polleau, the frenzy again taking him. "Soon they shall lie, dying! All of them—all of them! They die!"

He caught McKay by the shoulders, shook him like a child.

"Go tell them that!" he shouted. "Say to them that this very day we destroy them. Say to them it is *we* who will laugh when winter comes and we watch their round white bodies blaze in this hearth of ours and warm us! Go—tell them that!"

He spun McKay around, pushing him to the door, opened it and flung him staggering down the steps. He heard the tall son laugh, the door close. Blind with rage he rushed up the steps and hurled himself against the door. Again the tall son laughed. McKay beat at the door with clenched fists, cursing. The three within paid no heed. Despair began to dull his rage. Could the trees help him—counsel him? He turned and walked slowly down the field path to the little wood.

Slowly and ever more slowly he went as he neared it. He had failed. He was a messenger bearing a warrant of death. The birches were motionless; their leaves hung listlessly. It was as though they knew he had failed. He paused at the edge of the coppice. He looked at his watch, noted with faint surprise that already it was high noon. Short shrift enough had the little wood. The work of destruction would not be long delayed.

McKay squared his shoulders and passed in between the trees. It was strangely silent in the coppice. And it was mournful. He had a sense of life brooding around him, withdrawn into itself; sorrowing. He passed through the silent, mournful wood until he reached the spot where the rounded, gleaming barked tree stood close to the fir that held the withering birch. Still there was no sound, no movement. He laid his hands upon the cool bark of the rounded tree.

"Let me see again!" he whispered. "Let me hear! Speak to me!"

There was no answer. Again and again he called. The coppice was silent. He wandered through it, whispering, calling. The slim birches stood, passive with limbs and leaves adroop like listless arms and hands of captive maids awaiting with dull woe the will of conquerors. The firs seemed to crouch like hopeless men with heads in hands. His heart ached to the woe that filled the little wood, this hopeless submission of the trees.

When, he wondered, would Polleau strike? He looked at his watch again; an hour had gone by. How long would Polleau wait? He dropped to the moss, back against a smooth bole.

And suddenly it seemed to McKay that he was a madman—as mad as Polleau and his sons. Calmly, he went over the old peasant's indictment of the forest; recalled the face and eyes filled with the fanatic hate. Madness! After all, the trees were—only trees. Polleau and his sons—so he reasoned—had transferred to them the bitter hatred their forefathers had felt for those old lords who had enslaved them; had laid upon them too all the bitterness of their own struggle to exist in this high forest land. When they struck at the trees, it was the ghosts of these forefathers striking at the nobles who had oppressed them; it was themselves striking against their own destiny. The trees were but symbols. It was the warped minds of Polleau and his sons that clothed them in false semblance of conscious life in blind striving to wreak vengeance against the ancient masters and the destiny that had made their lives hard and unceasing battle against Nature. The nobles were long dead; destiny can be brought to grips by no man. But the trees were here and alive. Clothed in mirage, through them the driving lust for vengeance could be sated.

And he, McKay, was it not his own deep love and sympathy for the trees that similarly had clothed them in that false semblance of conscious life? Had he not built his own mirage? The trees did not really mourn, could not suffer, could not—know. It was his own sorrow that he had transferred to them; only his own sorrow that he felt echoing back to him from them.

The trees were—only trees.

Instantly, upon the heels of that thought, as though it were an answer, he was aware that the trunk against which he leaned was trembling; that the whole coppice was trembling; that all the little leaves were shaking, tremulously.

McKay, bewildered, leaped to his feet. Reason told him that it was the wind—yet there was no wind!

And as he stood there, a sighing arose as though a mournful breeze were blowing through the trees—and again there was no wind!

Louder grew the sighing and within it now faint wailings.

"They come! They come! Farewell sisters! Sisters—farewell!"

Clearly he heard the mournful whispers.

McKay began to run through the trees to the trail that led out to the fields of the old lodge. And as he ran the wood darkened as though clear shadows gathered in it, as though vast unseen wings hovered over it. The trembling of the coppice increased; bough touched bough, clung to each other; and louder became the sorrowful crying:

"Farewell sister! Sister—farewell!"

McKay burst out into the open. Halfway between him and the lodge were Polleau and his sons. They saw him; they pointed and lifted mockingly to him bright axes. He crouched, waiting for them to come, all fine spun theories gone and rising within him that same rage that hours before had sent him out to slay.

So crouching, he heard from the forested hills a roaring clamor. From every quarter it came, wrathful, menacing; like the voices of legions of great trees bellowing through the horns of tempest. The clamor maddened McKay; fanned the flame of rage to white heat.

If the three men heard it, they gave no sign. They came on steadily, jeering at him, waving their keen blades. He ran to meet them.

"Go back!" he shouted. "Go back, Polleau! I warn you!"

"He warns us!" jeered Polleau. "He—Pierre, Jean—he warns us!"

The old peasant's arm shot out and his hand caught McKay's shoulder with a grip that pinched to the bone. The arm flexed and hurled him against the unmaimed son. The son caught him, twisted him about and whirled him headlong a dozen yards, crashing him through the brush at the skirt of the wood.

McKay sprang to his feet howling like a wolf. The clamor of the forest had grown stronger.

"Kill!" it roared. "Kill!"

The unmaimed son had raised his axe. He brought it down upon the trunk of a birch, half splitting it with one blow. McKay heard a wail go up from the little wood. Before the axe could be withdrawn he had crashed a fist in the axe wielder's face. The head of Polleau's son rocked back; he yelped, and before McKay could strike again had wrapped strong arms around him, crushing breath from him. McKay relaxed, went limp, and the son loosened his grip. Instantly McKay slipped out of it and struck again, springing aside to avoid the rib breaking clasp. Polleau's son was quicker than he, the long arms caught him. But as the arms tightened, there was the sound of sharp splintering and the birch into which the axe had bitten toppled. It struck the ground directly behind the wrestling men. Its branches seemed to reach out and clutch at the feet of Polleau's son.

He tripped and fell backward, McKay upon him. The shock of the fall broke his grip and again McKay writhed free. Again he was upon his feet, and again Polleau's strong son, quick as he, faced him. Twice McKay's blows found their mark beneath his heart before once more the long arms trapped him. But their grip was weaker; McKay felt that now his strength was equal.

Round and round they rocked, McKay straining to break away. They fell, and over they rolled and over, arms and legs locked, each striving to free a hand to grip the other's throat. Around them ran Polleau and the one-eyed son, shouting encouragement to Pierre, yet neither daring to strike at McKay lest the blow miss and be taken by the other.

And all that time McKay heard the little wood shouting. Gone from it now was all mournfulness, all passive resignation. The wood was alive and raging. He saw the trees shake and bend as though torn by a tempest. Dimly he realized that the others must hear none of this, see none of it; as dimly wondered why this should be.

"Kill!" shouted the coppice—and over its tumult he heard the roar of the great forest:

"Kill! Kill!"

He became aware of two shadowy shapes, shadowy shapes of swarthy green clad men, that pressed close to him as he rolled and fought.

"Kill!" they whispered. "Let his blood flow! Kill! Let his blood flow!"

He tore a wrist free from the son's clutch. Instantly he felt within his hand the hilt of a knife.

"Kill!" whispered the shadowy men.

"Kill!" shrieked the coppice.

"Kill!" roared the forest.

McKay's free arm swept up and plunged the knife into the throat of Polleau's son! He heard a choking sob; heard Polleau shriek; felt the hot blood spurt in face and over hand; smelt its salt and faintly acrid odor. The encircling arms dropped from him; he reeled to his feet.

As though the blood had been a bridge, the shadowy men

leaped from immateriality into substances. One threw himself upon the man McKay had stabbed; the other hurled upon old Polleau. The maimed son turned and fled, howling with terror. A white woman sprang out from the shadow, threw herself at his feet, clutched them and brought him down. Another woman and another dropped upon him. The note of his shrieking changed from fear to agony; then died abruptly into silence.

And now McKay could see none of the three, neither old Polleau or his sons, for the green clad men and the white women covered them!

McKay stood stupidly, staring at his red hands. The roar of the forest had changed to a deep triumphal chanting. The coppice was mad with joy. The trees had become thin phantoms etched in emerald translucent air as they had been when first the green sorcery had emmeshed him. And all around him wove and danced the slim, gleaming woman of the wood.

They ringed him, their song bird-sweet and shrill; jubilant. Beyond them he saw gliding toward him the woman of the misty pillars whose kisses had poured the sweet green fire into his veins. Her arms were outstretched to him, her strange wide eyes were rapt on his, her white body gleamed with the moon radiance, her red lips were parted and smiling—a scarlet chalice filled with the promise of undreamed ecstasies. The dancing circle, chanting, broke to let her through.

Abruptly, a horror filled McKay. Not of this fair woman, not of her jubilant sisters—but of himself.

He had killed! And the wound the war had left in his soul, the wound he thought had healed, had opened.

He rushed through the broken circle, thrust the shining woman aside with his blood stained hands and ran, weeping, toward the lake shore. The singing ceased. He heard little cries, tender, appealing; little cries of pity; soft voices calling on him to stop, to return. Behind him was the sound of little racing feet, light as the fall of leaves upon the moss.

McKay ran on. The coppice lightened, the beach was before

him. He heard the fair woman call him, felt the touch of her hand upon his shoulder. He did not heed her. He ran across the narrow strip of beach, thrust his boat out into the water and wading through the shallows threw himself into it.

He lay there for a moment, sobbing; then drew himself up, caught at the oars. He looked back at the shore now a score of feet away. At the edge of the coppice stood the woman, staring at him with pitying, wise eyes. Behind her clustered the white faces of her sisters, the swarthy faces of the green clad men.

"Come back!" the woman whispered, and held out to him slender arms.

McKay hesitated, his horror lessening in that clear, wise, pitying gaze. He half swung the boat around. His gaze dropped upon his blood-stained hands and again the hysteria gripped him. One thought only was in his mind—to get far away from where Polleau's son lay with his throat ripped open, to put the lake between that body and him.

Head bent low, McKay bowed to the oars, skimming swiftly outward. When he looked up a curtain of mist had fallen between him and the shore. It hid the coppice and from beyond it there came to him no sound. He glanced behind him, back toward the inn. The mists swung there, too, concealing it.

McKay gave silent thanks for these vaporous curtains that hid him from both the dead and the alive. He slipped limply under the thwarts. After a while he leaned over the side of the boat and, shuddering, washed the blood from his hands. He scrubbed the oar blades where his hands had left red patches. He ripped the lining out of his coat and drenching it in the lake he cleansed his face. He took off the stained coat, wrapped it with the lining around the anchor stone in the skiff and sunk it in the lake. There were other stains upon his shirt; but these he would have to let be.

For a time he rowed aimlessly, finding in the exertion a lessening of his soul sickness. His numbed mind began to function, analyzing his plight, planning how to meet the future—how to save him.

What ought he do? Confess that he had killed Polleau's son? What reason could he give? Only that he had killed because the man had been about to cut down some trees—trees that were his father's to do with as he willed!

And if he told of the wood woman, the wood women, the shadowy shapes of their green gallants who had helped him—who would believe?

They would think him mad—mad as he half believed himself to be.

No, none would believe him. None! Nor would confession bring back life to him he had slain. No; he would not confess.

But stay—another thought came! Might he not be—accused? What actually had happened to old Polleau and his other son? He had taken it for granted that they were dead; that they had died under those bodies white and swarthy. But had they? While the green sorcery had meshed him he had held no doubt of this—else why the jubilance of the little wood, the triumphant chanting of the forest?

Were they dead—Polleau and the one-eyed son? Clearly it came to him that they had not heard as he had, had not seen as he had. To them McKay and his enemy had been but two men battling in a woodland glade; nothing more than that—until the last! Until the last? Had they seen more than that even then?

No, all that he could depend upon as real was that he had ripped out the throat of one of old Polleau's sons. That was the one unassailable verity. He had washed the blood of that man from his hands and his face.

All else might have been mirage—but one thing was true. He had murdered Polleau's son!

Remorse? He had thought that he had felt it. He knew now that he did not; that he had no shadow of remorse for what he had done. It had been panic that had shaken him, panic realization of the strangenesses, reaction from the battle lust, echoes of the war. He had been justified in that—execution. What right had those men to destroy the little wood; to wipe wantonly its beauty away?

None! He was glad that he had killed!

At that moment McKay would gladly have turned his boat and raced away to drink of the crimson chalice of the wood woman's lips. But the mists were rising. He saw that he was close to the landing of the inn. There was no one about. Now was his time to remove the last of those accusing stains. After that—

Quickly he drew up, fastened the skiff, slipped unseen to his room. He locked the door, started to undress. Then sudden sleep swept over him like a wave, drew him helplessly down into ocean depths of sleep.

A knocking at the door awakened McKay, and the innkeeper's voice summoned him to dinner. Sleepily, he answered, and as the old man's footsteps died away, he roused himself. His eyes fell upon his shirt and the great stains now rusty brown. Puzzled, he stared at them for a moment, then full memory clicked back in place.

He walked to the window. It was dusk. A wind was blowing and the trees were singing, all the little leaves dancing; the forest hummed a cheerful vespers. Gone was all the unease, all the inarticulate trouble and the fear. The forest was tranquil and it was happy.

He sought the coppice through the gathering twilight. Its demoiselles were dancing lightly in the wind, leafy hoods dipping, leafy skirts ablow. Beside them marched the green troubadours, carefree, waving their needled arms. Gay was the little wood, gay as when its beauty had first drawn him to it.

McKay undressed, hid the stained shirt in his travelling trunk, bathed and put on a fresh outfit, sauntered down to dinner. He ate excellently. Wonder now and then crossed his mind that he felt no regret, no sorrow even, for the man he had killed. Half he was inclined to believe it all a dream—so little of any emotion did he feel. He had even ceased to think of what discovery might mean.

His mind was quiet; he heard the forest chanting to him that there was nothing he need fear; and when he sat for a time that night upon the balcony a peace that was half an ecstasy stole in upon him from the murmuring woods and enfolded him. Cradled by it he slept dreamlessly.

McKay did not go far from the inn that next day. The little wood danced gaily and beckoned him, but he paid no heed. Something whispered to wait, to keep the lake between him and it until word came of what lay or had lain there. And the peace still was on him.

Only the old innkeeper seemed to grow uneasy as the hours went by. He went often to the landing, scanning the further shore.

"It is strange," he said at last to McKay as the sun was dipping behind the summits. "Polleau was to see me here today. He never breaks his word. If he could not come he would have sent one of his sons."

McKay nodded, carelessly.

"There is another thing I do not understand," went on the old man. "I have seen no smoke from the lodge all day. It is as though they were not there."

"Where could they be?" asked McKay, indifferently.

"I do not know," the voice was more perturbed. "It all troubles me, M'sieu. Polleau is hard, yes; but he is my neighbor. Perhaps an accident—"

"They would let you know soon enough if there was anything wrong," McKay said.

"Perhaps, but—" the old hesitated. "If he does not come tomorrow and again I see no smoke I will go to him," he ended.

McKay felt a little shock run through him—tomorrow then he would know, definitely know, what it was that had happened in the little wood.

"I would if I were you," he said. "I'd not wait too long either. After all—well, accidents do happen."

"Will you go with me, M'sieu," asked the old man.

"No!" whispered the warning voice within McKay. "No! Do not go!"

"Sorry," he said, aloud. "But I've some writing to do. If you should need me send back your man. I'll come."

And all that night he slept, again dreamlessly, while the crooning forest cradled him.

The morning passed without sign from the opposite shore. An hour after noon he watched the old innkeeper and his man row across the lake. And suddenly McKay's composure was shaken, his serene certainty wavered. He unstrapped his field glasses and kept them on the pair until they had beached the boat and entered the coppice. His heart was beating uncomfortably, his hands felt hot and his lips dry. He scanned the shore. How long had they been in the wood? It must have been an hour! What were they doing there? What had they found? He looked at his watch, incredulously. Less than fifteen minutes had passed.

Slowly the seconds ticked by. And it was all of an hour indeed before he saw them come out upon the shore and drag their boat into the water. McKay, throat curiously dry, a deafening pulse within his ears, steadied himself; forced himself to stroll leisurely down to the landing.

"Everything all right?" he called as they were near. They did not answer; but as the skiff warped against the landing they looked up at him and on their faces were stamped horror and a great wonder.

"They are dead, M'sieu," whispered the inkeeper. "Polleau and his two sons—all dead!"

McKay's heart gave a great leap, a swift faintness took him.

"Dead!" he cried. "What killed them?"

"What but the trees, M'sieu?" answered the old man, and McKay thought his gaze dwelt upon him strangely. "The trees killed them. See—we went up the little path through the wood, and close to the end we found it blocked by fallen trees. The flies buzzed round those trees, M'sieu, so we searched there. They were under them, Polleau and his sons. A fir had fallen upon Polleau and had crushed in his chest. Another son we found beneath a fir and upturned birches. They had broken his back, and an eye had been torn out—but that was no new wound, the latter."

He paused.

"It must have been a sudden wind," said his man. "Yet I never knew of a wind like that must have been. There were no trees down except those that lay upon them. And of those it was as though they had leaped out of the ground! Yes, as though they had leaped out of the ground upon them. Or it was as though giants had torn them out for clubs. They were not broken—their roots were bare—"

"But the other son—Polleau had two?"—try as he might, McKay could not keep the tremor out of his voice.

"Pierre," said the old man, and again McKay felt that strange quality in his gaze. "He lay beneath a fir. His throat was torn out!"

"His throat torn out!" whispered McKay. His knife! The knife that had been slipped into his hand by the shadowy shapes!

"His throat was torn out," repeated the innkeeper. "And in it still was the broken branch that had done it. A broken branch, M'sieu, pointed as a knife. It must have caught Pierre as the fir fell and ripping through his throat—been broken off as the tree crashed."

McKay stood, mind whirling in wild conjecture. "You said—a broken branch?" McKay asked through lips gone white.

"A broken branch, M'sieu," the innkeeper's eyes searched him. "It was very plain—what it was that happened. Jacques," he turned to his man. "Go up to the house."

He watched until the man shuffled out of sight.

"Yet not all plain, M'sieu," he spoke low to McKay. "For in Pierre's hand I found—this."

He reached into a pocket and drew out a button from which hung a strip of cloth. Cloth and button had once been part of that blood-stained coat which McKay had sunk within the lake; torn away no doubt when death had struck Polleau's son!

McKay strove to speak. The old man raised his hand. Button and cloth fell from it, into the water. A wave took it and floated it away; another and another. They watched it silently until it had vanished.

"Tell me nothing, M'sieu," the old innkeeper turned to him. "Polleau was hard and hard men, too, were his sons. The trees hated them. The trees killed them. And now the trees are happy. That is all. And the—souvenir—is gone. I have forgotten I saw it. Only M'sieu would better also—go."

That night McKay packed. When dawn had broken he stood at his window, looked long at the little wood. It was awakening, stirring sleepily like drowsy delicate demoiselles. He drank in its beauty—for the last time; waved it farewell.

McKay breakfasted well. He dropped into the driver's seat; set the engine humming. The old innkeeper and his wife, solicitous as ever for his welfare, bade him Godspeed. On both their faces was full friendliness—and in the old man's eyes somewhat of puzzled awe.

His road lay through the thick forest. Soon inn and lake were far behind him.

And singing went McKay, soft whisperings of leaves following him, glad chanting of needled pines; the voice of the forest tender, friendly, caressing—the forest pouring into him as farewell gift its peace, its happiness, its strength.

The Weird of Avoosl Wuthoqquan

by CLARK ASHTON SMITH

GIVE, GIVE, O magnanimous and liberal lord of the poor," cried the beggar.

Avoosl Wuthoqquan, the richest and most avaricious money-lender in all Commoriom, and, by that token, in the whole of Hyperborea, was startled from his train of revery by the sharp, eery, cicada-like voice. He eyed the supplicant with acidulous disfavor. His meditations, as he walked homeward that evening, had been splendidly replete with the shining of costly metals, with coins and ingots and gold-work and argentry, and the flaming or sparkling of many-tinted gems in rills, rivers and cascades, all flowing toward the coffers of Avoosl Wuthoqquan. Now the vision had flown; and this untimely and obstreperous voice was imploring him for alms.

"I have nothing for you." His tones were like the grating of a shut clasp.

"Only two *pazoors,* O generous one, and I will prophesy."

Avoosl Wuthoqquan gave the beggar a second glance. He had never seen so disreputable a specimen of the mendicant class in all his wayfarings through Commoriom. The man was preposterously old, and his mummy-brown skin, wherever visible, was ebbed with wrinkles that were like the heavy weaving of some giant jungle spider. His rags were no less than fabulous; and the beard that hung down and mingled with them was hoary as the moss of a primeval juniper.

"I do not require your prophecies."

"One *pazoor* then."

"No."

The eyes of the beggar became evil and malignant in their hollow sockets, like the heads of two poisonous little pit-vipers in their holes.

"Then, O Avoosl Wuthoqquan," he hissed, "I will prophesy gratis. Harken to your weird: the godless and exceeding love which you bear to all material things and your lust thereof, shall lead you on a strange quest and bring you to a doom whereof the stars and the sun will alike be ignorant. The hidden opulence of earth shall allure you and ensnare you; and earth itself shall devour you at the last."

"Begone," said Avoosl Wuthoqquan. "The weird is more than a trifle cryptic in its earlier clauses; and the final clause is somewhat platitudinous. I do not need a beggar to tell me the common fate of mortality."

It was many moons later, in that year which became known to pre-glacial historians as the year of the Black Tiger.

Avoosl Wuthoqquan sat in a lower chamber of his house, which was also his place of business. The room was obliquely shafted by the brief, aerial gold of the reddening sunset, which fell through a crystal window, lighting a serpentine line of irised sparks in the jewel-studded lamp that hung from copper chains, and touching to fiery life the tortuous threads of silver and similor in the dark arrases. Avoosl Wuthoqquan, seated in an umber shadow beyond the aisle of light, peered with an austere and ironic mien at his client, whose swarthy face and somber mantle were gilded by the passing glory.

The man was a stranger; possibly a travelling merchant from outland realms, the usurer thought—or else an outlander of more dubious occupation. His narrow, slanting, beryl-green eyes, his bluish, unkempt beard, and the uncouth cut of his sad raiment, were sufficient proof of his alienage in Commoriom.

"Three hundred *djals* is a large sum," said the moneylender thoughtfully. "Moreover, I do not know you. What security have you to offer?"

The visitor produced from the bosom of his garment a small bag of tiger-skin, tied at the mouth with sinew, and opening the bag with a deft movement, poured on the table before Avoosl Wuthoqquan two uncut emeralds of immense size and flawless purity. They flamed at the heart with a cold and ice-green fire as they caught the slanting sunset; and a greedy spark was kindled in the eyes of the usurer. But he spoke coolly and indifferently.

"It may be that I can loan you one hundred and fifty *djals*. Emeralds are hard to dispose of; and if you should not return to claim the gems and repay me the money, I might have reason to repent my generosity. But I will take the hazard."

"The loan I ask is a mere tithe of their value," protested the stranger. "Give me two hundred and fifty *djals*.... There are other money-lenders in Commoriom, I am told."

"Two hundred *djals* is the most I can offer. It is true that the gems are not without value. But you may have stolen them. How am I to know? It is not my habit to ask indiscreet questions."

"Take them," said the stranger, hastily. He accepted the

silver coins which Avoosl Wuthoqquan counted out, and offered no further protest. The usurer watched him with a sardonic smile as he departed, and drew his own inferences. He felt sure that the jewels had been stolen, but was in no wise perturbed or disquieted by this fact. No matter whom they had belonged to, or what their history, they would form a welcome and valuable addition to the coffers of Avoosl Wuthoqquan. Even the smaller of the two emeralds would have been absurdly cheap at three hundred *djals;* but the usurer felt no apprehension that the stranger would return to claim them at any time.... No, the man was plainly a thief, and had been glad to rid himself of the evidence of his guilt. As to the rightful ownership of the gems—that was hardly a matter to arouse the concern or the curiosity of the money-lender. They were his own property now, by virtue of the sum in silver which had been tacitly regarded by himself and the stranger as a price rather than a mere loan.

The sunset faded swiftly from the room and a brown twilight began to dull the metal broideries of the curtains and the colored eyes of the gems. Avoosl Wuthoqquan lit the fretted lamp; and then, opening a small brazen strongbox, he poured from it a flashing rill of jewels on the table beside the emeralds. There were pale and ice-clear topazes from Mhu Thulan, and gorgeous crystals of tourmaline from Tscho Vulpanomi; there were chill and furtive sapphires of the north, and arctic carnelians like frozen blood, and diamonds that were hearted with white stars. Red, unblinking rubies glared from the coruscating pile, chatoyants shone like the eyes of tigers, garnets and alabraundines gave their somber flames to the lamplight amid the restless hues of opals. Also, there were other emeralds, but none so large and flawless as the two that he had acquired that evening.

Avoosl Wuthoqquan sorted out the gems in gleaming rows and circles, as he had done so many times before; and he set apart all the emeralds with his new acquisitions at one end, like captains leading a file. He was well pleased with his bargain, well satisfied with his overflowing caskets. He regarded the jewels with an avaricious love, a miserly complacence; and one might have thought that his eyes were little beads of jasper, set in his leathery face as in the smoky parchment cover of some olden book of doubtful magic. Money and precious gems—these things alone, he thought, were immutable and non-volatile in a world of never-ceasing change and fugacity.

His reflections, at this point, were interrupted by a singular occurrence. Suddenly and without warning—for he had not touched or disturbed them in any manner—the two large emeralds started to roll away from their companions on the smooth, level table of black *ogga*-wood; and before the startled money-lender could put out his hand to stop them, they had vanished over the opposite edge and had fallen with a muffled rattling on the carpeted floor.

Such behavior was highly eccentric and peculiar, not to say unaccountable; but the usurer leapt to his feet with no other thought save to retrieve the jewels. He rounded the table in time to see that they had continued their mysterious rolling and were slipping through the outer door, which the stranger in departing had left slightly ajar. This door gave on a courtyard; and the courtyard, in turn, opened on the streets of Commoriom.

Avoosl Wuthoqquan was deeply alarmed, but was more concerned by the prospect of losing the emeralds than by the eeriness and mystery of their departure. He gave chase with an agility of which few would have believed him capable, and throwing open the door, he saw the fugitive emeralds gliding with an uncanny smoothness and swiftness across the rough, irregular flags of the courtyard. The twilight was deepening to a nocturnal blue; but the jewels seemed to wink derisively with a strange phosphoric luster as he followed them. Clearly visible in the gloom, they passed through the unbarred gate that gave on a principal avenue, and disappeared.

It began to occur to Avoosl Wuthoqquan that the jewels were bewitched; but not even in the face of an unknown sorcery was he willing to relinquish anything for which he had paid the munificent sum of two hundred *djals*. He gained the open street with a running leap, and paused only to make sure of the direction in which his emeralds had gone.

The dim avenue was almost entirely deserted; for the worthy citizens of Commoriom, at that hour, were preoccupied with the consumption of their evening meal. The jewels, gaining momentum, and skimming the ground lightly in their flight, were speeding away on the left toward the less reputable suburbs and the wild, luxuriant jungle beyond. Avoosl Wuthoqquan saw that he must redouble his pursuit if he were to overtake them.

Panting and wheezing valiantly with the unfamiliar exertion, he renewed the chase, but in spite of all his efforts, the jewels ran always at the same distance before him, with a maddening ease and eery volitation, tinkling musically at whiles on the pavement. The frantic and bewildered usurer was soon out of breath; and being compelled to slacken his speed, he feared to lose sight of the eloping gems; but strangely, thereafterward, they ran with a slowness that corresponded to his own, maintaining ever the same interval.

The money-lender grew desperate. The flight of the emeralds was leading him into an outlying quarter of Commoriom where thieves and murderers and beggars dwelt. Here he met a few passers, all of dubious character, who stared in stupefaction at the fleeing stones, but made no effort to stop them. Then the foul tenements among which he ran became smaller, with wider spaces between; and soon there were only sparse huts, where furtive lights gleamed out in the full-grown darkness, beneath the lowering frondage of high palms.

Still plainly visible, and shining with a mocking phosphorescence, the jewels fled before him on the dark road. It seemed to him, however, that he was gaining upon them a little. His flabby limbs and pursy body was faint with fatigue, and he was grievously winded; but he went on in renewed hope, gasping with eager avarice. A full moon, large and amber-tinted, rose beyond the jungle and began to light his way.

Commoriom was far behind him now; and there were no more huts on the lonely forest road, nor any other wayfarers. He shivered a little—either with fear or the chill night air; but he did not relax his pursuit. He was closing in on the emeralds, very gradually but surely; and he felt that he would recapture them soon. So engrossed was he in the weird chase, with his eyes on the ever-rolling gems, that he failed to perceive that he was no longer following an open highway. Somehow, somewhere, he had taken a narrow path that wound among monstrous trees whose foliage turned the moonlight to a mesh of quick-silver with heavy, fantastic raddlings of ebony. Crouching in grotesque menace, like giant retiarii, they seemed to close in upon him from all sides. But the money-lender was oblivious of their shadowy threats, and heeded not the sinister strangeness and solitude of the jungle path, nor the dank odors that lingered beneath the trees like unseen pools.

Nearer and nearer he came to the fleeting gems, till they ran and flickered tantalizingly a little beyond his reach, and seemed to look back at him like two greenish, glowing eyes, filled with allurement and mockery. Then, as he was about to fling himself forward in a last and supreme effort to secure them, they vanished abruptly from view, as if they had been swallowed by the forest shadows that lay like sable pythons athwart the moonlit way.

Baffled and disconcerted, Avoosl Wuthoqquan paused and peered in bewilderment at the place where they had disappeared. He saw that the path ended in a cavern-mouth yawning blackly and silently before him, and leading to unknown subterranean depths. It was a doubtful and suspicious-looking cavern, fanged with sharp stones and bearded with queer grasses; and Avoosl Wuthoqquan, in his cooler moments, would have hesitated a long while before entering it. But just then he was capable of no other impulse than the fervor of the chase and the prompting of avarice.

The cavern that had swallowed his emeralds in a fashion so nefarious was a steep incline running swiftly down into darkness. It was low and narrow, and slippery with noisome oozings; but the money-lender was heartened as he went on by a glimpse of the glowing jewels, which seemed to float beneath him in the black air, as if to illuminate his way. The incline led to a level, winding passage, in which Avoosl Wuthoqquan began to overtake his elusive property once more; and hope flared high in his panting bosom.

The emeralds were almost within reach; then, with sleightful suddenness, they slipped from his ken beyond an abrupt angle of the passage; and following them, he paused in wonder, as if halted by an irresistible hand. He was half blinded for some moments by the pale, mysterious, bluish light that poured from the roof and walls of the huge cavern into which he had emerged; and he was more than dazzled by the multi-tinted splendor that flamed and glowed and glistened and sparkled at his very feet.

He stood on a narrow ledge of stone; and the whole chamber before and beneath him, almost to the level of this ledge, was filled with jewels even as a granary is filled with grain! It was as if all the rubies, opals, beryls, diamonds, amethysts, emeralds, chrysolites and sapphires of the world had been gathered together and poured into an immense pit. He thought that he saw his own emeralds, lying tranquilly and decorously in a nearer mound of the undulant mass; but there were so many others of like size and flawlessness that he could not be sure of them.

For awhile, he could hardly believe the ineffable vision. Then, with a single cry of ecstasy, he leapt forward from the ledge, sinking almost to his knees in the shifting and tinkling and billowing gems. In great double handfuls, he lifted the flaming and scintillating stones and let them sift between his fingers, slowly and voluptuously, to fall with a light clash on the monstrous heap. Blinking joyously, he watched the royal lights and colors run in spreading or narrowing ripples; he saw them burn like steadfast coals and secret stars, or leap out in blazing eyes that seemed to catch fire from each other.

In his most audacious dreams, the usurer had never even suspected the existence of such riches. He babbled aloud in a rhapsody of delight, as he played with the numberless gems; and he failed to perceive that he was sinking deeper with every movement into the unfathomable pit. The jewels had risen above his knees, were engulfing his pudgy thighs, before his avaricious rapture was touched by any thought of peril.

Then, startled by the realization that he was sinking into his new-found wealth as into some treacherous quicksand, he sought to extricate himself and return to the safety of the ledge. He floundered helplessly; for the moving gems gave way beneath him, and he made no progress but went deeper still, till the bright, unstable heap had risen to his waist.

Avoosl Wuthoqquan began to feel a frantic terror amid the intolerable irony of his plight. He cried out; and as if in answer, there came a loud, unctuous, evil chuckle from the cavern behind him. Twisting his fat neck with painful effort, so that he could peer over his shoulder, he saw a most peculiar entity that was couching on a sort of shelf above the pit of jewels. The entity was wholly and outrageously unhuman; and neither did it resemble any species of animal, or any known god or demon of Hyperborea. Its aspect was not such as to lessen the alarm and panic of the money-lender; for it was very large and pale and squat, with a toad-like face and a swollen, squidgy body and numerous cuttlefish limbs or appendages. It lay flat on the shelf, with its chinless head and long slit-like mouth overhanging the pit, and its cold, lidless eyes peering obliquely at Avoosl Wuthoqquan. The usurer was not reassured when it began to speak in a thick and loathsome voice, like the molten tallow of corpses dripping from a wizard's kettle.

"Ho! what have we here?" it said. "By the black altar of

Tsathoggua, 'tis a fat money-lender, wallowing in my jewels like a lost pig in a quagmire!"

"Help me!" cried Avoosl Wuthoqquan. "See you not that I am sinking?"

The entity gave its oleaginous chuckle. "Yes, I see your predicament, of course.... What are you doing here?"

"I came in search of my emeralds—two fine and flawless stones for which I have just paid the sum of two hundred *djals.*"

"*Your* emeralds?" said the entity. "I fear that I must contradict you. The jewels are mine. They were stolen not long ago from this cavern, in which I have been wont to gather and guard my subterranean wealth for many ages. The thief was frightened away... when he saw me... and I suffered him to go. He had taken only the two emeralds; and I knew that they would return to me—as my jewels always return—whenever I choose to call them. The thief was lean and bony, and I did well to let him go; for now, in his place, there is a plump and well-fed usurer."

Avoosl Wuthoqquan, in his mounting fear, was barely able to comprehend the words or to grasp their implications. He had sunk slowly but steadily into the yielding pile; and green, yellow, red and violet gems were blinking gorgeously about his bosom and sifting with a light tinkle beneath his armpits.

"Help! help!" he wailed. "I shall be engulfed!"

Grinning sardonically, and showing the cloven tip of a fat white tongue, the singular entity slid from the shelf with boneless ease; and spreading its flat body on the pool of gems, into which it hardly sank, it slithered forward to a position from which it could reach the frantic usurer with its octopus-like members. It dragged him free with a single motion of incredible celerity. Then, without pause or preamble or further comment, in a leisurely and methodical fashion, it began to devour him.

The Valley of the Worm

by ROBERT E. HOWARD

I WILL tell you of Niord and the Worm. You have heard the tale before in many guises wherein the hero was named Tyr, or Perseus, or Siegfried, or Beowulf, or Saint George. But it was Niord who met the loathly demoniac thing that crawled hideously up from hell, and from which meeting sprang the cycle of hero-tales that revolves down the ages until the very substance of the truth is lost and passes into the limbo of all forgotten legends. I know whereof I speak, for I was Niord.

As I lie here awaiting death, which creeps slowly upon me like a blind slug, my dreams are filled with glittering visions and the pageantry of glory. It is not of the drab, disease-racked life of James Allison I dream, but all the gleaming figures of the mighty pageantry that have passed before, and shall come after; for I have faintly glimpsed, not merely the shapes that trail out behind, but shapes that come after, as a man in a long parade glimpses, far ahead, the line of figures that precede him winding over a distant hill, etched shadow-like against the sky. I am one and all the pageantry of shapes and guises and masks which have been, are, and shall be the visible manifestations of that illusive, intangible, but vitally existent spirit now promenading under the brief and temporary name of James Allison.

Each man on earth, each woman, is part and all of a similar caravan of shapes and beings. But they can not remember—their minds can not bridge the brief, awful gulfs of blackness which lie between those unstable shapes, and which the spirit, soul or ego, in spanning, shakes off its fleshly masks. I remember. Why I can remember is the strangest tale of all; but as I lie here with death's black wings slowly unfolding over me, all the dim folds of my previous lives are shaken out before my eyes, and I see myself in many forms and guises—braggart, swaggering, fearful, loving, foolish, all that men have been or will be.

I have been Man in many lands and many conditions; yet—and here is another strange thing—my line of reincarnation runs straight down one unerring channel. I have never been any but a man of that restless race men once called Nordheimr and later Aryans, and today name by many names and designations. Their history is my history, from the first mewling wail of a hairless white ape cub in the wastes of the Artic; to the death-cry of the last degenerate product of ultimate civilization, in some dim and unguessed future age.

My name has been Hialmar, Tyr, Bragi, Bran, Horsa, Eric, and John. I strode red-handed through the deserted streets of Rome behind the yellow-maned Brennus; I wandered through the violated plantations with Alaric and his Goths when the flame of burning villas lit the land like day and an empire was gasping its last under our sandalled feet; I waded sword in hand through the foaming surf from Hengist's galley to lay the foundations of England in blood and pillage; when Leif the Lucky sighted the broad white beaches of an unguessed world, I stood beside him in the bows of the dragon-ship, my golden beard blowing in the wind; and when Godfrey of Bouillon led his Crusaders over the walls of Jerusalem, I was among them in steel cap and brigandine.

But it is of none of these things I would speak. I would take you back with me into an age beside which that of Brennus and Rome is as yesterday. I would take you back through, not merely centuries and millenniums, but epochs and dim ages unguessed by the wildest philosopher. Oh far, far and far will you fare into the nighted Past before you win beyond the boundaries of my race, blue-eyed, yellow-haired, wanderers, slayers, lovers, mighty in rapine and wayfaring.

It is the adventure of Niord Worm's-bane of which I would speak—the root-stem of a whole cycle of hero-tales which has not yet reached its end, the grisly underlying reality that lurks behind time-distorted myths of dragons, fiends and monsters.

Yet it is not alone with the mouth of Niord that I will speak. I am James Allison no less than I was Niord, and as I unfold the tale, I will interpret some of his thoughts and dreams and deeds from the mouth of the modern I, so that the saga of Niord shall not be a meaningless chaos to you. His blood is your blood, who are sons of Aryan; but wide misty gulfs of eons lie horrifically between, and the deeds and dreams of Niord seem as alien to your deeds and dreams as the primordial and lion-haunted forest seems alien to the white-walled city street.

It was a strange world in which Niord lived and loved and fought, so long ago that even my eon-spanning memory can not recognize landmarks. Since then the surface of the earth has changed, not once but a score of times; continents have risen and sunk, seas have changed their beds and rivers their courses, glaciers have waxed and waned, and the very stars and constellations have altered and shifted.

It was so long ago that the cradle-land of my race was still in Nordheim. But the epic drifts of my people had already begun, and blue-eyed, yellow-maned tribes flowed eastward and southward and westward, on century-long treks that carried them around the world and left their bones and their traces in strange lands and wild waste places. On one of these drifts I grew from infancy to manhood. My knowledge of that northern homeland was dim memories, like half-remembered dreams, of blinding white snow plains and ice fields, of great fires roaring in the circle of hide tents, of yellow manes flying in great winds, and a sun setting in a lurid wallow of crimson clouds, blazing on trampled snow where still dark forms lay in pools that were redder than the sunset.

That last memory stands out clearer than the others. It was the field of Jotunheim, I was told in later years, whereon had just been fought that terrible battle which was the Armageddon of the Æsir-folk, the subject of a cycle of hero-songs for long ages, and which still lives today in dim dreams of Ragnarok and Goetterdaemmerung. I look on that battle as a mewling infant; so I must have lived about—but I will not name the age, for I would be called a madman, and historians and geologists alike would rise to dispute me.

But my memories of Nordheim were few and dim, paled by memories of that long, long trek upon which I have spent my life. We had not kept to a straight course, but our trend had been forever southward. Sometimes we had bided for a while in fertile upland valleys or rich river-traversed plains, but always we took up the trail again, and not always because of drought or famine. Often we left countries teeming with game and wild grain to push into wastelands. On our trail we moved endlessly, driven only by our restless whim, yet blindly following a cosmic law, the workings of which we never guessed, any more than the wild geese guess in their flights around the world. So at last we came into the Country of the Worm.

I will take up the tale at the time when we came into jungle-clad hills reeking with rot and teeming with spawning life, where the tom-toms of a savage people pushed incessantly through the hot breathless night. These people came forth to dispute our way—short, strongly built men, black-haired, painted, ferocious, but indisputably white men. We knew their breed of old. They were Picts, and of all alien races the fiercest. We had met their kind before in thick forests, and in upland valleys beside mountain lakes. But many moons had passed since those meetings.

I believe this particular tribe represented the easternmost drift of the race. They were the most primitive and ferocious of any I ever met. Already they were exhibiting hints of characteristics I have noted among black savages in jungle countries, though they had dwelt in these envisions only a few generations. The absymal jungle was engulfing them, was obliterating their pristine characteristics and shaping them in its own horrific mold. They were drifting into head-hunting, and cannibalism was but a step which I believe they must have taken before they became extinct. These things are natural adjuncts to the jungle; the Picts did not learn them from the black people, for then there were no blacks among those hills. In later years they came up from the south, and the Picts first enslaved and then were absorbed by them. But with that my saga of Niord is not concerned.

We came into that brutish hill country, with its squalling absyms of savagery and black primitiveness. We were a whole tribe marching on foot, old men, wolfish with their long beards and gaunt limbs, giant warriors in their prime, naked children running along the line of march, women with tousled yellow locks carrying babies which never cried—unless it were to scream from pure rage. I do not remember our numbers, except that there were some five hundred fighting-men—and by fighting-men I mean all males, from the child just strong enough to lift a bow, to the oldest of the old men. In that madly ferocious age all were fighters. Our women fought, when brought to bay, like tigresses, and I have seen a babe, not yet old enough to stammer articulate words, twist its head and sink its teeth in the foot that stamped out its life.

Oh, we were fighters! Let me speak of Niord. I am proud of him, the more when I consider the paltry crippled body of James Allison, the unstable mask I now wear. Niord was tall, with great shoulders, lean hips and mighty limbs. His muscles were long and swelling, denoting endurance and speed as well as strength. He could run all day without tiring, and he possessed a co-ordination that made his movements a blur of blinding speed. If I told you his full strength, you would brand me a liar. But there is no man on earth today strong enough to bend the bow Niord handled with ease. The longest arrow-flight on record is that of a Turkish archer who sent a shaft 482 yards. There was not a stripling in my tribe who could not have bettered that flight.

As we entered the jungle country we heard the tom-toms booming across the mysterious valley that slumbered between the brutish hills, and in a broad, open plateau we met our enemies. I do not believe these Picts knew us, even by legends, or they had never rushed so openly to the onset, though they outnumbered us. But there was no attempt at ambush. They swarmed out of the trees, dancing and singing their war-songs, yelling their barbarous threats. Our heads should hang in their idol-hut and our yellow-haired women should bear their sons. Ho! ho! ho! By Ymir, it was Niord who laughed then, not James Allison. Just so we of the Æsir laughed to hear their threats—deep thunderous laughter from broad and mighty chests. Our trail was laid in blood and embers through many lands. We were the slayers and ravishers, striding sword in hand across the world, and that these folk threatened us woke our rugged humor.

We went to meet them, naked but for our wolfhides, swinging our bronze swords, and our singing was like rolling thunder in the hills. They sent their arrows among us, and we gave back their fire. They could not match us in archery. Our arrows hissed in blinding clouds among them, dropping them like autumn leaves, until they howled and frothed like mad dogs and charged to hand-grips. And we, mad with the fighting joy, dropped our bows and ran to meet them, as a lover runs to his love.

By Ymir, it was a battle to madden and make drunken with the slaughter and the fury. The Picts were as ferocious as we, but ours was the superior physique, the keener wit, the more highly developed fighting-brain. We won because we were a superior race, but it was no easy victory. Corpses littered the blood-soaked earth; but at last they broke, and we cut them down as they ran, to the very edge of the trees. I tell of that fight in a few bald words. I can not paint the madness, the reek of sweat and blood, the panting, muscle-straining effort, the splintering of bones under mighty blows, the rending and hewing of quivering sentient flesh; above all the merciless, abysmal savagery of the whole affair, in which there was neither rule nor order, each man fighting as he would or could. If I might do so, you would recoil in horror; even the modern I, cognizant of my close kinship with those times, stand aghast as I review that butchery. Mercy was yet unborn, save as some individual's whim, and rules of warfare were as yet undreamed of. It was an age in which each tribe and each human fought tooth and fang from birth to death, and neither gave nor expected mercy.

So we cut down the fleeting Picts, and our women came out on the field to brain the wounded enemies with stones, or cut their throats with copper knives. We did not torture. We were no more cruel than life demanded. The rule of life was ruthlessness, but there is no more wanton cruelty today than ever we dreamed of. It was not wanton bloodthirstiness that made us butcher wounded and captive foes. It was because we knew our chances of survival increased with each enemy slain.

Yet there was occasionally a touch of individual mercy, and so it was in this fight. I had been occupied with a duel with an especially valiant enemy. His tousled thatch of black hair scarcely came above my chin, but he was a solid knot of steel-spring muscles, than which lightning scarcely moved faster. He had an iron sword and a hide-covered buckler. I had a knotty-headed bludgeon. That fight was one that glutted even my battle-lusting soul. I was bleeding from a score of flesh wounds before one of my terrible, lashing strokes smashed his shield like cardboard, and an instant later my bludgeon glanced from his unprotected head. Ymir! Even now I stop to laugh and marvel at the hardness of that Pict's skull. Men of that age were assuredly built on a rugged plan! That blow should have spattered his brains like water. It did lay his scalp open horribly, dashing him senseless to the earth, where I let him lie, supposing him to be dead, as I joined in the slaughter of the fleeing warriors.

When I returned reeking with sweat and blood, my club horribly clotted with blood and brains, I noticed that my antagonist was regaining consciousness, and that a naked tousle-headed girl was preparing to give him the finishing touch with a stone she could scarcely lift. A vagrant whim caused me to check the blow. I had enjoyed the fight, and I admired the adamantine quality of his skull.

We made camp a short distance away, burned our dead on a great pyre, and after looting the corpses of the enemy, we dragged them across the plateau and cast them down in a valley to make a feast for the hyenas, jackals and vultures which were already gathering. We kept close watch that night, but we were not attacked, though far away through the jungle we could make out the red gleam of fires, and could faintly hear, when the wind veered, the throb of tom-toms and demoniac screams and yells—keenings for the slain or mere animal squallings of fury.

Nor did they attack us in the days that followed. We bandaged our captive's wounds and quickly learned his primitive tongue, which, however, was so different from ours that I can not conceive of the two languages having ever had a common source.

His name was Grom, and he was a great hunter and fighter,

he boasted. He talked freely and held no grudge, grinning broadly and showing tusk-like teeth, his beady eyes glittering from under the tangled black mane that fell over his low forehead. His limbs were almost ape-like in their thickness.

He was vastly interested in his captors, though he could never understand why he had been spared; to the end it remained an inexplicable mystery to him. The Picts obeyed the law of survival even more rigidly than did the Æsir. They were the more practical, as shown by their more settled habits. They never roamed as far or as blindly as we. Yet in every line we were the superior race.

Grom, impressed by our intelligence and fighting qualities, volunteered to go into the hills and make peace for us with his people. It was immaterial to us, but we let him go. Slavery had not yet been dreamed of.

So Grom went back to his people, and we forgot about him, except that I went a trifle more cautiously about my hunting, expecting him to be lying in wait to put an arrow through my back. Then one day we heard a rattle of tom-toms, and Grom appeared at the edge of the jungle, his face split in his gorilla-grin, with the painted, skin-clad, feather-bedecked chiefs of the clans. Our ferocity had awed them, and our sparing of Grom further impressed them. They could not understand leniency; evidently we valued them too cheaply to bother about killing one when he was in our power.

So peace was made with much pow-wow, and sworn to with many strange oaths and rituals—we swore only by Ymir, and an Æsir never broke that vow. But they swore by the elements, by the idol which sat in the fetish-hut where fires burned for ever and a withered crone slapped a leather-covered drum all night long, and by another being too terrible to be named.

Then we all sat around the fires and gnawed meat-bones, and drank a fiery concoction they brewed from wild grain, and the wonder is that the feast did not end in a general massacre; for that liquor had devils in it and made maggots writhe in our brain. But no harm came of our vast drunkenness, and thereafter we dwelt at peace with our barbarous neighbors. They taught us many things, and learned many more from us. But they taught us iron-workings, into which they had been forced by the lack of copper in those hills, and we quickly excelled them.

We went freely among their villages—mud-walled clusters of huts in hilltop clearings, overshadowed by giant trees—and we allowed them to come at will among our camps—straggling lines of hide tents on the plateau where the battle had been fought. Our young men cared not for their squat beady-eyed women, and our rangy clean-limbed girls with their tousled yellow heads were not drawn to the hairy-breasted savages. Familiarity over a period of years would have reduced the repulsion on either side, until the two races would have flowed together to form one hybrid people, but long before that time the Æsir rose and departed, vanishing into the mysterious hazes of the haunted south. But before that exodus there came to pass the horror of the Worm.

I hunted with Grom and he led me into brooding, uninhabited valleys and up into silence-haunted hills where no men had set foot before us. But there was one valley, off in the mazes of the southwest, into which he would not go. Stumps of shattered columns, relics of a forgotten civilization, stood among the trees on the valley floor. Grom showed them to me, as we stood on the cliffs that flanked the mysterious vale, but he would not go down into it, and he dissuaded me when I would have gone alone. He would not speak plainly of the danger that lurked there, but it was greater than that of serpent or tiger, or the trumpeting elephants which occasionally wandered up in devastating droves from the south.

Of all beasts, Grom told me in the gutturals of his tongue, the Picts feared only Satha, the great snake, and they shunned the jungle where he lived. But there was another thing they feared, and it was connected in some manner with the Valley of Broken Stones, as the Picts called the crumbling pillars. Long ago, when his ancestors had first come into the country, they had dared that grim vale, and a whole clan of them had perished, suddenly, horribly, and unexplainably. At least Grom did not explain. The horror had come up out of the earth, somehow, and it was not good to talk of it, since it was believed that It might be summoned by speaking of It—whatever It was.

But Grom was ready to hunt with me anywhere else; for he was the greatest hunter among the Picts, and many and fearful were our adventurers. Once I killed, with the iron sword I had forged with my own hands, that most terrible of all beasts—old saber-tooth, which men today call a tiger because he was more like a tiger than anything else. In reality he was almost as much like a bear in build, save for his unmistakably feline head. Saber-tooth was massive-limbed, with a low-hung head, great, heavy body, and he vanished from the earth because he was too terrible a fighter, even for that grim age. As his muscles and ferocity grew, his brain dwindled until at last even the instinct of self-preservation vanished. Nature, who maintains her balance in such things, destroyed him because, had his super-fighting powers been allied with an intelligent brain, he would have destroyed all other forms of life on earth. He was a freak on the road of evolution—organic development gone mad and run to fangs and talons, to slaughter and destruction.

I killed saber-tooth in a battle that would make a saga in itself, and for months afterward I lay semi-delirious with ghastly wounds that made the toughest warriors shake their heads. The Picts said that never before had a man killed a saber-tooth single-handed. Yet I recovered, to the wonder of all.

While I lay at the doors of death there was a secession from the tribe. It was a peaceful secession, such as continually occurred and contributed greatly to the peopling of the world by yellow-haired tribes. Forty-five of the young men took themselves mates simultaneously and wandered off to found a clan of their own. There was no revolt; it was a racial custom which bore fruit in all the later ages, when tribes sprung from the same roots met, after centuries of separation, and cut one another's throats with joyous abandon. The tendency of the Aryan and the pre-Aryan was always toward disunity, clans splitting off the main stem, and scattering.

So these young men, led by one Bragi, my brother-in-arms, took their girls and venturing to the southwest, took up their abode in the Valley of Broken Stones. The Picts expostulated, hinting vaguely of a monstrous doom that haunted the vale, but the Æsir laughed. We had left our own demons and weirds in the icy wastes of the far blue north, and the devils of other races did not much impress us.

When my full strength was returned, and the grisly wounds were only scars, I girt on my weapons and strode over the plateau to visit Bragi's clan. Grom did not accompany me. He had not been in the Æsir camp for several days. But I knew the way. I remembered well the valley, from the cliffs of which I had looked down and seen the lake at the upper end, the trees thickening into forest at the lower extremity. The sides of the valley were high sheer cliffs, and a steep broad ridge at either end cut it off from the surrounding country. It was toward the lower or southwestern end that the valley-floor was dotted thickly with ruined columns, some towering high among the trees, some fallen into heaps of lichen-clad stones. What race reared them none knew. But Grom had hinted fearsomely of a hairy, apish monstrosity dancing loathsomely under the moon to a demoniac piping that induced horror and madness.

I crossed the plateau whereon our camp was pitched, descended the slope, traversed a shallow vegetation-choked valley, climbed another slope, and plunged into the hills. A half-day's leisurely travel brought me to the ridge on the other side of which lay the valley of the pillars. For many miles I had seen no sign of human life. The settlements of the Picts all lay many miles to the east. I toppled the ridge and looked down into the dreaming valley with its still blue lake, its brooding cliffs and its broken columns jutting among the trees. I looked for smoke. I saw none, but I saw vultures wheeling in the sky over a cluster of tents on the lake shore.

I came down the ridge, warily and approached the silent camp. In it I halted, frozen with terror. I was not easily moved. I had seen death in many forms, and had fled from or taken part in red massacres that spilled blood like water and heaped the earth with corpses. But here I was confronted with an organic devastation that staggered and appalled me. Of Bragi's embryonic clan, not one remained alive, and not one corpse was whole. Some of the hide tents still stood erect. Others were mashed down and flattened out, as if crushed by some monstrous weight, so that at first I wondered if a drove of elephants had stampeded across the camp. But no elephants ever wrought such destruction as I saw strewn on the bloody ground. The camp was a shambles, littered with bits of flesh and fragments of bodies—hands, feet, heads, pieces of human debris. Weapons lay about, some of them stained with a greenish slime like that which spurts from a crushed caterpillar.

No human foe could have committed this ghastly atrocity. I looked at the lake, wondering if nameless amphibian monsters had crawled from the calm waters whose deep blue told of unfathomed depths. Then I saw a print left by the destroyer. It was a track such as a titanic worm might leave, yards broad, winding back down the valley. The grass lay flat where it ran, and bushes and small trees had been crushed down into the earth, all horribly smeared with blood and greenish slime.

With berserk fury in my soul I drew my sword and started to follow it, when a call attracted me. I wheeled, to see a stocky form approaching me from the ridge. It was Grom the Pict, and when I think of the courage it must have taken for him to have overcome all the instincts planted in him by traditional teachings and personal experience, I realize the full depths of his friendship for me.

Squatting on the lake shore, spear in his hands, his black eyes ever roving fearfully down the brooding tree-waving reaches of the valley, Grom told me of the horror that had come upon Bragi's clan under the moon. But first he told me of it, as his sires had told the tale to him.

Long ago the Picts had drifted down from the northwest on a long, long trek, finally reaching these jungle-covered hills, where, because they were weary, and because the game and fruit were plentiful and there were no hostile tribes, they halted and built their mud-walled villages.

Some of them, a whole clan of that numerous tribe, took up their abode in the Valley of the Broken Stones. They found the columns and a great ruined temple back in the trees, and in that temple there was no shrine or altar, but the mouth of a shaft that vanished deep into the black earth, and in which there were no steps such as a human being would make and use. They built their village in the valley, and in the night, under the moon, horror came upon them and left only broken walls and bits of slime-smeared flesh.

In those days the Picts feared nothing. The warriors of the other clans gathered and sang their war-songs and danced their war dances, and followed a broad track of blood and slime to the shaft-mouth in the temple. They howled defiance and hurled down boulders which were never heard to strike bottom. Then began a thin demoniac piping, and up from the well pranced a hideous anthropomorphic figure dancing to the weird strains of a pipe it held in its monstrous hands. The horror of its aspect froze the fierce Picts with amazement, and close behind it a vast white bulk heaved up from the subterranean darkness. Out of the shaft came a slavering mad nightmare which arrows pierced but could not check, which swords carved but could not slay. It fell slobbering upon the warriors, crushing them to crimson pulp, tearing them to bits as an octopus might tear small fishes, sucking their blood from their mangled limbs and devouring them even as they screamed and struggled. The survivors fled, pursued to the very ridge, up which, apparently, the monster could not propel its quaking mountainous bulk.

After that they did not dare the silent valley. But the dead came to their shamans and old men in dreams and told them strange and terrible secrets. They spoke of an ancient, ancient race of semi-human beings which once inhabited that valley and reared those columns for their own weird inexplicable purpose. The white monster in the pits was their god, summoned up from the nighted abysses of mid-earth uncounted fathoms below the black mold, by sorcery unknown to the sons of men. The hairy anthropomorphic being was its servant, created to serve the god, a formless elemental spirit drawn up from below and cased in flesh, organic but beyond the understanding of humanity. The Old Ones had long vanished into the limbo from whence they crawled in the black dawn of the universe, but their bestial god and his inhuman slave lived on. Yet both were organic after a fashion, and could be wounded, though no human weapon had been found potent enough to slay them.

Bragi and his clan had dwelt for weeks in the valley before the horror struck. Only the night before, Grom, hunting above the cliffs, and by that token daring greatly, had been paralyzed by a high-pitched demon piping, and then by a mad clamor of human screaming. Stretched face down in the dirt, hiding his head in a tangle of grass, he had not dared to move, even when the shrieks died away in the slobbering, repulsive sounds of a hideous feast. When dawn broke he had crept shuddering to the cliffs to look down into the valley, and the sight of the devastation, even when seen from afar, had driven him in yammering flight far into the hills. But it had occurred to him, finally, that he should warn the rest of the tribe, and returning, on his way to the camp on the plateau, he had seen me entering the valley.

So spoke Grom, while I sat and brooded darkly, my chin on my mighty fist. I can not frame in modern words the clan-feeling that in those days was a living vital part of every man and woman. In a world where talon and fang were lifted on every hand, and the hands of all men raised against an individual, except those of his own clan, tribal instinct was more than the phase it is today. It was as much a part of a man as was his heart or his right hand. This was necessary, for only thus banded together in unbreakable groups could mankind have survived in the terrible environments of the primitive world. So now the personal grief I felt for Bragi and the clean-limbed young men and laughing white-skinned girls was drowned in a deeper sea of grief and fury that was cosmic in its depth and intensity. I sat grimly, while the Pict squatted anxiously beside me, his gaze roving from me to the menacing deeps of the valley where the accursed columns loomed like broken teeth of cackling hags among the waving leafy reaches.

I, Niord, was not one to use my brain over-much. I lived in a physical world, and there were the old men of the tribe to do my thinking. But I was one of a race destined to become dominant mentally as well as physically, and I was no mere muscular animal. So as I sat there there came dimly and then clearly a thought to me that brought a short fierce laugh from my lips.

Rising, I bade Grom aid me, and we built a pyre on the lake shore of dried wood, the ridge-poles of the tents, and the broken shafts of spears. Then we collected the grisly fragments that had been parts of Bragi's band, and we laid them on the pile, and struck flint and steel to it.

The thick sad smoke crawled serpent-like into the sky, and turning to Grom, I made him guide me to the jungle where lurked that scaly horror, Satha, the great serpent. Grom gaped at me; not the greatest hunters among the Picts sought out the mighty crawling one. But my will was like a wind that swept him along my course, and at last he led the way. We left the valley by the upper end, crossing the ridge, skirting the tall cliffs, and plunged into the fastnesses of the south, which was peopled only by the grim denizens of the jungle. Deep into the jungle we went, until we came to a low-lying expanse, dark and dark beneath the great creeper-festooned trees, where our feet sank deep into the spongy silt, carpeted by rotting vegetation, and slimy moisture oozed up beneath their pressure. This, Grom told me, was the realm haunted by Satha, the great serpent.

Let me speak of Satha. There is nothing like him on earth today, nor has there been for countless ages. Like the meat-eating dinosaur, like old saber-tooth, he was too terrible to exist. Even then he was a survival of a grimmer age when life and its forms were cruder and more hideous. There were not many of his kind then, though they may have existed in great numbers in the reeking ooze of the vast jungled-tangled swamps still farther south. He was larger than any python of modern ages, and his fangs dripped with poison a thousand times more deadly than that of a king cobra.

He was never worshipped by the pure-blood Picts, though the blacks that came later defied him, and that adoration persisted in the hybrid race that sprang from the Negroes and their white conquerors. But to other peoples he was the nadir of evil horror, and the tales of him became twisted into demonology; so in later ages Satha became the veritable devil of the white races, and the Stygians first worshipped, and then, when they became Egyptians, abhorred him under the name of Set, the Old Serpent, while to the Semites he became Leviathan and Satan. He was terrible enough to be a god, for he was a crawling death. I had seen a bull elephant fall dead in his tracks from Satha's bite. I had seen him, had glimped him writhing his horrific way through the dense jungle, had seen him take his prey, but had never hunted him. He was too grim, even for the slayer of old saber-tooth.

But now I hunted him, plunging farther and farther into the hot, breathless reek of his jungle, even when friendship for me could not drive Grom farther. He urged me to paint my body and sing my death-song before I advanced farther, but I pushed on unheeding.

In a natural runway that wound between the shouldering trees, I set a trap. I found a large tree, soft and spongy of fiber, but thick-boled and heavy, and I hacked through its base close to the ground with my great sword, directing its fall so that when it toppled, its top crashed into the branches of a smaller tree, leaving it leaning across the runway, one end resting on the earth, the other caught in the small tree. Then I cut away the branches on the under side, and cutting a slim tough sapling I trimmed it and stuck it upright like a prop-pole under the leaning tree. Then, cutting away the tree which supported it, I left the great trunk poised precariously on the prop-pole, to which I fastened a long vine, as thick as my wrist.

Then I went alone through the primordial twilight jungle until an overpowering fetid odor assailed my nostrils, and from the rank vegetation in front of me, Satha reared up his hideous head, swaying lethally from side to side, while his forked tongue jetted in and out, and his great yellow terrible eyes burned icily on me with all the evil wisdom of the black elder world that was when man was not. I backed away, feeling no fear, only an icy sensation along my spine, and Satha came sinuously after me, his shining eighty-foot barrel rippling over the rotting vegetation in mesmeric silence. His wedge-shaped head was bigger than the head of the hugest stallion, his trunk was thicker than a man's body, and his scales shimmered with a thousand changing scintillations. I was to Satha as a mouse is to a king cobra, but I was fanged as no mouse ever was. Quick as I was, I knew I could not avoid the lightning stroke of that great triangular head; so I dared not let him come too close. Subtly I fled down the runway, and behind me the rush of the great supple body was like the sweep of wind through the grass.

He was not far behind me when I raced beneath the deadfall, and as the great shining length glided under the trap, I gripped the vine with both hands and jerked desperately. With a crash the great trunk fell across Satha's scaly back, some six feet back of his wedge-shaped head.

I had hoped to break his spine but I do not think it did, for the great body coiled and knotted, the mighty tail lashed and thrashed, mowing down the bushes as if with a giant flail. At the instant of the fall, the huge head had whipped about and struck the tree with a terrific impact, the mighty fangs shearing through bark and wood like scimitars. Now, as if aware he fought an inanimate foe, Satha turned on me, standing out of his reach. The scaly neck writhed and arched, the mighty jaws gaped, disclosing fangs a foot in length, from which dripped venom that might have burned through solid stone.

I believe, what of his stupendous strength, that Satha would have writhed from under the trunk, but for a broken branch that had been driven deep into his side, holding him like a barb. The sound of his hissing filled the jungle and his eyes glared at me with such concentrated evil I shook despite myself. Oh, he knew it was I who had trapped him! Now I came as close as I dared, and with a sudden powerful cast of my spear, transfixed his neck just below the gaping jaws, nailing him to the tree-trunk. Then I dared greatly, for he was far from dead, and I knew he would in an instant tear the spear from the wood and be free to strike. But in that instant I ran in, and swinging my sword with all my great power, I hewed off his terrible head.

The heavings and contortions of Satha's prisoned form in life were naught to the convulsions of his headless length in death. I retreated, dragging the gigantic head after me with a crooked pole, and a safe distance from the lashing, flying tail, I set to work. I worked with naked death then, and no man ever toiled more gingerly than did I. For I cut out the poison sacs at the base of the great fangs, and in the terrible venom I soaked the heads of eleven arrows, being careful that only the bronze points were in the liquid, which else had corroded away the wood of the tough shafts. While I was doing this, Grom, driven by comradeship and curiosity, came stealing nervously through the jungle, and his mouth gaped as he looked on the head of Satha.

For hours I seeped the arrowheads in the poison, until they were caked with a horrible green scum, and showed tiny flecks of corrosion where the venom had eaten into the solid bronze.

I wrapped them carefully in broad, thick, rubber-like leaves, and then, though night had fallen and the hunting beasts were roaring on every hand, I went back through the jungled hills, Grom with me, until at dawn we came again to the high cliffs that loomed above the Valley of Broken Stones.

At the mouth of the valley I broke my spear, and I took all the unpoisoned shafts from my quiver, and snapped them. I painted my face and limbs as the Æsir painted themselves only when they went forth to certain doom, and I sang my death-song to the sun as it rose over the cliffs, my yellow mane blowing in the morning wind.

Then I went down into the valley, bow in hand.

Grom could not drive himself to follow me. He lay on his belly in the dust and howled like a dying dog.

I passed the lake and the silent camp where the pyre-ashes still smoldered, and came under the thickening trees beyond. About me the columns loomed, mere shapeless heaps from the ravages of staggering eons. The trees grew more dense, and under their vast leafy branches the very light was dusky and evil. As in twilight shadow I saw the ruined temple, cyclopean walls staggering up from masses of decaying masonry and fallen blocks of stone. About six hundred yards in front of it a great column reared up in an open glade, eighty or ninety feet in height. It was so worn and pitted by weather and time that any child of my tribe could have climbed it, and I marked it and changed my plan.

I came to the ruins and saw huge crumbling walls upholding a domed roof from which many stones had fallen, so that it seemed like the lichen-grown ribs of some mythical monster's skeleton arching above me. Titanic columns flanked the open doorway through which ten elephants could have stalked abreast. Once there might have been inscriptions and hieroglyphics on the pillars and walls, but they were long worn away. Around the great room, on the inner side, ran columns in better state of preservation. On each of these columns was a flat pedestal, and some dim instinctive memory vaguely resurrected a shadowy scene wherein black drums roared madly, and on these pedestals monstrous beings squatted loathsomely in inexplicable rituals rooted in the black dawn of the universe.

There was no altar—only the mouth of a great well-like shaft in the stone stone floor, with strange obscene carvings all about the rim. I tore great pieces of stone from the rotting floor and cast them down the shaft which slanted down into utter darkness. I heard them bound along the side, but I did not hear them strike bottom. I cast down stone after stone, each with a searing curse, and at last I heard a sound that was not the dwindling rumble of the falling stones. Up from the well floated a weird demon-piping that was a symphony of madness. Far down in the darkness I glimpsed the faint fearful glimmering of a vast white bulk.

I retreated slowly as the piping grew louder, falling back through the broad doorway. I heard a scratching, scrambling noise, and up from the shaft and out of the doorway between the colossal columns came a prancing incredible figure. It went erect like a man, but it was covered with fur, that was shaggiest where its face should have been. If it had ears, nose and a mouth I did not discover them. Only a pair of staring red eyes leered from the furry mask. Its misshapen hands held a strange set of pipes, on which it blew weirdly as it pranced toward me with many a grotesque caper and leap.

Behind it I heard a repulsive obscene noise as of a quaking unstable mass heaving up out of a well. Then I nocked an arrow, drew the cord and sent the shaft singing through the furry beast of the dancing monstrosity. It went down as though struck by a thunderbolt, but to my horror the piping continued, though the pipes had fallen from the malformed hands. Then I turned and ran fleetly to the column, up which I swarmed before I looked back. When I reached the pinnacle I looked, and because of the shock and surprise of what I saw, I almost fell from my dizzy perch.

Out of the temple the monstrous dweller in the darkness

had come, and I, who had expected a horror yet cast in some terrestrial mold, looked on the spawn of nightmare. From what subterranean hell it crawled in the long ago I know not, nor what black age it represented. But it was not a beast, as humanity knows beasts. I call it a worm for lack of a better term. There is no earthly language which has a name for it. I can only say it looked somewhat more like a worm than it did an octopus, a serpent or a dinosaur.

It was white and pulpy, and drew its quaking bulk along the ground, worm-fashion. But it had wide flat tentacles, and fleshly feelers, and other adjuncts the use of which I am unable to explain. And it had a long proboscis which it curled and uncurled like an elephant's trunk. Its forty eyes, set in a horrific circle, were composed of thousands of facets of as many scintillant colors which changed and altered in never-ending transmutation. But through all interplay of hue and glint, they retained their evil intelligence—intelligence there was behind those flickering facets, not human nor yet bestial, but a night-born demoniac intelligence such as men in dreams vaguely sense throbbing titanically in the black gulfs outside our material universe. In size the monster was mountainous; its bulk would have dwarfed a mastodon.

But even as I shook with the cosmic horror of the thing, I drew a feathered shaft to my ear and arched it singing on its way. Grass and bushes were crushed flat as the monster came toward me like a moving mountain and shaft after shaft I sent with terrific force and deadly precision. I could not miss so huge a target. The arrows sank to the feathers or clear out of sight in the unstable bulk, each bearing enough poison to have stricken dead a bull elephant. Yet on it came, swiftly, appallingly, apparently heedless of both the shafts and the venom in which they were steeped. And all the time the hideous music played a maddening accompaniment, whining thinly from the pipes that lay untouched on the ground.

My confidence faded; even the poison of Satha was futile against this uncanny being. I drove my last shaft almost straight downward into the quaking white mountain, so close was the monster under my perch. Then suddenly its color altered. A wave of ghastly blue surged over it, and the vast bulk heaved in earthquake-like convulsions. With a terrible plunge it struck the lower part of the column, which crashed to falling shards of stone. But even with the impact, I leaped far out and fell through the empty air full upon the monster's back.

The spongy skin yielded and gave beneath my feet, and I drove my sword hilt deep, dragging it through the pulpy flesh, ripping a horrible yard-long wound, from which oozed a green slime. Then a flip of a cable-like tentacle flicked me from the titan's back and spun me three hundred feet through the air to crash among a cluster of giant trees.

The impact must have splintered half the bones in my frame, for when I sought to grasp my sword again and crawl anew to the combat, I could not move hand or foot, could only writhe helplessly with my broken back. But I could see the monster and I knew that I had won, even in defeat. The mountainous bulk was heaving and billowing, the tentacles were lashing madly, the antennae writhing and knotting, and the nauseous whiteness had changed to a pale and grisly green. It turned ponderously and lurched back toward the temple, rolling like a crippled ship in a heavy swell. Trees crashed and splintered as it lumbered against them.

I wept with pure fury because I could not catch my sword and rush in to die glutting my berserk madness in mighty strokes. But the worm-god was death-stricken and needed not my futile sword. The demon pipes on the ground kept up their infernal tune, and it was like the fiend's death-dirge. Then as the monster veered and floundered, I saw it catch up the corpse of its hairy slave. For an instant the apish form dangled in midair, gripped round by the trunk-like proboscis, then was dashed against the temple wall with a force that reduced the hairy body to a mere shapeless pulp. At that the pipes screamed out horribly, and fell silent for ever.

The titan staggered on the brink of the shaft, then another

change came over it—a frightful transfiguration the nature of which I can not yet describe. Even now when I try to think of it clearly, I am only chaotically conscious of a blasphemous, unnatural transmutation of form and substance, shocking and indescribable. Then the strangely altered bulk tumbled into the shaft to roll down into the ultimate darkness from whence it came, and I knew that it was dead. And as it vanished into the well, with a rending, grinding groan the ruined walls quivered from dome to base. They bent inward and buckled with deafening reverberation, the column splintered, and with a cataclysmic crash the dome itself came thundering down. For an instant the air seemed veiled with flying debris and stone-dust, through which the tree-tops lashed madly as in a storm or an earthquake convulsion. Then all was clear again and I stared, shaking the blood from my eyes. Where the temple had stood there lay only a colossal pile of shattered masonry and broken stones, and every column in the valley had fallen, to lie in crumbling shards.

In the silence that followed I heard Grom wailing to dirge over me. I bade him lay my sword in my hand, and he did so, and bent close to hear what I had to say, for I was passing swiftly.

"Let my tribe remember," I said, speaking slowly. "Let the tale be told from village to village, from camp to camp, from tribe to tribe, so that men may know that no man nor beast nor devil may prey in safety on the golden-haired people of Asgard. Let them build me a cairn where I lie and lay me therein with my bow and sword at hand, to guard this valley for ever; so if the ghost of the god I slew comes up from below, my ghost will ever be ready to give it battle."

And while Grom howled and beat his hairy breast, death came to me in the Valley of the Worm.

Black God's Kiss

by C. L. MOORE

THEY BROUGHT in Joiry's tall commander, struggling between two men-at-arms who tightly gripped the ropes which bound their captive's mailed arms. They picked their way between mounds of dead as they crossed the great hall toward the dais where the conqueror sat, and twice they slipped a little in the blood that spattered the flags. When they came to a halt before the mailed figure on the dais, Joiry's commander was breathing hard, and the voice that echoed hollowly under the helmet's confines was hoarse with fury and despair.

Guillaume the conqueror leaned on his mighty sword, hands crossed on its hilt, grinning down from his height upon the furious captive before him. He was a big man, Guillaume, and he looked bigger still in his spattered armor. There was blood on his hard, scarred face, and he was grinning a white grin that split his short, curly beard glitteringly. Very splendid and very dangerous he looked, leaning on his great sword and smiling down upon fallen Joiry's lord, struggling between the stolid men-at-arms.

"Unshell me this lobster," said Guillaume in his deep, lazy voice. "We'll see what sort of face the fellow has who gave us such a battle. Off with his helmet, you."

But a third man had to come up and slash the straps which held the iron helmet on, for the struggles of Joiry's commander were too fierce, even with bound arms, for either of the guards to release their hold. There was a moment of sharp struggle; then the straps parted and the helmet rolled loudly across the flagstones.

Guillaume's white teeth clicked on a startled oath. He stared. Joiry's lady glared back at him from between her captors, wild red hair tousled, wild lion-yellow eyes ablaze.

"God curse you!" snarled the lady of Joiry between clenched teeth. "God blast your black heart!"

Guillaume scarcely heard her. He was still staring, as most men stared when they first set eyes upon Jirel of Joiry. She was as tall as most men, and as savage as the wildest of them, and the fall of Joiry was bitter enough to break her heart as she stood snarling curses up at her tall conqueror. The face above her mail might not have been fair in a woman's headdress, but in the steel setting of her armor it had a biting, sword-edge beauty as keen as the flash of blades. The red hair was short upon her high, defiant head, and the yellow blaze of her eyes held fury as a crucible holds fire.

Guillaume's stare melted into a slow smile. A little light kindled behind his eyes as he swept the long, strong lines of her with a practiced gaze. The smile broadened, and suddenly he burst into full-throated laughter, a deep bull bellow of amusement and delight.

"By the Nails!" he roared. "Here's welcome for the warrior! and what forfeit d'ye offer, pretty one, for your life?"

She blazed a curse at him.

"So? Naughty words for a mouth so fair, my lady. Well, we'll not deny you put up a gallant battle. No man could have done better, and many have done worse. But against Guillaume—" He inflated his splendid chest and grinned down at her from the depths of his jutting beard. "Come to me, pretty one," he commanded. "I'll wager your mouth is sweeter than your words."

Jirel drove a spurred heel into the shin of one guard and twisted from his grip as he howled, bringing up an iron knee into the abdomen of the other. She had writhed from their grip and made three long strides toward the door before Guillaume caught her. She felt his arms closing about her from behind, and lashed out with both spiked heels in a futile assault upon his leg armor, twisting like a maniac, fighting with her knees and spurs, straining hopelessly at the ropes which bound her arms. Guillaume laughed and whirled her round, grinning down into the blaze of her yellow eyes. Then deliberately he set a fist under her chin and tilted her mouth up to his. There was a cessation of her hoarse curses.

"By Heaven, that's like kissing a sword-blade," said Guillaume, lifting his lips at last.

Jirel choked something that was mercifully muffled as she darted her head sidewise, like a serpent striking, and sank her teeth into his neck. She missed the jugular by a fraction of an inch.

Guillaume said nothing, then. He sought her head with a steady hand, found it despite her wild writhing, sank iron fingers deep into the hinges of her jaw, forcing her teeth relentlessly apart. When he had her free he glared down into the yellow hell of her eyes for an instant. The blaze of them was hot enough to scorch his scarred face. He grinned and lifted his ungauntleted hand, and with one heavy blow in the face he knocked her halfway across the room. She lay still upon the flags.

Jirel opened her yellow eyes upon darkness. She lay quiet for a while, collecting her scattered thoughts. By degrees it came back to her, and she muffled upon her arm a sound that was half curse and half sob. Joiry had fallen. For a time she lay rigid in the dark, forcing herself to the realization.

The sound of feet shifting on stone near by brought her out of that particular misery. She sat up cautiously, feeling about her to determine in what part of Joiry its liege lady was imprisoned. She knew that the sound she had heard must be a sentry, and by the dank smell of the darkness that she was underground. In one of the little dungeon cells, of course. With careful quietness she got to her feet, muttering a curse as her head reeled for an instant and then began to throb. In the utter dark she felt around the cell. Presently she came to a little wooden stool in a corner, and was satisfied. She gripped one leg of it with firm fingers and made her soundless way around the wall until she had located the door.

The sentry remembered, afterward, that he had heard the wildest shriek for help which had ever rung in his ears, and he remembered unbolting the door. Afterward, until they found him lying inside the locked cell with a cracked skull, he remembered nothing.

Jirel crept up the dark stairs of the north turret, murder in her heart. Many little hatreds she had known in her life, but no such blaze as this. Before her eyes in the night she could see Guillaume's scornful, scarred face laughing, the little jutting beard split with the whiteness of his mirth. Upon her mouth she felt the remembered weight of his, about her the strength of his arms. And such a blast of hot fury came over her that she reeled a little and clutched at the wall for support. She went on in a haze of red anger, and something like madness burning in her brain as a resolve slowly took shape out of the chaos of her hate. When that thought came to her she paused again, mid-step upon the stairs, and was conscious of a little coldness blowing over her. Then it was gone, and she shivered a little, shook her shoulders and grinned wolfishly, and went on.

By the stars she could see through the arrow-slits in the wall it must be near to midnight. She went softly on the stairs, and she encountered no one. Her little tower room at the top was empty. Even the straw pallet where the serving-wench slept had not been used that night. Jirel got herself out of her armor alone, somehow, after much striving and twisting. Her doeskin shirt was stiff with sweat and stained with blood. She tossed it disdainfully into a corner. The fury in her eyes had cooled now to a contained and secret flame. She smiled to herself as she slipped a fresh shirt of doeskin over her tousled red head and donned a brief tunic of link-mail. On her legs she buckled the greaves of some forgotten legionary, relic of the not long past days when Rome still ruled the world. She thrust a dagger through her belt and took her own long two-handed sword barebladed in her grip. Then she went down the stairs again.

She knew there must have been revelry and feasting in the great hall that night, and by the silence hanging so heavily now she was sure that most of her enemies lay still in drunken slumber, and she experienced a swift regret for the gallons of her good French wine so wasted. And the thought flashed through her head that a determined woman with a sharp sword might work some little damage among the drunken sleepers before she was overpowered. But she put that idea by, for Guillaume would have posted sentries to spare, and she must not give up her secret freedom so fruitlessly.

Down the dark stairs she went, and crossed one corner of the vast central hall whose darkness she was sure hid wine-deadened sleepers, and so into the lesser dimness of the rough little chapel that Joiry boasted. She had been sure she would find Father Gervase there, and she was not mistaken. He rose from his knees before the altar, dark in his robe, the starlight through the narrow window shining upon his tonsure.

"My daughter!" he whispered. "My daughter! How have you escaped? Shall I find you a mount? If you can pass the sentries you should be in your cousin's castle by daybreak."

She hushed him with a lifted hand.

"No," she said. "It is not outside I go this night. I have a more perilous journey even than that to make. Shrive me, father."

He stared at her.

"What is it?"

She dropped to her knees before him and gripped the rough cloth of his habit with urgent fingers.

"Shrive me, I say! I go down into hell tonight to pray the devil for a weapon, and it may be I shall not return."

Gervase bent and gripped her shoulders with hands that shook.

"Look at me!" he demanded. "Do you know what you're saying? You go—"

"Down!" She said it firmly. "Only you and I know that passage, father—and not even we can be sure of what lies beyond. But to gain a weapon against that man I would venture into perils even worse than that."

"If I thought you meant it," he whispered, "I would waken Guillaume now and give you into his arms. It would be a kinder fate, my daughter."

"It's that I would walk through hell to escape," she whispered back fiercely. "Can't you see? Oh, God knows I'm not innocent of the ways of light loving—but to be any man's fancy, for a night or two, before he snaps my neck or sells me into slavery—and above all, if that man were Guillaume! Can't you understand?"

"That would be shame enough," nodded Gervase. "But think, Jirel! For that shame there is atonement and absolution, and for that death the gates of heaven open wide. But this other—Jirel, Jirel, never through all eternity may you come out, body or soul, if you venture—down!"

She shrugged.

"To wreak my vengeance upon Guillaume I would go if I knew I should burn in hell forever."

"But Jirel, I do not think you understand. This is a worse fate than the deepest depths of hell-fire. This is—this is beyond all the bounds of the hells we know. And I think Satan's hottest flames were the breath of paradise, compared to what may befall there."

"I know. Do you think I'd venture down if I could not be sure? Where else would I find such a weapon as I need, save outside God's dominion?"

"Jirel, you shall not!"

"Gervase, I go! Will you shrive me?" The hot yellow eyes blazed into his, lambent in the starlight.

After a moment he dropped his head. "You are my lady. I will give you God's blessing, but it will not avail you—there."

She went down into the dungeons again. She went down a long way through utter dark, over stones that were oozy and odorous with moisture, through blackness that had never known the light of day. She might have been a little afraid at other times, but that steady flame of hatred burning behind her eyes was a torch to light the way, and she could not wipe from her memory the feel of Guillaume's arms about her, the scornful press of his lips on her mouth. She whimpered a little, low in her throat, and a hot gust of hate went over her.

In the solid blackness she came at length to a wall, and she set herself to pulling the loose stones from this with her free hand, for she would not lay down the sword. They had never been laid in mortar, and they came out easily. When the way was clear she stepped through and found her feet upon a downward-sloping ramp of smooth stone. She cleared the rubble away from the hole in the wall, and enlarged it enough for a quick passage; for when she came back this way—if she did—it might well be that she would come very fast.

At the bottom of the slope she dropped to her knees on the cold floor and felt about. Her fingers traced the outline of a circle, the veriest crack in the stone. She felt until she found the ring in its center. That ring was of the coldest metal she had ever known, and the smoothest. She could put no name to it. The daylight had never shone upon such metal.

She tugged. The stone was reluctant, and at last she took her sword in her teeth and put both hands to the lifting. Even then it taxed the limit of her strength, and she was strong as many men. But at last it rose, with the strangest sighing sound, and a little prickle of gooseflesh rippled over her.

Now she took the sword back into her hand and knelt on the rim of the invisible blackness below. She had gone this path once before and once only, and never thought to find any necessity in life strong enough to drive her down again. The way was the strangest she had ever known. There was, she thought, no such passage in all the world save here. It had not been built for human feet to travel. It had not been built for feet at all. It was a narrow, polished shaft that corkscrewed round and round in dizzy circles—but no snake on earth was big enough to fill that shaft. No human travelers had worn the sides of the spiral so smooth, and she did not care to speculate on what creatures had polished it so, through what ages of passage.

She might never have made that first trip down, nor anyone after her, had not some unknown human hacked the notches which made it possible to descend slowly; that is, she thought it must have been a human. At any rate, the notches were roughly shaped for hands and feet, and spaced not too far apart; but who and when and how she could not even guess. As to the beings who made the shaft, in long-forgotten ages—well, there were devils on earth before man, and the world was very old.

She turned on her face and slid feet-first into the curving tunnel. That first time she and Gervase had gone down in sweating terror of what lay below, and with devils tugging at their heels. Now she slid easily, not bothering to find toeholds, but slipping swiftly round and round the long spirals with only her hands to break the speed when she went too fast. Round and round she went, round and round.

It was a long way down. Before she had gone very far the curious dizziness she had known before came over her again, a dizziness not entirely induced by the spirals she whirled around, but a deeper, atomic unsteadiness as if not only she but also the substances around her were shifting. There was something queer about the angles of those curves. She was no scholar in geometry or aught else, but she felt intuitively that the bend and slant of the way she went were somehow outside any other angles or bends she had ever known. They led into the unknown and the dark, but it seemed to her obscurely that they led into deeper darkness and mystery than the merely physical, as if, though she could not put it clearly even into thoughts, the peculiar and exact lines of the tunnel had been carefully angled to lead through poly-dimensional space as well as through the underground—perhaps through time, too. She did not know she was thinking such things; but all about her was a blurred dizziness as she shot down and round, and she knew that the way she went took her on a stranger journey than any other way she had ever traveled.

Down, and down. She was sliding fast, but she knew how long it would be. On that first trip they had taken alarm as the passage spiraled so endlessly and with thoughts of the long climb back had tried to stop before it was too late. They had found it impossible. Once embarked, there was no halting. She had tried, and such waves of sick blurring had come over her that she came near to unconsciousness. It was as if she had tried to halt some inexorable process of nature, half finished. They could only go on. The very atoms of their bodies shrieked in rebellion against a reversal of the change.

And the way up, when they returned, had not been difficult. They had had visions of a back-breaking climb up interminable curves, but again the uncanny difference of those angles from those they knew was manifested. In a queer way they seemed to defy gravity, or perhaps led through some way outside the power of it. They had been sick and dizzy on the return, as on the way down, but through the clouds of that confusion it had seemed to them that they slipped as easily up the shaft as they had gone down; or perhaps that, once in the tunnel, there was neither up nor down.

The passage leveled gradually. This was the worst part for a human to travel, though it must have eased the speed of whatever beings the shaft was made for. It was too narrow for her to turn in, and she had to lever herself face down and feet first, along the horizontal smoothness of the floor, pushing with her hands. She was glad when her questing heels met open space and she slid from the mouth of the shaft and stood upright in the dark.

Here she paused to collect herself. Yes, this was the beginning of the long passage she and Father Gervase had traveled on that long-ago journey of exploration. By the veriest accident they had found the place, and only the veriest bravado had brought them thus far. He had gone on a greater distance than she—she was younger then, and more amenable to authority—and had come back white-faced in the torchlight and hurried her up the shaft again.

She went on carefully, feeling her way, remembering what she herself had seen in the darkness a little farther on, wondering in spite of herself, and with a tiny catch at her heart, what it was that had sent Father Gervase so hastily back. She had never been entirely satisfied with his explanations. It had been about here—or was it a little farther on? The stillness was like a roaring in her ears.

Then ahead of her the darkness moved. It was just that—a vast, imponderable shifting of the solid dark. Jesu! This was new! She gripped the cross at her throat with one hand and her sword-hilt with the other. Then it was upon her, striking like a hurricane, whirling her against the walls and shrieking in her ears like a thousand wind-devils—a wild cyclone of the dark that buffeted her mercilessly and tore at her flying hair and raved in her ears with the myriad voices of all lost things crying in the night. The voices were piteous in their terror and loneliness. Tears came to her eyes even as she shivered with nameless dread, for the whirlwind was alive with a dreadful instinct, an animate thing sweeping through the dark of the underground; an unholy thing that made her flesh crawl even though it touched her to the heart with its pitiful little lost voices wailing in the wind where no wind could possibly be.

And then it was gone. In that one flash of an instant it vanished, leaving no whisper to commemorate its passage. Only in the heart of it could one hear the sad little voices wailing or the wild shriek of the wind. She found herself standing stunned, her sword yet gripped futilely in one hand and the tears running down her face. Poor little lost voices, wailing. She wiped the tears away with a shaking hand and set her teeth hard against the weakness of reaction that flooded her. Yet it was a good five minutes before she could force herself on. After a few steps her knees ceased to tremble.

The floor was dry and smooth underfoot. It sloped a little downward, and she wondered into what unplumbed deeps she had descended by now. The silence had fallen heavily again, and she found herself straining for some other sound than the soft padding of her own boots. Then her foot slipped in sudden wetness. She bent, exploring fingers outstretched, feeling without reason that the wetness would be red if she could see it. But her fingers traced the immense outline of a footprint—splayed and three-toed like a frog's, but of monster size. It was a fresh footprint. She had a vivid flash of memory—that thing she had glimpsed in the torchlight on the other trip down. But she had had light then, and now she was blind in the dark, the creature's natural habitat....

For a moment she was not Jirel of Joiry, vengeful fury on the trail of a devilish weapon, but a frightened woman alone in the unholy dark. That memory had been so vivid.... Then she saw Guillaume's scornful, laughing face again, the little beard dark along the line of his jaw, the strong teeth white with his laughter; and something hot and sustaining swept over her like a thin flame, and she was Joiry again, vengeful and resolute. She went on more slowly, her sword swinging in a semicircle before every third step, that she might not be surprised too suddenly by some nightmare monster clasping her in smothering arms. But the flesh crept upon her unprotected back.

The smooth passage went on and on. She could feel the cold walls on either hand, and her upswung sword grazed the roof. It was like crawling through some worm's tunnel, blindly under the weight of countless tons of earth. She felt the pressure of it above and about her, overwhelming, and found herself praying that the end of this tunnel-crawling might come soon, whatever the end might bring.

But when it came it was a stranger thing than she had ever dreamed. Abruptly she felt the immense, imponderable oppression cease. No longer was she conscious of the tons of earth pressing about her. The walls had fallen away and her feet struck a sudden rubble instead of the smooth floor. But the darkness that had bandaged her eyes was changed, too, indescribably. It was no longer darkness, but void; not an absence of light, but simple nothingness. Abysses opened around her, yet she could see nothing. She only knew that she stood at the threshold of some immense space, and sensed nameless things about her, and battled vainly against that nothingness which was all her straining eyes could see. And at her throat something constricted painfully.

She lifted her hand and found the chain of her crucifix taut and vibrant around her neck. At that she smiled a little grimly, for she began to understand. The crucifix. She found her hand shaking despite herself, but she unfastened the chain and dropped the cross to the ground. Then she gasped.

All about her, as suddenly as the awakening from a dream, the nothingness had opened out into undreamed-of distances.

She stood high on a hilltop under a sky spangled with strange stars. Below she caught glimpses of misty plains and valleys with mountain peaks rising far away. And at her feet a ravening circle of small, slavering, blind things leaped with clashing teeth.

They were obscene and hard to distinguish against the darkness of the hillside, and the noise they made was revolting. Her sword swung up of itself, almost, and slashed furiously at the little dark horrors leaping up around her legs. They died squashily, splattering her bare thighs with unpleasantness, and after a few had gone silent under the blade the rest fled into the dark with quick, frightened pantings, their feet making a queer splashing noise on the stones.

Jirel gathered a handful of the coarse grass which grew there and wiped her legs of the obscene splatters, looking about with quickened breath upon this land so unholy that one who bore a cross might not even see it. Here, if anywhere, one might find a weapon such as she sought. Behind her in the hillside was the low tunnel opening from which she had emerged. Overhead the strange stars shone. She did not recognize a single constellation, and if the brighter sparks were planets they were strange ones, tinged with violet and green and yellow. One was vividly crimson, like a point of fire. Far out over the rolling land below she could discern a mighty column of light. It did not blaze, nor illuminate the dark about. It cast no shadows. It simply was a great pillar of luminance towering high in the night. It seemed artificial—perhaps man-made, though she scarcely dared hope for men here.

She had half expected, despite her brave words, to come out upon the storied and familiar red-hot pave of hell, and this pleasant, starlit land surprised her and made her more wary. The things that build the tunnel could not have been human. She had no right to expect men here. She was a little stunned by finding open sky so far underground, though she was intelligent enough to realize that however she had come, she was not underground now. No cavity in the earth could contain this starry sky. She came of a credulous age, and she accepted her surroundings without too much questioning, though she was a little disappointed, if the truth were known, in the pleasantness of the mistily starlit place. The fiery streets of hell would have been a likelier locality in which to find a weapon against Guillaume.

When she had cleansed her sword on the grass and wiped her legs clean, she turned slowly down the hill. The distant column beckoned her, and after a moment of indecision she turned toward it. She had no time to waste, and this was the likeliest place to find what she sought.

The coarse grass brushed her legs and whispered round her feet. She stumbled now and then on the rubble, for the hill was steep, but she reached the bottom without mishap, and struck out across the meadows toward that blaze of faraway brilliance. It seemed to her that she walked more lightly, somehow. The grass scarcely bent underfoot, and she found she could take long sailing strides like one who runs with wings on his heels. It felt like a dream. The gravity pull of the place must have been less than she was accustomed to, but she only knew that she was skimming over the ground with amazing speed.

Traveling so, she passed through the meadows over the strange, coarse grass, over a brook or two that spoke endlessly to itself in a curious language that was almost speech, certainly not the usual gurgle of earth's running water. Once she ran into a blotch of darkness, like some pocket of void in the air, and struggled through gasping and blinking outraged eyes. She was beginning to realize that the land was not so innocently normal as it looked.

On and on she went, at that surprising speed, while the meadows skimmed past beneath her flying feet and gradually the light drew nearer. She saw now that it was a round tower of sheeted luminance, as if walls of solid flame rose up from the ground. Yet it semeed to be steady, nor did it cast any illumination upon the sky.

Before much time had elapsed, with her dreamlike speed she had almost reached her goal. The ground was becoming marshy underfoot, and presently the smell of swamps rose in her nostrils and she saw that between her and the light stretched a belt of unstable ground tufted with black reedy grass. Here and there she could see dim white blotches moving. They might be beasts, or only wisps of mist. The starlight was not very illuminating.

She began to pick her way carefully across the black, quaking morasses. Where the tufts of grass rose she found firmer ground, and she leaped from clump to clump with that amazing lightness, so that her feet barely touched the black ooze. Here and there slow bubbles rose through the mud and broke thickly. She did not like the place.

Halfway across, she saw one of the white blotches approaching her with slow, erratic movements. It bumped along unevenly, and at first she thought it might be inanimate, its approach was so indirect and purposeless. Then it blundered nearer, with that queer bumpy gait, making sucking noises in the ooze and splashing as it came. In the starlight she saw suddenly what it was, and for an instant her heart paused and sickness rose overwhelmingly in her throat. It was a woman—a beautiful woman whose white bare body had the curves and loveliness of some marble statue. She was crouching like a frog, and as Jirel watched in stupefaction she straightened her legs abruptly and leaped as a frog leaps, only more clumsily, falling forward into the ooze a little distance beyond the watching woman. She did not seem to see Jirel. The mud-spattered face was blank. She blundered on through the mud in awkward steps. Jirel watched until the woman was no more than a white wandering blue in the dark, and above the shock of that sight pity was rising, and uncomprehending resentment against whatever had brought so lovely a creature into this—into this—into blundering in frog leaps aimless through the mud, with empty mind and blind, staring eyes. For the second time that night she knew the sting of unaccustomed tears as she went on.

The sight, though, had given her reassurance. The human form was not unknown here. There might be leathery devils with hoofs and horns, such as she still half expected, but she would not be alone in her humanity; though if all the rest were as piteously mindless as the one she had seen—she did not follow that thought. It was too unpleasant. She was glad when the marsh was past and she need not see any longer the awkward white shapes bumping along through the dark.

She struck out across the narrow space which lay between her and the tower. She saw now that it was a building, and that the light composed it. She could not understand that, but she saw it. Walls and columns outlined the tower, solid sheets of light with definite boundaries, not radiant. As she came nearer she saw that it was in motion, apparently spurting up from some source underground as if the light illuminated sheets of water rushing upward under great pressure. Yet she felt intuitively that it was not water, but incarnate light.

She came forward hesitantly, gripping her sword. The area around the tremendous pillar was paved with something black and smooth that did not reflect the light. Out of it sprang the uprushing walls of brilliance with their sharply defined edges. The magnitude of the thing dwarfed her to infinitesimal size. She stared upward with undazzled eyes, trying to understand. If there could be such a thing as solid, non-radiating light, this was it.

She was very near under the mighty tower before she could see the details of the building clearly. They were strange to her—great pillars and arches around the base, and one stupendous portal, all molded out of the rushing, prisoned light.

She turned toward the opening after a moment, for the light had a tangible look. She did not believe she could have walked through it even had she dared.

When that tremendous portal arched over her she peered in, affrighted by the very size of the place. She thought she could hear the hiss and spurt of the light surging upward. She was looking into a mighty globe inside, a hall shaped like the interior of a bubble, though the curve was so vast she was scarcely aware of it. And in the very center of the globe floated a light. Jirel blinked. A light, dwelling in a bubble of light. It glowed there in midair with a pale, steady flame that was somehow alive and animate, and brighter than the serene illumination of the building, for it hurt her eyes to look at it directly.

She stood on the threshold and stared, not quite daring to venture in. And as she hesitated a change came over the light. A flash of rose tinged its pallor. The rose deepened and darkened until it took on the color of blood. And the shape underwent strange changes. It lengthened, drew itself out narrowly, split at the bottom in two branches, put out two tendrils from the top. The blood-red paled again, and the light somehow lost its brilliance, receded into the depths of the thing that was forming. Jirel clutched her sword and forgot to breathe, watching. The light was taking on the shape of a human being—of a woman—of a tall woman in mail, her red hair tousled and her eyes staring straight into the duplicate eyes at the portal....

"Welcome," said the Jirel suspended in the center of the globe, her voice deep and resonant and clear in spite of the distance between them. Jirel at the door held her breath, wondering and afraid. This was herself, in every detail, a mirrored Jirel—that was it, a Jirel mirrored upon a surface which blazed and smoldered with barely repressed light, so that the eyes gleamed with it and the whole figure seemed to hold its shape by an effort, only by that effort restraining itself from resolving into pure, formless light again. But the voice was not her own. It shook and resounded with a knowledge as alien as the light-built walls. It mocked her. It said,

"Welcome! Enter into the portals, woman!"

She looked up warily at the rushing walls about her. Instinctively she drew back.

"Enter, enter!" urged that mocking voice from her own mirrored lips. And there was a note in it she did not like.

"Enter!" cried the voice again, this time a command.

Jirel's eyes narrowed. Something intuitive warned her back, and yet—she drew the dagger she had thrust in her belt and with a quick motion she tossed it into the great globe-shaped hall. It struck the floor without a sound, and a brilliant light flared up around it, so brilliant she could not look upon what was happening; but it seemed to her that the knife expanded, grew large and nebulous and ringed with dazzling light. In less time than it takes to tell, it had faded out of sight as if the very atoms which composed it had flown apart and dispersed in the golden glow of that mighty bubble. The dazzle faded with the knife, leaving Jirel staring dazedly at a bare floor.

That other Jirel laughed a rich, resonant laugh of scorn and malice.

"Stay out, then," said the voice. "You've more intelligence than I thought. Well, what would you here?"

Jirel found her voice with an effort.

"I seek a weapon," she said, "a weapon against a man I so hate that upon earth there is none terrible enough for my need."

"You so hate him, eh?" mused the voice.

"With all my heart!"

"With all your heart!" echoed the voice, and there was an undernote of laughter in it that she did not understand. The echoes of that mirth ran round and round the great globe. Jirel felt her cheeks burn with resentment against some implication in the derision which she could not put a name to. When the echoes of the laugh had faded the voice said indifferently.

"Give the man what you find at the black temple in the lake. I make you a gift of it."

The lips that were Jirel's twisted into a laugh of purest mockery; then all about that figure so perfectly her own the light flared out. She saw the outlines melting fluidly as she turned her dazzled eyes away. Before the echoes of that derision had died, a blinding, formless light burned once more in the midst of the bubble.

Jirel turned and stumbled away under the mighty column of the tower, a hand to her dazzled eyes. Not until she had reached the edge of the black, unreflecting circle that paved the ground around the pillar did she realize that she knew no way of finding the lake where her weapon lay. And not until then did she remember how fatal it is said to be to accept a gift from a demon. Buy it, or earn it, but never accept the gift. Well—she shrugged and stepped out upon the grass. She must surely be damned by now, for having ventured down of her own will into this curious place for such a purpose as hers. The soul can be lost but once.

She turned her face up to the strange stars and wondered in what direction her course lay. The sky looked blankly down upon her with its myriad meaningless eyes. A star fell as she watched, and in her superstitious soul she took it for an omen, and set off boldly over the dark meadows in the direction where the bright streak had faded. No swamps guarded the way here, and she was soon skimming along over the grass with that strange, dancing gait that the lightness of the place allowed her. And as she went she was remembering, as from long ago in some other far world, a man's arrogant mirth and the press of his mouth on hers. Hatred bubbled up hotly within her and broke from her lips in a little savage laugh of anticipation. What dreadful thing awaited her in the temple in the lake, what punishment from hell to be loosed by her own hands upon Guillaume? And though her soul was the price it cost her, she would count it a fair bargain if she could drive the laughter from his mouth and bring terror into the eyes that mocked her.

Thoughts like these kept her company for a long way upon her journey. She did not think to be lonely or afraid in the uncanny darkness across which no shadows fell from that mighty column behind her. The unchanging meadows flew past underfoot, lightly as meadows in a dream. It might almost have been that the earth moved instead of herself, so effortlessly did she go. She was sure now that she was heading in the right direction, for two more stars had fallen in the same arc across the sky.

The meadows were not untenanted. Sometimes she felt presences near her in the dark, and once she ran full-tilt into a nest of little yapping horrors like those on the hilltop. They lunged up about her with clicking teeth, mad with a blind ferocity, and she swung her sword in frantic circles, sickened by the noise of them lunging splashily through the grass and splattering her sword with their deaths. She beat them off and went on, fighting her own sickness, for she had never known anything quite so nauseating as these little monstrosities.

She crossed a brook that talked to itself in the darkness with that queer murmuring which came so near to speech, and a few strides beyond it she paused suddenly, feeling the ground tremble with the rolling thunder of hoofbeats approaching. She stood still, searching the dark anxiously, and presently the earth-shaking beat grew louder and she saw a white blur flung wide across the dimness to her left, and the sound of hoofs deepened and grew. Then out of the night swept a herd of snow-white horses. Magnificently they ran, manes tossing, tails streaming, feet pounding a rhythmic, heart-stirring roll along the ground. She caught her breath at the beauty of their motion. They swept by a little distance away, tossing their heads, spurning the ground with scornful feet.

But as they came abreast of her she saw one blunder a little and stumble against the next, and that one shook his head bewilderedly; and suddenly she realized that they were blind—all running so splendidly in a deeper dark than even she groped through. And she saw, too, their coats were roughened with sweat, and foam dripped from their lips, and their nostrils were flaring pools of scarlet. Now and again one stumbled from pure exhaustion. Yet they ran, frantically, blindly through the dark, driven by something outside their comprehension.

As the last one of all swept by her, sweat-crusted and staggering, she saw him toss his head high, spattering foam, and whinny shrilly to the stars. And it seemed to her that the sound was strangely articulate. Almost she heard the echoes of a name—"Julienne! Julienne!"—in that high, despairing sound. And the incongruity of it, the bitter despair, clutched at her heart so sharply that for the third time that night she knew the sting of tears.

The dreadful humanity of that cry echoed in her ears as the thunder died away. She went on, blinking back the tears for that beautiful blind creature, staggering with exhaustion, calling a girl's name hopelessly from a beast's throat into the blank darkness wherein it was forever lost.

Then another star fell across the sky, and she hurried ahead, closing her mind to the strange, incomprehensible pathos that made an undernote of tears to the starry dark of this land. And the thought was growing in her mind that, though she had come into no brimstone pit where horned devils pranced over flames, yet perhaps it was after all a sort of hell through which she ran.

Presently in the distance she caught a glimmer of something bright. The ground dipped after that and she lost it, and skimmed through a hollow where pale things wavered away from her into the deeper dark. She never knew what they were, and was glad. When she came up onto higher ground again she saw it more clearly, an expanse of dim brilliance ahead. She hoped it was a lake, and ran more swiftly.

It *was* a lake—a lake that could never have existed outside some obscure hell like this. She stood on the brink doubtfully, wondering if this could be the place the light-devil had meant. Black, shining water stretched out before her, heaving gently with a motion unlike that of any water she had ever seen before. And in the depths of it, like fireflies caught in ice, gleamed myriad small lights. They were fixed there immovably, not stirring with the motion of the water. As she watched, something hissed above her and a streak of light split the dark air. She looked up in time to see something bright curving across the sky to fall without a splash into the water, and small ripples of phosphorescence spread sluggishly toward the shore, where they broke at her feet with the queerest whispering sound, as if each succeeding ripple spoke the syllable of a word.

She looked up, trying to locate the origin of the falling lights, but the strange stars looked down upon her blankly. She bent and stared down into the center of the spreading ripples, and where the thing had fallen she thought a new light twinkled through the water. She could not determine what it was, and after a curious moment she gave the question up and began to cast about for the temple the light-devil had spoken of.

After a moment she thought she saw something dark in the center of the lake, and when she had stared for a few minutes it gradually became clearer, an arch of darkness against the starry background of the water. It might be a temple. She strolled slowly along the brim of the lake, trying to get a closer view of it, for the thing was no more than a darkness against the spangles of light, like some void in the sky where no stars shine. And presently she stumbled over something in the grass.

She looked down with startled yellow eyes, and saw a strange, indistinguishable darkness. It had solidity to the feel but scarcely to the eye, for she could not quite focus upon it. It was like trying to see something that did not exist save as a void, a darkness in the grass. It had the shape of a step, and when she followed with her eyes she saw that it was the beginning of a dim bridge stretching out over the lake, narrow and curved and made out of nothingness. It seemed to have no surface, and its edges were difficult to distinguish from the lesser gloom surrounding it. But the thing was tangible—an arch carved out of the solid dark—and it led out in the direction she wished to go. For she was naïvely sure now that the dim blot in the center of the lake was the temple she was searching for. The falling stars had guided her, and she could not have gone astray.

So she set her teeth and gripped her sword and put her foot upon the bridge. It was rock-firm under her, but scarcely more than a foot or so wide, and without rails. When she had gone a step or two she began to feel dizzy; for under her the water heaved with a motion that made her head swim, and the stars twinkled eerily in its depths. She dared not look away for fear of missing her footing on the narrow arch of darkness. It was like walking a bridge flung across the void, with stars underfoot and nothing but an unstable strip of nothingness to bear her up. Halfway across, the heaving of the water and the illusion of vast, constellated spaces beneath and the look her bridge had of being no more than empty space ahead, combined to send her head reeling; and as she stumbled on, the bridge seemed to be wavering with her, swinging in gigantic arcs across the starry void below.

Now she could see the temple more closely, though scarcely more clearly than from the shore. It looked to be no more than an outlined emptiness against the star-crowded brilliance behind it, etching its arches and columns of blankness upon the twinkling waters. The bridge came down in a long dim swoop to its doorway. Jirel took the last few yards at a reckless run and stopped breathless under the arch that made the temple's vague doorway. She stood there panting and staring about narrow-eyed, sword poised in her hand. For though the place was empty and very still she felt a presence even as she set her foot upon the floor of it.

She was staring about a little space of blankness in the starry lake. It seemed to be no more than that. She could see the walls and columns where they were outlined against the water and where they made darknesses in the star-flecked sky, but where there was only dark behind them she could see nothing. It was a tiny place, no more than a few square yards of emptiness upon the face of the twinkling waters. And in its center an image stood.

She stared at it in silence, feeling a curious compulsion growing within her, like a vague command from something outside herself. The image was of some substance of nameless black, unlike the material which composed the building, for even in the dark she could see it clearly. It was a semi-human figure, crouching forward with out-thrust head, sexless and strange. Its one central eye was closed as if in rapture, and its mouth was pursed for a kiss. And though it was but an image and without even the semblance of life, she felt unmistakably the presence of something alive in the temple, something so alien and innominate that instinctively she drew away.

She stood there for a full minute, reluctant to enter the place where so alien a being dwelt, half-conscious of that voiceless compulsion growing up within her. And slowly she became aware that all the lines and angles of the half-seen building were curved to make the image their center and focus. The very bridge swooped its long arc to complete the centering. As she watched, it seemed to her that through the arches of the columns even the stars in lake and sky were grouped in patterns which took the image for their focus. Every line and curve in the dim world seemed to sweep round toward the squatting thing before her with its closed eye and expectant mouth.

Gradually the universal focusing of lines began to exert its influence upon her. She took a hesitant step forward without realizing the motion. But that step was all the dormant urge within her needed. With her one motion forward the compulsion closed down upon her with whirlwind impetuosity. Helplessly she felt herself advancing, helplessly with one small, sane portion of her mind she realized the madness that was gripping her, the blind, irresistible urge to do what every visible line in the temple's construction was made to compel. With stars swirling around her she advanced across the floor and laid her hands upon the rounded shoulders of the image—the sword, forgotten, making a sort of accolade against its hunched neck—and lifted her red head and laid her mouth blindly against the pursed lips of the image.

In a dream she took that kiss. In a dream of dizziness and confusion she seemed to feel the iron-cold lips stirring under hers. And through the union of that kiss—warm-blooded woman with image of nameless stone—through the meeting of their mouths something entered into her very soul; something cold and stunning; somcthing alien beyond any words. It lay upon her shuddering soul like some frigid weight from the void, a bubble holding something unthinkably alien and dreadful. She could feel the heaviness of it upon some intangible part of her that shrank from the touch. It was like the weight of remorse or despair, only far colder and stranger and—somehow—more ominous, as if this weight were but the egg from which things might hatch too dreadful to put even into thoughts.

The moment of the kiss could have been no longer than a breath's space, but to her it was timeless. In a dream she felt the compulsion falling from her at last. In a dim dream she dropped her hands from its shoulders, finding the sword heavy in her grasp and staring dully at it for a while before clarity began its return to her cloudy mind. When she became completely aware of herself once more she was standing with slack body and dragging head before the blind, rapturous image, that dead weight upon her heart as dreary as an old sorrow, and more coldly ominous than anything she could find words for.

And with returning clarity the most staggering terror came over her, swiftly and suddenly—terror of the image and the temple of darkness, and the coldly spangled lake and of the whole, wide, dim, dreadful world about her. Desperately she longed for home again, even the red fury of hatred and the press of Guillaume's mouth and the hot arrogance of his eyes again. Anything but this. She found herself running without knowing why. Her feet skimmed over the narrow bridge lightly as a gull's wings dipping the water. In a brief instant the starry void of the lake flashed by beneath her and the solid earth was underfoot. She saw the great column of light far away across the dark meadows and beyond it a hilltop against the stars. And she ran.

She ran with terror at her heels and devils howling in the wind her own speed made. She ran from her own curiously alien body, heavy with its weight of inexplicable doom. She passed through the hollow where pale things wavered away, she fled over the uneven meadows in a frenzy of terror. She ran and ran, in those long light bounds the lesser gravity allowed her, fleeter than a deer, and her own panic choked in her throat and that weight upon her soul dragged at her too drearily for tears. She fled to escape it, and could not; and the ominous certainty that she carried something too dreadful to think of grew and grew.

For a long while she skimmed over the grass, tirelessly, wing-heeled, her red hair flying. The panic died after a while, but that sense of heavy disaster did not die. She felt somehow that tears would ease her, but something in the frigid darkness of her soul froze her tears in the ice of that gray and alien chill.

And gradually, through the inner dark, a fierce anticipation took form in her mind. Revenge upon Guillaume! She had taken from the temple only a kiss, so it was that which she must deliver to him. And savagely she exulted in the thought of what that kiss would release upon him, unsuspecting. She did not know, but it filled her with fierce joy to guess.

She had passed the column and skirted the morass where the white, blundering forms still bumped along awkwardly through the ooze, and was crossing the coarse grass toward the nearing hill when the sky began to pale along the horizon.

And with that pallor a fresh terror took hold upon her, a wild horror of daylight in this unholy land. She was not sure if it was the light itself she so dreaded, or what that light would reveal in the dark stretches she had traversed so blindly—what unknown horrors she had skirted in the night. But she knew instinctively that if she valued her sanity she must be gone before the light had risen over the land. And she redoubled her efforts, spurring her wearying limbs to yet more skimming speed. But it would be a close race, for already the stars were blurring out, and a flush of curious green was broadening along the sky, and around her the air was turning to a vague, unpleasant gray.

She toiled up the steep hillside breathlessly. When she was halfway up, her own shadow began to take form upon the rocks, and it was unfamiliar and dreadfully significant of something just outside her range of understanding. She averted her eyes from it, afraid that at any moment the meaning might break upon her outraged brain.

She could see the top of the hill above her, dark against the paling sky, and she toiled up in frantic haste, clutching her sword and feeling that if she had to look in the full light upon the dreadful little abominations that had snapped around her feet when she first emerged she would collapse into screaming hysteria.

The cave-mouth yawned before her, invitingly black, a refuge from the dawning light behind her. She knew an almost irresistible desire to turn and look back from this vantage point across the land she had traversed, and gripped her sword hard to conquer the pervasive longing. There was a scuffling in the rocks at her feet, and she set her teeth in her underlip and swung viciously in brief arcs, without looking down. She heard small squeakings and the splashy sound of feet upon the stones, and felt her blade shear thrice through semi-solidity, to the click of little vicious teeth. Then they broke and ran off over the hillside, and she stumbled on, choking back the scream that wanted so fiercely to break from her lips.

She fought that growing desire all the way to the cave-mouth, for she knew that if she gave way she would never cease shrieking until her throat went raw.

Blood was trickling from her bitten lip with the effort at silence when she reached the cave. And there, twinkling upon the stones, lay something small and bright and dearly familiar. With a sob of relief she bent and snatched up the crucifix she had torn from her throat when she came out into this land. And as her fingers shut upon it a vast, protecting darkness swooped around her. Gasping with relief, she groped her way the step or two that separated her from the cave.

Dark lay like a blanket over her eyes, and she welcomed it gladly, remembering how her shadow had lain so awfully upon the hillside as she climbed, remembering the first rays of savage sunlight beating upon her shoulders. She stumbled through the blackness, slowly getting control again over her shaking body and laboring lungs, slowly stilling the panic that the dawning day had roused so inexplicably within her. And as that terror died, the dull weight upon her spirit became strong again. She had all but forgotten it in her panic, but now the impending and unknown dreadfulness grew heavier and more oppressive in the darkness of the underground, and she groped along in a dull stupor of her own depression, slow with the weight of the strange doom she carried.

Nothing barred her way. In the dullness of her stupor she scarcely realized it, or expected any of the vague horrors that peopled the place to leap out upon her. Empty and unmenacing, the way stretched before her blindly stumbling feet. Only once did she hear the sound of another presence—the rasp of hoarse breathing and the scrape of a scaly hide against the stone—but it must have been outside the range of her own passage, for she encountered nothing.

When she had come to the end and a cold wall rose up before her, it was scarcely more than automatic habit that made her search along it with groping hand until she came to the mouth of the shaft. It sloped gently up into the dark. She crawled in, trailing her sword, until the rising incline and lowering roof forced her down upon her face. Then with toes and fingers she began to force herself up the spiral, slippery way.

Before she had gone very far she was advancing without effort, scarcely realizing that it was against gravity she moved. The curious dizziness of the shaft had come over her, the strange feeling of change in the very substance of her body, and through the cloudy numbness of it she felt herself sliding round and round the spirals, without effort. Again, obscurely, she had the feeling that in the peculiar angles of this shaft was neither up nor down. And for a long while the dizzy circling went on.

When the end came at last, and she felt her fingers gripping the edge of that upper opening which lay beneath the door of Joiry's lowest dungeons, she heaved herself up warily and lay for awhile on the cold floor in the dark, while slowly the clouds of dizziness passed from her mind, leaving only that ominous weight within. When the darkness had ceased to circle about her, and the floor steadied, she got up dully and swung the cover back over the opening, her hands shuddering from the feel of the cold, smooth ring which had never seen daylight.

When she turned from this task she was aware of the reason for the lessening in the gloom around her. A guttering light outlined the hole in the wall from which she had pulled the stones—was it a century ago? The brilliance all but blinded her after her long sojourn through blackness, and she stood there awhile, swaying a little, one hand to her eyes, but she went out into the familiar torchlight she knew waited her beyond. Father Gervase, she was sure, anxiously waiting her return. But even he had not dared to follow her through the hole in the wall, down to the brink of the shaft.

Somehow she felt that she should be giddy with relief at this safe homecoming, back to humanity again. But as she stumbled over the upward slope toward light and safety she was conscious of no more than the dullness of whatever unreleased horror it was which still lay so ominously upon her stunned soul.

She came through the gaping hole in the masonry into the full glare of torches awaiting her, remembering with a wry inward smile how wide she had made the opening in anticipation of flight from something dreadful when she came back that way. Well, there was no flight from the horror she bore within her. It seemed to her that her heart was slowing, too, missing a beat now and then and staggering like a weary runner.

She came out into the torchlight, stumbling with exhaustion, her mouth scarlet from the blood of her bitten lip and her bare greaved legs and bare sword-blade foul with the deaths of those little horrors that swarmed around the cave-mouth. From the tangle of red hair her eyes stared out with a bleak, frozen, inward look, as of one who has seen nameless things. That keen, steel-bright beauty which had been hers was as dull and fouled as her sword-blade, and at the look in her eyes Father Gervase shuddered and crossed himself.

They were waiting for her in an uneasy group—the priest anxious and dark, Guillaume splendid in the torchlight, tall and arrogant, a handful of men-at-arms holding the guttering lights and shifting uneasily from one foot to the other. When she saw Guillaume the light that flared up in her eyes blotted out for a moment the bleak dreadfulness behind them, and her slowing heart leaped like a spurred horse, sending the blood riotously through her veins. Guillaume, magnificent in his armor, leaning upon his sword and staring down at her from his scornful height, the little black beard jutting. Guillaume, to whom Joiry had fallen. Guillaume.

That which she carried at the core of her being was heavier than anything else in the world, so heavy she could scarcely keep her knees from bending, so heavy her heart labored under its weight. Almost irresistibly she wanted to give way beneath it, to sink down and down under the crushing load, to lie prone and vanquished in the ice-gray bleak place she was so dimly aware of through the clouds that were rising about her. But there was Guillaume, grim and grinning, and she hated him so very bitterly—she must make the effort. She must, at whatever cost, for she was coming to know that death lay in wait for her if she bore this burden long, that it was a two-edged weapon which could strike at its wielder if the blow were delayed too long. She knew this through the dim mists that were thickening in her brain, and she put all her strength into the immense effort it cost to cross the floor toward him. She stumbled a little, and made one faltering step and then another, and dropped her sword with a clang as she lifted her arms to him.

He caught her strongly, in a hard, warm clasp, and she heard his laugh triumphant and hateful as he bent his head to take the kiss she was raising her mouth to offer. He must have seen, in that last moment before their lips met, the savage glare of victory in her eyes, and been startled. But he did not hesitate. His mouth was heavy upon hers.

It was a long kiss. She felt him stiffen in her arms. She felt a coldness in the lips upon hers, and slowly the dark weight of what she bore lightened, lifted, cleared away from her cloudy mind. Strength flowed back through her richly. The whole world came alive to her once more. Presently she loosed his slack arms and stepped away, looking up into his face with a keen and dreadful triumph upon her own.

She saw the ruddiness of him draining away, and the rigidity of stone coming over his scarred features. Only his eyes remained alive, and there was torment in them, and understanding. She was glad—she had wanted him to understand what it cost to take Jirel's kiss unbidden. She smiled thinly into his tortured eyes, watching. And she saw something cold and alien seeping through him, permeating him slowly with some unnamable emotion which no man could ever have experienced before. She could not name it, but she saw it in his eyes—some dreadful emotion never made for flesh and blood to know, some iron despair such as only an unguessable being from the gray, formless void could ever have felt before—too hideously alien for any human creature to endure. Even she shuddered from the dreadful, cold bleakness looking out of his eyes, and knew as she watched that there must be many emotions and many fears and joys too far outside man's comprehension for any being of flesh to undergo, and live. Grayly she saw it spreading through him, and the very substance of his body shuddered under that iron weight.

And now came a visible, physical change. Watching, she was aghast to think that in her own body and upon her own soul she had borne the seed of this dreadful flowering, and did not wonder that her heart had slowed under the unbearable weight of it. He was standing rigidly with arms half bent, just as he stood when she slid from his embrace. And now great shudders began to go over him, as if he were wavering in the torchlight, some gray-faced wraith in armor with torment in his eyes. She saw the sweat beading his forehead. She saw a trickle of blood from his mouth, as if he had bitten through his lip in the agony of this new, incomprehensible emotion. Then a last shiver went over him violently, and he flung up his head, the little curling beard jutting ceilingward and the muscles of his strong throat corded, and from his lips broke a long, low cry of such utter, inhuman strangeness that Jirel felt coldness rippling through her veins and she put up her hands to her ears to shut it out. It meant something—it expressed some dreadful emotion that was neither sorrow nor despair nor anger, but infinitely alien and infinitely sad. Then his long legs buckled at the knees and he dropped with a clatter of mail and lay still on the stone floor.

They knew he was dead. That was unmistakable in the way he lay. Jirel stood very still, looking down upon him, and strangely it seemed to her that all the lights in the world had gone out. A moment before he had been so big and vital, so magnificent in the torchlight—she could still feel his kiss upon her mouth, and the hard warmth of his arms....

Suddenly and blindingly it came upon her what she had done. She knew now why such heady violence had flooded her whenever she thought of him—knew why the light-devil in her own form had laughed so derisively—knew the price she must pay for taking a gift from a demon. She knew that there was no light anywhere in the world, now that Guillaume was gone.

Father Gervase took her arm gently. She shook him off with an impatient shrug and dropped to one knee beside Guillaume's body, bending her head so that the red hair fell forward to hide her tears.

The Silver Key

by H. P. LOVECRAFT

WHEN RANDOLPH CARTER was thirty he lost the key of the gate of dreams. Prior to that time he had made up for the prosiness of life by nightly excursions to strange and ancient cities beyond space, and lovely, unbelievable garden lands across ethereal seas; but as middle age hardened upon him he felt those liberties slipping away little by little, until at last he was cut off altogether. No more could his galleys sail up the river Oukranos past the gilded spires of Thran, or his elephant caravans tramp through perfumed jungles in Kled, where forgotten palaces with veined ivory columns sleep lovely and unbroken under the moon.

He had read much of things as they are, and talked with too many people. Well-meaning philosophers had taught him to look into the logical relations of things, and analyze the processes which shaped his thoughts and fancies. Wonder had gone away, and he had forgotten that all life is only a set of pictures in the brain, among which there is no difference betwixt those born of real things and those born of inward dreamings, and no cause to value the one above the other. Custom had dinned into his ears a superstitious reverence for that which tangibly and physically exist, and had made him secretly ashamed to dwell in visions. Wise men told him his simple fancies were inane and childish, and even more absurd because their actors persist in fancying them full of meaning and purpose as the blind cosmos grinds aimlessly on from nothing to something and from something back to nothing again, neither heeding nor knowing the wishes or existence of the minds that flicker for a second now and then in the darkness.

They had chained him down to things that are, and had then explained the workings of those things till mystery had gone out of the world. When he complained, and longed to escape into twilight realms where magic moulded all the little vivid fragments and prized associations of his mind into vistas of breathless expectancy and unquenchable delight, they turned him instead toward the newfound prodigies of science, bidding him find wonder in the atom's vortex and mystery in the sky's dimensions. And when he had failed to find these boons in things whose laws are known and measurable, they told him he lacked imagination, and was immature because he preferred dream-illusions to the illusions of our physical creation.

So Carter had tried to do as others did, and pretended that the common events and emotions of earthly minds were more important than the fantasies of rare and delicate souls. He did not dissent when they told him that the animal pain of a struck pig or dyspeptic ploughman in real life is a greater thing than the peerless beauty of Narath with its hundred carven gates and domes of chalcedony, which he dimly remembered from his dreams; and under their guidance he cultivated a painstaking sense of pity and tragedy.

Once in a while, though, he could not help seeing how shallow, fickle, and meaningless all human aspirations are, and how emptily our real impulses contrast with those pompous ideals we profess to hold. Then he would have recourse to the polite laughter they had taught him to use against the extravagance and artificiality of dreams; for he saw that the daily life of our world is every inch as extravagant and artificial, and far less worthy of respect because of its poverty in beauty and its silly reluctance to admit its own lack of reason and purpose. In this way he became a kind of humorist, for he did not see that even humor is empty in a mindless universe devoid of any true standard of consistency or inconsistency.

In the first days of his bondage he had turned to the gentle churchly faith endeared to him by the naive trust of his fathers, for thence stretched mystic avenues which seemed to promise escape from life. Only on closer view did he mark the starved fancy and beauty, the stale and prosy triteness, and the owlish gravity and grotesque claims of solid truth which reigned boresomely and overwhelmingly among most of its professors; or feel to the full the awkwardness with which it sought to keep alive as literal fact the outgrown fears and guesses of a primal race confronting the unknown. It wearied Carter to see how solemnly people tried to make earthly reality out of old myths which every step of their boasted science confuted, and this misplaced seriousness killed the attachment he might have kept for the ancient creeds had they been content to offer the sonorous rites and emotional outlets in their true guise of ethereal fantasy.

But when he came to study those who had thrown off the old myths, he found them even more ugly than those who had not. They did not know that beauty lies in harmony, and that loveliness of life has no standard amidst an aimless cosmos save only its harmony with the dreams and the feelings which have gone before and blindly moulded our little spheres out of the rest of chaos. They did not see that good and evil and beauty and ugliness are only ornamental fruits of perspective, whose sole value lies in their linkage to what chance made our fathers think and feel, and whose finer details are different for every race and culture. Instead, they either denied these things altogether or transferred them to the crude, vague instincts which they shared with the beasts and peasants; so that their lives were dragged malodorously out in pain, ugliness, and disproportion, yet filled with a ludicrous pride at having escaped from something no more unsound than that which still held them. They had traded the false gods of fear and blind piety for those of license and anarchy.

Carter did not taste deeply of these modern freedoms; for their cheapness and squalor sickened a spirit loving beauty alone while his reason rebelled at the flimsy logic with which their champions tried to gild brute impulse with a sacredness stripped from the idols they had discarded. He saw that most of them, in common with their cast-off priestcraft, could not escape from the delusion that life has a meaning apart from that which men dream into it; and could not lay aside the crude notion of ethics and obligations beyond those of beauty, even when all Nature shrieked of its unconsciousness and impersonal unmorality in the light of their scientific discoveries. Warped and bigoted with preconceived illusions of justice, freedom, and consistency, they cast off the old lore and the old way with the old beliefs; nor ever stopped to think that that lore and those ways were the sole makers of their present thoughts and judgments, and the sole guides and standards in a meaningless universe without fixed aims or stable points of reference. Having lost these artificial settings, their lives grew void of direction and dramatic interest; till at length they strove to drown their ennui in bustle and pretended usefulness, noise and excitement, barbaric display and animal sensation. When these things palled, disappointed, or grew nauseous through revulsion, they cultivated irony and bitterness, and found fault with the social order. Never could they realize that their brute foundations were as shifting and contradictory as the gods of their elders, and that the satisfaction of one moment is the bane of the next. Calm, lasting beauty comes only in dream, and this solace the world had thrown away when in its worship of the real it threw away the secrets of childhood and innocence.

Amidst this chaos of hollowness and unrest Carter tried to live as befitted a man of keen thought and good heritage. With his dreams fading under the ridicule of the age he could not believe in anything, but the love of harmony kept him close to the ways of his race and station. He walked impassive through the cities of men, and sighed because no vista seemed fully real; because every flash of yellow sunlight on tall roofs and every glimpse of balustraded plazas in the first lamps of evening served only to remind him of dreams he had once known, and to make him homesick for ethereal lands he no longer knew how to find. Travel was only a mockery; and even the Great War stirred him but little, though he served from the first in the Foreign Legion of France. For a while he sought friends, but soon grew weary of the crudeness of their emotions, and the sameness and earthiness of their visions. He felt vaguely glad that all his relatives were distant and out of touch with him, for they would not have understood his mental life. That is, none but his grandfather and great-uncle Christopher could, and they were long dead.

Then he began once more the writing of books, which he had left off when dreams first failed him. But here, too, was there no satisfaction or fulfillment; for the touch of earth was upon his mind, and he could not think of lovely things as he had done of yore. Ironic humor dragged down all the twilight minarets he reared, and the earthy fear of improbability blasted all the delicate and amazing flowers in his faery gardens. The convention of assumed pity spilt mawkishness on his characters, while the myth of an important reality and significant human events and emotions debased all his high fantasy into thin-veiled allegory and cheap social satire. His new novels were successful as his old ones had never been; and because he knew how empty they must be to please an empty herd, he burned them and ceased his writing. They were very graceful novels, in which he urbanely laughed at the dreams he lightly sketched; but he saw that their sophistication had sapped all their life away.

It was after this that he cultivated deliberate illusion, and dabbled in the notions of the bizarre and the eccentric as an antidote for the commonplace. Most of these, however, soon showed their poverty and barrenness; and he saw that the popular doctrines of occultism are as dry and inflexible as those of science, yet without even the slender palliative of truth to redeem them. Gross stupidity, falsehood, and muddled thinking are not dream; and form no escape from life to a mind trained above their own level. So Carter bought stranger books and sought out deeper and more terrible men of fantastic erudition; delving into arcana of consciousness that few have trod, and learning things about the secret pits of life, legend, and immemorial antiquity which disturbed him ever afterward. He decided to live on a rare plane, and furnished his Boston home to suit his changing moods; one room for each, hung in appropriate colors, furnished with befitting books and objects, and provided with sources of the proper sensations of light, heat, sound, taste, and odor.

Once he heard of a man in the south who was shunned and feared for the blasphemous things he read in prehistoric books and clay tablets smuggled from India and Arabia. Him he visited, living with him and sharing his studies for seven years, till horror overtook them one midnight in an unknown and archaic graveyard, and only one emerged where two had entered. Then he went back to Arkham, the terrible witch-haunted old town of his forefathers in New England, and had experiences in the dark, amidst the hoary willows and tottering gambrel roofs, which made him seal forever certain pages in the diary of a wildminded ancestor. But these horrors took him only to the edge of reality, and were not of the true dream country he had known in youth; so that at fifty he despaired of any rest or contentment in a world grown too busy for beauty and too shrewd for dreams.

Having perceived at last the hollowness and futility of real things, Carter spent his days in retirement, and in wistful disjointed memories of his dream-filled youth. He thought it rather silly that he bothered to keep on living at all, and got from a South American acquaintance a very curious liquid to take him to oblivion without suffering. Inertia and force of habit, however, caused him to defer action; and he lingered indecisively among thoughts of old times, taking down the strange hangings from his walls and refitting the house as it was in his early boyhood—purple panes, Victorian furniture, and all.

With the passage of time he became almost glad he had lingered, for his relics of youth and his cleavage from the world made life and sophistication seem very distant and unreal; so much so that a touch of magic and expectancy stole back into his nightly slumbers. For years those slumbers had known only such twisted reflections of everyday things as the commonest slumbers know, but now there returned a flicker of something stranger and wilder; something of vaguely awesome imminence which took the form of tensely clear pictures from his childhood days, and made him think of little inconsequential things he had long forgotten. He would often awake calling for his mother and grandfather, both in their graves a quarter of a century.

Then one night his grandfather reminded him of the key. The gray old scholar, as vivid as in life, spoke long and earnestly of their ancient line, and of the strange visions of the delicate and sensitive men who composed it. He spoke of the flame-eyed Crusader who learnt wild secrets of the Saracens that held him captive; and of the first Sir Randolph Carter who studied magic when Elizabeth was queen. He spoke, too, of that Edmund Carter who had just escaped hanging in the Salem witchcraft, and who had placed in an antique box a great silver key handed down from his ancestors. Before Carter awakened, the gentle visitant had told him where to find that box; that carved oak box of archaic wonder whose grotesque lid no hand had raised for two centuries.

In the dust and shadows of the great attic he found it, remote and forgotten at the back of a drawer in a tall chest. It was about a foot square, and its Gothic carvings were so fearful that he did not marvel no person since Edmund Carter had dared to open it. It gave forth no noise when shaken, but was mystic with the scent of unremembered spices. That it held a key was indeed only a dim legend, and Randolph Carter's father had never known such a box existed. It was bound in rusty iron, and no means was provided for working the formidable lock. Carter vaguely understood that he would find within it some key to the lost gate of dreams, but of where and how to use it his grandfather had told him nothing.

An old servant forced the carven lid, shaking as he did so at the hideous faces leering from the blackened wood, and at some unplaced familiarity. Inside, wrapped in a discolored parchment, was a huge key of tarnished silver covered with cryptical arabesques; but of any legible explanation there was none. The parchment was voluminous, and held only the strange hieroglyphs of an unknown tongue written with an antique reed. Carter recognized the characters as those he had seen on a certain papyrus scroll belonging to that terrible scholar of the South who had vanished one midnight in a nameless cemetery. The man had always shivered when he read this scroll, and Carter shivered now.

But he cleaned the key, and kept it by him nightly in its aromatic box of ancient oak. His dreams were meanwhile increasing in vividness, and though showing him none of the strange cities and incredible gardens of the old days, were assuming a definite cast whose purpose could not be mistaken. They were calling him back along the years, and with the mingled wills of all his fathers were pulling him toward some hidden and ancestral source. Then he knew he must go into the past and merge himself with old things, and day after day he thought of the hills to the north where haunted Arkham and the rushing Miskatonic and the lonely rustic homestead of his people lay.

In the brooding fire of autumn Carter took the old remembered way past graceful lines of rolling hiss and stone-walled meadow, distant vale and hanging woodland, curving road and nestling farmstead, and the crystal windings of the Miskatonic, crossed here and there by rustic bridges of wood or stone. At one bend he saw the group of giant elms among which an ancestor had oddly vanished a century and a half before, and shuddered as the wind blew meaningly through them. Then there was the crumbling farmhouse of old Goody Fowler the witch, with its little evil windows and great roof sloping nearly to the ground on the north side. He speeded up his car as he passed it, and did not slacken till he had mounted the hill where his mother and her fathers before her were born, and where the old white house still looked proudly across the road at the breathlessly lovely panorama of rocky slope and verdant valley, with the distant spires of Kingsport on the horizon, and hints of the archaic, dream-laden sea in the farthest background.

Then came the steeper slope that held the old Carter place he had not seen in over forty years. Afternoon was far gone when he reached the foot, and at the bend half way up he paused to scan the outspread countryside golden and glorified in the slanting floods of magic poured out by a western sun. All the strangeness and expectancy of his recent dreams seemed present in this hushed and unearthly landscape, and he thought of the unknown solitudes of other planets as his eyes traced out the velvet and deserted lawns shining undulant between their tumbled walls, and clumps of faery forest setting off far lines of purple hills beyond hills, and the spectral wooded valley dipping down in shadow to dank hollows where trickling waters crooned and gurgled among swollen and distorted roots.

Something made him feel that motors did not belong in the realm he was seeking, so he left his car at the edge of the forest, and putting the great key in his coat pocket walked on up the hill. Woods now engulfed him utterly, though he knew the house was on a high knoll that cleared the trees except to the north. He wondered how it would look, for it had been left vacant and untended through his neglect since the death of his strange great-uncle Christopher thirty years before. In his boyhood he had revelled through long visits there, and had found weird marvels in the woods beyond the orchard.

Shadows thickened around him, for the night was neat. Once a gap in the trees opened up to the right, so that he saw off across leagues of twilight meadow and spied the old Congregational steeple on Central Hill in Kingsport; pink with the last flush of day, the panes of the little round windows blazing with reflected fire. Then, when he was in deep shadow again, he recalled with a start that the glimpse must have come from childish memory alone, since the old white church had long been torn down to make room for the Congregational Hospital. He had read of it with interest, for the paper had told about some strange burrows or passages found in the rocky hill beneath.

Through his puzzlement a voice piped, and he started again at its familiarity after long years. Old Benijah Corey had been his Uncle Christopher's hired man, and was aged even in those far-off times of his boyhood visits. Now he must be well over a hundred, but that piping voice could come from no one else. He could distinguish no words, yet the tone was haunting and unmistakable. To think that "old Benijy" should still be alive!

"Mister Randy! Mister Randy! Wharbe ye? D'ye want to skeer yer Aunt Marthy plumb to death? Hain't she tuld ye to keep nigh the place in the arternoon an' git back afur dark? Randy! Ran...dee!...He's the beatin'est boy fer runnin' off in the woods I ever see; haff the time a-settin' moonin' raound that snake-den in the upper timberlot!...Hey yew, Ran...dee!"

Randolph Carter stopped in the pitch darkness and rubbed his hand across his eyes. Something was queer. He had been somewhere he ought not to be; had strayed very far away to places where he had not belonged, and was now inexcusably late. He had not noticed the time on the Kingsport steeple, though he could easily have made it out with his pocket telescope; but he knew his lateness was something very strange and unprecedented. He was not sure he had his little telescope with him, and put his hand in his blouse pocket to see. No, it was not there, but there was the big silver key he had found in a box somewhere. Uncle Chris had told him something odd once about an old unopened box with a key in it, but Aunt Martha had stopped the story abruptly, saying it was no kind of thing to tell a child whose head was already too full of queer fancies. He tried to recall just where he had found the key, but something seemed very confused. He guessed it was in the attic at home in Boston, and dimly remembered bribing Parks with half his week's allowance to help him open the box and keep quiet about it; but when he remembered this, the face of Parks came up very strangely, as if the wrinkles of long years had fallen upon the brisk little Cockney.

"Ran...dee! Ran...dee! Hi! Hi! Randy!"

A swaying lantern came around the back bend, and old Benijah pounced on the silent and bewildered form of the pilgrim.

"Durn ye, boy, so thar ye be! Ain't ye got a tongue in yer head, that ye can't answer a body? I ben callin' this haff hour, an' ye must a heerd me long ago! Dun't ye know yer Aunt Marthy's all a-fidget over yer bein' off arter dark? Wait till I tell yer Uncle Chris when he gits hum! Ye'd orta know these here woods ain't no fitten place to be traipsin' this hour! They's things abroad what dun't do nobody no good, as my gran'-sir' knowed afur me. Come, Mister Randy, or Hannah wunt keep supper no longer!"

So Randolph Carter was marched up the road where wondering stars glimmered through high autumn boughs. And dogs barked as the yellow light of small-paned windows shone out at the farther turn, and the Pleiades twinkled across the open knoll where a great gambrel roof stood black against the dim west. Aunt Martha was in the doorway, and did not scold too hard when Benijah shoved the truant in. She knew Uncle

Chris well enough to expect such things of the Carter blood. Randolph did not show his key, but ate his supper in silence and protested only when bedtime came. He sometimes dreamed better when awake, and he wanted to use that key.

In the morning Randolph was up early, and would have run off to the upper timber lot if Uncle Chris had not caught him and forced him into his chair by the breakfast table. He looked impatiently around the low-pitched room with the rag carpet and exposed beams and corner-posts, and smiled only when the orchard boughs scratched at the leaded panes of the rear window. The trees and the hills were close to him, and formed the gates of that timeless realm which was his true country.

Then, when he was free, he felt in his blouse pocket for the key; and being reassured, skipped off across the orchard to the rise beyond, where the wooded hill climbed again to heights above even the treeless knoll. The floor of the forest was mossy and mysterious, and great lichened rocks rose vaguely here and there in the dim light like Druid monoliths among the swollen and twisted trunks of a sacred grove. Once in his ascent Randolph crossed a rushing stream whose falls a little way off sang runic incantations to the lurking fauns and aegipans and dryads.

Then he came to the strange cave in the forest slope, the dreaded "snake-den" which country folk shunned, and away from which Benijah had warned him again and again. It was deep; far deeper than anyone but Randolph suspected, for the boy had found a fissure in the farthermost black corner that led to a loftier grotto beyond—a haunting sepulchral place whose granite walls held a curious illusion of conscious artifice. On this occasion he crawled in as usual, lighting his way with matches filched from the sitting-room match-safe, and edging through the final crevice with an eagerness hard to explain even to himself. He could not tell why he approached the farther wall so confidently, or why he instinctively drew forth the great silver key as he did so. But on he went, and when he danced back to the house that night he offered no excuses for his lateness, nor heeded in the least the reproofs he gained for ignoring the noontide dinner-horn altogether.

Now it is agreed by all the distant relatives of Randolph Carter that something occurred to heighten his imagination in his tenth year. His cousin, Ernest B. Aspinwall, Esq., of Chicago, is fully ten years his senior; and distinctly recalls a change in the boy after the autumn of 1883. Randolph had looked on scenes of Fantasy that few others can ever have beheld, and stranger still were some of the qualities which he showed in relation to very mundane things. He seemed, in fine, to have picked up an odd gift or prophecy; and reacted unusually to things which, though at the time without meaning, were later found to justify the singular impressions. In subsequent decades as new inventions, new names, and new events appeared one by one in the book of history, people would now and then recall wonderingly how Carter had years before let fall some careless word of undoubted connection with what was then far in the future. He did not understand these words, or know why certain things made him feel certain emotions; but fancied that some unremembered dream must be responsible. It was as early as 1897 that he turned pale when some traveller mentioned the French town of Belloy-en-Santerre, and friends remembered it when he was almost mortally wounded there in 1916, while serving with the Foreign Legion in the Great War.

Carter's relatives talk much of these things because he has lately disappeared. His little old servant Parks, who for years bore patiently with his vagaries, last saw him on the morning he drove off alone in his car with a key he had recently found. Parks had helped him get the key from the old box containing it, and had felt strangely affected by the grotesque carvings on the box, and by some other odd quality he could not name. When Carter left, he had said he was going to visit his old ancestral country around Arkham.

Halfway up Elm Mountain, on the way to the ruins of the old Carter place, they found his motor set carefully by the roadside; and in it was a box of fragrant wood with carvings that frightened the countrymen who stumbled on it. The box held only a queer parchment whose characters no linguist or paleographer has been able to decipher or identify. Rain had long effaced any possible footprints, though Boston investigators had something to say about evidence of disturbances among the fallen timbers of the Carter place. It was, they averred, as though someone had groped about the ruins at no distant period. A common white handkerchief found among forest rocks on the hillside beyond cannot be identified as belonging to the missing man.

There is talk of apportioning Randolph Carter's estate among his heirs, but I shall stand firmly against this course because I do not believe he is dead. There are twists of time and space, of vision and reality, which only a dreamer can divine; and from what I know of Carter I think he had merely found a way to traverse these mazes. Whether or not he will ever come back, I cannot say. He wanted the lands of dream he had lost, and yearned for the days of his childhood. Then he found a key, and I somehow believe he was able to use it to strange advantage.

I shall ask him when I see him, for I expect to meet him shortly in a certain dream-city we both used to haunt. It is rumored in Ulthar, beyond the River Skai, that a new king reigns on the opal throne of Ilek-Vad, that fabulous town of turrets atop the hollow cliffs of glass overlooking the twilight sea wherein the bearded and finny Gnorri build their singular labyrinths, and I believe I know how to interpret this rumor. Certainly, I look forward impatiently to the sight of that great silver key, for in its cryptical arabesques there may stand symbolized all the aims and mysteries of a blindly impersonal cosmos.

Nothing in the Rules

by L. SPRAGUE DE CAMP

NOT MANY spectators turn out for a meet between two minor women's swimming clubs, and this one was no exception. Louis Connaught, looking up at the balcony, thought casually that the single row of seats around it was about half full, mostly with the usual bored-looking assortment of husbands and boy friends, and some of the Hotel Creston's guests who had wandered in for want of anything better to do. One of the bellboys was asking an evening-gowned female not to smoke, and she was showing irritation. Mr. Santalucia and the little Santalucias were there as usual to see mamma perform. They waved down at Connaught.

Connaught—a dark devilish-looking little man—glanced over to the other side of the pool. The girls were coming out of the shower rooms, and their shrill conversation was blurred by the acoustics of the pool room into a continuous buzz. The air was faintly steamy. The stout party in white duck pants was Laird, coach of the Knickerbockers and Connaught's arch rival. He saw Connaught and boomed: "Hi, Louie!" The words rattled from wall to wall with a sound like a stick being drawn swiftly along a picket fence. Wambach of the A. A. U. Committee, who was refereeing, came in with his overcoat still on and greeted Laird, but the booming reverberations drowned his words before they got over to Connaught.

Then something else came through the door; or rather, a knot of people crowded through it all at once, facing inward, some in bathing suits and some in street clothes. It was a few seconds before Coach Connaught saw what they were looking at. He blinked and looked more closely, standing with his mouth half open.

But not for long. "*Hey!*" he yelled in a voice that made the pool room sound like the inside of a snare drum in use. "Protest! PROTEST! *You can't do that!*"

It had been the preceding evening when Herbert Laird opened his front door and shouted, "H'lo, Mark, come on in." The chill March wind was making a good deal of racket but not so much as all that. Laird was given to shouting on general principle. He was stocky and bald.

Mark Vining came in and deposited his briefcase. He was younger than Laird—just thirty, in fact—with octagonal glasses and rather thin, severe features, which made him look more serious than he was.

"Glad you could come, Mark," said Laird. "Listen, can you make our meet with the Crestons tomorrow night?"

Vining pursed his lips thoughtfully. "I guess so. Loomis decided not to appeal, so I don't have to work nights for a few days anyhow. Is something special up?"

Laird looked sly. "Maybe. Listen, you know that Mrs. Santalucia that Louie Connaught has been cleaning up with for the past couple of years? I think I've got that fixed. But I want you along to think up legal reasons why my scheme's okay."

"Why," said Vining cautiously, "what's your scheme?"

"Can't tell you now. I promised not to. But if Louie can win by entering a freak—a woman with webbed fingers—"

"Oh, look here, Herb, you know those webs don't really help her—"

"Yes, yes, I know all the arguments. You've already got more water resistance to your arms than you've got muscle to overcome it with, and so forth. But I know Mrs. Santalucia has webbed fingers, and I know she's the best damned woman swimmer in New York. And I don't like it. It's bad for my prestige as a coach." He turned and shouted into the gloom: "Iantha!"

"Yes?"

"Come here, will you please? I want you to meet my friend Mr. Vining. Here, we need some light."

The light showed the living room as usual buried under disorderly piles of boxes and bathing suits and other swimming equipment, the sale of which furnished Herbert Laird with most of his income. It also showed a young woman coming in in a wheelchair.

One look gave Vining a feeling that, he knew, boded no good for him. He was unfortunate in being a pushover for any reasonably attractive girl and at the same time being cursed with an almost pathological shyness where women were concerned. The fact that both he and Laird were bachelors and took their swimming seriously was the main tie between them.

This girl was more than reasonably attractive. She was, thought the dazzled Vining, a wow, a ten-strike, a direct sixteen-inch hit. Her smooth, rather flat features and high cheekbones had a hint of Asian or American Indian and went oddly with her light-gold hair, which, Vining could have sworn, had a faint greenish tinge. A blanket was wrapped around her legs.

He came out of his trance as Laird introduced the exquisite creature as "Miss Delfoiros."

Miss Delfoiros did not seem exactly overcome. As she extended her hand, she said with a noticeable accent: "You are not from the newspapers, Mr. Vining?"

"No," said Vining. "Just a lawyer. I specialize in wills and probates and things. Not thinking of drawing up yours, are you?"

She relaxed visibly and laughed. "No. I 'ope I shall not need one for a long, long time."

"Still," said Vining seriously, "you never know—"

Laird bellowed: "Wonder what's keeping that sister of mine. Dinner ought to be ready. *Martha!*" He marched out, and Vining heard Miss Laird's voice, something about "—but Herb, I had to let those things cool down—"

Vining wondered with a great wonder what he should say to Miss Delfoiros. Finally he said, "Smoke?"

"Oh, no, thank you very much. I do not do it."

"Mind if I do?"

"No, not at all."

"Whereabouts do you hail from?" Vining thought the question sounded both brusque and silly. He never did get the hang of talking easily under these circumstances.

"Oh, I am from Kip—Cyprus, I mean. You know, the island."

"Will you be at this swimming meet?"

"Yes, I think so."

"You don't"—he lowered his voice—"know what scheme Herb's got up his sleeve to beat La Santalucia?"

"Yes...no...I do not...what I mean is, I must not tell."

More mystery, thought Vining. What he really wanted to know was why she was confined to a wheelchair; whether the cause was temporary or permanent. But you couldn't ask a person right out, and he was still trying to concoct a leading question when Laird's bellow wafted in: "All right, folks, soup's on!" Vining would have pushed the wheelchair in, but before he had a chance, the girl had spun the chair around and was halfway to the dining room.

Vining said: "Hello, Martha, how's the schoolteaching business?" But he was not really paying much attention to Laird's capable spinster sister. He was gaping at Miss Delfoiros, who was quite calmly emptying a teaspoonful of salt into her water glass and stirring.

"What... what?" he gulped.

"I 'ave to," she said. "Fresh water makes me—like what you call drunk."

"Listen, Mark!" roared his friend. "Are you sure you can be there on time tomorrow night? There are some questions of eligibility to be cleared up, and I'm likely to need you badly."

"Will Miss Delfoiros be there?" Vining grinned, feeling very foolish inside.

"Oh, sure. Iantha's our... say, listen, you know that little eighteen-year-old Clara Havranek? She did the hundred in one-oh-five yesterday. She's championship material. We'll clean the Creston Club yet—" He went on, loud and fast, about what he was going to do to Louis Connaught's girls. The while, Mark Vining tried to concentrate on his own food, which was good, and on Iantha Delfoiros, who was charming but evasive.

There seemed to be something special about Miss Delfoiros' food, to judge by the way Martha Laird had served it. Vining looked closely and saw that it had the peculiarly dead and clammy look that a dinner once hot but now cold has. He asked about it.

"Yes," she said, "I like it cold."

"You mean you don't eat *anything* hot?"

She made a face. "'Ot food? No, I do not like it. To us it is—"

"Listen, Mark! I hear the W. S. A. is going to throw a post-season meet in April for novices only—"

Vining's dessert lay before him a full minute before he noticed it. He was too busy thinking how delightful Miss Delfoiros' accent was.

When dinner was over, Laird said, "Listen, Mark, you know something about these laws against owning gold? Well, look here—" He led the way to a candy box on a table in the living room. The box contained, not candy, but gold and silver coins. Laird handed the lawyer several of them. The first one he examined was a silver crown, bearing the inscription "Carolus II Dei Gra" encircling the head of England's Merry Monarch with a wreath in his hair—or, more probably, in his wig. The second was an eighteenth-century Spanish dollar. The third was a Louis d'Or.

"I didn't know you went in for coin collecting, Herb," said Vining. "I suppose these are all genuine?"

"They're genuine all right. But I'm not collecting 'em. You might say I'm taking 'em in trade. I have a chance to sell ten thousand bathing caps, if I can take payment in those things."

"I shouldn't think the U. S. Rubber Company would like the idea much."

"That's just the point. What'll I do with 'em after I get 'em? Will the government put me in jail for having 'em?"

"You needn't worry about that. I don't think the law covers old coins, though I'll look it up to make sure. Better call up the American Numismatic Society—they're in the phone book—and they can tell you how to dispose of them. But look here, what the devil is this? Ten thousand bathing caps to be paid for in pieces-of-eight? I never heard of such a thing."

"That's it exactly. Just ask the little lady here." Laird turned to Iantha, who was nervously trying to signal him to keep quiet. "The deal's her doing."

"I did...did—" She looked as if she were going to cry. "'Erbert, you should not have said that. You see," she said to Vining, "we do not like to 'ave a lot to do with people. Always it causes us troubles."

"Who," asked Vining, "do you mean by 'we'?"

She shut her mouth obstinately. Vining almost melted, but his legal instincts came to the surface. If you don't get a grip on yourself, he thought, you'll be in love with her in another five minutes, and that might be a disaster. He said firmly:

"Herb, the more I see of this business, the crazier it looks.

Whatever's going on, you seem to be trying to get me into it. But I'm damned if I'll let you unless I know what it's all about."

"Might as well tell him, Iantha," said Laird. "He'll know when he sees you swim tomorrow, anyhow."

She said: "You will not tell the newspaper men, Mr. Vining?"

"No, I won't say anything to anybody."

"You promise?"

"Of course. You can depend on a lawyer to keep things under his hat."

"Under his— I suppose you mean, not to tell. So, look." She reached down and pulled up the lower end of the blanket.

Vining looked. Where he expected to see feet, there was a pair of horizontal flukes, like those of a porpoise.

Louis Connaught's having kittens, when he saw what his rival coach had sprung on him, can thus be easily explained. First he doubted his own senses; then he doubted whether there was any justice in the world.

Meanwhile, Mark Vining proudly pushed Iantha's wheelchair in among the cluster of judges and timekeepers at the starting end of the pool. Iantha herself, in a bright green bathing cap, held her blanket around her shoulders, but the slate-gray tail with its flukes was plain for all to see. The skin of the tail was smooth and the flukes were horizontal; artists who show mermaids with scales and a vertical tail fin, like a fish's, simply do not know their zoology.

"All right, all right," bellowed Laird. "Don't crowd around. Everybody get back to where they belong. Everybody, please."

One of the spectators, leaning over the rail of the balcony to see, dropped a fountain pen into the pool. One of Connaught's girls, a Miss Black, dove in after it.

Ogden Wambach, the referee, poked a finger at the skin of the tail. He was a well-groomed, gray-haired man.

"Laird," he said, "is this a joke?"

"Not at all. She's entered in the back stroke and all the free styles, just like any other club member. She's even registered with the A. A. U."

"But...but...I mean, is it alive? Is it real?"

Iantha spoke up. "Why do you not ask me those questions, Mr....Mr....I do not know you—"

"Good grief," said Wambach. "It talks! I'm the referee, Miss—"

"Delfoiros. Iantha Delfoiros."

"My word. Upon my word. That means—let's see—Violet Porpoise-tail, doesn't it? *Delphis* plus *oura*—"

"You know Greek? Oh, 'ow nice!" She broke into a string of *dimotiki.*

Wambach gulped a little. "Too fast for me, I'm afraid. And that's *modern* Greek, isn't it?"

"Why, yes. I am modern, am I not?"

"Dear me. I suppose so. But is that tail really real? I mean, it's not just a piece of costumery?"

"Oh, but yes." Iantha threw off the blanket and waved her flukes. Everyone in the pool seemed to have turned into a pair of eyeballs to which a body and a pair of legs were vaguely attached.

"Dear me," said Ogden Wambach. "Where are my glasses? You understand, I just want to make sure there's nothing spurious about this."

Mrs. Santalucia, a muscular-looking lady with a visible mustache and fingers webbed down to the first joint, said, "You mean I gotta swim against *her?*"

Louis Connaught had been sizzling like a dynamite fuse. "You can't do it!" he shrilled. "This is a woman's meet! I protest!"

"So what?" said Laird.

"But you can't enter a fish in a woman's swimming meet! Can you, Mr. Wambach?"

Mark Vining spoke up. He had just taken a bunch of papers

clipped together out of his pocket and was running through them.

"Miss Delfoiros," he asserted, "is not a fish. She's a mammal."

"How do you figure that?" yelled Connaught.

"*Look* at her."

"Um-m-m," said Ogden Wambach. "I see what you mean."

"But," howled Connaught, "she still ain't human!"

"There is a question about that, Mr. Vining," said Wambach.

"No question at all. There's nothing in the rules against entering a mermaid, and there's nothing that says the competitors have to be human."

Connaught was hopping about like an overwrought cricket. He was now waving a copy of the current A. A. U. swimming, diving, and water polo rules. "I still protest! Look here! All through here it only talks about two kinds of meets, men's and women's. She ain't a woman, and she certainly ain't a man. If the Union had wanted to have meets for mermaids they'd have said so."

"Not a woman?" asked Vining in a manner that juries learned meant a rapier thrust at an opponent. "I beg your pardon, Mr. Connaught. I looked the question up." He frowned at his sheaf of papers. "Webster's International Dictionary, Second Edition, defines a woman as 'any female person.' And it further defines 'person' as 'a being characterized by conscious apprehension, rationality, and a moral sense.'" He turned to Wambach. "Sir, I think you'll agree that Miss Delfoiros has exhibited conscious apprehension and rationality during her conversation with you, won't you?"

"My word...I really don't know what to say, Mr. Vining...I suppose she has, but I couldn't say—"

Horwitz, the scorekeeper, spoke up. "You might ask her to give the multiplication table." Nobody paid him any attention.

Connaught exhibited symptoms of apoplexy. "But you

can't—What the hell you talking about—conscious ap-ap—"

"Please, Mr. Connaught!" said Wambach. "When you shout that way I can't understand you because of the echoes."

Connaught mastered himself with a visible effort. Then he looked crafty. "How do I know she's got a moral sense?"

Vining turned to Iantha. "Have you ever been in jail, Iantha?"

Iantha laughed. "What a funny question, Mark! But of course, I have not."

"That's what *she* says," sneered Connaught. "How you gonna prove it?"

"We don't have to," said Vining loftily. "The burden of proof is on the accuser, and the accused is legally innocent until proved guilty. That principle was well established by the time of King Edward the First."

"Oh, damn King Edward the First," cried Connaught. "That wasn't the kind of moral sense I meant anyway. How about what they call moral turp-turp— You know what I mean."

"Hey," growled Laird, "what's the idea? Are you trying to cast— What's the word, Mark?"

"Aspersions?"

"—cast aspersions on one of my swimmers? You watch out, Louie. If I hear you be— What's the word, Mark?"

"Besmirching her fair name?"

"—besmirching her fair name, I'll drown you in your own tank."

"And after that," said Vining, "we'll slap a suit on you for slander."

"Gentlemen! Gentlemen!" said Wambach. "Let's not have any more personalities, please. This is a swimming meet, not a lawsuit. Let's get to the point."

"We've made ours," said Vining with dignity. "We've shown that Iantha Delfoiros is a woman, and Mr. Connaught has stated, himself, that this is a woman's meet. Therefore, Miss Delfoiros is eligible. Q.E.D."

"Ahem," said Wambach. "I don't quite know—I never had a case like this to decide before."

Louis Connaught almost had tears in his eyes; at least he sounded as if he did. "Mr. Wambach, you can't let Herb Laird do this to me. I'll be a laughingstock."

Laird snorted. "How about your beating me with your Mrs. Santalucia? I didn't get any sympathy from you when people laughed at me on account of that. And how much good did it do me to protest against her fingers?"

"But," wailed Connaught, "if he can enter this Miss Delfoiros, what's to stop somebody from entering a trained sea lion or something? Do you want to make competitive swimming into a circus?"

Laird grinned. "Go ahead, Louie. Nobody's stopping you from entering anything you like. How about it, Ogden? Is she a woman?"

"Well...really...oh, dear—"

"Please!" Iantha Delfoiros rolled her violet-blue eyes at the bewildered referee. "I should so like to swim in this nice pool with all these nice people!"

Wambach sighed. "All right, my dear, you shall!"

"Whoopee!" cried Laird, the cry being taken up by Vining, the members of the Knickerbocker Swimming Club, the other officials, and lastly the spectators. The noise in the enclosed space made sensitive eardrums wince.

"Wait a minute," yelped Connaught when the echoes had died. "Look here, page 19 of the rules. 'Regulation Costume, Women: Suits must be of dark color, with skirt attached. Leg is to reach—' and so forth. Right here it says it. She can't swim the way she is, not in a sanctioned meet."

"That's true," said Wambach. "Let's see—"

Horwitz looked up from his little scoresheet-littered table. "Maybe one of the girls has a halter she could borrow," he suggested. "That would be something."

"Halter, phooey!" snapped Connaught. "This means a regular suit with legs and a skirt, and everybody knows it."

"But she hasn't got any legs!" cried Laird. "How could she get into—"

"That's just the point! If she can't wear a suit with legs, and the rules say you gotta have legs, she can't wear the regulation suit, and she can't compete! I gotcha that time! Haha, I'm sneering!"

"I'm afraid not, Louie," said Vining, thumbing his own copy of the rule book. He held it up to the light and read: "'Note.— These rules are approximate, the idea being to bar costumes which are immodest, or will attract undue attention and comment. The referee shall have the power'—et cetera, et cetera. If we cut the legs out of a regular suit, and she pulled the rest of it on over her head, that would be modest enough for all practical purposes. Wouldn't it, Mr. Wambach?"

"Dear me—I don't know—I suppose it would."

Laird hissed to one of his pupils, "Hey, listen, Miss Havranek! You know where my suitcase is? Well, you get one of the extra suits out of it, and there's a pair of scissors in with the first-aid things. You fix that suit up so Iantha can wear it."

Connaught subsided. "I see now," he said bitterly, "why you guys wanted to finish with a 300-yard free style instead of a relay. If I'da' known what you were planning—and, you, Mark Vining, if I ever get in a jam, I'll go to jail before I hire you for a lawyer, so help me!"

Mrs. Santalucia had been glowering at Iantha Delfoiros. Suddenly she turned to Connaught. "Thissa no fair. I swim against people. I no-gotta swim against mermaids."

"Please, Maria, don't *you* desert me," wailed Connaught.

"I no swim tonight."

Connaught looked up appealingly to the balcony. Mr. Santalucia and the little Santalucias, guessing what was happening, burst into a chorus of: "Go on, mamma! You show them, mamma!"

"Aw right. I swim one, maybe two races. If I see I no got a chance, I no swim no more."

"That's better, Maria. It wouldn't really count if she beat you anyway." Connaught headed for the door, saying something about "telephone" on the way.

Despite the delays in starting the meet, nobody left the pool room through boredom. In fact, the empty seats in the balcony were full by this time and people were standing up behind them. Word had gotten around the Hotel Creston that something was up.

By the time Louis Connaught returned, Laird and Vining were pulling the altered bathing suit on over Iantha's head. It did not reach quite so far as they expected, having been designed for a slightly slimmer swimmer. Not that Iantha was fat. But her human part, if not exactly plump, was at least comfortably upholstered, so that no bones showed. Iantha squirmed around in the suit a good deal and threw a laughing remark in Greek to Wambach, whose expression showed that he hoped it did not mean what he suspected it did.

Laird said, "Now listen, Iantha, remember not to move till the gun goes off. And remember that you swim directly over the black line on the bottom, not between two lines."

"Are they going to shoot a gun? Oh, I am afraid of shooting!"

"It's nothing to be afraid of; just blank cartridges. They don't hurt anybody. And it won't be so loud inside that cap."

"Herb," said Vining, "won't she lose time getting off, not being able to make a flat dive like the others?"

"She will. But it won't matter. She can swim a mile in *four* minutes, without really trying."

Ritchey, the starter, announced the fifty-yard free style. He called: "All right, everybody, line up."

Iantha slithered off her chair and crawled over to the starting platform. The other girls were all standing with feet together, bodies bent forward at the hips and arms pointing backward. Iantha got into a curious position of her own, with her tail bent under her and her weight resting on her hand and flukes.

"Hey! Protest!" shouted Connaught. "The rules say that all races, except back strokes, are started with dives. What kind of a dive do you call that?"

"Oh, dear," said Wambach. "What—"

"That," said Vining urbanely, "is a mermaid dive. You couldn't expect her to stand upright on her tail."

"But that's just it!" cried Connaught. "First you enter a nonregulation swimmer. Then you put a nonregulation suit on her. Then you start her off with a nonregulation dive. Ain't there anything you guys do like other people?"

"But," said Vining, looking through the rule book, "it doesn't say—here it is. 'The start in all races shall be made with a dive.' But there's nothing in the rules about what kind of dive shall be used. And the dictionary defines a dive simply as 'a plunge into water.' So if you jump in feet first holding your nose, that's a dive for the purpose of the discussion. And in my years of watching swimming meets, I've seen some funnier starting dives than Miss Delfoiros'."

"I suppose he's right," said Wambach.

"Okay, okay," snarled Connaught. "But the next time I have a meet with you and Herb, I bring a lawyer along too, see?"

Ritchey's gun went off. Vining noticed that Iantha flinched a little at the report and was perhaps slowed down a trifle in getting off by it. The other girls' bodies shot out horizontally to smack the water loudly, but Iantha slipped in with the smooth, unhurried motion of a diving seal. Lacking the advantage of feet to push off with, she was several yards behind the other swimmers before she really got started. Mrs. Santalucia had taken her usual lead, foaming along with the slow strokes of her webbed hands.

Iantha did not bother to come to the surface except at the turn, where she had been specifically ordered to come up so that the judge of the turns would not raise arguments as to whether she had touched the end, and at the finish. She hardly used her arms at all, except for an occasional flip of her trailing hands to steer her. The swift up-and-down flutter of the powerful tail flukes sent her through the water like a torpedo, her wake appearing on the surface six or eight feet behind her. As she shot through the as yet unruffled waters at the far end of the pool on the first leg, Vining, who had gone around to the side to watch, noticed that she had the power of closing her nostrils tightly underwater, like a seal or a hippopotamus.

Mrs. Santalucia finished the race in the very creditable time of 29.8 seconds. But Iantha Delfoiros arrived, not merely first, but in the time of 8.0 seconds. At the finish she did not reach up to touch the starting platform and then hoist herself out by her arms the way human swimmers do. She simply angled up sharply, left the water like a leaping trout, and came down with a most smack on the concrete, almost bowling over a timekeeper. By the time the other contestants had completed the turn she was sitting on the platform with her tail curled under her. As the girls foamed laboriously down the final leg, she smiled dazzlingly at Vining, who had had to run to be in at the finish.

"That," she said, "was much fun, Mark. I am so glad you and 'Erbert put me in these races."

Mrs. Santalucia climbed out and walked over to Horwitz's table. That young man was staring in disbelief at the figures he had just written.

"Yes," he said, "that's what it says. Miss Iantha Delfoiros, 8.0; Mrs. Maria Santalucia, 29.8. Please don't drip on my score sheets, lady. Say, Wambach, isn't this a world's record or something?"

"My word!" said Wambach. "It's less than half the existing short-course record. Less than a third, maybe; I'd have to check it. Dear me! I'll have to take it up with the Committee. I don't know whether they'd allow it; I don't think they will, even though there isn't any specific rule against mermaids."

Vining spoke up. "I think we've complied with all the requirements to have records recognized, Mr. Wambach. Miss Delfoiros was entered in advance like all the others."

"Yes, yes, Mr. Vining, but don't you see, a record's a serious matter? No ordinary human being could ever come near a time like that."

"Unless he used an outboard motor," said Connaught. "If you allow contestants to use tail fins like Miss Delfoiros, you oughta let 'em use propellers. I don't see why these guys should be the only ones to be let bust rules all over the place, and then think up lawyer arguments why it's okay. I'm gonna get me a lawyer, too."

"That's all right, Ogden," said Laird. "You take it up with the Committee, but we don't really care much about the records anyway, so long as we can lick Louie here." He smiled indulgently at Connaught, who sputtered with fury.

"I no swim," announced Mrs. Santalucia. "This is all crazy business. I no got a chance."

"Now, Maria," said Connaught, taking her aside, "just once more, won't you please? My reputation—" The rest of his words were drowned in the general reverberation of the pool room. But at the end of them the redoubtable female appeared to have given in to his entreaties.

The hundred-yard free style started in much the same manner as the fifty-yard. Iantha did not flinch at the gun this time and got off to a good start. She skimmed along just below the surface, raising a wake like a tuna clipper. These waves confused the swimmer in the adjacent lane, who happened to be Miss Breitenfeld of the Creston Club. As a result, on her first return leg, Iantha met Miss Breitenfeld swimming athwart her—Iantha's—lane, and rammed the unfortunate girl amidships. Miss Breitenfeld went down without even a gurgle, spewing bubbles.

Connaught shrieked: "Foul! Foul!" although in the general uproar it sounded like "Wow! Wow!" Several swimmers who were not racing dove in to the rescue, and the race came to a stop in general confusion and pandemonium. When Miss Breitenfeld was hauled out, it was found that she had merely had the wind knocked out of her and had swallowed considerable water.

Mark Vining, looking around for Iantha, found her holding on to the edge of the pool and shaking her head. Presently she crawled out, crying:

"Is she 'urt? Is she 'urt? Oh, I am so sorree! I did not think there would be anybody in my lane, so I did not look ahead."

"See?" yelled Connaught. "See, Wambach? See what happens? They ain't satisfied to walk away with the races with their fishwoman. No, they gotta try to cripple my swimmers by butting their slats in. Herb," he went on nastily, "why dontcha get a pet swordfish. Then when you rammed one of my poor girls she'd be out of competition for good!"

"Oh," said Iantha, "I did not mean—it was an accident!"

"Accident my foot!"

"But it was. Mr. Referee, I do not want to bump people. My 'ead 'urts, and my neck also. You think I try to break my neck on purpose?" Iantha's altered suit had crawled up under her armpits, but nobody noticed particularly.

"Sure it was an accident," bellowed Laird. "Anybody could see that. And listen, if anybody was fouled it was Miss Delfoiros."

"Certainly," chimed in Vining. "She was in her own lane, and the other girl wasn't."

"Oh dear me," said Wambach. "I suppose they're right again. This'll have to be re-swum anyway. Does Miss Breitenfeld want to compete?"

Miss Breitenfeld did not, but the others lined up again. This time the race went off without untoward incident. Iantha again made a spectacular leaping finish, just as the other three swimmers were halfway down the second of their four legs.

When Mrs. Santalucia emerged this time, she said to Connaught: "I no swim no more. That is final."

"Oh, but Maria—" It got him nowhere. Finally he said, "Will you swim in the races that she don't enter?"

"Is there any?"

"I think so. Hey, Horwitz, Miss Delfoiros ain't entered in the breast stroke, is she?"

Horwitz looked. "No, she isn't," he said.

"That's something. Say, Herb, how come you didn't put your fishwoman in the breast stroke?"

Vining answered for Laird. "Look at your rules, Louie. 'The feet shall be drawn up simultaneously, the knees bent and open,' et cetera. The rules for back stroke and free style don't say anything about how the legs shall be used, but those for breast stroke do. So no legs, no breast stroke. We aren't giving you a chance to make any legitimate protests."

"Legitimate protests!" Connaught turned away, sputtering.

While the dives were being run off, Vining, watching, became aware of an ethereal melody. First he thought it was in his head. Then he was sure it was coming from one of the spectators. He finally located the source; it was Iantha Delfoiros, sitting in her wheelchair and singing softly. By leaning nearer he could make out the words:

Die schoenste Jungfrau sitzet
Dort ober wunderbar;
Ihr goldnes Geschmeide blitzet;
Sie kaemmt ihr goldenes Haar.

Vining went over quietly. "Iantha," he said. "Pull your bathing suit down, and don't sing."

She complied, looking up at him with a giggle. "But that is a nice song! I learn it from a wrecked German sailor. It is about one of my people."

"I know, but it'll distract the judges. They have to watch the dives closely, and the place is too noisy as it is."

"Such a nice man you are, Mark, but so serious!" She giggled again.

Vining wondered at the subtle change in the mermaid's manner. Then a horrible thought struck him.

"Herb!" he whispered. "Didn't she say something last night about getting drunk on fresh water?"

Laird looked up. "Yes. She—My God, the water in the pool's fresh! I never thought of that. Is she showing signs?"

"I think she is."

"Listen, Mark, what'll we do?"

"I don't know. She's entered in two more events, isn't she? Back stroke and 300-yard free style?"

"Yes."

"Well, why not withdraw her from the back stroke, and give her a chance to sober up before the final event?"

"Can't. Even with all her firsts, we aren't going to win by any big margin. Louie has the edge on us in the dives, and Mrs. Santalucia'll win the breast stroke. In the events Iantha's in, if she takes first and Louie's girls take second and third, that means five points for us but four for him, so we have an advantage of only one point. And her world's record time don't give us any more points."

"Guess we'll have to keep her in and take a chance," said Vining glumly.

Iantha's demeanor was sober enough in lining up for the back stroke. Again she lost a fraction of a second in getting started by not having feet to push off with. But once she got started, the contest was even more one-sided than the free-style races had been. The human part of her body was practically out of water, skimming the surface like the front half of a speedboat. She made paddling motions with her arms, but that was merely for technical reasons; the power was all furnished by the flukes. She did not jump out on to the starting platform this time; for a flash Vining's heart almost stopped as the emerald-green bathing cap seemed about to crash into the tiles at the end of the pool. But Iantha had judged the distance to a fraction of an inch, and braked to a stop with her flukes just before striking.

The breast stroke was won easily by Mrs. Santalucia, although her slow plodding stroke was less spectacular than the butterfly of her competitors. The shrill cheers of the little Santalucias could be heard over the general hubbub. When the winner climbed out, she glowered at Iantha and said to Connaught:

"Louie, if you ever put me in a meet wit' mermaids again, I no swim for you again, never. Now I go home." With which she marched off to the shower room.

Ritchey was just about to announce the final event, the 300-yard free style, when Connaught plucked his sleeve. "Jack," he said, "wait a second. One of my swimmers is gonna be delayed a coupla minutes." He went out a door.

Laird said to Vining: "Wonder what Louie's grinning about. He's got something nasty, I bet. He was phoning earlier, you remember."

"We'll soon see—What's that?" A hoarse bark wafted in from somewhere and rebounded from the walls.

Connaught reappeared carrying two buckets. Behind him was a little round man in three sweaters. Behind the little round man gallumped a glossy California sea lion. At the sight of the gently rippling, jade-green pool, the animal barked joyously and skidded into the water, swam swiftly about, and popped out on the landing platform, barking. The bark had a peculiarly nerve-racking effect in the echoing pool room.

Ogden Wambach seized two handfuls of his sleek gray hair and tugged. "Connaught!" he shouted. "What is that?"

"Oh, that's just one of my swimmers, Mr. Wambach."

"Hey, listen!" rumbled Laird. "We're going to protest this time. Miss Delfoiros is at least a woman, even if she's a kind of peculiar one. But you can't call *that* a woman."

Connaught grinned like Satan looking over a new shipment of sinners. "Didn't you say to go ahead and enter a sea lion if I wanted to?"

"I don't remember saying—"

"Yes, Herbert," said Wambach, looking haggard. "You did say it. There didn't used to be any trouble in deciding whether a swimmer was a woman or not. But now that you've brought in Miss Delfoiros, there doesn't seem to be any place we can draw a line."

"But look here, Ogden, there is such a thing as going too far—"

"That's just what I said about you!" shrilled Connaught.

Wambach took a deep breath. "Let's not shout, please. Herbert, technically you may have an argument. But after we allowed Miss Delfoiros to enter, I think it would only be sporting to let Louie have his seal. Especially after you told him to get one if he could."

Vining spoke up. "Oh, we're always glad to do the sporting thing. But I'm afraid the sea lion wasn't entered at the beginning of the meet as is required by the rules. We don't want to catch hell from the Committee—"

"Oh, yes, she was," said Connaught. "See!" He pointed to one of Horwitz's sheets. "Her name's Alice Black, and there it is."

"But," protested Vining, "I thought *that* was Alice Black." He pointed to a slim dark girl in a bathing suit who was sitting on a window ledge.

"It is," grinned Connaught. "It's just a coincidence that they both got the same name."

"You don't expect us to believe *that?*"

"I don't care whether you believe it or not. It's so. Ain't the sea lion's name Alice Black?" He turned to the little fat man, who nodded.

"Let it pass," moaned Wambach. "We can't take time off to get this animal's birth certificate."

"Well, then," said Vining, "how about the regulation suit? Maybe you'd like to try to put a suit on your sea lion?"

"Don't have to. She's got one already. It grows on her. Yah, yah, yah, gotcha that time."

"I suppose," said Wambach, "that you *could* consider a natural sealskin pelt as equivalent to a bathing suit."

"Sure you could. That's the point. Anyway, the idea of suits is to be modest, and nobody gives a damn about a sea lion's modesty."

Vining made a final point. "You refer to the animal as 'her,' but how do we know it's a female? Even Mr. Wambach wouldn't let you enter a male sea lion in a women's meet."

Wambach spoke: "How do you tell on a sea lion?"

Connaught looked at the little fat man. "Well, maybe we had better not go into that here. How would it be if I put up a ten-dollar bond that Alice is a female, and you checked on her sex later?"

"That seems fair," said Wambach.

Vining and Laird looked at each other. "Shall we let 'em get away with that, Mark?" asked the latter.

Vining rocked on his heels for a few seconds. Then he said, "I think we might as well. Can I see you outside a minute, Herb? You people don't mind holding up the race a couple of minutes more, do you? We'll be right back."

Connaught started to protest about further delay but thought better of it. Laird presently reappeared, looking unwontedly cheerful.

"'Erbert!" said Iantha.

"Yes?" he put his head down.

"I'm afraid—"

"You're afraid Alice might bite you in the water? Well, I wouldn't want that—"

"Oh, no, not afraid that way. Alice, poof! If she gets nasty I give her one with the tail. But I am afraid she can swim faster than me."

"Listen, Iantha, you just go ahead and swim the best you can. Twelve legs, remember. And don't be surprised, no matter what happens."

"What you two saying?" asked Connaught suspiciously.

"None of your business, Louie. Whatcha got in that pail? *Fish?* I see how you're going to work this. Wanta give up and concede the meet now?"

Connaught merely snorted.

The only competitors in the 300-yard free-style race were Iantha Delfoiros and the sea lion, allegedly named Alice. The normal members of both clubs declared that nothing would induce them to get into the pool with the animal. Not even the importance of collecting a third-place point would move them.

Iantha got into her usual starting position. Beside her, the little round man maneuvered Alice, holding her by an improvised leash made of a length of rope. At the far end, Connaught had placed himself and one of the buckets.

Ritchey fired his gun; the little man slipped the leash and said: "Go get 'em, Alice!" Connaught took a fish out of his bucket and waved it. But Alice, frightened by the shot, set up a furious barking and stayed where she was. Not till Iantha had almost reached the far end of the pool did Alice sight the fish at the other end. Then she slid off and shot down the water like a streak. Those who have seen sea lions merely loafing about a pool in a zoo or aquarium have no conception of how fast they can go when they try. Fast as the mermaid was, the sea lion was faster. She made two bucking jumps out of water before she arrived and oozed out onto the concrete. One gulp and the fish had vanished.

Alice spotted the bucket and tried to get her head into it. Connaught fended her off as best he could with his feet. At the starting end, the little round man had taken a fish out of the other bucket and was waving it, calling: "Here Alice!"

Alice did not get the idea until Iantha had finished her second leg. Then she made up for lost time.

The same trouble occurred at the starting end of the pool; Alice failed to see why she should swim twenty-five yards for a fish when there were plenty of them a few feet away. The result was that, at the halfway mark, Iantha was two legs ahead. But then Alice caught on. She caught up with and passed Iantha in the middle of her eighth leg, droozling out of the water at each end long enough to gulp a fish and then speeding down to the other end. In the middle of the tenth leg, she was ten yards ahead of the mermaid.

At that point, Mark Vining appeared through the door, running. In each hand he held a bowl of goldfish by the edge. Behind him came Miss Havranek and Miss Tufts, also of the Knickerbockers, both similarly burdened. The guests of the Hotel Creston had been mildly curious when a dark, severe-looking young man and two girls in bathing suits had dashed into the lobby and made off with the six bowls. But they had been too well-bred to inquire directly about the rape of the goldfish.

Vining ran down the side of the pool to a point near the far end. There he extended his arms and inverted the bowls. Water and fish cascaded into the pool. Miss Havranek and Miss Tufts did likewise at other points along the edge of the pool.

Results were immediate. The bowls had been large, and each had contained about six or eight fair-sized goldfish. The forty-odd bright-colored fish, terrified by their rough handling, darted hither and thither about the pool, or at least went as fast as their inefficient build would permit them.

Alice, in the middle of her ninth leg, angled off sharply. Nobody saw her snatch the fish; one second it was there, and the next it was not. Alice doubled with a swirl of flippers and shot diagonally across the pool. Another fish vanished. Forgotten were her master and Louis Connaught and their buckets. This was much more fun. Meanwhile, Iantha finished her race, narrowly avoiding a collision with the sea lion on her last leg.

Connaught hurled the fish he was holding as far as he could. Alice snapped it up and went on hunting. Connaught ran toward the starting platform, yelling: "Foul! Foul! Protest! Protest! Foul! Foul!"

He arrived to find the timekeepers comparing watches on Iantha's swim, Laird and Vining doing a kind of war dance, and Ogden Wambach looking like the March Hare on the twenty-eighth of February.

"Stop!" cried the referee. "Stop, Louie! If you shout like that you'll drive me mad! I'm almost mad now! I know what you're going to say."

"Well... well... why don't you do something, then? Why don't you tell these crooks where to head in? Why don't you have 'em expelled from the Union? Why don't you—"

"Relax, Louie," said Vining. "We haven't done anything illegal."

What? Why, you dirty—"

"Easy, easy." Vining looked speculatively at his fist. The little man followed his glance and quieted somewhat. "There's nothing in the rules about putting fish into a pool. Intelligent swimmers, like Miss Delfoiros, know enough to ignore them when they're swimming a race."

"But—what—why you—"

Vining walked off, leaving the two coaches and the referee to fight it out. He looked for Iantha. She was sitting on the edge of the pool, paddling in the water with her flukes. Beside her were four feebly flopping goldfish laid out in a row on the tiles. As he approached, she picked one up and put the front end of it in her mouth. There was a flash of pearly teeth and a spasmodic flutter of the fish's tail, and the front half of the fish was gone. The other half followed immediately.

At that instant Alice spotted the three remaining fish. The sea lion had cleaned out the pool and was now slithering around on the concrete, barking and looking for more prey. She gallumped past Vining toward the mermaid.

Iantha saw her coming. The mermaid hoisted her tail out of the water, pivoted where she sat, swung the tail up in a curve, and brought the flukes down on the sea lion's head with a loud *spat.* Vining, who was twenty feet off, could have sworn he felt the wind of the blow.

Alice gave a squawk of pain and astonishment and slithered

away, shaking her head. She darted past Vining again, and for reasons best known to herself hobbled over to the center of argument and bit Ogden Wambach in the leg. The referee screeched and climbed up on Horwitz's table.

"Hey," said the scorekeeper. "You're scattering my papers!"

"I still say they're publicity-hunting crooks!" yelled Connaught, waving his copy of the rule book at Wambach.

"Bunk!" bellowed Laird. "He's just sore because we can think up more stunts than he can. He started it, with his web-fingered woman."

"Damn your complaints!" screamed Wambach. "Damn your sea lions! Damn your papers! Damn your mermaids! Damn your web-fingered women! Damn your swimming clubs! Damn all of you! I'm going mad! You hear? Mad, mad, mad! One more word out of either of you and I'll have you suspended from the Union!"

"Ow, ow, ow!" barked Alice.

Iantha had finished her fish. She started to pull the bathing suit down again; changed her mind, pulled it off over her head, rolled it up, and threw it across the pool. Halfway across it unfolded and floated down onto the water. The mermaid then cleared her throat, took a deep breath, and, in a clear ringing soprano, launched into the heart-wrenching strains of:

Rheingold!
Reines Gold,
Wie lauter und hell
Leuchtest hold du uns!
Um dich, du klares—

"Iantha!"

"What is it, Markee?" she giggled.

"I said, it's getting time to go home!"

"Oh, but I do not want to go home. I am having much fun.

Nun wir klagen!
Gebt uns das Gold—

"No, really, Iantha, we've got to go." He laid a hand on her shoulder. The touch made his blood tingle. At the same time, it was plain that the remains of Iantha's carefully husbanded sobriety had gone. That last race in fresh water had been like three oversized Manhattans. Through Vining's head ran a paraphrase of an old song:

What shall we do with a drunken mermaid
At three o'clock in the morning?

"Oh, Markee, always you are so serious when people are 'aving fun. But if you say please I will come."

"Very well, please come. Here, put your arm around my neck, and I'll carry you to your chair."

Such, indeed, was Mark Vining's intention. He got one hand around her waist and another under her tail. Then he tried to straighten up. He had forgotten that Iantha's tail was a good deal heavier than it looked. In fact, that long and powerful structure of bone, muscle, and cartilage ran the mermaid's total weight up to the surprising figure of over two hundred and fifty pounds. The result of his attempt was to send himself and his burden headlong into the pool. To the spectators it looked as though he had picked Iantha up and then deliberately dived in with her.

He came up and shook the water out of his head. Iantha popped up in front of him.

"So!" she gurgled. "You are 'aving fun with Iantha! I think you are serious, but you want to play games! All right, I show you!" She brought her palm down smartly, filling Vining's mouth and nose with water. He struck out blindly for the edge of the pool. He was a powerful swimmer, but his street clothes hampered him. Another splash cascaded over his luckless head. He got his eyes clear in time to see Iantha's head go down and her flukes up.

"Markeeee!" The voice was behind him. He turned, and saw Iantha holding a large black block of soft rubber. This object was a plaything for users of the Hotel Creston's pool, and it had been left lying on the bottom during the meet.

"Catch!" cried Iantha gaily, and let drive. The block took Vining neatly between the eyes.

The next thing he knew, he was lying on the wet concrete. He sat up and sneezed. His head seemed to be full of ammonia. Louis Connaught put away the smelling-salts bottle, and Laird shoved a glass containing a snort of whiskey at him. Beside him was Iantha, sitting on her curled tail. She was actually crying.

"Oh, Markee, you are not dead? You are all right? Oh, I am so sorry! I did not mean to 'it you."

"I'm all right, I guess," he said thickly. "Just an accident. Don't worry."

"Oh, I am so glad!" she grabbed his neck and gave it a hug that made its vertebrae creak alarmingly.

'Now," he said, "if I could dry out my clothes. Louie, could you—uh—"

"Sure," said Connaught, helping him up. "We'll put your clothes on the radiator in the men's shower room, and I can lend you a pair of pants and a sweatshirt while they're drying."

When Vining came out in his borrowed garments, he had to push his way through the throng that crowded the starting end of the pool room. He was relieved to note that Alice had disappeared. In the crowd, Iantha was holding court in her wheelchair. In front of her stood a large man in a dinner jacket and a black cloak, with his back to the pool.

"Permit me," he was saying. "I am Joseph Clement. Under my management, nothing you wished in the way of a dramatic or musical career would be beyond you. I heard you sing, and I know that with but little training, even the doors of the Metropolitan would fly open at your approach."

"No, Mr. Clement. It would be nice, but tomorrow I 'ave to leave for 'ome." She giggled.

"But my dear Miss Delfoiros—where is your home, if I may presume to ask?"

"Cyprus."

"Cyprus? Hm-m-m—let's see, where's that?"

"You do not know where Cyprus is? You are not a nice man. I do not like you. Go away."

"Oh, but my dear, dear Miss Del—"

"Go away, I said. Scram."

"But—"

Iantha's tail came up and lashed out, catching the cloaked man in the solar plexus.

Little Miss Havranek looked at her teammate Miss Tufts, as she prepared to make her third rescue of the evening. "Poisonally," she said, "I am getting damn sick of pulling dopes out of this pool."

The sky was just turning gray the next morning when Laird drove his huge old limousine out into the driveway of his house in the Bronx. The wind was driving a heavy rain almost horizontally.

He got out and helped Vining carry Iantha into the car. Vining got in the back with the mermaid. He spoke into the voice tube: "Jones Beach, Chauncey."

"Aye, aye, sir," came the reply. "Listen, Mark, you sure we remembered everything?"

"I made a list and checked it." He yawned. "I could have done with some more sleep last night. Are you sure you won't fall asleep at the wheel?"

"Listen, Mark, with all the coffee I got sloshing around in me, I won't get to sleep for a week."

"We certainly picked a nice time to leave."

"I know we did. In a coupla hours, the place'll be covered six deep with reporters. If it weren't for the weather, they might be arriving now. When they do, they'll find the horse has stolen the stable door—that isn't what I mean, but you get the idea. Listen, you better pull down some of those curtains until we get out on Long Island."

"Righto, Herb."

Iantha spoke up in a small voice. "Was I very bad last night when I was drunk, Mark?"

"Not very. At least, not worse than I'd be if I went swimming in a tank of sherry."

"I am so sorry—always I try to be nice, but the fresh water gets me out of my head. And that poor Mr. Clement, that I pushed in the water—"

"Oh, he's used to temperamental people. That's his business. But I don't know that it was such a good idea on the way home to stick your tail out of the car and biff that cop under the chin with it."

She giggled. "But he looked so surprised!"

"I'll say he did! But a surprised cop is sometimes a tough customer."

"Will that make trouble for you?"

"I don't think so. If he's a wise cop, he won't report it at all. You know how the report would read: "Attacked by mermaid at corner Broadway and Ninety-eighth Street, 11:45 P.M.' And *where* did you learn the unexpurgated version of 'Barnacle Bill the Sailor'?"

"A Greek sponge diver I met in Florida told me. 'E is a friend of us mer-folk, and he taught me my first English. 'E used to joke me about my Cypriot accent when we talked Greek. It is a pretty song, is it not?"

"I don't think 'pretty' is exactly the word I'd use."

"'Oo won the meet? I never did 'ear."

"Oh, Louie and Herb talked it over, and decided they'd both get so much publicity out of it that it didn't much matter. They're leaving it up to the A. A. U., who will get a first-class headache. For instance, we'll claim we didn't foul Alice, because Louie had already disqualified her by his calling and fish-waving. You see that's coaching, and coaching a competitor during an event is illegal.

"But look here, Iantha, why do you have to leave so abruptly?"

She shrugged. "My business with 'Erbert is over, and I promised to be back to Cyprus for my sister's baby being born."

"You don't lay eggs? But of course you don't. Didn't I just prove last night you were mammals?"

"Markee, what an idea! Anyway, I do not want to stay around. I like you and I like 'Erbert, but I do not like living on land. You just imagine living in water for yourself, and you get an idea. And if I stay, the newspapers come, and soon all New York knows about me. We mer-folk do not believe in letting the land men know about us."

"Why?"

"We used to be friends with them sometimes, and always it made trouble. And now they 'ave guns and go around shooting things a mile away, to collect them. My great-uncle was shot in the tail last year by some aviator man who thought he was a porpoise or something. We don't like being collected. So when we see a boat or an airplane coming, we duck down and swim away quick."

"I suppose," said Vining slowly, "that that's why there were plenty reports of mer-folk up to a few centuries ago, and then they stopped, so that now people don't believe they exist."

"Yes. We are smart, and we can see as far as the land men can. So you do not catch us very often. That is why this business with 'Erbert, to buy ten thousand bathing caps for the mer-folk, 'as to be secret. Not even his company will know about it. But they will not care if they get their money. And we shall not 'ave to sit on rocks drying our 'air so much. Maybe later we can arrange to buy some good knives and spears the same way. They would be better than the shell things we use now."

"I suppose you get all these old coins out of wrecks?"

"Yes. I know of one just off—no, I must not tell you. If the land men know about a wreck, they come with divers. Of course, the very deep ones we do not care about, because we cannot dive down that far. We 'ave to come up for air, like a whale."

"How did Herb happen to suck you in on that swimming meet?"

"Oh, I promised him when he asked—when I did not know 'ow much what-you-call-it fuss there would be. When I found out, he would not let me go back on my promise. I think he 'as a conscience about that, and that is why he gave me that nice fish spear."

"Do you ever expect to get back this way?"

"No, I do not think so. We 'ad a committee to see about the caps, and they chose me to represent them. But now that is arranged, and there is no more reason for me going out on land again."

He was silent for a while. Then he burst out: "Damn it all, Iantha, I just can't believe that you're starting off this morning to swim the Atlantic, and I'll never see you again."

She patted his hand. "Maybe you cannot, but that is so. Remember, friendships between my folk and yours always make people un'appy. I shall remember you a long time, but that is all there will ever be to it."

He growled something in his throat, looking straight in front of him.

She said, "Mark, you know I like you, and I think you like me. 'Erbert 'as a moving-picture machine in his house, and he showed me some pictures of 'ow the land folk live.

"These pictures showed a custom of the people in this country, when they like each other. It is called—kissing, I think. I should like to learn that custom."

"Huh? You mean *me?*" To a man of Vining's temperament, the shock was almost physically painful. But her arms were already sliding around his neck. Presently twenty firecrackers, six Roman candles, and a skyrocket seemed to go off inside him.

"Here we are, folks," called Laird. Getting no response, he repeated the statement more loudly. A faint and unenthusiastic "Yeah" came through the voice tube.

Jones Beach was bleak under the lowering March clouds. The wind drove the rain against the car windows.

They drove down the beach road a way, till the tall tower was lost in the rain. Nobody was in sight.

The men carried Iantha down on the beach and brought the things she was taking. These consisted of a boxful of cans of sardines, with a strap to go over the shoulders; a similar but smaller container with her personal belongings, and the fish spear, with which she might be able to pick up lunch on the way.

Iantha peeled off her land-woman's clothes and pulled on the emerald bathing cap. Vining, watching her with the skirt of his overcoat whipping about his legs, felt as if his heart was running out of his damp shoes onto the sand.

They shook hands, and Iantha kissed them both. She squirmed down the sand and into the water. Then she was gone. Vining thought he saw her wave back from the crest of a wave, but in that visibility he couldn't be sure.

They walked back to the car, squinting against the drops. Laird said: "Listen, Mark, you look as if you'd just taken a right to the button."

Vining merely grunted. He had gotten in front with Laird and was drying his glasses with his handkerchief, as if that were an important and delicate operation.

"Don't tell me you're hooked?"

"So what?"

"Well, I suppose you know there's absolutely nothing you can do about it."

"Herb!" Vining snapped angrily. "Do you have to point out the obvious?"

Laird, sympathizing with his friend's feelings, did not take offense. After they had driven a while, Vining spoke on his own initiative.

"That," he said, "is the only woman I've ever known that made me feel at ease. I could talk to her."

Later, he said, "I never felt so damn mixed up in my life. I doubt whether anybody else ever did, either. Maybe I ought to feel relieved it's over. But I don't."

Pause. Then: "You'll drop me in Manhattan on your way back, won't you?"

"Sure, anywhere you say. Your apartment?"

"Anywhere near Times Square will do. There's a bar there I like."

So, thought Laird, at least the normal male's instincts were functioning correctly in the crisis.

A Gnome There Was

by HENRY KUTTNER

TIM CROCKETT should never have sneaked into the mine on Dornsef Mountain. What is winked at in California may have disastrous results in the coal mines of Pennsylvania. Especially when gnomes are involved.

Not that Tim Crockett knew about the gnomes. He was just investigating conditions among the lower classes, to use his own rather ill-chosen words. He was one of a group of southern Californians who had decided that labor needed them. They were wrong. They needed labor—at least eight hours of it a day.

Crockett, like his colleagues, considered the laborer a combination of a gorilla and The Man with the Hoe, probably numbering the Kallikaks among his ancestors. He spoke fierily of down-trodden minorities, wrote incendiary articles for the group's organ, *Earth,* and deftly maneuvered himself out of entering his father's law office as a clerk. He had, he said, a mission. Unfortunately, he got little sympathy from either the workers or their oppressors.

A psychologist could have analyzed Crockett easily enough. He was a tall, thin, intense-looking young man, with rather beady little eyes, and a nice taste in neckties. All he needed was a vigorous kick in the pants.

But definitely not administered by a gnome!

He was junketing through the country, on his father's money, investigating labor conditions, to the profound annoyance of such laborers as he encountered. It was with this idea in mind that he surreptitiously got into the Ajax coal mine—or, at least, one shaft of it—after disguising himself as a miner and rubbing his face well with black dust. Going down in the lift, he looked singularly untidy in the midst of a group of well-scrubbed faces. Miners look dirty only after a day's work.

Dornsef Mountain is honeycombed, but not with the shafts of the Ajax Company. The gnomes have ways of blocking their tunnels when humans dig too close. The whole place was a complete confusion to Crockett. He let himself drift along with the others, till they began to work. A filled car rumbled past on its tracks. Crockett hesitated, and then sidled over to a husky specimen who seemed to have the marks of a great sorrow stamped on his face.

"Look," he said, "I want to talk to you."

"Inglis?" asked the other inquiringly. "Viskey. Chin. Vine. Hell."

Having thus demonstrated his somewhat incomplete command of English, he bellowed hoarsely with laughter and returned to work, ignoring the baffled Crockett, who turned away to find another victim. But this section of the mine seemed deserted. Another loaded car rumbled past, and Crockett decided to see where it came from. He found out, after banging his head painfully and falling flat at least five times.

It came from a hole in the wall. Crockett entered it, and simultaneously heard a hoarse cry from behind him. The unknown requested Crockett to come back.

"So I can break your slab-sided neck," he promised, adding

a stream of sizzling profanity. "Come outa there!"

Crockett cast one glance back, saw a gorillalike shadow lurching after him, and instantly decided that his stratagem had been discovered. The owners of the Ajax mine had sent a strong-arm man to murder him—or, at least, to beat him to a senseless pulp. Terror lent wings to Crockett's flying feet. He rushed on, frantically searching for a side tunnel in which he might lose himself. The bellowing from behind re-echoed against the walls. Abruptly Crockett caught a significant sentence clearly.

"—before that dynamite goes off!"

It was at that exact moment that the dynamite went off.

Crockett, however, did not know it. He discovered, quite briefly, that he was flying. Then he was halted, with painful suddenness, by the roof. After that he knew nothing at all, till he recovered to find a head regarding him steadfastly.

It was not a comforting sort of head—not one at which you would instinctively clutch for companionship. It was, in fact, a singularly odd, if not actually revolting, head. Crockett was too much engrossed with staring at it to realize that he was actually seeing in the dark.

How long had he been unconscious? For some obscure reason Crockett felt that it had been quite a while. The explosion had—what?

Buried him here behind a fallen roof of rock? Crockett would have felt little better had he known that he was in a used-up shaft, valueless now, which had been abandoned long since. The miners, blasting to open a new shaft, had realized that the old one would be collapsed, but that didn't matter.

Except to Tim Crockett.

He blinked, and when he reopened his eyes, the head had vanished. This was a relief. Crockett immediately decided the unpleasant thing had been a delusion. Indeed, it was difficult to remember what it had looked like. There was only a vague impression of a turnip-shaped outline, large, luminous eyes, and an incredibly broad slit of a mouth.

Crockett sat up, groaning. Where was this curious silvery radiance coming from? It was like daylight on a foggy afternoon, coming from nowhere in particular, and throwing no shadows. "Radium," thought Crockett, who knew very little of mineralogy.

He was in a shaft that stretched ahead into dimness till it made a sharp turn perhaps fifty feet away. Behind him—behind him the roof had fallen. Instantly Crockett began to experience difficulty in breathing. He flung himself upon the rubbly mound, tossing rocks frantically here and there, gasping and making hoarse, inarticulate noises.

He became aware, presently, of his hands. His movements slowed till he remained perfectly motionless, in a half-crouching posture, glaring at the large, knobbly, and surprising objects that grew from his wrists. Could he, during his period of unconsciousness, have acquired mittens? Even as the thought came to him, Crockett realized that no mittens ever knitted resembled in the slightest degree what he had a right to believe to be his hands. They twitched slightly.

Possibly they were caked with mud—no. It wasn't that. His hands had—altered. They were huge, gnarled, brown objects, like knotted oak roots. Sparse black hairs sprouted on their backs. The nails were definitely in need of a manicure—preferably with a chisel.

Crockett looked down at himself. He made soft cheeping noises, indicative of disbelief. He had squat bow legs, thick and strong, and no more than two feet long—less, if anything. Uncertain with disbelief, Crockett explored his body. It had changed—certainly not for the better.

He was slightly more than four feet high, and about three feet wide, with a barrel chest, enormous splay feet, stubby thick legs, and no neck whatsoever. He was wearing red sandals, blue shorts, and a red tunic which left his lean but sinewy arms bare. His head—

Turnip-shaped. The mouth—*Yipe!* Crockett had inadvertently put his fist clear into it. He withdrew the offending hand instantly, stared around in a dazed fashion, and collapsed on the ground. It couldn't be happening. It was quite impossible. Hallucinations. He was dying of asphyxiation, and delusions were preceding his death.

Crockett shut his eyes, again convinced that his lungs were laboring for breath. "I'm dying," he said. "I can't breathe."

A contemptuous voice said, "I hope you don't think you're breathing *air!*"

"I'm n-not—" Crockett didn't finish the sentence. His eyes popped again. He was hearing things.

He heard it again. "You're a singularly lousy specimen of gnome," the voice said. "But under Nid's law we can't pick and choose. Still, you won't be put to digging hard metals, I can see that. Anthracite's about your speed. What're you staring at? You're *very* much uglier than I am."

Crockett, endeavoring to lick his dry lips, was horrified to discover the end of his moist tongue dragging limply over his eyes. He whipped it back, with a loud smacking noise, and managed to sit up. Then he remained perfectly motionless, staring.

The head had reappeared. This time there was a body under it.

"I'm Gru Magru," said the head chattily. "You'll be given a gnomic name, of course, unless your own is guttural enough. What is it?"

"Crockett," the man responded, in a stunned, automatic manner.

"Hey?"

"Crockett."

"Stop making noises like a frog and—oh, I see. Crockett. Fair enough. Now get up and follow me or I'll kick the pants off you."

But Crockett did not immediately rise. He was watching

Gru Magru—obviously a gnome. Short, squat and stunted, the being's figure resembled a bulging little barrel, topped by an inverted turnip. The hair grew up thickly to a peak—the root, as it were. In the turnip face was a loose, immense slit of a mouth, a button of a nose, and two very large eyes.

"Get *up!*" Gru Magru said.

This time Crockett obeyed, but the effort exhausted him completely. If he moved again, he thought, he would go mad. It would be just as well. Gnomes—

Gru Magru planted a large splay foot where it would do the most good, and Crockett described an arc which ended at a jagged boulder fallen from the roof. "Get up," the gnome said, with gratuitous bad temper, "or I'll kick you again. It's bad enough to have an outlying prospect patrol, where I might run into a man any time, without—*Up!* Or—"

Crockett got up. Gru Magru took his arm and impelled him into the depths of the tunnel.

"Well, you're a gnome now," he said. "It's the Nid law. Sometimes I wonder if it's worth the trouble. But I suppose it is—since gnomes can't propagate, and the average population has to be kept up somehow."

"I want to die," Crockett said wildly.

Gru Magru laughed. "Gnomes *can't* die. They're immortal, till the Day. Judgment Day, I mean."

"You're not logical," Crockett pointed out, as though by disproving one factor he could automatically disprove the whole fantastic business. "You're either flesh and blood and have to die eventually, or you're not, and then you're not real."

"Oh, we're flesh and blood, right enough," Gru Magru said. "But we're not mortal. There's a distinction. Not that I've anything against some mortals," he hastened to explain. "Bats, now—and owls—they're fine. But men!" he shuddered. "No gnome can stand the sight of a man."

Crockett clutched at a straw. "I'm a man."

"You were, you mean," Gru said. "Not a very good specimen, either, for my ore. But you're a gnome now. It's the Nid law."

"You keep talking about the Nid law," Crockett complained.

"Of course you don't understand," said Gru Magru, in a patronizing fashion. "It's this way. Back in ancient times, it was decreed that if any humans got lost in underearth, a tithe of them would be transformed into gnomes. The first gnome emperor, Podrang the Third, arranged that. He saw that fairies could kidnap human children and keep them, and spoke to the authorities about it. Said it was unfair. So when miners and such-like are lost underneath, a tithe of them are transformed into gnomes and join us. That's what happened to you. See?"

"No," Crockett said weakly. "Look. You said Podrang was the first gnome emperor. Why was he called Podrang the Third?"

"No time for questions," Gru Magru snapped. "Hurry!"

He was almost running now, dragging the wretched Crockett after him. The new gnome had not yet mastered his rather unusual limbs, and, due to the extreme wideness of his sandals, he trod heavily on his right hand, but after that learned to keep his arms bent and close to his sides. The walls, illuminated with that queer silvery radiance, spun past dizzily.

"W-what's that light?" Crockett managed to gasp. "Where's it coming from?"

"Light?" Gru Magru inquired. "It isn't light."

"Well, it isn't dark—"

"Of course it's dark," the gnome snapped. "How could we see if it wasn't dark?"

There was no possible answer to this, except, Crockett thought wildly, a frantic shriek. And he needed all his breath for running. They were in a labyrinth now, turning and twisting and doubling through innumerable tunnels, and Crockett knew he could never retrace his steps. He regretted having left the scene of the cave-in. But how could he have helped doing so?

"Hurry!" Gru Magru urged. "Hurry!"

"Why?" Crockett got out breathlessly.

"There's a fight going on!" the gnome said.

Just then they rounded a corner and almost blundered into the fight. A seething mass of gnomes filled the tunnel, battling with frantic fury. Red and blue pants and tunics moved in swift patchwork frenzy; turnip heads popped up and down vigorously. It was apparently a free-for-all.

"See!" Gru gloated. "A fight! I could smell it six tunnels away. Oh, a beauty!" He ducked as a malicious-looking little gnome sprang out of the huddle to seize a rock and hurl it with vicious accuracy. The missile missed its mark, and Gru, neglecting his captive, immediately hurled himself upon the little gnome, bore him down on the cave floor, and began to beat his head against it. Both parties shrieked at the top of their voices, which were lost in the deafening din that resounded through the tunnel.

"Oh—my," Crockett said weakly. He stood staring, which was a mistake. A very large gnome emerged from the pile, seized Crockett by the feet, and threw him away. The terrified inadvertent projectile sailed through the tunnel to crash heavily into something which said, *"Whoo-doof!"* There was a tangle of malformed arms and legs.

Crockett arose to find that he had downed a vicious-looking gnome with flaming red hair and four large diamond buttons on his tunic. This repulsive creature lay motionless, out for the count. Crockett took stock of his injuries—there were none. His new body was hardy, anyway.

"You saved me!" said a new voice. It belonged to a—lady gnome. Crockett decided that if there was anything uglier than a gnome, it was the female of the species. The creature stood crouching just behind him, clutching a large rock in one capable hand.

Crockett ducked.

"I won't hurt you," the other howled above the din that filled the passage. "You saved me! Mugza was trying to pull my ears off—oh! He's waking up!"

The red-haired gnome was indeed recovering consciousness. His first act was to draw up his feet and, without rising, kick Crockett clear acorss the tunnel. The feminine gnome immediately sat on Mugza's chest and pounded his head with the rock till he subsided.

Then she arose. "You're not hurt? Good! I'm Brockle Buhn...Oh, look! He'll have his head off in a minute!"

Crockett turned to see that his erstwhile guide, Gru Magru, was gnomefully tugging at the head of an unidentified opponent, attempting, apparently, to twist it clear off. "What's it all about?" Crockett howled. "Uh—Brockle Buhn! *Brockle Buhn!*"

She turned unwillingly. "What?"

"The fight! What started it?"

"I did," she explained. "I said, 'Let's have a fight.'"

"Oh, that was all?".

"Then we started." Brockle Buhn nodded. "What's your name?"

"Crockett."

"You're new here, aren't you? Oh—I know. You were a human being!" Suddenly a new light appeared in her bulging eyes. "Crockett, maybe you can tell me something. What's a kiss?"

"A—kiss?" Crockett repeated, in a baffled manner.

"Yes. I was listening inside a knoll once, and heard two human beings talking—male and female, by their voices. I didn't dare look at them, of course, but the man asked the woman for a kiss."

"Oh," Crockett said, rather blankly. "He asked for a kiss, eh?"

"And then there was a smacking noise and the woman said it was wonderful. I've wondered ever since. Because if any gnome asked me for a kiss, I wouldn't know what he meant."

"Gnomes don't kiss?" Crockett asked in perfunctory way.

"Gnomes dig," said Brockle Buhn. "And we eat. I like to eat. Is a kiss like mud soup?"

"Well, not exactly." Somehow Crockett managed to explain the mechanics of osculation.

The gnome remained silent, pondering deeply. At last she said, with the air of one bestowing mud soup upon a hungry applicant, "I'll give you a kiss."

Crockett had a nightmare picture of his whole head being engulfed in that enormous maw. He backed away. "N-no," he got out. "I—I'd rather not."

"Then let's fight," said Brockle Buhn, without rancor, and swung a knotted fist which smacked painfully athwart Crockett's ear. "Oh, no," she said regretfully, turning away. "The fight's over. It wasn't very long, was it?"

Crockett, rubbing his mangled ear, saw that in every direction gnomes were picking themselves up and hurrying off about their business. They seemed to have forgotten all about the recent conflict. The tunnel was once more silent, save for the pad-padding of gnomes' feet on the rock. Gru Magru came over, grinning happily.

"Hello, Brockle Buhn," he greeted. "A good fight. Who's this?" He looked down at the prostrate body of Mugza, the red-haired gnome.

"Mugza," said Brockle Buhn. "He's still out. Let's kick him."

They proceeded to do it with vast enthusiasm, while Crockett watched and decided never to allow himself to be knocked unconscious. It definitely wasn't safe. At last, however, Gru Magru tired of the sport and took Crockett by the arm again. "Come along," he said, and they sauntered along the tunnel, leaving Brockle Buhn jumping up and down on the senseless Magza's stomach.

"You don't seem to mind hitting people when they're knocked out," Crockett hazarded.

"It's *much* more fun," Gru said happily. "That way you can

tell just where you want to hit 'em. Come along. You'll have to be inducted. Another day, another gnome. Keeps the population stable," he explained, and fell to humming a little song.

"Look," Crockett said. "I just thought of something. You say human beings are turned into gnomes to keep the population stable. But if gnomes don't die, doesn't that mean that there are more gnomes now than ever? The population keeps rising, doesn't it?"

"Be still," Gru Magru commanded. "I'm singing."

It was a singularly tuneless song. Crockett, his thoughts veering madly, wondered if the gnomes had a national anthem. Probably "Rock Me to Sleep." Oh, well.

"We're going to see the Emperor," Gru said at last. "He always sees the new gnomes. You'd better make a good impression, or he'll put you to placer-mining lava."

"Uh—" Crockett glanced down at his grimy tunic. "Hadn't I better clean up a bit? That fight made me a mess."

"It wasn't the fight," Gru said insultingly. "What's wrong with you, anyway? I don't see anything amiss."

"My clothes—they're dirty."

"Don't worry about that," said the other. "It's good filthy dirt, isn't it? Here!" He halted, and, stooping, seized a handful of dust, which he rubbed into Crockett's face and hair. "That'll fix you up."

"I—*pffht!*... Thanks... *pffh!*" said the newest gnome. "I hope I'm dreaming. Because if I'm not—" He didn't finish. Crockett was feeling unwell.

They went through a labyrinth, far under Dornsef Mountain, and emerged at last in a bare, huge chamber with a throne of rock at one end of it. A small gnome was sitting on the throne paring his toenails. "Bottom of the day to you," Gru said. "Where's the Emperor?"

"Taking a bath," said the other. "I hope he drowns. Mud, mud, mud—morning, noon and night. First it's too hot. Then it's too cold. Then it's too thick. I work my fingers to the bone mixing his mud baths, and all I get is a kick," the small gnome continued plaintively. "There's such a thing as being *too* dirty. Three mud baths a day—that's carrying it too far. And never a thought for me! Oh, no. I'm a mud puppy, that's what I am. He called me that today. Said there were lumps in the mud. Well, why not? That damned loam we've been getting is enough to turn a worm's stomach. You'll find His Majesty in there," the little gnome finished, jerking his foot toward an archway in the wall.

Crockett was dragged into the next room, where, in a sunken bath filled with steaming, brown mud, a very fat gnome sat, only his eyes discernible through the oozy coating that covered him. He was filling his hands with mud and letting it drip over his head, chuckling in a senile sort of way as he did so.

"Mud," he remarked pleasantly to Gru Magru, in a voice like a lion's bellow. "Nothing like it. Good rich mud. *Ah!*"

Gru was bumping his head on the floor, his large, capable hand around Crockett's neck forcing the other to follow suit.

"Oh, get up," said the Emperor. "What's this? What's this gnome been up to? Out with it."

"He's new," Gru explained. "I found him topside. The Nid law, you know."

"Yes, of course. Let's have a look at you. Ugh! I'm Podrang the Second, Emperor of the Gnomes. What have you to say to that?"

All Crockett could think of was: "How—how can you be Podrang the Second? I thought Podrang the Third was the first emperor."

"A chatterbox," said Podrang II, disappearing beneath the surface of the mud and spouting as he rose again. "Take care of him, Gru. Easy work at first. Digging anthracite. Mind you don't eat any while you're on the job," he cautioned the dazed Crockett. "After you've been here a century, you're allowed one mud bath a day. Nothing like 'em," he added, bringing up a gluey handful to smear over his face.

Abruptly he stiffened. His lion's bellow rang out.

"Drook! *Drook!*"

The little gnome Crockett had seen in the throne room scurried in, wringing his hands. "Your Majesty! Isn't the mud warm enough?"

"You crawling blob!" roared Podrang II. "You slobbering, offspring of six thousand individual offensive stenches! You mica-eyed, incompetent, draggle-eared, writhing blot on the good name of gnomes! You geological mistake! You—you—"

Drook took advantage of his master's temporary inarticulacy. "It's the best mud, Your Majesty! I refined it myself. Oh, Your Majesty, what's wrong?"

"There's a worm in it!" His Majesty bellowed, and launched into a stream of profanity so horrendous that it practically made the mud boil. Clutching his singed ears, Crockett allowed Gru Magru to drag him away.

"I'd like to get the old boy in a fight," Gru remarked, when they were safely in the depths of a tunnel, "but he'd use magic, of course. That's the way he is. Best emperor we've ever had. Not a scrap of fair play in his bloated body."

"Oh," Crockett said blankly. "Well, what next?"

"You heard Podrang, didn't you? You dig anthracite. And if you eat any, I'll kick your teeth in."

Brooding over the apparent bad tempers of gnomes, Crockett allowed himself to be conducted to a gallery where dozens of gnomes, both male and female, were using picks and mattocks with furious vigor. "This is it," Gru said. "Now! You dig anthracite. You work twenty hours, and then sleep six."

"Then what?"

"Then you start digging again," Gru explained. "You have a brief rest once every ten hours. You mustn't stop digging in between, unless it's for a fight. Now, here's the way you locate coal. Just think of it."

"Eh?"

"How do you think I found you?" Gru asked impatiently.

"Gnomes have—certain senses. There's a legend that fairy folk can locate water by using a forked stick. Well, we're attracted to metals. Think of anthracite," he finished, and Crockett obeyed. Instantly he found himself turning to the wall of the tunnel nearest him.

"See how it works?" Gru grinned. "It's a natural evolution, I suppose. Functional. We have to know where the underneath deposits are, so the authorities gave us this sense when we were created. Think of ore—or any deposit in the ground—and you'll be attracted to it. Just as there's a repulsion in all gnomes against daylight."

"Eh?" Crockett started slightly. "What was that?"

"Negative and positive. We need ores, so we're attracted to them. Daylight is harmful to us, so if we think we're getting too close to the surface, we think of light, and it repels us. Try it!"

Crockett obeyed. Something seemed to be pressing down the top of his head.

"Straight up," Gru nodded. "But it's a long way. I saw daylight once. And—a man, too." He stared at the other. "I forgot to explain. Gnomes can't stand the sight of human beings. They—well, there's a limit to how much ugliness a gnome can look at. Now you're one of us, you'll feel the same way. Keep away from daylight, and never look at a man. It's as much as your sanity is worth."

There was a thought stirring in Crockett's mind. He could, then, find his way out of this maze of tunnels, simply by employing his new sense to lead him to daylight. After that—well, at least he would be above ground.

Gru Magru shoved Crockett into a place between two busy gnomes and thrust a pick into his hands. "There. Get to work."

"Thanks for—" Crockett began, when Gru suddenly kicked him and then took his departure, humming happily to himself. Another gnome came up, saw Crockett standing motionless, and told him to get busy, accompanying the command with a blow on his already tender ear. Perforce Crockett seized the pick and began to chop anthracite out of the wall.

"Crockett!" said a familiar voice. "It's you! I thought they'd send you here."

It was Brockle Buhn, the feminine gnome Crockett had already encountered. She was swinging a pick with the others, but dropped it now to grin at her companion.

"You won't be here long," she consoled. "Ten years or so. Unless you run into trouble, and then you'll be put at really hard work."

Crockett's arms were already aching. "*Hard* work! My arms are going to fall off in a minute."

He leaned on his pick. "Is this your regular job?"

"Yes—but I'm seldom here. Usually I'm being punished. I'm a troublemaker, I am. I eat anthracite."

She demonstrated, and Crockett shuddered at the audible crunching sound. Just then the overseer came up. Brockle Buhn swallowed hastily.

"What's this?" he snarled. "Why aren't you at work?"

"We were just going to fight," Brockle Buhn explained.

"Oh—just the two of you? Or can I join in?"

"Free for all," the unladylike gnome offered, and struck the unsuspecting Crockett over the head with her pick. He went out like a light.

Awakening some time later, he investigated bruised ribs and decided Brockle Buhn must have kicked him after he'd lost consciousness. What a gnome! Crockett sat up, finding himself in the same tunnel, dozens of gnomes busily digging anthracite.

The overseer came toward him. "Awake, eh? Get to work!"

Dazedly Crockett obeyed. Brockle Buhn flashed him a delighted grin. "You missed it. I got an ear—see?" She exhibited it. Crockett hastily lifted an exploring hand. It wasn't his.

Dig...dig...dig...the hours dragged past. Crockett had never worked so hard in his life. But, he noticed, not a gnome complained. Twenty hours of toil, with one brief rest period—he'd slept through that. Dig...dig...dig...

Without ceasing her work, Brockle Buhn said, "I think you'll make a good gnome, Crockett. You're toughening up already. Nobody'd ever believe you were once a man."

"Oh—no?"

"No. What were you, a miner?"

"I was—" Crockett paused suddenly. A curious light came into his eyes.

"I was a labor organizer," he finished.

"What's that?"

"Ever heard of a union?" Crockett asked, his gaze intent.

"Is it an ore?" Brockle Buhn shook her head. "No, I've never heard of it. What's a union?"

Crockett explained. No genuine labor organizer would have accepted that explanation. It was, to say the least, biased.

Brockle Buhn seemed puzzled. "I don't see what you mean, exactly, but I suppose it's all right."

"Try another tack," Crockett said. "Don't you ever get tired of working twenty hours a day?"

"Sure. Who wouldn't?"

"Then why do it?"

"We always have," Brockle Buhn said indulgently. "We can't stop."

"Suppose you did?"

"I'd be punished—beaten with stalacites, or something."

"Suppose you all did," Crockett insisted. "Every damn gnome. Suppose you had a sit-down strike."

"You're crazy," Brockle Buhn said. "Such a thing's never happened. It—it's *human.*"

"Kisses never happened underground, either," said Crockett. "No, I don't want one! And I don't want to fight, either. Good heavens, let me get the set-up here. Most of the gnomes work to support the privileged classes."

"No. We just work."

"But why?"

"We always have. And the Emperor wants us to."

"Has the Emperor ever worked?" Crockett demanded, with an air of triumph. "No! He just takes mud baths! Why shouldn't every gnome have the same privilege? Why—"

He talked on, at great length, as he worked. Brockle Buhn listened with increasing interest. And eventually she swallowed the bait—hook, line and sinker.

An hour later she was nodding agreeably. "I'll pass the word along. Tonight. In the Roaring Cave. Right after work."

"Wait a minute," Crockett objected. "How many gnomes can we get?"

"Well—not very many. Thirty?"

"We'll have to organize first. We'll need a definite plan."

Brockle Buhn went off at a tangent. "Let's fight."

"No! Will you listen? We need a—a council. Who's the worst troublemaker here?"

"Mugza, I think," she said. "The red-haired gnome you knocked out when he hit me."

Crockett frowned slightly. Would Mugza hold a grudge? Probably not, he decided. Or, rather, he'd be no more ill tempered than other gnomes. Mugza might attempt to throttle Crockett on sight, but he'd no doubt do the same to any other gnome. Besides, as Brockle Buhn went on to explain, Mugza was the gnomic equivalent of a duke. His support would be valuable.

"And Gru Magru," she suggested. "He loves new things, especially if they make trouble."

"Yeah." These were not the two Crockett would have chosen, but at least he could think of no other candidates. "If we could get somebody who's close to the Emperor... What about Drook—the guy who gives Podrang his mud baths?"

"Why not? I'll fix it." Brockle Buhn lost interest and surreptitiously began to eat anthracite. Since the overseer was watching, this resulted in a violent quarrel, from which Crockett emerged with a black eye. Whispering profanity under his breath, he went back to digging.

But he had time for a few more words with Brockle Buhn. She'd arrange it. That night there would be a secret meeting of the conspirators.

Crockett had been looking forward to exhausted slumber, but this chance was too good to miss. He had no wish to continue his unpleasant job digging anthracite. His body ached fearfully. Besides, if he could induce the gnomes to strike, he might be able to put the squeeze on Podrang II. Gru Magru had said the Emperor was a magician. Couldn't he, then, transform Crockett back into a man?

"He's never done that," Brockle Buhn said, and Crockett realized he had spoken his thought aloud.

"Couldn't he, though—if he wanted?"

Brockle Buhn merely shuddered, but Crockett had a little gleam of hope. To be human again!

Dig...dig...dig...dig...with monotonous, deadening regularity. Crockett sank into a stupor. Unless he got the gnomes to strike, he was faced with an eternity of arduous toil. He was scarcely conscious of knocking off, of feeling Brockle Buhn's gnarled hand under his arm, of being led through passages to a tiny cubicle, which was his new home. The gnome left him there, and he crawled into a stony bunk and went to sleep.

Presently a casual kick aroused him. Blinking, Crockett sat up, instinctively dodging the blow Gru Magru was aiming at his head. He had four guests—Gru, Brockle Buhn, Drook and the red-haired Mugza.

"Sorry I woke up too soon," Crockett said bitterly. "If I hadn't, you could have got in another kick."

"There's lots of time," Gru said. "Now, what's this all about? I wanted to sleep, but Brockle Buhn here said there was going to be a fight. A *big* one, huh?"

"Eat first," Brockle Buhn said firmly. "I'll fix mud soup for everybody." She bustled away, and presently was busy in a corner, preparing refreshments. The other gnomes squatted on their haunches, and Crockett sat on the edge of his bunk, still dazed with sleep.

But he managed to explain his idea of the union. It was received with interest—chiefly, he felt, because it involved the possibility of a tremendous scrap.

"You mean every Dornsef gnome jumps the Emperor?" Gru asked.

"No, no! Peaceful arbitration. We just refuse to work. All of us."

"*I* can't," Drook said. "Podrang's got to have his mud baths, the bloated old slug. He'd send me to the fumaroles till I was roasted."

"Who'd take you there?" Crockett asked.

"Oh—the guards, I suppose."

"But they'd be on strike, too. *Nobody'd* obey Podrang, till he gave in."

"Then he'd enchant me," Drook said.

"He can't enchant us all," Crockett countered.

"But he could enchant *me,*" Drook said with great firmness. "Besides, he *could* put a spell on every gnome in Dornsef. Turn us into stalacites or something."

"Then what? He wouldn't have any gnomes at all. Half a loaf is better than none. We'll just use logic on him. Wouldn't he rather have a little less work done than none at all?"

"Not him," Gru put in. "He'd rather enchant us. Oh, he's a bad one, he is," the gnome finished approvingly.

But Crockett couldn't quite believe this. It was too alien to his understanding of psychology—human psychology, of course. He turned to Mugza, who was glowering furiously.

"What do you think about it?"

"I want to fight," the other said rancorously. "I want to kick somebody."

"Wouldn't you rather have mud baths three times a day?"

Mugza grunted. "Sure. But the Emperor won't let me."

"Why not?"

"Because I want 'em."

"You can't be contented," Crockett said desperately. "There's more to life than—than digging."

"Sure. There's fighting. Podrang lets us fight whenever we want."

Crockett had a sudden inspiration. "But that's just it. He's going to stop all fighting! He's going to pass a new law forbidding fighting except to himself."

It was an effective shot in the dark. Every gnome jumped.

"Stop—*fighting!*" That was Gru, angry and disbelieving. "Why, we've always fought."

"Well, you'll have to stop," Crockett insisted.

"Won't!"

"Exactly! Why should you? Every gnome's entitled to life, liberty and the pursuit of—of pugilism."

"Let's go and beat up Podrang," Mugza offered, accepting a steaming bowl of mud soup from Brockle Buhn.

"No, that's not the way—no, thanks, Brockle Buhn—not the way at all. A strike's the thing. We'll peaceably force Podrang to give us what we want."

He turned to Drook. "Just what can Podrang do about it if we all sit down and refuse to work?"

The little gnome considered. "He'd swear. And kick me."

"Yeah—and then what?"

"Then he'd go off and enchant everybody, tunnel by tunnel."

"Uh-huh." Crockett nodded. "A good point. Solidarity is what we need. If Podrang finds a few gnomes together, he can scare the hell out of them. But if we're all together—that's it! When the strike's called, we'll all meet in the biggest cave in the joint."

"That's the Council Chamber," Gru said. "Next to Podrang's throne room."

"O.K. We'll meet there. How many gnomes will join us?"

"All of 'em," Mugza grunted, throwing his soup bowl at Drook's head. "The Emperor can't stop us fighting."

"And what weapons can Podrang use, Drook?"

"He might use the Cockatrice Eggs," the other said doubtfully.

"What are those?"

"They're not really eggs," Gru broke in. "They're magic jewels for wholesale enchantments. Different spells in each one. The green ones, I think, are for turning people into earthworms. Podrang just breaks one, and the spell spreads out for twenty feet or so. The red ones are—let's see. Transforming gnomes into human beings—though that's a bit *too* rough. No...yes. The blue ones—"

"Into *human beings!*" Crockett's eyes widened. "Where are the eggs kept?"

"Let's fight," Mugza offered, and hurled himself bodily on Drook, who squeaked frantically and beat his attacker over the head with his soup bowl, which broke. Brockle Buhn added to the excitement by kicking both battlers impartially, till felled by Gru Magru. Within a few moments the room resounded with the excited screams of gnomic battle. Inevitably Crockett was sucked in...

Of all the perverted, incredible forms of life that had ever existed, gnomes were about the oddest. It was impossible to understand their philosophy. Their minds worked along different paths from human intelligences. Self-preservation and survival of the race—these two vital human instincts were lacking in gnomes. They neither died nor propagated. They just worked and fought. Bad-tempered little monsters, Crockett thought irritably. Yet they had existed for—ages. Since the beginning, maybe. Their social organism was the result of evolution far older than man's. It might be well suited to gnomes. Crockett might be throwing the unnecessary monkey wrench in the machinery.

So what? He wasn't going to spend eternity digging anthracite, even though, in retrospect, he remembered feeling a curious thrill of obscure pleasure as he worked. Digging might be fun for gnomes. Certainly it was their *raison d'être.* In time Crockett himself might lose his human affiliations, and be metamorphosed completely into a gnome. What had happened to other humans who had undergone such an—alteration as he had done? All gnomes look alike. But maybe Gru Magru had once been human—or Drook—or Brockle Buhn.

They were gnomes now, at any rate, thinking and existing completely as gnomes. And in time he himself would be exactly like them. Already he had acquired the strange tropism that attracted him to metals and repelled him from daylight. But he didn't *like* to dig!

He tried to recall the little he knew about gnomes—miners, metalsmiths, living underground. There was something about the Picts—dwarfish men who hid underground when invaders came to England, centuries ago. That seemed to tie in vaguely with the gnomes' dread of human beings. But the gnomes themselves were certainly not descended from Picts. Very likely the two separate races and species had become identified through occupying the same habitat.

Well, that was no help. What about the Emperor? He wasn't, apparently, a gnome with a high I.Q., but he *was* a magician. Those jewels—Cockatrice Eggs—were significant. If he could get hold of the ones that transformed gnomes into men...

But obviously he couldn't, at present. Better wait. Till the strike had been called. The strike...

Crockett went to sleep.

He was roused, painfully, by Brockle Buhn, who seemed to have adopted him. Very likely it was her curiosity about the matter of a kiss. From time to time she offered to give Crockett one, but he steadfastly refused. In lieu of it, she supplied him with breakfast. At least, he thought grimly, he'd get plenty of iron in his system, even though the rusty chips rather resembled corn flakes. As a special inducement Brockle Buhn sprinkled coal dust over the mess.

Well, no doubt his digestive system had also altered. Crockett wished he could get an X-ray picture of his insides. Then he decided it would be much too disturbing. Better not to know. But he could not help wondering. Gears in his stomach? Small millstones? What would happen if he inadvertently swallowed some emery dust? Maybe he could sabotage the Emperor that way.

Perceiving that his thoughts were beginning to veer wildly, Crockett gulped the last of his meal and followed Brockle Buhn to the anthracite tunnel.

"How about the strike? How's it coming?"

"Fine, Crockett." She smiled, and Crockett winced at the sight. "Tonight all the gnomes will meet in the Roaring Cave. Just after work."

There was no time for more conversation. The overseer appeared, and the gnomes snatched up their picks. Dig...dig...dig...It kept up at the same pace. Crockett sweated and toiled. It wouldn't be for long. His mind slipped a cog, so that he relapsed into a waking slumber, his muscles responding automatically to the need. Dig, dig, dig. Sometimes a fight. Once a rest period. Then dig again.

Five centuries later the day ended. It was time to sleep.

But there was something much more important. The union meeting in the Roaring Cave. Brockle Buhn conducted Crockett there, a huge cavern hung with glittering green stalactites. Gnomes came pouring into it. Gnomes and more gnomes. The turnip heads were everywhere. A dozen fights started. Gru Magru, Mugza and Drook found places near Crockett. During a lull Brockle Buhn urged him to a platform of rock jutting from the floor.

"Now," she whispered. "They all know about it. Tell them what you want."

Crockett was looking out over the bobbing heads, the red and blue garments, all lit by that eerie silver glow. "Fellow gnomes," he began weakly.

"Fellow gnomes!" The words roared out, magnified by the acoustics of the cavern. That bull bellow gave Crocket courage. He plunged on.

"Why should you work twenty hours a day? Why should you be forbidden to eat the anthracite you dig, while Podrang squats in his bath and laughs at you? Fellow gnomes, the Emperor is only one; you are many! He can't make you work. How would you like mud soup three times a day? The Emperor can't fight you all. If you refuse to work—all of you—he'll have to give in! He'll have to!"

"Tell 'em about the non-fighting edict," Gru Magru called.

Crockett obeyed. That got 'em. Fighting was dear to every gnomic heart. And Crockett kept on talking.

"Podrang will try to back down, you know. He'll pretend he never intended to forbid fighting. That'll show he's afraid of you! We hold the whip hand! We'll strike—and the Emperor can't do a damn thing about it. When he runs out of mud for his baths, he'll capitulate soon enough."

"He'll enchant us all," Drook muttered sadly.

"He won't dare! What good would that do? He knows which side his—ugh—which side his mud is buttered on. Podrang is unfair to gnomes! That's our watchword!"

It ended, of course, in a brawl. But Crockett was satisfied. The gnomes would not go to work tomorrow. They would, instead, meet in the Council Chamber, adjoining Podrang's throne room—and sit down.

That night he slept well.

In the morning Crockett went, with Brockle Buhn, to the Council Chamber, a cavern gigantic enough to hold the thousands of gnomes who thronged it. In the silver light their red and blue garments had a curiously elfin quality. Or, perhaps, naturally enough, Crockett thought. Were gnomes, strictly speaking, elves?

Drook came up. "I didn't draw Podrang's mud bath," he confided hoarsely. "Oh, but he'll be furious. Listen to him."

And, indeed, a distant crackling of profanity was coming through an archway in one wall of the cavern.

Mugza and Gru Magru joined them. "He'll be along directly," the latter said. "What a fight there'll be!"

"Let's fight now," Mugza suggested. "I want to kick somebody. Hard."

"There's a gnome who's asleep," Crockett said. "If you sneak up on him, you can land a good one right in his face."

Mugza, drooling slightly, departed on his errand, and simultaneously Podrang II, Emperor of the Dornsef Gnomes, stumped into the cavern. It was the first time Crockett had seen the ruler without a coating of mud, and he could not help gulping at the sight. Podrang was *very* ugly. He combined in himself the most repulsive qualities of every gnome Crockett had previously seen. The result was perfectly indescribable.

"Ah," said Podrang, halting and swaying on his short bow legs. "I have guests. Drook! Where in the name of the nine steaming hells is my bath?" But Drook had ducked from sight.

The Emperor nodded. "I see. Well, I won't lose my temper, *I won't lose my temper!* I WON'T—"

He paused as a stalactite was dislodged from the roof and crashed down. In the momentary silence, Crockett stepped forward, cringing slightly.

"W-we're on strike," he announced. "It's a sit-down strike. We won't work till—"

"*Yaah!*" screamed the infuriated Emperor. "You won't work, eh? Why, you boggle-eyed, flap-tongued, drag-bellied offspring of unmentionable algae! You seething little leprous blotch of bat-nibbled fungus! You cringing parasite on the underside of a dwarfish and ignoble worm. *Yaaah!*"

"Fight!" the irrepressible Mugza yelled, and flung himself on Podrang, only to be felled by a well-placed foul blow.

Crockett's throat felt dry. He raised his voice, trying to keep it steady.

"Your Majesty! If you'll just wait a minute—"

"You mushroom-nosed spawn of degenerate black bats," the enraged Emperor shrieked at the top of his voice. "I'll enchant you all! I'll turn you into naiads! Strike, will you! Stop me from having my mud bath, will you? By Kronos, Nid, Ymir and Loki, you'll have cause to regret this! *Yah!*" he finished, inarticulate with fury.

"Quick!" Crockett whispered to Gru and Brockle Buhn. "Get between him and the door, so he can't get hold of the Cockatrice Eggs."

"They're not in the throne room," Gru Magru explained unhelpfully. "Podrang just grabs them out of the air."

"Oh!" the harassed Crockett groaned. At that strategic moment Brockle Buhn's worst instincts overcame her. With a loud shriek of delight she knocked Crockett down, kicked him twice and sprang for the Emperor.

She got in one good blow before Podrang hammered her atop the head with one gnarled fist, and instantly her turnip-shaped skull seemed to prolapse into her torso. The Emperor, bright purple with fury, reached out—and a yellow crystal appeared in his hand.

It was one of the Cockatrice Eggs.

Bellowing like a *musth* elephant, Podrang hurled it. A circle of twenty feet was instantly cleared among the massed gnomes. But it wasn't vacant. Dozens of bats rose and fluttered about, adding to the confusion.

Confusion became chaos. With yells of delighted fury, the gnomes rolled forward toward their ruler. "Fight!" the cry thundered out, reverberating from the roof. "*Fight!*"

Podrang snatched another crystal from nothingness—a green one, this time. Thirty-seven gnomes were instantly transformed into earthworms, and were trampled. The Emperor went down under an avalanche of attackers, who abruptly disappeared, turned into mice by another of the Cockatrice Eggs.

Crockett saw one of the crystals sailing toward him, and ran like hell. He found a hiding place behind a stalagmite, and from there watched the carnage. It was definitely a sight worth seeing, though it could not be recommended to a nervous man.

The Cockatrice Eggs exploded in an incessant stream. Whenever that happened, the spell spread out for twenty feet or more before losing its efficacy. Those caught on the fringes of the circle were only partially transformed. Crockett saw one gnome with a mole's head. Another was a worm from the waist down. Another was—*ulp!* Some of the spell patterns were not, apparently, drawn even from known mythology.

The fury of noise that filled the cavern brought stalactites crashing down incessantly from the roof. Every so often Podrang's battered head would reappear, only to go down again as more gnomes sprang to the attack—to be enchanted. Mice, moles, bats and other things filled the Council Chamber. Crockett shut his eyes and prayed.

He opened them in time to see Podrang snatch a red crystal out of the air, pause and then deposit it gently behind him. A purple Cockatrice Egg came next. This crashed against the floor, and thirty gnomes turned into tree toads.

Apparently only Podrang was immune to his own magic. The thousands who had filled the cavern were rapidly thinning, for the Cockatrice Eggs seemed to come from an inexhaustible source of supply. How long would it be before Crockett's own turn came? He couldn't hide here forever.

His gaze riveted to the red crystal Podrang had so carefully put down. He was remembering something—the Cockatrice Egg that would transform gnomes into human beings. Of course! Podrang wouldn't use *that,* since the very sight of men was so distressing to gnomes. If Crockett could get his hands on that red crystal...

He tried it, sneaking through the confusion, sticking close to the wall of the cavern, till he neared Podrang. The Emperor was swept away by another onrush of gnomes, who abruptly changed into dormice, and Crockettt got the red jewel. It felt abnormally cold.

He almost broke it at his feet before a thought stopped and

chilled him. He was far under Dornsef Mountain, in a labyrinth of caverns. No human being could find his way out. But a gnome could, with the aid of his strange tropism to daylight.

A bat flew against Crockett's face. He was almost certain it squeaked, "What a fight!" in a parody of Brockle Buhn's voice, but he couldn't be sure. He cast one glance over the cavern before turning to flee.

It was a complete and utter chaos. Bats, moles, worms, ducks, eels and a dozen other species crawled, flew, ran, bit, shrieked, snarled, grunted, whooped and croaked all over the place. From all directions the remaining gnomes—only about a thousand now—were converging on a surging mound of gnomes that marked where the Emperor was. As Crockett stared the mound dissolved, and a number of gecko lizards ran to safety.

"Strike, will you!" Podrang bellowed. *"I'll show you!"*

Crockett turned and fled. The throne room was deserted, and he ducked into the first tunnel. There, he concentrated on thinking of daylight. His left ear felt compressed. He sped on till he saw a side passage on the left, slanting up, and turned into it at top speed. The muffled noise of combat died behind him.

He clutched the red Cockatrice Egg tightly. What had gone wrong? Podrang should have stopped to parley. Only—only he hadn't. A singularly bad-tempered and short-sighted gnome. He probably wouldn't stop till he'd depopulated his entire kingdom. At the thought Crockett hurried along faster.

The tropism guided him. Sometimes he took the wrong tunnel, but always, whenever he thought of daylight, he would *feel* the nearest daylight pressing against him. His short, bowed legs were surprisingly hardy.

Then he heard someone running after him.

He didn't turn. The sizzling blast of profanity that curled his ears told him the identity of the pursuer. Podrang had no doubt cleared the Council Chamber, to the last gnome, and was now intending to tear Crockett apart pinch by pinch. That was only one of the things he promised.

Crockett ran. He shot along the tunnel like a bullet. The tropism guided him, but he was terrified lest he reach a dead end. The clamor from behind grew louder. If Crockett hadn't known better, he would have imagined that an army of gnomes pursued him.

Faster! Faster! But now Podrang was in sight. His roars shook the very walls. Crockett sprinted, rounded a corner, and saw a wall of flaming light—a circle of it, in the distance. It was daylight, as it appeared to gnomic eyes.

He could not reach it in time. Podrang was too close. A few more seconds, and those gnarled, terrible hands would close on Crockett's throat.

Then Crockett remembered the Cockatrice Egg. If he transformed himself into a man now, Podrang would not dare touch him. And he was almost at the tunnel's mouth.

He stopped, whirling and lifted the jewel. Simultaneously the Emperor, seeing his intention, reached out with both hands, and snatched six or seven of the crystals out of the air. He threw them directly at Crockett, a fusillade of rainbow colors.

But Crockett had already slammed the red gem down on the rock at his feet. There was an ear-splitting crash. Jewels seemed to burst all around Crockett—but the red one had been broken first.

The roof fell in.

A short while later, Crockett dragged himself painfully from the debris. A glance showed him that the way to the outer world was still open. And—thank heaven!—daylight looked normal again, not that flaming blaze of eye-searing white.

He looked toward the depths of the tunnel, and froze. Podrang was emerging, with some difficulty, from a mound of rubble. His low curses had lost none of their fire.

Crockett turned to run, stumbled over a rock, and fell flat.

As he sprang up, he saw that Podrang had seen him.

The gnome stood transfixed for a moment. Then he yelled, spun on his heel, and fled into the darkness. He was gone. The sound of his rapid footfalls died.

Crockett swallowed with difficulty. *Gnomes are afraid of men—whew!* That had been a close squeak. But now...

He was more relieved than he had thought. Subconsciously he must have been wondering whether the spell would work, since Podrang had flung six or seven Cockatrice Eggs at him. But he had smashed the red one first. Even the strange, silvery gnome-light was gone. The depths of the cave were utterly black—and silent.

Crockett headed for the entrance. He pulled himself out, luxuriating the warmth of the afternoon sun. He was near the foot of Dornsef Mountain, in a patch of brambles. A hundred feet away a farmer was plowing one terrace of a field.

Crockett stumbled toward him. As he approached, the man turned.

He stood transfixed for a moment. Then he yelled, spun on his heel, and fled.

His shrieks drifted back up the mountain as Crockett, remembering the Cockatrice Eggs, forced himself to look down at his own body.

Then he screamed too. But the sound was not one that could ever have emerged from a human throat.

Still, that was natural enough—under the circumstances.

Snulbug

by ANTHONY BOUCHER

"THAT'S A hell of a spell you're using," said the demon, "if I'm the best you can call up."

He wasn't much, Bill Hitchens had to admit. He looked lost in the center of that pentacle. His basic design was impressive enough—snakes for hair, curling tusks, a sharp-tipped tail, all the works—but he was something under an inch tall.

Bill had chanted the words and lit the powder with the highest hopes. Even after the feeble flickering flash and the damp fizzling *zzzt* which had replaced the expected thunder and lightning, he had still had hopes. He had stared up at the space above the pentacle waiting to be awe-struck until he had heard that plaintive little voice from the floor wailing, "Here I am."

"Nobody's wasted time and power on a misfit like me for years," the demon went on. "Where'd you get the spell?"

"Just a little something I whipped up," said Bill modestly.

The demon grunted and muttered something about people that thought they were magicians.

"But I'm not a magician," Bill explained. "I'm a biochemist."

The demon shuddered. "I land the damnedest cases," he mourned. "Working for that psychiatrist wasn't bad enough, I should draw a biochemist. Whatever that is."

Bill couldn't check his curiosity. "And what did you do for a psychiatrist?"

"He showed me to people who were followed by little men and told them I'd chase the little men away." The demon pantomimed shooting motions.

"And did they go away?"

"Sure. Only then the people decided they'd sooner have little men than me. It didn't work so good. Nothing ever does," he added woefully. "Yours won't either."

Bill sat down and filled his pipe. Calling up demons wasn't so terrifying after all. Something quiet and homey about it. "Oh, yes it will," he said. "This is foolproof."

"That's what they all think. People—" The demon wistfully eyed the match as Bill lit his pipe. "But we might as well get it over with. What do you want?"

"I want a laboratory for my embolism experiments. If this method works, it's going to mean that a doctor can spot an embolus in the blood stream long before it's dangerous and remove it safely. My ex-boss, that screwball old occultist Reuben Choatsby, said it wasn't practical—meaning there wasn't a fortune in it for him—and fired me. Everybody else thinks I'm wacky too, and I can't get any backing. So I need ten thousand dollars."

"There!" the demon sighed with satisfaction. "I told you it wouldn't work. That's out for me. They can't start fetching money on demand till three grades higher than me. I told you."

"But you don't," Bill insisted, "appreciate all my fiendish subtlety. Look— Say, what is your name?"

The demon hesitated. "You haven't got another of those things?"

"What things?"

"Matches."

"Sure."

"Light me one, please?"

Bill tossed the burning match into the center of the pentacle. The demon scrambled eagerly out of the now cold ashes of the powder and dived into the flame, rubbing himself with the brisk vigor of a man under a needle-shower. "There!" he gasped joyously. "That's more like it."

"And now what's your name?"

The demon's face fell again. "My name? You really want to know?"

"I've got to call you something."

"Oh, no you don't. I'm going home. No money games for me."

"But I haven't explained yet what you are to do. What's your name?"

"Snulbug." The demon's voice dropped almost too low to be heard.

"Snulbug?" Bill laughed.

"Uh-huh. I've got a cavity in one tusk, my snakes are falling out, I haven't got enough troubles, I should be named Snulbug."

"All right. Now listen, Snulbug, can you travel into the future?"

"A little. I don't like it much, though. It makes you itch in the memory."

"Look, my fine snake-haired friend. It isn't a question of what you like. How would you like to be left there in that pentacle with nobody to throw matches at you?" Snulbug shuddered. "I thought so. Now, you can travel into the future?"

"I said a little."

"And," Bill leaned forward and puffed hard at his corncob as he asked the vital question, "can you bring back material objects?" If the answer was no, all the fine febrile fertility of his spell-making was useless. And if that was useless, heaven alone knew how the Hitchens Embolus Diagnosis would ever succeed in ringing down the halls of history, and incidentally saving a few thousand lives annually.

Snulbug seemed more interested in the warm clouds of pipe smoke than in the question. "Sure," he said. "Within reason I can—" He broke off and stared up piteously. "You don't mean— You can't be going to pull that old gag again?"

"Look, baby. You do what I tell you and leave the worrying to me. You can bring back material objects?"

"Sure. But I warn you—"

Bill cut him off short. "Then as soon as I release you from that pentacle, you're to bring me tomorrow's newspaper."

Snulbug sat down on the burned match and tapped his forehead sorrowfully with his tail tip. "I knew it," he wailed. "I knew it. Three times already this happens to me. I've got limited powers, I'm a runt, I've got a funny name, so I should run foolish errands."

"Foolish errands?" Bill rose and began to pace about the bare attic. "Sir, if I may call you that, I resent such an imputation. I've spent weeks on this idea. Think of the limitless power in knowing the future. Think of what could be done with it: swaying the course of empire, dominating mankind. All I want is to take this stream of unlimited power, turn it into the simple channel of humanitarian research, and get me $10,000; and you call that a foolish errand!"

"That Spaniard," Snulbug moaned. "He was a nice guy, even if his spell was lousy. Had a solid, comfortable brazier where an imp could keep warm. Fine fellow. And he has to ask to see tomorrow's newspaper. I'm warning you—"

"I know," said Bill hastily. "I've been over in my mind all the things that can go wrong. And that's why I'm laying three conditions on you before you get out of that pentacle. I'm not falling for the easy snares."

"All right." Snulbug sounded almost resigned. "Let's hear 'em. Not that they'll do any good."

"First: This newspaper must not contain a notice of my

own death or of any other disaster that would frustrate what I can do with it."

"But shucks," Snulbug protested. "I can't guarantee that. If you're slated to die between now and tomorrow, what can I do about it? Not that I guess you're important enough to crash the paper."

"Courtesy, Snulbug. Courtesy to your master. But I tell you what: When you go into the future, you'll know then if I'm going to die? Right. Well, if I am, come back and tell me and we'll work out other plans. This errand will be off."

"People," Snulbug observed, "make such an effort to make trouble for themselves. Go on."

"Second: The newspaper must be of this city and in English. I can just imagine you and your little friends presenting some dope with the Omsk and Tomsk *Daily Vuskutsukt.*"

"We should take so much trouble," said Snulbug.

"And third: The newspaper must belong to this space-time continuum, to this spiral of the serial universe, to this Wheel of If. However you want to put it. It must be a newspaper of the tomorrow that I myself shall experience, not of some other, to me hypothetical, tomorrow."

"Throw me another match," said Snulbug.

"Those three conditions should cover it, I think. There's not a loophole there, and the Hitchens Laboratory is guaranteed."

Snulbug grunted. "You'll find out."

Bill took a sharp blade and duly cut a line of the pentacle with cold steel. But Snulbug simply dived in and out of the flame of his second match, twitching his tail happily and seemed not to give a rap that the way to freedom was now open.

"Come on!" Bill snapped impatiently. "Or I'll take the match away."

Snulbug got as far as the opening and hesitated. "Twenty-four hours is a long way."

"You can make it."

"I don't know. Look." He shook his head, and a microscopic dead snake fell to the floor. "I'm not at my best. I'm shot to pieces lately, I am. Tap my tail."

"Do what?"

"Go on. Tap it with your fingernail right there where it joins on."

Bill grinned and obeyed. "Nothing happens."

"Sure nothing happens. My reflexes are all haywire. I don't know as I can make twenty-four hours." He brooded, and his snakes curled up into a concentrated clump. "Look. All you want is tomorrow's newspaper, huh? Just tomorrow's, not the edition that'll be out exactly twenty-four hours from now?"

"It's noon now," Bill reflected. "Sure, I guess tomorrow morning's paper'll do."

"OK. What's the date today?"

"August 21."

"Fine. I'll bring you a paper for August 22. Only I'm warning you: It won't do any good. But here goes nothing. Goodbye now. Hello again. Here you are." There was a string in Snulbug's horny hand, and on the end of the string was a newspaper.

"But hey!" Bill protested. "You haven't been gone."

"People," said Snulbug feelingly, "are dopes. Why should it take any time out of the present to go into the future? I leave this point, I come back to this point. I spent two hours hunting for this damned paper but that doesn't mean two hours of your time here. People—" he snorted.

Bill scratched his head. "I guess it's all right. Let's see the paper. And I know; You're warning me." He turned quickly to the obituaries to check. No Hitchens. "And I wasn't dead in the time you were in?"

"No," Snulbug admitted. "Not *dead,*" he added, with the most pessimistic implications possible.

"What was I, then? Was I—"

"I had salamander blood," Snulbug complained. "They thought I was an undine like my mother and they put me in the cold-water incubator when any dope knows salamandery is a dominant. So I'm a runt and good for nothing but to run errands, and now I should make prophecies! You read your paper and see how much good it does you."

Bill laid down his pipe and folded the paper back from the obituaries to the front page. He had not expected to find anything useful there—what advantage could he gain from knowing who won the next naval engagement or which cities were bombed?—but he was scientifically methodical. And this time method was rewarded. There it was, streaming across the front page in vast black blocks:

MAYOR ASSASSINATED
FIFTH COLUMN KILLS CRUSADER

Bill snapped his fingers. This was it. This was his chance. He jammed his pipe in his mouth, hastily pulled a coat on his shoulders, crammed the priceless paper into a pocket, and started out of the attic. Then he paused and looked around. He'd forgotten Snulbug. Shouldn't there be some sort of formal discharge?

The dismal demon was nowhere in sight. Not in the pentacle or out of it. Not a sign or a trace of him. Bill frowned. This was definitely not methodical. He struck a match and held it over the bowl of his pipe.

A warm sigh of pleasure came from inside the corncob.

Bill took the pipe from his mouth and stared at it. "So that's where you are!" he said musingly.

"I told you salamandery was a dominant," said Snulbug, peering out of the bowl. "I want to go along. I want to see just what kind of a fool you make of yourself." He withdrew his head into the glowing tobacco, muttering about newspapers, spells, and, with a wealth of unhappy scorn, people.

The crusading mayor of Granton was a national figure of splendid proportions. Without hysteria, red baiting, or strike-breaking, he had launched a quietly purposeful and well-directed program against subversive elements which had rapidly converted Granton into the safest and most American city in the country. He was also a persistent advocate of national, state, and municipal subsidy of the arts and sciences—the ideal man to wangle an endowment for the Hitchens Laboratory, if he were not so surrounded by overly skeptical assistants that Bill had never been able to lay the program before him.

This would do it. Rescue him from assassination in the very nick of time—in itself an act worth calling up demons to perform—and then when he asks, "And how, Mr. Hitchens, can I possibly repay you?" come forth with the whole great plan of research. It couldn't miss.

No sound came from the pipe bowl, but Bill clearly heard the words, "Couldn't it just?" ringing in his mind.

He braked his car to a fast stop in the red zone before the city hall, jumped out without even slamming the door, and dashed up the marble steps so rapidly, so purposefully, that pure momentum carried him up three flights and through four suites of offices before anybody had the courage to stop him and say, "What goes?"

The man with the courage was a huge bull-necked plainclothes man, whose bulk made Bill feel relatively about the size of Snulbug. "All right, there," this hulk rumbled. "All right. Where's the fire?"

"In an assassin's gun," said Bill. "And it had better stay there."

Bullneck had not expected a literal answer. He hesitated long enough for Bill to push him to the door marked MAYOR—PRIVATE. But though the husky's brain might move slowly, his muscles made up for the lag. Just as Bill started to shove the door open, a five-pronged mound of flesh lit on his neck and jerked.

Bill crawled from under a desk, ducked Bullneck's left, reached the door, executed a second backward flip, climbed down from the table, ducked a right, reached the door, sailed back in reverse, and lowered himself nimbly from the chandelier.

Bullneck took up a stand in front of the door, spread his legs in ready balance, and drew a service automatic from its holster. "You ain't going in there," he said, to make the situation perfectly clear.

Bill spat out a tooth, wiped the blood from his eyes, picked up the shattered remains of his pipe, and said, "Look. It's now 12:30. At 12:32 a redheaded hunchback is going to come out on that balcony across the street and aim through the open window into the mayor's office. At 12:33 His Honor is going to be slumped over his desk, dead. Unless you help me get him out of range."

"Yeah?" said Bullneck. "And who says so?"

"It says so here. Look. In the paper."

Bullneck guffawed. "How can a paper say what ain't even happened yet? You're nuts, brother, if you ain't something worse. Now go on. Scram. Go peddle your paper."

Bill's glance darted out the window. There was the balcony facing the mayor's office. And there coming out on it—

"Look!" he cried. "If you won't believe me, look out the window. See on that balcony? The redheaded hunchback? Just like I told you. Quick!"

Bullneck stared despite himself. He saw the hunchback peer across into the office. He saw the sudden glint of metal in the hunchback's hand. "Brother," he said to Bill, I'll tend to you later."

The hunchback had his rifle halfway to his shoulder when Bullneck's automatic spat and Bill braked his car in the red zone, jumped out, and dashed through four suites of offices before anybody had the courage to stop him.

The man with the courage was a huge bull-necked plainclothes man who rumbled, "Where's the fire?"

"In an assassin's gun," said Bill, and took advantage of Bullneck's confusion to reach the door marked MAYOR—PRIVATE.

But just as he started to push it open, a vast hand lit on his neck and jerked.

As Bill descended from the chandelier after his third try, Bullneck took up a stand in front of the door, with straddled legs and drawn gun. "You ain't going in," he said clarifyingly.

Bill spat out a tooth and outlined the situation. "—12:33," he ended. "His Honor is going to be slumped over the desk dead. Unless you help me get him out of range. See? It says so here. In the paper."

"How can it? Gwan. Go peddle your paper."

Bill's glance darted to the balcony. "Look, if you won't believe me. See the redheaded hunchback? Just like I told you. Quick! We've got to—"

Bullneck started. He saw the sudden glint of metal in the hunchback's hand. "Brother," he said, "I'll tend to you later."

The hunchback had his rifle halfway to his shoulder when Bullneck's automatic spat and Bill braked his car in the red zone, jumped out, and dashed through four suites before anybody stopped him.

The man who did was a bull-necked plain-clothes man, who rumbled—

"Don't you think," said Snulbug, "you've had enough of this?"

Bill agreed mentally, and there he was sitting in his roadster in front of the city hall. His clothes were umrumpled, his eyes were bloodless, his teeth were all there, and his corncob was still intact. "And just what," he demanded of his pipe bowl, "has been going on?"

Snulbug popped his snaky head out. "Light this again, will you? It's getting cold. Thanks."

"What happened?" Bill insisted.

"People!" Snulbug moaned. "No sense. Don't you see? So long as the newspaper was in the future, it was only a possibility. If you'd had, say, a hunch that the mayor was in danger, maybe you could have saved him. But when I brought it into now, it became a fact. You can't possibly make it untrue."

"But how about man's free will? Can't I do whatever I want to do?"

"Sure. It was your precious free will that brought the newspaper into now. You can't undo your own will. And, anyway, your will's still free. You're free to go getting thrown around chandeliers as often as you want. You probably like it. You can do anything up to the point where it would change what's in that paper. Then you have to start in again and again and again until you make up your mind to be sensible."

"But that—" Bill fumbled for words, "that's just as bad as...as fate or predestination. If my soul wills to—"

"Newspapers aren't enough. Time theory isn't enough. So I should tell him about his soul! People—" and Snulbug withdrew into the bowl.

Bill looked up at the city hall regretfully and shrugged his resignation. Then he folded his paper to the sports page and studied it carefully.

Snulbug thrust his head out again as they stopped in the many-acred parking lot. "Where is it this time?" he wanted to know. "Not that it matters."

"The racetrack."

"Oh—" Snulbug groaned, "I might have known it. You're all alike. No sense in the whole caboodle. I suppose you found a long shot?"

"Darned tooting I did. Alhazred at twenty to one in the fourth. I've got $500, the only money I've got left on earth. Plunk on Alhazred's nose it goes, and there's our $10,000."

Snulbug grunted. "I hear his lousy spell, I watch him get caught on a merry-go-round, it isn't enough, I should see him lay a bet on a long shot."

"But there isn't a loophole in this. I'm not interfering with the future; I'm just taking advantage of it. Alhazred'll win this race whether I bet on him or not. Five pretty hundred-dollar parimutuel tickets, and behold: The Hitchens Laboratory!" Bill jumped spryly out of his car and strutted along joyously. Suddenly he paused and addressed his pipe: "Hey! Why do I feel so good?"

Snulbug sighed dismally. "Why should anybody?"

"No, but I mean: I took a hell of a shellacking from that plug-ugly in the office. And I haven't got a pain or an ache."

"Of course not. It never happened."

"But I felt it then."

"Sure. In a future that never was. You changed your mind, didn't you? You decided not to go up there?"

"O.K., but that was after I'd already been beaten up."

"Uh-uh," said Snulbug firmly. "It was before you hadn't been." And he withdrew again into the pipe.

There was a band somewhere in the distance and the racous burble of an announcer's voice. Crowds clustered around the $2 windows, and the $5 weren't doing bad business. But the $100 window, where the five beautiful pasteboards lived that were to create an embolism laboratory, was almost deserted.

Bill buttonholed a stranger with a purple nose. "What's the next race?"

"Second, Mac."

Swell, Bill thought. Lots of time. And from now on—He hastened to the $100 window and shoved across the five bills that he had drawn from the bank that morning. "Alhazred, on the nose," he said.

The clerk frowned with surprise, but took the money and turned to get the tickets.

Bill buttonholed a stranger with a purple nose. "What's the next race?"

"Second, Mac."

Swell, Bill thought. And then he yelled, "Hey!"

A stranger with a purple nose paused and said, "'Smatter, Mac?"

"Nothing," Bill groaned. "Just everything."

The stranger hesitated. "Ain't I seen you someplace before?"

"No," said Bill hurriedly. "You were going to, but you haven't. I changed my mind."

The stranger walked away shaking his head and muttering how the ponies could get a guy.

Not till Bill was back in his roadster did he take the corncob from his mouth and glare at it. "All right!" he barked. "What was wrong this time? Why did I get on a merry-go-round again? I didn't try to change the future!"

Snulbug popped his head out and yawned a tuskful yawn. "I warn him, I explain it, I warn him again, now he wants I should explain it all over."

"But what did I do?"

"What did he do? You changed the odds, you dope. That much folding money on a long shot at a parimutuel track, and the odds change. It wouldn't have paid off at twenty to one, the way it said in the paper."

"Nuts," Bill muttered. "And I suppose that applies to anything? If I study the stock market in this paper and try to invest my $500 according to tomorrow's market—"

"Same thing. The quotations wouldn't be quite the same if you started in playing. I warned you. You're stuck," said Snulbug. "You're stymied. It's no use." He sounded almost cheerful.

"Isn't it?" Bill mused. "Now look, Snulbug. Me, I'm a great believer in Man. This universe doesn't hold a problem that Man can't eventually solve. And I'm no dumber than the average."

"That's saying a lot, that is," Snulbug sneered. "People—"

"I've got a responsibility now. It's more than just my $10,000. I've got to redeem the honor of Man. You say this is the insoluble problem. I say there *is* no insoluble problem."

"I say you talk a lot."

Bill's mind was racing furiously. How can a man take advantage of the future without in any smallest way altering that future? There must be an answer somewhere, and a man who devised the Hitchens Embolus Diagnosis could certainly crack a little nut like this. Man cannot refuse a challenge.

Unthinking, he reached for his tobacco pouch and tapped out his pipe on the sole of his foot. There was a microscopic thud as Snulbug crashed onto the floor of the car.

Bill looked down half-smiling. The tiny demon's tail was lashing madly, and every separate snake stood on end. "This is too much!" Snulbug screamed. "Dumb gags aren't enough, insults aren't enough. I should get thrown around like a damned soul. This is the last straw. Give me my dismissal!"

Bill snapped his fingers gleefully. "Dismissal!" he cried. "I've got it, Snully. We're all set."

Snulbug looked up puzzled and slowly let his snakes droop more amicably. "It won't work," he said, with an ominisciently sad shake of his serpentine head.

It was the dashing act again that carried Bill through the Choatsby Laboratories, where he had been employed so recently, and on up to the very anteroom of old R. C.'s office.

But where you can do battle with a bull-necked guard, there is not a thing you can oppose against the brisk competence of a young lady who says, "I shall find out if Mr. Choatsby will see you." There was nothing to do but wait.

"And what's the brilliant idea this time?" Snulbug obviously feared the worst.

"R. C.'s nuts," said Bill. "He's an astrologer and a pyramidologist and a British Israelite—American Branch Reformed—and Heaven knows what else. He... why, he'll even believe in you."

"That's more than I do," said Snulbug. "It's a waste of energy."

"He'll buy this paper. He'll pay anything for it. There's nothing he loves more than futzing around with the occult. He'll never be able to resist a good solid slice of the future, with illusions of a fortune thrown in."

"You better hurry, then."

"Why such a rush? It's only 2:30 now. Lots of time. And while that girl's gone there's nothing for us to do but cool our heels."

"You might at least," said Snulbug, "warm the heel of your pipe."

The girl returned at last. "Mr. Choatsby will see you."

Reuben Choatsby overflowed the outsize chair behind his desk. His little face, like a baby's head balanced on a giant suet pudding, beamed as Bill entered. "Changed your mind, eh?" His words came in sudden soft blobs, like the abrupt glugs of pouring syrup. "Good. Need you in K-39. Lab's not the same since you left."

Bill groped for the exactly right words. "That's not it, R. C. I'm on my own now and I'm doing all right."

The baby face soured. "Damned cheek. Competitor of mine, eh? What you want now? Waste my time?"

"Not at all." With a pretty shaky assumption of confidence, Bill perched on the edge of the desk. "R. C.," he said, slowly and impressively, "what would you give for a glimpse into the future?"

Mr. Choatsby glugged vigorously. "Ribbing me? Get out of here! Have you thrown out— Hold on! You're the one—Used to read queer books. Had a grimoire here once." The baby face grew earnest. "What d'you mean?"

"Just what I said, R. C. What would you give for a glimpse into the future?"

Mr. Choatsby hesitated. "How? Time travel? Pyramid? You figured out the King's Chamber?"

"Much simpler than that. I have here"—he took it out of his pocket and folded it so that only the name and the date line were visible—"tomorrow's newspaper."

Mr. Choatsby grabbed. "Let me see."

"Uh-uh. Naughty. You'll see after we discuss terms. But there it is."

"Trick. Had some printer fake it. Don't believe it."

"All right. I never expected you, R. C., to descend to such

unenlightened skepticism. But if that's all the faith you have—" Bill stuffed the paper back in his pocket and started for the door.

"Wait!" Mr. Choatsby lowered his voice. "How'd you do it? Sell your soul?"

"That wasn't necessary."

"How? Spells? Cantrips? Incantations? Prove it to me. Show me it's real. Then we'll talk terms."

Bill walked casually to the desk and emptied his pipe into the ash tray.

"I'm underdeveloped. I run errands. I'm named Snulbug. It isn't enough—now I should be a testimonial!"

Mr. Choatsby stared rapt at the furious little demon raging in his ash tray. He watched reverently as Bill held out the pipe for its inmate, filled it with tobacco, and lit it. He listened awe-struck as Snulbug moaned with delight at the flame.

"No more questions," he said. "What terms?"

"Fifteen thousand dollars." Bill was ready for bargaining.

"Don't put it too high," Snulbug warned. "You better hurry."

But Mr. Choatsby had pulled out his checkbook and was scribbling hastily. He blotted the check and handed it over. "It's a deal." He grabbed up the paper. "You're a fool, young man. Fifteen thousand! *Hmf!*" He had it open already at the financial page. "With what I make on the market tomorrow, never notice $15,000. Pennies."

"Hurry up," Snulbug urged.

"Goodbye, sir," Bill began politely, "and thank you for—" But Reuben Choatsby wasn't even listening.

"What's all this hurry?" Bill demanded as he reached the elevator.

"People!" Snulbug sighed. "Never you mind what's the hurry. You get to your bank and deposit that check."

So Bill, with Snulbug's incessant prodding, made a dash to the bank worthy of his descents on the city hall and on the

Choatsby Laboratories. He just made it, by stop-watch fractions of a second. The door was already closing as he shoved his way through at three o'clock sharp.

He made his deposit, watched the teller's eyes bug out at the size of the check, and delayed long enough to enjoy the incomparable thrill of changing the account from William Hitchens to The Hitchens Research Laboratory.

Then he climbed once more into his car, where he could talk with his pipe in peace. "Now," he asked as he drove home, "what was the rush?"

"He'd stop payment."

"You mean when he found out about the merry-go-round? But I didn't promise him anything. I just sold him tomorrow's paper. I didn't guarantee he'd make a fortune of it."

"That's all right. But—"

"Sure, you warned me. But where's the hitch? R. C.'s a bandit, but he's honest. He wouldn't stop payment."

"Wouldn't he?"

The car was waiting for a stop signal. The newsboy in the intersection was yelling "Uxtruh!" Bill glanced casually at the headline, did a double take, and instantly thrust out a nickel and seized a paper.

He turned into a side street, stopped the car, and went through this paper. Front page: MAYOR ASSASSINATED. Sports page: Alhazred at twenty to one. Obituaries: The same list he'd read at noon. He turned back to the date line. August 22. Tomorrow.

"I warned you," Snulbug was explaining. "I told you I wasn't strong enough to go far into the future. I'm not a well demon, I'm not. And an itch in the memory is something fierce. I just went far enough ahead to get a paper with tomorrow's date on it. And any dope knows that a Tuesday paper comes out Monday afternoon."

For a moment Bill was dazed. His magic paper, his fifteen-thousand-dollar paper, was being hawked by newsies on every corner. Small wonder R. C. might have stopped payment! And then he saw the other side. He started to laugh. He couldn't stop.

"Look out!" Snulbug shrilled. "You'll drop my pipe. And what's so funny?"

Bill wiped tears from his eyes. "I was right. Don't you see, Snulbug? Man can't be licked. My magic was lousy. All it could call up was you. You brought me what was practically a fake, and I got caught on the merry-go-round of time trying to use it. You were right enough there; no good could come out of that magic.

"But without the magic, just using human psychology, knowing a man's weaknesses, playing on them, I made a syrup-voiced old bandit endow the very research he'd tabooed, and do more good for humanity than he's done in all the rest of his life. I was right, Snulbug. You can't lick Man."

Snulbug's snakes writhed into knots of scorn. "People!" he snorted. "You'll find out." And he shook his head with dismal satisfaction.

The Words of Guru

by C. M. KORNBLUTH

YESTERDAY, WHEN I was going to meet Guru in the woods a man stopped me and said: "Child, what are you doing out at one in the morning? Does your mother know where you are? How old are you, walking around this late?"

I looked at him, and saw that he was white-haired, so I laughed. Old men never see; in fact men hardly see at all. Sometimes young women see part, but men rarely ever see at all. "I'm twleve on my next birthday," I said. And then, because I would not let him live to tell people, I said, "and I'm out this late to see Guru."

"Guru?" he asked. "Who is Guru? Some foreigner, I suppose? Bad business mixing with foreigners, young fellow. Who is Guru?"

So I told him who Guru was, and just as he began talking about cheap magazines and fairy tales I said one of the words that Guru taught me and he stopped talking. Because he was an old man and his joints were stiff he didn't crumple up but fell in one piece, hitting his head on the stone. Then I went on.

Even though I'm going to be only twelve on my next birthday I know many things that old people don't. And I remember things that other boys can't. I remember being born out of darkness, and I remember the noises that people made about me. Then when I was two months old I began to understand that the noises meant things like the things that were going on inside my head. I found out that I could make the noises too, and everybody was very much surprised. "Talking!" they said, again and again. "And so very young! Clara, what do you make of it?" Clara was my mother.

And Clara would say: "I'm sure I don't know. There never was any genius in my family, and I'm sure there was none in Joe's." Joe was my father.

Once Clara showed me a man I had never seen before, and told me that he was a reporter—that he wrote things in newspapers. The reporter tried to talk to me as if I were an ordinary baby; I didn't even answer him, but just kept looking at him until his eyes fell and he went away. Later Clara scolded me and read me a little piece in the reporter's newspaper that was supposed to be funny—about the reporter asking me very complicated questions and me answering with baby noises. It was not true, of course. I didn't say a word to the reporter, and he didn't ask me even one of the questions.

I heard her read the little piece, but while I listened I was watching the slug crawling on the wall. When Clara was finished I asked her: "What is that gray thing?"

She looked where I pointed, but couldn't see it. "What grey thing, Peter?" she asked. I had her call me by my whole name, Peter, instead of anything silly like Petey. "What gray thing?"

"It's as big as your hand, Clara, but soft. I don't think it has any bones at all. It's crawling up, but I don't see any face on the topwards side. And there aren't any legs."

I think she was worried, but she tried to baby me by putting her hand on the wall and trying to find out where it was. I called out whether she was right or left of the thing. Finally she put her hand right through the slug. And then I realized that she really couldn't see it, and didn't believe it was there. I stopped talking about it then and only asked her a few days later: "Clara, what do you call a thing which one person can see and another person can't?"

"An illusion, Peter," she said. "If that's what you mean." I said nothing, but let her put me to bed as usual, but when she turned out the light and went away I waited a little while and then called out softly. "Illusion! Illusion!"

At once Guru came for the first time. He bowed, the way he always has since, and said: "I have been waiting."

"I didn't know that was the way to call you," I said.

"Whenever you want me I will be ready. I will teach you, Peter—if you want to learn. Do you know what I will teach you?"

"If you will teach me about the gray thing on the wall," I said, "I will listen. And if you will teach me about real things and unreal things I will listen."

"These things," he said thoughtfully, "very few wish to learn. And there are some things that nobody ever wished to learn. And there are some things that I will not teach."

Then I said: "The things nobody has ever wished to learn I will learn. And I will even learn the things you do not wish to teach."

He smiled mockingly. "A master has come," he said, half-laughing. "A master of Guru."

That was how I learned his name. And that night he taught me a word which would do little things, like spoiling food.

From that day to the time I saw him last night he has not changed at all, though now I am as tall as he is. His skin is still as dry and shiny as ever it was, and his face is still bony, crowned by a head of very coarse, black hair.

When I was ten years old I went to bed one night only long enough to make Joe and Clara suppose I was fast asleep. I left in my place something which appears when you say one of the words of Guru and went down the drainpipe outside my window. It always was easy to climb down and up, ever since I was eight years old.

I met Guru in Inwood Hill Park. "You're late," he said.

"Not too late," I answered. "I know it's never too late for one of these things."

"How do you know?" he asked sharply. "This is your first."

"And maybe my last," I replied. "I don't like the idea of it. If I have nothing more to learn from my second than my first I shan't go to another."

"You don't know," he said. "You don't know what it's like—the voices, and the bodies slick with unguent, leaping flames; mind-filling ritual! You can have no idea at all until you've taken part."

"We'll see," I said. "Can we leave from here?"

"Yes," he said. Then he taught me the word I would need to know, and we both said it together.

The place we were in next was lit with red lights, and I think that the walls were of rock. Though of course there was no real seeing there, and so the lights only seemed to be red, and it was not real rock.

As we were going to the fire one of them stopped us. "Who's with you?" she asked, calling Guru by another name. I did not know that he was also the person bearing that name, for it was a very powerful one.

He cast a hasty, sidewise glance at me and then said: "This is Peter of whom I have often told you."

She looked at me then and smiled, stretching out her oily arms. "Ah," she said, softly, like the cats when they talk at night to me. "Ah, this is Peter. Will you come to me when I call you, Peter? And sometimes call for me—in the dark—when you are alone?"

"Don't do that!" said Guru, angrily pushing past her. "He's very young—you might spoil him for his work."

She screeched at our backs: "Guru and his pupil—fine pair!

Boy, he's no more real than I am—you're the only real thing here!"

"Don't listen to her," said Guru. "She's wild and raving. They're always tight-strung when this time comes around."

We came near the fires then, and sat down on rocks. They were killing animals and birds and doing things with their bodies. The blood was being collected in a basin of stone, which passed through the crowd. The one to my left handed it to me. "Drink," she said, grinning to show me her fine, white teeth. I swallowed twice from it and passed it to Guru.

When the bowl had passed all around we took off our clothes. Some, like Guru, did not wear them, but many did. The one to my left sat closer to me, breathing heavily at my face. I moved away. "Tell her to stop, Guru," I said. "This isn't part of it, I know."

Guru spoke to her sharply in their own language, and she changed her seat, snarling.

Then we all began to chant, clapping our hands and beating our thighs. One of them rose slowly and circled about the fires in a slow pace, her eyes rolling wildly. She worked her jaws and flung her arms about so sharply that I could hear the elbows crack. Still shuffling her feet against the rock floor she bent her body backwards down to her feet. Her belly muscles were bands nearly standing out from her skin, and the oil rolled down her body and legs. As the palms of her hands touched the ground, she collapsed in a twitching heap and began to set up a thin wailing noise against the steady chant and hand beat that the rest of us were keeping up. Another of them did the same as the first, and we chanted louder for her and still louder for the third. Then, while we still beat our hands and thighs, one of them took up the third, laid her across the altar, and made her ready with a stone knife. The fire's light gleamed off the chipped edge of obsidian. As her blood drained down the groove, cut as a gutter into the rock of the altar, we stopped our chant and the fires were snuffed out.

But still we could see what was going on, for these things

were, of course, not happening at all—only seeming to happen, really, just as all the people and things there only seemed to be what they were. Only I was real. That must be why they desired me so.

As the last of the fires died Guru excitedly whispered: "The Presence!" He was deeply moved.

From the pool of blood from the third dancer's body there issued the Presence. It was the tallest one there, and when it spoke its voice was deeper, and when it commanded its commands were obeyed.

"Let blood!" it commanded, and we gashed ourselves with flints. It smiled and showed teeth bigger and sharper and whiter than any of the others.

"Make water!" it commanded, and we all spat on each other. It flapped its wings and rolled its eyes, which were bigger and redder than any of the others.

"Pass flame!" it commanded, and we breathed smoke and fire on our limbs. It stamped its feet, let blue flames roar from its mouth, and they were bigger and wilder than any of the others.

Then it returned to the pool of blood and we lit the fires again. Guru was staring straight before him; I tugged his arm. He bowed as though we were meeting for the first time that night.

"What are you thinking of?" I asked. "We shall go now."

"Yes," he said heavily. "Now we shall go." Then we said the word that had brought us there.

The first man I killed was Brother Paul, at the school where I went to learn the things that Guru did not teach me.

It was less than a year ago, but it seems like a very long time. I have killed so many times since then.

"You're a very bright boy, Peter," said the brother.

"Thank you, brother."

"But there are things about you that I don't understand. Normally I'd ask your parents but—I feel that they don't understand either. You were an infant prodigy, weren't you?"

"Yes, brother."

"There's nothing very unusual about that—glands, I'm told. You know what glands are?"

Then I was alarmed. I had heard of them, but I was not certain whether they were the short, thick green men who wear only metal or the things with many legs with whom I talked in the woods.

"How did you find out?" I asked him.

"But Peter! You look positively frightened, lad! I don't know a thing about them myself, but Father Frederick does. He has whole books about them, though I sometimes doubt whether he believes them himself."

"They aren't good books, brother," I said. "They ought to be burned."

"That's a savage thought, my son. But to return to your own problem—"

I could not let him go any further knowing what he did about me. I said one of the words Guru taught me and he looked at first very surprised and then seemed to be in great pain. He dropped across his desk and I felt his wrist to make sure, for I had not used that word before. But he was dead.

There was a heavy step outside and I made myself invisible. Stout Father Frederick entered, and I nearly killed him too with the word, but I knew that would be very curious. I decided to wait, and went through the door as Father Frederick bent over the dead monk. He thought he was asleep.

I went down the corridor to the book-lined office of the stout priest and, working quickly, piled all his books in the center of the room and lit them with my breath. Then I went down to the schoolyard and made myself visible again when there was nobody looking. It was very easy. I killed a man I passed on the street the next day.

There was a girl named Mary who lived near us. She was fourteen then, and I desired her as those in the Cavern out of Time and Space had desired me.

So when I saw Guru and he had bowed, I told him of it, and

he looked at me in great surprise. "You are growing older, Peter," he said.

"I am, Guru. And there will come a time when your words will not be strong enough for me."

He laughed. "Come, Peter," he said. "Follow me if you wish. There is something that is going to be done—" He licked his thin, purple lips and said: "I have told you what it will be like."

"I shall come," I said. "Teach me the word." So he taught me the word and we said it together.

The place we were in next was not like any of the other places I had been to before with Guru. It was No-place. Always before there had been the seeming passage of time and matter, but here there was not even that. Here Guru and the others cast off their forms and were what they were, and No-place was the only place where they could do this.

It was not like the Cavern, for the Cavern had been out of Time and Space, and this place was not enough of a place even for that. It was No-place.

What happened there does not bear telling, but I was made known to certain ones who never departed from there. All came to them as they existed. They had not color or the seeming of color, or any seeming of shape.

There I learned that eventually I would join with them; that I had been selected as the one of my planet who was to dwell without being forever in that No-place.

Guru and I left, having said the word.

"Well?" demanded Guru, staring me in the eye.

"I am willing," I said. "But teach me one word now—"

"Ah," he said grinning. "The girl?"

"Yes," I said. "The word that will mean much to her."

Still grinning, he taught me the word.

Mary, who had been fourteen, is now fifteen and what they call incurably mad.

Last night I saw Guru again and for the last time. He bowed as I approached him. "Peter," he said warmly.

"Teach me the word," said I.

"It is not too late."

"Teach me the word."

"You can withdraw—with what you master you can master also this world. Gold without reckoning; sardonyx and gems, Peter! Rich crushed velvet—stiff, scraping, embroidered tapestries!"

"Teach me the word."

"Think, Peter, of the house you could build. It could be of white marble, and every slab centered by a winking ruby. Its gate could be of beaten gold within and without and it could be built about one slender tower of carven ivory, rising mile after mile into the turquoise sky. You could see the clouds float underneath your eyes."

"Teach me the word."

"Your tongue could crush the grapes that taste like melted silver. You could hear always the song of the bulbul and the lark that sounds like the dawn star made musical. Spikenard that will bloom a thousand thousand years could be ever in your nostrils. Your hands could feel the down of purple Himalayan swans that is softer than a sunset cloud."

"Teach me the word."

"You could have women whose skin would be from the black of ebony to the white of snow. You could have women who would be as hard as flints or as soft as a sunset cloud."

"Teach me the word."

Guru grinned and said the word.

Now, I do not know whether I will say that word, which was the last Guru taught me, today or tomorrow or until a year has passed.

It is a word that will explode this planet like a stick of dynamite in a rotten apple.

Homecoming

by RAY BRADBURY

"HERE THEY come," said Cecy, lying there flat in her bed. "Where are they?" cried Timothy from the doorway. "Some of them are over Europe, some over Asia, some of them over the Island, some over South America!" said Cecy, her eyes closed, the lashes long, brown, and quivering.

Timothy came forward upon the bare plankings of the upstairs room. "Who are they?"

"Uncle Einar and Uncle Fry, and there's Cousin William, and I see Frulda and Helgar and Aunt Morgiana and Cousin Vivian, and I see Uncle Johann! They're all coming fast!"

"Are they up in the sky?" cried Timothy, his little gray eyes flashing. Standing by the bed, he looked no more than his fourteen years. The wind blew outside, the house was dark and lit only by starlight.

"They're coming through the air and traveling along the ground, in many forms," said Cecy, in her sleeping. She did not move on the bed; she thought inward on herself and told what she saw. "I see a wolflike thing coming over a dark river—at the shallows—just above a waterfall, the starlight shining up his pelt. I see a brown oak leaf blowing far up in the sky. I see a small bat flying. I see many other things, running through the forest trees and slipping through the highest branches; and they're *all* coming this way!"

"Will they be here by tomorrow night?" Timothy clutched the bedclothes. The spider on his lapel swung like a black pendulum, excitedly dancing. He leaned over his sister. "Will they all be here in time for the Homecoming?"

"Yes, yes, Timothy, yes," sighed Cecy. She stiffened. "Ask no more of me. Go away now. Let me travel in the places I like best."

"Thanks, Cecy," he said. Out in the hall, he ran to his room. He hurriedly made his bed. He had just awakened a few minutes ago, at sunset, and as the first stars had risen, he had gone to let his excitement about the party run with Cecy. Now she slept so quietly there was not a sound. The spider hung on a silvery lasso about Timothy's slender neck as he washed his face. "Just think, Spid, tomorrow night is Allhallows' Eve!"

He lifted his face and looked into the mirror. His was the only mirror allowed in the house. It was his mother's concession to his illness. Oh, if only he were not so afflicted! He opened his mouth, surveyed the poor, inadequate teeth nature had given him. No more than so many corn kernels—round, soft and pale in his jaws. Some of the high spirit died in him.

It was now totally dark and he lit a candle to see by. He felt exhausted. This past week the whole family had lived in the fashion of the old country. Sleeping by day, rousing at sunset to move about. There were blue hollows under his eyes. "Spid, I'm no good," he said, quietly, to the little creature. "I can't even get used to sleeping days like the others."

He took up the candleholder. Oh, to have strong teeth, with incisors like steel spikes. Or strong hands, even, or a strong mind. Even to have the power to send one's mind out, free, as Cecy did. But, no, he was the imperfect one, the sick one.

He was even—he shivered and drew the candle flame closer—afraid of the dark. His brothers snorted at him. Bion and Leonard and Sam. They laughed at him because he slept in a bed. With Cecy it was different; her bed was part of her comfort for the composure necessary to send her mind abroad to hunt. But Timothy, did he sleep in the wonderful polished boxes like the others? He did not! Mother let him have his own bed, his own room, his own mirror. No wonder the family skirted him like a holy man's crucifix. If only the wings would sprout from his shoulder blades. He bared his back, stared at it. He sighed again. No chance. Never.

Downstairs were exciting and mysterious sounds. The slithering sound of black crepe going up in all the halls and on the ceilings and doors. The smell of burning black tapers crept up the banistered stair well. Mother's voice, high and firm. Father's voice, echoing from the damp cellar. Bion walking from outside the old country house lugging vast two-gallon jugs.

"I've just got to go to the party, Spid," said Timothy. The spider whirled at the end of its silk, and Timothy felt alone. He would polish cases, fetch toadstools and spiders, hang crepe, but when the party started he'd be ignored. The less seen or said of the imperfect son the better.

All through the house below, Laura ran.

"The Homecoming!" she shouted gaily. "The Homecoming!" Her footsteps everywhere at once.

Timothy passed Cecy's room again, and she was sleeping quietly. Once a month she went belowstairs. Always she stayed in bed. Lovely Cecy. He felt like asking her, "Where are you now, Cecy? And *in* who? And what's happening? Are you beyond the hills? And what goes on there?" But he went on to Ellen's room instead.

Ellen sat at her desk, sorting out many kinds of blond, red and black hair and little scimitars of fingernail gathered from her manicurist job at the Mellin Village beauty parlor fifteen miles over. A sturdy mahogany case lay in one corner with her name on it.

"Go away," she said, not even looking at him. "I can't work with you gawking."

"Allhallows' Eve, Ellen; just think!" he said, trying to be friendly.

"Hunh!" She put some fingernail clippings in a small white sack, labeled them. "What can it mean to you? What do you know of it? It'll scare the hell out of you. Go back to bed."

His cheeks burned. "I'm needed to polish and work and help serve."

"If you don't go, you'll find a dozen raw oysters in your bed tomorrow," said Ellen, matter-of-factly. "Good-by, Timothy."

In his anger, rushing downstairs, he bumped into Laura.

"Watch where you're going!" she shrieked from clenched teeth.

She swept away. He ran to the open cellar door, smelled the channel of moist earthy air rising from below. "Father?"

"It's about time," Father shouted up the steps. "Hurry down, or they'll be here before we're ready!"

Timothy hesitated only long enough to hear the million other sounds in the house. Brothers came and went like trains in a station, talking and arguing. If you stood in one spot long enough the entire household passed with their pale hands full of things. Leonard with his little black medical case, Samuel with his large, dusty ebon-bound book under his arm, bearing more black crepe, and Bion excursioning to the car outside and bringing in many more gallons of liquid.

Father stopped polishing to give Timothy a rag and a scowl. He thumped the huge mahogany box. "Come on, shine this up, so we can start on another. Sleep your life away."

While waxing the surface, Timothy looked inside.

"Uncle Einar's a big man, isn't he, Papa?"

"Unh."

"How big is he?"

"The size of the box'll tell you."

"I was only asking. Seven feet tall?"

"You talk a lot."

About nine o'clock Timothy went out into the October weather. For two hours in the now-warm, now-cold wind he walked the meadows collecting toadstools and spiders. His heart began to beat with anticipation again. How many relatives had Mother said would come? Seventy? One hundred? He passed a farmhouse. If only you knew what was happening at our house, he said to the glowing windows. He climbed a hill and looked at the town, miles away, settling into sleep, the town hall clock high and round white in the distance. The town did not know, either. He brought home many jars of toadstools and spiders.

In the little chapel belowstairs a brief ceremony was celebrated. It was like all the other rituals over the years, with Father chanting the dark lines, Mother's beautiful white ivory hands moving in the reverse blessings, and all the children gathered except Cecy, who lay upstairs in bed. But Cecy was present. You saw her peering, now from Bion's eyes, now Sauel's, now Mother's, and you felt a movement and now she was in you, fleetingly, and gone.

Timothy prayed to the Dark One with a tightened stomach. "Please, please, help me grow up, help me be like my sisters and brothers. Don't let me be different. If only I could put the hair in the plastic images as Ellen does, or make people fall in love with me as Laura does with people, or read strange books as Sam does, or work in a respected job like Leonard and Bion do. Or even raise a family one day, as Mother and Father have done...."

At midnight a storm hammered the house. Lightning struck outside in amazing, snow-white bolts. There was a sound of an approaching, probing, sucking tornardo, funneling and nuzzling the moist night earth. Then the front door, blasted half off its hinges, hung stiff and discarded, and in trooped Grandmama and Grandpapa, all the way from the old country!

From then on people arrived each hour. There was a flutter at the side window, a rap on the front porch, a knock at the back. There were fey noises from the cellar; autumn wind piped down the chimney throat, chanting, Mother filled the large crystal punch bowl with a scarlet fluid poured from the jugs Bion had carried home. Father swept from room to room lighting more tapers. Laura and Ellen hammered up more wolfsbane. And Timothy stood amidst this wild excitement, no expression to his face, his hands trembling at his sides, gazing now here, now there. Banging of doors, laughter, the sound of liquid pouring, darkness, sound of wind, the webbed thunder of wings, the padding of feet, the welcoming bursts of talk at the entrances, the transparent rattlings of casements, the shadows passing, coming, going, wavering.

"Well, well, and *this* must be Timothy!"

"What?"

A chilly hand took his hand. A long hairy face leaned down over him. "A good lad, a fine lad," said the stranger.

"Timothy," said his mother. "This is Uncle Jason."

"Hello, Uncle Jason."

"And over here—" Mother drifted Uncle Jason away. Uncle Jason peered back at Timothy over his caped shoulder, and winked.

Timothy stood alone.

From off a thousand miles in the candled darkness, he heard a high fluting voice; that was Ellen. "And my brothers, they *are* clever. Can you guess their occupations, Aunt Morgiana?"

"I have no idea."

"They operate the undertaking establishment in town."

"What!" A gasp.

"Yes!" Shrill laughter. "Isn't that priceless!"

Timothy stood very still.

A pause in the laughter. "They bring home sustenance for Mama, Papa and all of us," said Laura. "Except, of course, Timothy. . . ."

An uneasy silence. Uncle Jason's voice demanded. "Well? Come now. What about Timothy?"

"Oh, Laura, your tongue," said Mother.

Laura went on with it. Timothy shut his eyes. "Timothy doesn't—well—doesn't *like* blood. He's delicate."

"He'll learn," said Mother. "He'll learn," she said very firmly. "He's my son, and he'll learn. He's only fourteen."

"But I was raised on the stuff," said Uncle Jason, his voice passing from one room on into another. The wind played the trees outside like harps. A little rain spatted on the windows—"raised on the stuff," passing away into faintness.

Timothy bit his lips and opened his eyes.

"Well, it was all my fault." Mother was showing them into the kitchen now. "I tried forcing him. You can't force children, you only make them sick, and then they never get a taste for things. Look at Bion, now, he was thirteen before he..."

"I understand," murmured Uncle Jason. "Timothy will come around."

"I'm sure he will," said Mother, defiantly.

Candle flames quivered as shadows crossed and recrossed the dozen musty rooms. Timothy was cold. He smelled the hot tallow in his nostrils and instinctively he grabbed at a candle and walked with it around and about the house, pretending to straighten the crepe.

"*Timothy,*" someone whispered behind a patterned wall, hissing and sizzling and sighing the words, "*Timothy is afraid of the dark.*"

Leonard's voice. Hateful Leonard!

"I like the candle, that's all," said Timothy in a reproachful whisper.

More noise, more laughter, and thunder. Cascades of roaring laughter. Bangings and clickings and shouts and rustles of clothing. Clammy fog swept through the front door. Out of the fog, settling his wings, stalked a tall man.

"Uncle Einar!"

Timothy propelled himself on his thin legs straight through the fog, under the green webbing shadows. He threw himself across Einar's arms. Einar lifted him.

"You've wings, Timothy!" He tossed the boy light as thistles. "Wings, Timothy; fly!" Faces wheeled under. Darkness rotated. The house blew away. Timothy felt breezelike. He flapped his arms. Einar's fingers caught and threw him once more to the ceiling. The ceiling rushed down like a charred wall. "Fly, Timothy!" shouted Einar, loud and deep. "Fly with wings! Wings!"

He felt an exquisite ecstasy in his shoulder blades, as if roots grew, burst to explode and blossom into new, moist membrane. He babbled wild stuff; again Einar hurled him high.

The autumn wind broke in a tide on the house, rain crashed down, shaking the beams, causing chandeliers to tilt their enraged candle lights. And the one hundred relatives peered out from every black, enchanted room, circling inward, all shapes and sizes, to where Einar balanced the child like a baton in the roaring spaces.

"Enough!" shouted Einar, at last.

Timothy, deposited on the floor timbers, exaltedly, exhaustedly fell against Uncle Einar, sobbing happily. "Uncle, uncle, uncle!"

"Was it good, flying? Eh, Timothy?" said Uncle Einar, bending down, patting Timothy's head. "Good, good."

It was coming toward dawn. Most had arrived and were ready to bed down for the daylight, sleep motionlessly with no sound until the following sunset, when they would shout out of their mahogany boxes for the revelry.

Uncle Einar, followed by dozens of others, moved toward the cellar. Mother directed them downward to the crowded row on row of highly polished boxes. Einar, his wings like sea-green tarpaulins tented behind him, moved with a curious whistling and through the passageway; where his wings touched they made a sound of drumheads gently beaten.

Upstairs, Timothy lay wearily thinking, trying to like the darkness. There was so much you could do in darkness that people couldn't criticize you for, because they never saw you.

He *did* like the night, but it was a qualified liking; sometimes there was so much night he cried out in rebellion.

In the cellar, mahogany doors sealed downward, drawn in by pale hands. In corners, certain relatives circled three times to lie down, heads on paws, eyelids shut. The sun rose. There was a sleeping.

Sunset. The revel exploded like a bat nest struck full, shrieking out, fluttering, spreading. Box doors banked wide. Steps rushed up from cellar damp. More late guests, kicking on front and back portals, were admitted.

It rained, and sodden visitors laid their capes, their water-pelleted hats, their sprinkled veils upon Timothy who bore them to a closet. The rooms were crowd-packed. The laughter of one cousin shot from one room, angled off the wall of another, ricocheted, banked and returned to Timothy's ears from a fourth room, accurate and cynical.

A mouse ran across the floor.

"I know you, Niece Leibersrouter!" exclaimed Father.

The mouse spiraled three women's feet and vanished into a corner. Moments later a beautiful woman rose up out of nothing and stood in the corner, smiling her white smile at them all.

Something huddled against the flooded pane of the kitchen window. It sighed and wept and tapped continually, pressed against the glass, but Timothy could make nothing of it, he saw nothing. In imagination he was outside staring in. The rain was on him; the wind at him, and the taper-dotted darkness inside was inviting. Waltzes were being danced; tall thin figures pirouetted to outlandish music. Stars of light flickered off lifted bottles; small clods of earth crumbled from casques, and a spider fell and went silently legging over the floor.

Timothy shivered. He was inside the house again. Mother was calling him to run here, run there, help, serve, out to the kitchen now, fetch this, fetch that, bring the plates, heap the food—on and on—the party happened around him but not to him. The dozens of towering people pressed in against him, elbowed him, ignored him.

Finally, he turned and slipped away up the stairs.

He called softly. "Cecy. Where are you now, Cecy?"

She waited a long while before answering. "In the Imperial Valley," she murmured faintly. "Beside the Salton Sea, near the mud pots and the stream and the quiet. I'm inside a farmer's wife. I'm sitting on a front porch. I can make her move if I want, or do anything or think anything. The sun's going down."

"What's it like, Cecy?"

"You can hear mud pots hissing," she said, slowly, as if speaking in a church. "Little gray heads of steam push up the mud like bald men rising in the thick syrup, head first, out in the broiling channels. The gray heads rip like rubber fabric, collapse with noises like wet lips moving. And feathery plumes of steam escape from the ripped tissue. And there is a smell of deep sulphurous burning and old time. The dinosaur has been abroiling here ten million years."

"Is he done yet, Cecy?"

"Yes, he's done. Quite done." Cecy's calm sleeper's lips turned up. The languid words fell slowly from her shaping mouth. "Inside this woman's skull I am, looking out, watching the sea that does not move, and is so quiet it makes you afraid. I sit on the porch and wait for my husband to come home. Occasionally, a fish leaps, falls back, starlight edging it. The valley, the sea, the few cars, the wooden porch, my rocking chair, myself, the silence."

"What now, Cecy?"

"I'm getting up from my rocking chair," she said.

"Yes?"

"I'm walking off the porch, toward the mud pots. Planes fly over, like primordial birds. Then it is quiet, so quiet."

"How long will you stay inside her, Cecy?"

"Until I've listened and looked and felt enough: until I've

changed her life some way. I'm walking off the porch and along the wooden boards. My feet knock on the planks, tiredly, slowly."

"And now?"

"Now the sulphur fumes are all around me. I stare at the bubbles as they break and smooth. A bird darts by my temple, shrieking. Suddenly I am in the bird and fly away! And as I fly, inside my new small glass-bead eyes I see a woman below me, on a boardwalk, take one two three steps forward into the mud pots. I hear a sound as of a boulder plunged into molten depths. I keep flying, circle back. I see a white hand, like a spider, wriggle and disappear into the gray lava pool. The lava seals over. Now I'm flying home, swift, swift, swift!"

Something clapped hard against the window. Timothy started.

Cecy flicked her eyes wide, bright, full, happy, exhilarated. "Now I'm *home!*" she said.

After a pause, Timothy ventured, "The Homecoming's on. And everybody's here."

"Then why are you upstairs?" She took his hand. "Well, ask me." She smiled slyly. "Ask me what you came to ask."

"I didn't come to ask anything," he said. "Well, almost nothing. Well, oh, Cecy!" It came from him in one long rapid flow. "I want to do something at the party to make them look at me, something to make me good as them, something to make me belong, but there's nothing I can do and I feel funny and, well, I thought you might..."

"I might," She said, closing her eyes, smiling inwardly. "Stand up straight. Stand very still." He obeyed. "Now shut your eyes and blank out your thoughts."

He stood very straight and thought of nothing, or at least thought of thinking nothing.

She sighed. "Shall we go downstairs now, Timothy?" Like a hand into a glove, Cecy was within him.

"Look everybody!" Timothy held the glass of warm red

liquid. He held up the glass so that the whole house turned to watch him. Aunts, uncles, cousins, brothers, sisters!

He drank it straight down.

He jerked a hand at his sister Laura. He held her gaze, whispering to her in a subtle voice that kept her silent, frozen. He felt tall as the trees as he walked to her. The party now slowed. It waited on all sides of him, watching. From all the room doors the faces peered. They were not laughing. Mother's face was astonished. Dad looked bewildered, but pleased and getting prouder every instant.

He nipped her, gently, over the neck vein. The candle flames swayed drunkenly. The wind climbed around on the roof outside. The relatives stared from all the doors. He popped toadstools into his mouth, swallowed, then beat his arms against his flanks and circled. "Look, Uncle Einer! I can fly, at last!" Beat went his hands. Up and down pumped his feet. The faces flashed past him.

At the top of the stairs before knowing it, flapping. Timothy heard his mother cry, "Stop, Timothy!" far below. "Hey!" shouted Timothy, and leaped off the top of the well, thrashing.

Halfway down, the wings he thought he owned dissolved. He screamed. Uncle Einar caught him.

Timothy flailed whitely in the receiving arms. A voice burst out of his lips unbidden. "This is Cecy! This is Cecy!" it announced, shrilly. "Cecy! Come see me, all of you, upstairs, first room on the left!" Followed by a long trill of high laughter. Timothy tried to cut it off with his tongue, his lips.

Everybody was laughing. Einar set him down. Running through the crowding blackness as the relatives flowed upstairs toward Cecy's room to congratulate her, Timothy banged the front door open. Mother called out behind him, anxiously.

"Cecy, I hate you, I hate you!"

By the sycamore tree, in deep shadow, Timothy spewed out his dinner, sobbed bitterly and threshed in a pile of autumn leaves. Then he lay still. From his blouse pocket, from the protection of the matchbox he used for his retreat, the spider crawled forth. Spid walked along Timothy's arm. Spid explored up his neck to his ear and climbed in the ear to tickle it. Timothy shook his head. "Don't, Spid. Don't."

The feathery touch of a tentative feeler probing his eardrum set Timothy shivering. "Don't, Spid!" He sobbed somewhat less.

The spider traveled down his cheek, took a station under the boy's nose, looked up into the nostrils as if to seek the brain, and then clambered softly up over the rim of the nose to sit, to squat there peering at Timothy with green gem eyes until Timothy filled with ridiculous laughter. "Go away, Spid!"

Timothy sat up, rustling the leaves. The land was very bright with the moon. In the house he could hear the faint ribaldry as Mirror, Mirror was played. Celebrants shouted, dimly muffled, as they tried to identify those of themselves whose reflections did not, had not ever appeared in a glass.

"Timothy." Uncle Einar's wings spread and twitched and came in with a sound like kettledrums. Timothy felt himself plucked up like a thimble and set upon Einar's shoulder. "Don't feel badly, Nephew Timothy. Each to his own, each in his own way. How much better things are for you. How rich. The world's dead for us. We've seen so much of it, believe me. Life's best to those who live the least of it. It's worth more per ounce, Timothy, remember that."

The rest of the black morning, from midnight on, Uncle Einar led him about the house, from room to room, weaving and singing. A horde of late arrivals set the entire hilarity off afresh. Great-great-great-great and a thousand more great-greats Grandmother was there, wrapped in Egyptian cerements. She said not a word, but lay straight as a burnt ironing board against the wall, her eye hollows cupping a distant, wise, silent glimmering. At the breakfast, at four in the morning, one-thousand-odd-greats Grandmama was stiffly seated at the head of the longest table.

The numerous young cousins caroused at the crystal punch

bowl. Their shiny olive-pit eyes, their conical, devilish faces and curly bronze hair hovered over the drinking table, their hard-soft, half-girl half-boy bodies wrestling against each other as they got unpleasantly, sullenly drunk. The wind got higher, the stars burned with fiery intensity, the noises redoubled, the dances quickened, the drinking became more positive. To Timothy there were thousands of things to hear and watch. The many darknesses roiled, bubbled, the many faces passed and repassed....

"Listen!"

The party held its breath. Far away the town clock struck its chimes, saying six o'clock. The party was ending. As if at a cue, in time to the rhythm of the clock striking, their one hundred voices began to sing songs that were four hundred years old, songs Timothy could not know. They twined their arms around one another, circling slowly, and sang, and somewhere in the cold distance of morning the town clock finished out its chimes and quieted.

Good-bys were said, there was a great rustling. Mother and Father and the brothers and sisters lined up at the door to shake hands and kiss each departing relative in turn. The sky beyond the open door colored and shone in the east. A cold wind entered.

The shouting and the laughing bit by bit faded and went away. Dawn grew more apparent. Everybody was embracing and crying and thinking how the world was becoming less a place for them. There had been a time when they had met every year, but now decades passed with no reconciliation. "Don't forget, we meet in Salem in 1970!" someone cried.

Salem. Timothy's numbed mind turned the word over. Salem, 1970. And there would be Uncle Fry and Grandma and Grandfather and a thousand-times-great Grandmother in her withered cerements. And Mother and Father and Ellen and Laura and Cecy and Leonard and Bion and Sam and all the rest. But would he be there? Would he be alive that long? Could he be certain of living until then?

With one last withering wind blast, away they all went, so many scarves, so many fluttery mammals, so many sere leaves, so many wolves loping, so many whinings and clustering noises, so many midnights and ideas and insanities.

Mother shut the door. Laura picked up a broom.

"No," said Mother, "we'll clean up tonight. We need sleep first."

Father walked down into the cellar, followed by Laura and Bion and Sam. Ellen walked upstairs, as did Leonard.

Timothy walked across the crepe-littered hall. His head was down, and in passing a party mirror he saw himself, the pale mortality of his face. He was cold and trembling.

"Timothy!" said Mother.

He stopped at the stair well. She came to him, laid a hand on his face. "Son," she said. "We love you. Remember that. We all love you. No matter how different you are, no matter if you leave us one day," she said. She kissed his cheek. "And if and when you die, your bones will lie undisturbed, we'll see to that. You'll lie at ease forever, and I'll come see you every Allhallows' Eve and tuck you in the more secure."

The house was silent. Far away the wind went over a hill with its last cargo of small dark bats echoing, chittering.

He walked up the steps, one by one, crying to himself all the way.

Mazirian the Magician

by JACK VANCE

DEEP IN thought, Mazirian the Magician walked his garden. Trees fruited with many intoxications overhung his path, and flowers bowed obsequiously as he passed. An inch above the ground, dull as agates, the eyes of mandrakes followed the tread of his black-slippered feet. Such was Mazirian's garden—three terraces growing with strange and wonderful vegetations. Certain plants swam with changing iridescences; others held up blooms pulsing like sea-anemones, purple, green, lilac, pink, yellow. Here grew trees like feather parasols, trees with transparent trunks threaded with red and yellow veins, trees with foilage like metal foil, each leaf a different metal—copper, silver, blue tantalum, bronze, green iridium. Here blooms like bubbles tugged gently upward from glazed green leaves, there a shrub bore a thousand pipe-shaped blossoms, each whistling softly to make music of the ancient Earth, of the ruby-red sunlight, water seeping through black soil, the languid winds. And beyond the roqual hedge the trees of the forest made a tall wall of mystery. In this waning hour of Earth's life no man could count himself familiar with the glens, the glades, the dells and deeps, the secluded clearings, the ruined pavilions, the sun-dappled pleasances, the gullys and heights, the various brooks, freshets, ponds, the meadows, thickets, brakes and rocky outcrops.

Mazirian paced his garden with a brow frowning in thought. His step was slow and his arms were clenched behind his back. There was one who had brought him puzzlement, doubt, and a great desire: a delightful woman-creature who dwelt in the woods. She came to his garden half-laughing and always wary, riding a black horse with eyes like golden crystals. Many times had Mazirian tried to take her; always her horse had borne her from his varied enticements, threats, and subterfuges.

Agonized screaming jarred the garden. Mazirian, hastening his step, found a mole chewing the stalk of a plant-animal hybrid. He killed the marauder, and the screams subsided to a dull gasping. Mazirian stroked a furry leaf and the red mouth hissed in pleasure.

Then: "K-k-k-k-k-k-k," spoke the plant. Mazirian stooped, held the rodent to the red mouth. The mouth sucked, the small body slid into the stomach-bladder underground. The plant gurgled, eructated, and Mazirian watched with satisfaction.

The sun had swung low in the sky, so dim and red that the stars could be seen. And now Mazirian felt a watching presence. It would be the woman of the forest, for thus had she disturbed him before. He paused in his stride, feeling for the direction of the gaze.

He shouted a spell of immobilization. Behind him the plant-animal froze to rigidity and a great green moth wafted to the ground. He whirled around. There she was, at the edge of the forest, closer than ever she had approached before. Nor did she move as he advanced. Mazirian's young-old eyes shone. He would take her to his manse and keep her in a prison of green glass. He would test her brain with fire, with cold, with pain and with joy. She should serve him with wine and make the eighteen motions of allurement by yellow lamp-light. Perhaps she was spying on him; if so, the Magician would discover immediately, for he could call no man friend and had forever to guard his garden.

She was but twenty paces distant—then there was a thud and pound of black hooves as she wheeled her mount and fled into the forest.

The Magician flung down his cloak in rage. She held a guard—a counter-spell, a rune of protection—and always she came when he was ill-prepared to follow. He peered into the murky depths, glimpsed the wanness of her body flitting through a shaft of red light, then black shade and she was gone... Was she a witch? Did she come of her own volition, or—more likely—had an enemy sent her to deal him inquietude? If so, who might be guiding her? There was Prince Kandive the Golden, of Kaiin, whom Mazirian had bilked of his secret of renewed youth. There was Azvan the Astronomer, there was Turjan—hardly Turjan, and here Mazirian's face lit in a pleasing recollection... He put the thought aside. Azvan, at least, he could test. He turned his steps to his workshop, went to a table where rested a cube of clear crystal, shimmering with a red and blue aureole. From a cabinet he brought a bronze gong and a silver hammer. He tapped on the gong and the mellow tone sang through the room and out, away and beyond. He tapped again and again. Suddenly Azvan's face shone from the crystal, beaded with pain and great terror.

"Stay the strokes, Mazirian!" cried Azvan. "Strike no more on the gong of my life!"

Mazirian paused, his hand poised over the gong.

"Do you spy on me, Azvan? Do you send a woman to regain the gong?"

"Not I, Master, not I. I fear you too well."

"You must deliver me the woman, Azvan; I insist."

"Impossible, Master! I know not who or what she is!"

Mazirian made as if to strike. Azvan poured forth such a torrent of supplication that Mazirian with a gesture of disgust threw down the hammer and restored the gong to its place. Azvan's face drifted slowly away, and the fine cube of crystal shone blank as before.

Mazirian stroked his chin. Apparently he must capture the girl himself. Later, when black night lay across the forest, he would seek through his books for spells to guard him through the unpredictable glades. They would be poignant corrosive spells, of such a nature that one would daunt the brain of an ordinary man and two render him mad. Mazirian, by dint of stringent exercise, could encompass four of the most formidable, or six of the lesser spells.

He put the project from his mind and went to a long vat bathed in a flood of green light. Under a wash of clear fluid lay the body of a man, ghastly below the green glare, but of great physical beauty. His torso tapered from wide shoulders through lean flanks to long strong legs and arched feet; his face was clean and cold with hard flat features. Dusty golden hair clung about his head.

Mazirian stared at the thing, which he had cultivated from a single cell. It needed only intelligence, and this he knew not how to provide. Turjan of Miir held the knowledge, and Turjan—Mazirian glanced with a grim narrowing of the eyes at a trap in the floor—refused to part with his secret.

Mazirian pondered the creature in the vat. It was a perfect body; therefore might not the brain be ordered and pliant? He would discover. He set in motion a device to draw off the liquid and presently the body lay stark to the direct rays. Mazirian injected a minim of drug into the neck. The body twitched. The eyes opened, winced in the glare. Mazirian turned away the projector.

Feebly the creature in the vat moved its arms and feet, as if unaware of their use. Mazirian watched intently; perhaps he had stumbled on the right synthesis for the brain.

"Sit up!" commanded the Magician.

The creature fixed its eyes upon him, and reflexes joined muscle to muscle. It gave a throaty roar and sprang from the vat at Mazirian's throat. In spite of Mazirian's strength it caught him and shook him like a doll.

For all Mazirian's magic he was helpless. The mesmeric spell had been expended, and he had none other in his brain. In any event he could not have uttered the space-twisting syllables with that mindless clutch at his throat.

His hand closed on the neck of a leaden carboy. He swung and struck the head of his creature, which slumped to the floor.

Mazirian, not entirely dissatisfied, studied the glistening body at his feet. The spinal coordination had functioned well. At his table he mixed a white potion, and, lifting the golden head, poured the fluid into the lax mouth. The creature stirred, opened its eyes, propped itself on its elbows. The madness had left its face—but Mazirian sought in vain for the glimmer of intelligence. The eyes were as vacant as those of a lizard.

Mazirian shook his head in annoyance. He went to the window and his brooding profile was cut black against the oval panes... Turjan once more? Under the most dire inquiry Turjan had kept his secret close. Mazirian's thin mouth curved wryly. Perhaps if he inserted another angle in the passage...

The sun had gone from the sky and there was dimness in Mazirian's garden. His white night-blossoms opened and their captive gray mouths fluttered from bloom to bloom. Mazirian pulled open the trap in the floor and descended stone stairs. Down, down, down... At last a passage intercepted at right angles, lit with the yellow light of eternal lamps. To the left were his fungus beds, to the right a stout oak and iron door, locked with three locks. Down and ahead the stone steps continued, dropping into blackness.

Mazirian unlocked the three locks, flung wide the door. The room within was bare except for a stone pedestal supporting a glass-topped box. The box measured a yard on a side and was four or five inches high. Within the box—actually a squared passageway, a run with four right angles—moved two small creatures, one seeking, the other evading. The predator was a small dragon with furious red eyes and a monstrous fanged mouth. It waddled along the passage on six splayed legs, twitching its tail as it went. The other stood only half the size of the dragon—a strong-featured man, stark naked, with a copper fillet binding his long black hair. He moved slightly faster than his pursuer, which still kept relentless chase, using a measure of craft, speeding, doubling back, lurking at the angle in case the man should unwarily step around. By holding himself continually alert, the man was able to stay beyond the reach of the fangs. The man was Turjan, whom Mazirian by trickery had captured several weeks before, reduced in size and thus imprisoned.

Mazirian watched with pleasure as the reptile sprang upon the momentarily relaxing man, who jerked himself clear by the thickness of his skin. It was time, Mazirian thought, to give both rest and nourishment. He dropped panels across the passage, separating it into halves, isolating man from beast. To both he gave meat and pannikins of water.

Turjan slumped in the passage.

"Ah," said Mazirian, "you are fatigued. You desire rest?"

Turjan remained silent, his eyes closed. Time and the world had lost meaning for him. The only realities were the gray passage and the interminable flight. At unknown intervals came food and a few hours rest.

"Think of the blue sky," said Mazirian, "the white stars, your castle Miir by the river Derna; think of wandering free in the meadows."

The muscles at Turjan's mouth twitched.

"Consider you might crush the little dragon under your heel."

Turjan looked up. "I would prefer to crush your neck, Mazirian."

Mazirian was unperturbed. "Tell me, how do you invest your vat creatures with intelligence? Speak, and you go free."

Turjan laughed, and there was madness in his laughter.

"Tell you? And then? You would kill me with hot oil in a moment."

Mazirian's thin mouth drooped petulantly.

"Wretched man, I know how to make you speak. If your mouth were stuffed, waxed and sealed, you would speak! Tomorrow I take a nerve from your arm and draw coarse cloth along its length."

The small Turjan, sitting with his legs across the passageway, drank his water and said nothing.

"Tonight," said Mazirian with studied malevolence, "I add an angle and change your run to a pentagon."

Turjan paused and looked up through the glass cover at his enemy. Then he slowly sipped his water. With five angles there would be less time to evade the charge of the monster, less of the hall in view from one angle.

"Tomorrow," said Mazirian, "you will need all your agility." But another matter occurred to him. He eyed Turjan speculatively. "Yet even this I spare you if you assist me with another problem."

"What is your difficulty, febrile Magician?"

"The image of a woman-creature haunts my brain, and I would capture her." Mazirian's eyes went misty at the thought. "Late afternoon she comes to the edge of my garden riding a great black horse—you know her, Turjan?"

"Not I, Mazirian." Turjan sipped his water.

Mazirian continued. "She has sorcery enough to ward away Felojun's Second Hypnotic Spell—or perhaps she has some protective rune. When I approach, she flees into the forest."

"So then?" asked Turjan, nibbling the meat Mazirian had provided.

"Who may this woman be?" demanded Mazirian, peering down his long nose at the tiny captive.

"How can I say?"

"I must capture her," said Mazirian abstractedly: "What spells, what spells?"

Turjan looked up, although he could see the Magician only indistinctly through the cover of glass.

"Release me, Mazirian, and on my word as a Chosen Hierarch of the Maram-Or, I will deliver you this girl."

"How would you do this?" asked the suspicious Mazirian.

"Pursue her into the forest with my best Live Boots and a headful of spells."

"You would fare no better than I," retorted the Magician. "I give you freedom when I know the synthesis of your vat-things. I myself will pursue the woman."

Turjan lowered his head that the Magician might not read his eyes.

"And as for me, Mazirian?" he inquired after a moment.

"I will treat with you when I return."

"And if you do not return?"

Mazirian stroked his chin and smiled, revealing fine white teeth. "The dragon could devour you now, if it were not for your cursed secret."

The Magician climbed the stairs. Midnight found him in his study, poring through leather-bound tomes and untidy portfolios...At one time a thousand or more runes, spells, incantations, curses and sorceries had been known. The reach of Grand Motholam—Ascolais, the Ide of Kauchique, Almery to the South, the Land of the Falling Wall to the East—swarmed with sorcerers of every description, of whom the chief was the Arch-Necromancer Phandaal. A hundred spells Phandaal personally had formulated—though rumor said that demons whispered at his ear when he wrought magic. Pontecilla the Pious, then ruler of Grand Motholam, put Phandaal to torment, and after a terrible night, he killed Phandaal and outlawed sorcery throughout the land. The wizards of Grand Motholam fled like beetles under a strong light; the lore was dispersed and forgotten, until now, at this dim time, with the sun dark, wilderness obscuring Ascolais, and the white city

Kaiin half in ruins, only a few more than a hundred spells remained to the knowledge of man. Of these, Mazirian had access to seventy-three, and gradually, by stratagem and negotiation, was securing the others.

Mazirian made a selection from his books, and with great effort forced five spells upon his brain: Phandaal's Gyrator, Felojun's Second Hypnotic Spell, The Excellent Prismatic Spray, the Charm of Untiring Nourishment, and the Spell of the Omnipotent Sphere. This accomplished, Mazirian drank wine and retired to his couch.

The following day, when the sun hung low, Mazirian went to walk in his garden. He had but short time to wait. As he loosened the earth at the roots of his moon geraniums a soft rustle and stamp told that the object of his desire had appeared.

She sat upright in the saddle, a young woman of exquisite configuration. Mazirian slowly stooped, as not to startle her, put his feet into the Live Boots and secured them above the knee.

He stood up. "Ho, girl," he cried, "you have come again. Why are you here of evenings? Do you admire the roses? They are vividly red because live red blood flows in their petals. If today you do not flee, I will make you the gift of one."

Mazirian plucked a rose from the shuddering bush and advanced toward her, fighting the surge of the Live Boots. He had taken but four steps when the woman dug her knees into the ribs of her mount and so plunged off through the trees.

Mazirian allowed full scope to the life in his boots. They gave a great bound, and another, and another, and he was off in full chase.

So Mazirian entered the forest of fable. On all sides mossy boles twisted up to support the high panoply of leaves. At intervals shafts of sunshine drifted through to lay carmine blots on the turf. In the shade long-stemmed flowers and fragile fungi sprang from the humus; in this ebbing hour of Earth nature was mild and relaxed.

Mazirian in his Live Boots bounded with great speed through

the forest, yet the black horse, running with no strain, stayed easily ahead.

For several leagues the woman rode, her hair flying behind like a pennon. She looked back and Mazirian saw the face over her shoulder as a face in a dream. Then she bent forward; the golden-eyed horse thundered ahead and soon was lost to sight. Mazirian followed by tracing the trail in the sod.

The spring and drive began to leave the Live Boots, for they had come far and at great speed. The monstrous leaps became shorter and heavier, but the strides of the horse, shown by the tracks, were also shorter and slower. Presently Mazirian entered a meadow and saw the horse, riderless, cropping grass. He stopped short. The entire expanse of tender herbiage lay before him. The trail of the horse leading into the glade was clear, but there was no trail leaving. The woman therefore had dismounted somewhere behind—how far he had no means of knowing. He walked toward the horse, but the creature shied and bolted through the trees. Mazirian made one effort to follow, and discovered that his Boots hung lax and flaccid—dead.

He kicked them away, cursing the day and his ill-fortune. Shaking the cloak free behind him, a baleful tension shining on his face, he started back along the trail.

In this section of the forest, outcroppings of black and green rock, basalt and serpentine, were frequent—forerunners of the crags over the River Derna. On one of these rocks Mazirian saw a tiny man-thing mounted on a dragon-fly. He had skin of a greenish cast; he wore a gauzy smock and carried a lance twice his own length.

Mazirian stopped. The Twk-man looked down stolidly.

"Have you seen a woman of my race passing by, Twk-man?"

"I have seen such a woman," responded the Twk-man after a moment of deliberation.

"Where may she be found?"

"What may I expect for the information?"

"Salt—as much as you can bear away."

The Twk-man flourished his lance. "Salt? No. Liane the Wayfarer provides the chieftain Dandanflores salt for all the tribe."

Mazirian could surmise the services for which the bandit-troubadour paid salt. The Twk-men, flying fast on their dragon-flies, saw all that happened in the forest.

"A vial of oil from my telanxis blooms?"

"Good," said the Twk-man. "Show me the vial."

Mazirian did so.

"She left the trail at the lightning-blasted oak lying a little before you. She made directly for the river valley, the shortest route to the lake."

Mazirian laid the vial beside the dragon-fly and went off toward the river oak. The Twk-man watched him go, then dismounted and lashed the vial to the underside of the dragon-fly, next to the skein of fine haft the woman had given him thus to direct Mazirian.

The Magician turned at the oak and soon discovered the trail over the dead leaves. A long open glade lay before him, sloping gently to the river. Trees towered to either side and the long sundown rays steeped one side in blood, left the other deep in black shadow. So deep was the shade that Mazirian did not see the creature seated on a fallen tree; and he sensed it only as it prepared to leap on his back.

Mazirian sprang about to face the thing, which subsided again to sitting posture. It was a Deodand, formed and featured like a handsome man, finely muscled, but with a dead black lusterless skin and long slit eyes.

"Ah, Mazirian, you roam the woods far from home," the black thing's soft voice rose through the glade.

The Deodand, Mazirian knew, craved his body for meat. How had the girl escaped? Her trail led directly past.

"I come seeking, Deodand. Answer my questions, and I undertake to feed you much flesh."

The Deodand's eyes glinted, flitting over Mazirian's body. "You may in any event, Mazirian. Are you with powerful spells today?"

"I am. Tell me, how long has it been since the girl passed? Went she fast, slow, alone or in company? Answer, and I give you meat at such time as you desire."

The Deodand's lips curled mockingly. "Blind Magician! She has not left the glade." He pointed, and Mazirian followed the direction of the dead black arm. But he jumped back as the Deodand sprang. From his mouth gushed the syllables of Phandaal's Gyrator Spell. The Deodand was jerked off his feet and flung high in the air, where he hung whirling, high and low, faster and slower, up to the treetops, low to the ground. Mazirian watched with a half-smile. After a moment he brought the Deodand low and caused the rotations to slacken.

"Will you die quickly or slow?" asked Mazirian. "Help me and I kill you at once. Otherwise you shall rise high where the pelgrane fly."

Fury and fear choked the Deodand.

"May dark Thial spike your eyes! May Kraan hold your living brain in acid!" And it added such charges that Mazirian felt forced to mutter countercurses.

"Up then," said Mazirian at last, with a wave of his hand. The black sprawling body jerked high above the tree-tops to revolve slowly in the crimson bask of setting sun. In a moment a mottled bat-shaped thing with hooked snout swept close and its beak tore the black leg before the crying Deodand could kick it away. Another and another of the shapes flitted across the sun.

"Down, Mazirian!" came the faint call. "I tell what I know."

Mazirian brought him close to earth.

"She passed alone before you came. I made to attack her but she repelled me with a handful of thyle-dust. She went to the end of the glade and took the trail to the river. This trail leads also past the lair of Thrang. So is she lost, for he will sate himself on her till she dies."

Mazirian rubbed his chin. "Had she spells with her?"

"I know not. She will need strong magic to escape the demon Thrang."

"Is there anything else to tell?"

"Nothing."

"Then you may die." And Mazirian caused the creature to revolve at ever greater speed, faster and faster, until there was only a blur. A strangled, wailing came and presently the Deodand's frame parted. The head shot like a bullet far down the glade; arms, legs, viscera flew in all directions.

Mazirian went his way. At the end of the glade the trail led steeply down ledges of dark green serpentine to the River Derna. The sun had set and shade filled the valley. Mazirian gained the riverside and set off downstream toward a far shimmer known as Sanra Water, the Lake of Dreams.

An evil odor came to the air, a stink of putrescence and filth. Mazirian went ahead more cautiously, for the lair of Thrang the ghoul-bear was near, and in the air was the feel of magic—strong brutal sorcery his own more subtle spells might not contain.

The sound of voices reached him, the throaty tones of Thrang and gasping cries of terror. Mazirian stepped around a shoulder of rock, inspected the origin of the sounds.

Thrang's lair was an alcove in the rock, where a fetid pile of grass and skins served him for a couch. He had built a rude pen to cage three women, these wearing many bruises on their bodies and the effects of much horror on their faces. Thrang had taken them from the tribe that dwelt in silk-hung barges along the lake-shore. Now they watched as he struggled to subdue the woman he had just captured. His round gray man's face was contorted and he tore away her jerkin with his human hands. But she held away the great sweating body with an amazing dexterity. Mazirian's eyes narrowed. Magic, magic!

So he stood watching, considering how to destroy Thrang with no harm to the woman. But she spied him over Thrang's shoulder.

"See," she panted, "Mazirian has come to kill you."

Thrang twisted about. He saw Mazirian and came charging on all fours, venting roars of wild passion. Mazirian later wondered if the ghoul had cast some sort of spell, for a strange paralysis strove to bind his brain. Perhaps the spell lay in the sight of Thrang's raging graywhite face, the great arms thrust out to grasp.

Mazirian shook off the spell, if such it were, and uttered a spell of his own, and all the valley was lit by streaming darts of fire, lashing in from all directions to split Thrang's blundering body in a thousand places. This was the Excellent Prismatic Spray—many-colored, stabbing lines. Thrang was dead almost at once, purple blood flowing from countless holes where the radiant rain had pierced him.

But Mazirian heeded little. The girl had fled. Mazirian saw her white form running along the river toward the lake, and took up the chase, heedless of the piteous cries of the three women in the pen.

The lake presently lay before him, a great sheet of water whose further rim was but dimly visible. Mazirian came down to the sandy shore and stood seeking across the dark face of Sanra Water, the Lake of Dreams, Deep night with only a verge of afterglow ruled the sky, and stars glistened on the smooth surface. The water lay cool and still, tideless as all Earth's waters had been since the moon had departed the sky.

Where was the woman? There, a pale white form, quiet in the shadow across the river. Mazirian stood on the riverbank, tall and commanding, a light breeze ruffling the cloak around his legs.

"Ho, girl," he called. "It is I, Mazirian, who saved you from Thrang. Come close, that I may speak to you."

"At this distance I hear you well, Magician," she replied. "The closer I approach the farther I must flee."

"Why then do you flee? Return with me and you shall be mistress of many secrets and hold much power."

She laughed. "If I wanted these, Mazirian, would I have fled so far?"

"Who are you then that you desire not the secrets of magic?"

"To you, Mazirian, I am nameless, lest you curse me. Now I go where you may not come." She ran down the shore, waded slowly out till the water circled her waist, then sank out of sight. She was gone.

Mazirian paused indecisively. It was not good to use so many spells and thus shear himself of power. What might exist below the lake? The sense of quiet magic was there, and though he was not at enmity with the Lake Lord, other beings might resent a trespass. However, when the figure of the girl did not break the surface, he uttered the Charm of Untiring Nourishment and entered the cool waters.

He plunged deep through the Lake of Dreams, and as he stood on the bottom, his lungs at ease by virtue of the charm, he marveled at the fey place he had come upon. Instead of blackness a green light glowed everywhere and the water was but little less clear than air. Plants undulated to the current and with them moved the lake flowers, soft with blossoms of red, blue and yellow. In and out swam large-eyed fish of many shapes.

The bottom dropped by rocky steps to a wide plain where trees of the underlake floated up from slender stalks to elaborate fronds and purple water-fruits, and so till the misty wet distance veiled all. He saw the woman, a white water nymph now, her hair like dark fog. She half-swam, half-ran across the sandy floor of the water-world, occasionally looking back over her shoulder. Mazirian came after, his cloak streaming out behind.

He drew nearer to her, exulting. He must punish her for leading him so far... The ancient stone stairs below his workroom led deep and at last opened into chambers that grew ever vaster as one went deeper. Mazirian had found a rusted cage in one of these chambers. A week or two locked in the blackness would curb her willfulness. And once he had dwindled a woman small as his thumb and kept her in a little glass bottle with two buzzing flies...

A ruined white temple showed through the green. There were many columns, some toppled, some still upholding the pediment. The woman entered the great portico under the shadow of the architrave. Perhaps she was attempting to elude him; he must follow closely. The white body glimmered at the far end of the nave, swimming now over the rostrum and into a semicircular alcove behind.

Mazirian followed as fast as he was able, half-swimming, half-walking through the solemn dimness. He peered across the murk. Smaller columns here precariously upheld a dome from which the keystone had dropped. A sudden fear smote him, then realization as he saw the flash of movement from above. On all sides the columns toppled in, and an avalanche of marble blocks tumbled at his head. He jumped frantically back.

The commotion ceased, the white dust of the ancient mortar drifted away. On the pediment of the main temple the women kneeled on slender knees, staring down to see how well she had killed Mazirian.

She had failed. Two columns, by sheerest luck, had crashed to either side of him, and a slab had protected his body from the blocks. He moved his head painfully. Through a chink in the tumbled marble he could see the woman, leaning to discern his body. So she would kill him? He, Mazirian, who had already lived more years than he could easily reckon? So much more would she hate and fear him later. He called his charm, the Spell of the Omnipotent Sphere. A film of force formed around his body, expanding to push aside all that resisted. When the marble ruins had been thrust back, he destroyed the sphere, regained his feet, and glared about for the woman. She was almost out of sight, behind a brake of long purple kelp, climbing the slope to the shore. With all his power he set out in pursuit.

* * *

T'sain dragged herself up on the beach. Still behind her came Mazirian the Magician, whose power had defeated each of her plans. The memory of his face passed before her and she shivered. He must not take her now.

Fatigue and despair slowed her feet. She had set out with but two spells, the Charm of Untiring Nourishment and a spell affording strength to her arms—the last permitting her to hold off Thrang and tumble the temple upon Mazirian. These were exhausted; she was bare of protection; but, on the other hand, Mazirian could have nothing left.

Perhaps he was ignorant of the vampire-weed. She ran up the slope and stood behind a patch of pale, wind-beaten grass. And now Mazirian came from the lake, a spare form visible against the shimmer of the water.

She retreated, keeping the innocent patch of grass between them. If the grass failed—her mind quailed at the thought of what she must do.

Mazirian strode into the grass. The sickly blades became sinewy fingers. They twined about his ankles, holding him in an unbreakable grip, while others sought to find his skin.

So Mazirian chanted his last spell—the incantation of paralysis, and the vampire grass grew lax and slid limply to earth. T'sain watched with dead hope. He was now close upon her, his cloak flapping behind. Had he no weakness? Did not his fibers ache, did not his breath come short? She whirled and fled across the meadow, toward a grove of black trees. Her skin chilled at the deep shadows, the somber frames. But the thud of the Magician's feet was loud. She plunged into the dread shade. Before all in the grove awoke she must go as far as possible.

Snap! A thong lashed at her. She continued to run. Another and another—she fell. Another great whip and another beat at her. She staggered up, and on, holding her arms before her face. Sna-- Snap! The flails whistled through the air, and the last blow twisted her around. So she saw Mazirian.

He fought. As the blows rained on him, he tried to seize the whips and break them. But they were supple and springy beyond his powers, and jerked away to beat at him again. Infuriated by his resistance, they concentrated on the unfortunate Magician, who foamed and fought with transcendent fury, and T'sain was permitted to crawl to the edge of the grove with her life.

She looked back in awe at the expression of Mazirian's lust for life. He staggered about in a cloud of whips, his furious obstinate figure dimly silhouetted. He weakened and tried to flee, and then he fell. The blows pelted at him—on his head, shoulders, the long legs. He tried to rise but fell back.

T'sain closed her eyes in lassitude. She felt the blood oozing from her broken flesh. But the most vital mission yet remained. She reached her feet, and reelingly set forth. For a long time the thunder of many blows reached her ears.

Mazirian's garden was surpassingly beautiful by night. The star-blossoms spread wide, each of magic perfection, and the captive half-vegetable moths flew back and forth. Phosphorescent water-lillies floated like charming faces on the pond and the bush which Mazirian had brought from far Almery in the south tinctured the air with sweet fruity perfume.

T'sain, weaving and gasping, now came groping through the garden. Certain of the flowers awoke and regarded her curiously. The half-animal hybrid sleepily chittered at her, thinking to recognize Mazirian's step. Faintly to be heard was the wistful music of the blue-cupped flowers singing of ancient nights when a white moon swam the sky, the great storms and clouds and thunder ruled the seasons.

T'sain passed unheeding. She entered Mazirian's house, found the workroom where glowed the eternal yellow lamps. Mazirian's golden-haired vat-thing sat up suddenly and stared at her with his beautiful vacant eyes.

She found Mazirian's keys in the cabinet, and managed to claw open the trap door. Here she slumped to rest and let the pink gloom pass from her eyes. Visions began to come—Mazirian, tall and arrogant, stepping out to kill Thrang; the strange-hued flowers under the lake; Mazirian, his magic lost, fighting the whips...She was brought from the half-trance by the vat-thing timidly fumbling with her hair.

She shook herself awake, and half-walked, half-fell down the stairs. She unlocked the thrice-bound door, thrust it open with almost the last desperate urge of her body. She wandered in to clutch at the pedestal where the glass-topped box stood and Turjan and the dragon were playing their desperate game. She flung the glass crashing to the floor, gently lifted Turjan out and set him down.

The spell was disrupted by the touch of the rune at her wrist, and Turjan became a man again. He looked aghast at the nearly unrecognizable T'sain.

She tried to smile up at him.

"Turjan—you are free—"

"And Mazirian?"

"He is dead." She slumped wearily to the stone floor and lay limp. Turjan surveyed her with an odd emotion in his eyes.

"T'sain, dear creature of my mind," he whispered, "more noble are you than I, who used the only life you knew for my freedom."

He lifted her body in his arms.

"But I shall restore you to the vats. With your brain I build another T'sain, as lovely as you. We go."

He bore her up the stone stairs.

O Ugly Bird!

by MANLY WADE WELLMAN

I SWEAR I'm licked before I start, trying to tell you all what Mr. Onselm looked like. Words give out—for instance, you're frozen to death for fit words to tell the favor of the girl you love. And Mr. Onselm and I pure poison hated each other. That's how love and hate are alike.

He was what country folks call a low man, more than calling him short or small; a low man is low otherwise than by inches. Mr. Onselm's shoulders didn't wide out as far as his big ears, and they sank and sagged. His thin legs bowed in at the knee and out at the shank, like two sickles point to point. On his carrot-thin neck, his head looked like a swollen pale gourd. Thin, moss-gray hair. Loose mouth, a bit open to show long, even teeth. Not much chin. The right eye squinted, mean and dark, while the hike of his brow twitched the left one wide. His good clothes fitted his mean body like they were cut to it. Those good clothes were almost as much out of match to the rest of him as his long, soft, pink hands, the hands of a man who never had to work a tap.

You see what I mean, I can't say how he looked, only he was hateful.

I first met him when I came down from the high mountain's comb, along an animal trail—maybe a deer made it. Through the trees I saw, here and there in the valley below, patch-places and cabins and yards. I hoped I'd get fed at one of them, for I'd run clear out of eating some spell back. I had no money. Only my hickory shirt and blue duckin pants and torn old army shoes, and my guitar on its sling cord. But I knew the mountain folks. If they've got ary thing to eat, a decent spoken stranger can get the half part of it. Towns aren't always the same way.

Downslope I picked, favoring the guitar in case I slipped and fell, and in an hour made it to the first patch. Early fall was browning the corn out of the green. The cabin was two-room, dog-trotted open in the middle. Beyond was a shed and a pigpen. In the yard the man of the house talked to who I found out later was Mr. Onselm.

"No meat at all?" said Mr. Onselm. His voice was the last you'd expect him to have, full of broad low music, like an organ in a town church. I decided against asking him to sing when I glimpsed him closer, sickle-legged and gourd-headed and pale and puny in his fine-fitting clothes. For he looked mad and dangerous; and the man of the place, though he was a big, strong old gentleman with a square jaw, looked afraid.

"I been short this year, Mr. Onselm," he said, begging like. "The last bit of meat I fished out of the brine on Tuesday. And I don't want to have to kill the pig till December."

Mr. Onselm tramped over to the pen. The pig was a friendly one, it reared its front feet against the boards and grunted up to him. Mr. Onselm spit into the pen. "All right," he said, "but I want some meal."

He sickle-legged back to the cabin. A brown barrel stood in the dog trot. Mr. Onselm lifted the cover and pinched some meal between his pink fingertips. "Get me a sack," he told the man.

The man went indoors and brought out the sack. Mr. Onselm held it open while the man scooped out meal enough to fill it. Then Mr. Onselm held it tight shut while the man lashed the neck with twine. Finally Mr. Onselm looked up and saw me standing there.

"Who are you?" he asked, sort of crooning.

"My name's John," I said.

"John what?" Then, without waiting for my answer, "Where did you steal that guitar?"

"It was given to me," I replied. "I strung it with silver wires myself."

"Silver," he said, and opened his squint eye by a trifle.

With my left hand I clamped a chord. With my right thumb I picked a whisper from the silver strings. I began to make a song:

Mister Onselm,
They do what you tell 'em—

"That will do," said Mr. Onselm, not so musically, and I stopped playing. He relaxed. "They do what I tell 'em," he said, half to himself. "Not bad."

We studied each other a few ticks of time. Then he turned and tramped out of the yard in among the trees. When he was out of sight the man of the place asked, right friendly, what he could do for me.

"I'm just walking through," I said. I didn't want to ask right off for some dinner.

"I heard you name yourself John," he said. "So happens my name's John too, John Bristow."

"Nice place you've got," I said, looking around. "Cropper or tenant?"

"I own the house and the land," he told me, and I was surprised; for Mr. Onselm had treated him the way a mean boss treats a cropper.

"Then that Mr. Onselm was just a visitor," I said.

"Visitor?" Mr. Bristow snorted. "He visits everybody here

around. Lets them know what he wants, and they pass it to him. Thought you knew him, you sang about him so ready."

"Shucks, I made that up." I touched the silver strings again. "I sing a many a new song that comes to me."

"I love the old songs better," he said, and smiled, so I sang one:

I had been in Georgia
Not a many more weeks than three,
When I fell in love with a pretty fair girl,
And she fell in love with me.

Her lips were red as red could be,
Her eyes were brown as brown,
Her hair was like the thundercloud
Before the rain comes down.

You should have seen Mr. Bristow's face shine. He said: "By God, you sure enough can sing it and play it."

"Do my possible best," I said. "But Mr. Onselm don't like it." I thought a moment, then asked: "What way can he get everything he wants in this valley?"

"Shoo, can't tell you way. Just done it for years, he has."

"Anybody refuse him?"

"Once Old Jim Desbro refused him a chicken. Mr. Onselm pointed his finger at Old Jim's mules, they was plowing. Them mules couldn't move ary foot, not till Mr. Onselm had the chicken. Another time, Miss Tilly Parmer hid a cake when she seen him come. He pointed a finger and dumbed her. She never spoke one mumbling word from that day to when she died. Could hear and understand, but when she tried to talk she could just wheeze."

"He's a hoodoo man," I said, "which means the law can't do anything."

"Not even if the law worried about anything this far from the county seat." He looked at the meal back against the cabin.

"About time for the Ugly Bird to fetch Mr. Onselm's meal."

"What's the Ugly Bird?" I asked, but he didn't have to answer.

It must have hung over us, high and quiet, and now it dropped into the yard like a fish hawk into a pond.

First out I saw it was dark, heavy-winged, bigger than a buzzard. Then I saw the shiny gray-black of the body, like wet slate, and how it seemed to have feathers only on its wide wings. Then I made out the thin snaky neck, the bulgy head and long stork beak, the eyes set in front of its head—man-fashion in front, not to each side.

The feet that taloned onto the sack showed pink and smooth with five graspy toes. The wings snapped like a tablecloth in a wind, and it churned away over the trees with the meal sack.

"That's the Ugly Bird," said Mr. Bristow. I barely heard him. "Mr. Onselm has companioned with it ever since I recollect."

"I never saw such a bird," I said, "Must be a scarce one. You know what struck me while I watched it?"

"I do know, John. Its feet look like Mr. Onselm's hands."

"Might it be," I asked, "that a hoodoo man like Mr. Onselm knows what way to shape himself into a bird?"

He shook his head. "It's known that when he's at one place, the Ugly Bird's been sighted at another." He tried to change the subject. "Silver strings on your guitar—never heard of any but steel strings."

"In the olden days," I told him, "silver was used a many times for strings. It gives a more singy sound."

In my mind I had it the subject wouldn't be changed. I tried a chord on my guitar, and began to sing:

You all have heard of the Ugly Bird
So curious and so queer,
That flies its flight by day and night
And fills folks' hearts with fear.

I never come here to hide from fear,
And I give you my promised word

That I soon expect to twist the neck
Of the God damn Ugly Bird.

When I finished, Mr. Bristow felt in his pocket.

"I was going to bid you eat with me," he said, "but—here, maybe you better buy something."

He gave me a quarter and a dime. I about gave them back, but I thanked him and walked away down the same trail Mr. Onselm had gone. Mr. Bristow watched me go, looking shrunk up. My song had scared him, so I kept singing it.

O Ugly Bird! O Ugly Bird!
You snoop and sneak and thieve!
This place can't be for you and me,
And one of us got to leave.

Singing, I tried to remember all I'd heard or read or guessed that might help toward my Ugly Bird study.

Didn't witch people have partner animals? I'd read and heard tell about the animals called familiars—mostly cats or black dogs or the like, but sometimes birds.

That might be the secret, or a right much of it, for the Ugly Bird wasn't Mr. Onselm's other self. Mr. Bristow had said the two of them were seen different places at one time. Mr. Onselm didn't turn into the Ugly Bird then. They were just close partners. Brothers. With the Ugly Bird's feet like Mr. Onselm's hands.

I awared of something in the sky, the big black V of a flying creature. It quartered over me, half as high as the highest woolly scrap of cloud. Once or twice it seemed like it would stoop for me, like a hawk, for a rabbit, but it didn't. Looking up and letting my feet find the trail, I rounded a bunch of bushes and there, on a rotten log in a clearing, sat Mr. Onselm.

His gourd-head sank on his thin neck. His elbows set on his knees, and the soft, pink, long hands hid his face, as if he was miserable. His look made me feel disgusted. I came toward him.

"You don't feel so brash, do you?" I asked.

"Go away," he sort of gulped, soft and sick.

"Why?" I wanted to know. "I like it here." Sitting on the log, I pulled my guitar across me. "I feel like singing, Mr. Onselm."

> *His father got hung for horse stealing,*
> *His mother got burned for a witch,*
> *And his only friend is the Ugly Bird,*
> *The dirty son of—*

Something hit me like a shooting star from overhead.

It hit my back and shoulder, and knocked me floundering forward on one hand ond one knee. It was only the mercy of God I didn't fall on my guitar and smash it. I crawled forward a few scrambles and made to get up, shaky and dizzy.

The Ugly Bird had flown down and dropped the sack of meal on me. Now it skimmed across the clearing, at the height of the low branches, its eyes glinting at me, and its mouth came open a little. I saw teeth, sharp and mean, like a garpike's teeth. It swooped for me, and the wind of its wings was colder than a winter storm.

Without stopping to think, I flung up my both hands to box it off from me, and it gave back, flew backwards like the biggest, devilishest humming bird ever seen in a nightmare. I was too dizzy and scared to wonder why it gave back; I had barely the wit to be thankful.

"Get out of here," moaned Mr. Onselm, who hadn't stirred.

I shame to say that I got. I kept my hands up and backed across the clearing and into the trail beyond. Then I half realized where my luck had been. My hands had lifted the guitar toward the Ugly Bird, and somehow it hadn't liked the guitar.

Just once I looked back. The Ugly Bird was perching on the log and it sort of nuzzled up to Mr. Onselm, most horrible. They were sure enough close together. I stumbled off away.

I found a stream, with stones to make steps across. I turned and walked down to where it made a wide pool. There I knelt and washed my face—it looked pallid in the water image—and sat with my back to a tree and hugged my guitar and rested. I shook all over. I must have felt as bad for a while as Mr. Onselm looked like he felt, sitting on the log waiting for his Ugly Bird and—what else?

Had he been hungry? Sick? Or just evil? I couldn't say which.

After a while I walked back to the trail and along it again, till I came to what must have been the only store thereabouts.

It faced one way on a rough road that could carry wagon and car traffic, and the trail joined on and reached the door. The building wasn't big but it was good, made of sawed planks well painted. It rested on big rocks instead of posts; and had a roofed open front like a porch, with a bench where people could sit.

Opening the door, I went in. You'll find a many such stores in back country places through the land. Counters. Shelves of cans and packages. Smoked meat hung one corner, a glass-front icebox for fresh meat another. One point, sign says U. S. POST OFFICE, with half a dozen pigeonholes for letters and a couple of cigar boxes for stamps and money-order blanks. The proprietor wasn't in. Only a girl, scared and shaking, and Mr. Onselm, there ahead of me, telling her what he wanted.

He wanted her.

"I don't care if Sam Heaver did leave you in charge here," he said with the music in his voice. "He won't stop my taking you with me."

Then he swung around and fixed his squint eye and wide open eye on me, like two mismated gun muzzles. "You again," he said.

He looked hale and hearty. I strayed my hands over the guitar strings, and he twisted up his face as if it colicked him.

"Winnie, he said to the girl, "wait on him and get him out of here."

Her eyes were round in her scared face. I never saw as sweet a face as hers, or as scared. Her hair was dark and thick. It was like the thundercloud before the rain comes down. It made her paleness look paler. She was small, and she cowered for fear of Mr. Onselm.

"Yes sir?" she said to me.

"Box of crackers," I decided, pointing to a near shelf. "And a can of those sardine fish."

She put them on the counter. I dug out the quarter Mr. Bristow had given me, and slapped it down on the counter top between the girl and Mr. Onselm.

"Get away!" he squeaked, shrill and mean as a bat. He had jumped back, almost halfway across the floor. And for once both of his eyes were big.

"What's the matter?" I asked him, purely wondering. "This is a good silver quarter." And I picked it up and held it out for him to take and study.

But he ran out of the store like a rabbit. A rabbit with the dogs after it.

The girl he'd called Winnie just leaned against the wall as if she was tired. I asked: "Why did he light out like that?"

She took the quarter. "It doesn't scare me much," she said, and rung it up on the old cash register. "All that scares me is—Mr. Onselm."

I picked up the crackers and sardines. "He's courting you?"

She shuddered, though it was warm. "I'd sooner be in a hole with a snake than be courted by Mr. Onselm."

"Why not just tell him to leave you be?"

"He'd not listen. He always does what pleases him. Nobody dares stop him."

"I know, I heard about the mules he stopped and the poor lady he dumbed." I returned to the other subject. "Why did he squinch away from money? I'd reckon he loved money."

She shook her head. The thundercloud hair stirred. "He never needs any. Takes what he wants without paying."

"Including you?"

"Not including me yet. But he'll do that later."

I laid down my dime I had left. "Let's have a coke drink, you and me."

She rang up the dime too. There was a sort of dry chuckle at the door, like a stone rattling down the well. I looked quick, and saw two long, dark wings flop away from the door. The Ugly Bird had spied.

But the girl Winnie smiled over her coke drink. I asked permission to open my fish and crackers on the bench outside. She nodded yes. Out there, I worried open the can with my pocket knife and had my meal. When I finished I put the trash in a garbage barrel and tuned my guitar. Winnie came out and harked while I sang about the girl whose hair was like the thundercloud before the rain comes down, and she blushed till she was pale no more.

Then we talked about Mr. Onselm and the Ugly Bird, and how they had been seen in two different places at once—

"But," said Winnie, "who's seen them together?"

"Shoo, I have," I told her. "Not long ago." And I told how Mr. Onselm sat, all sick and miserable, and the conjer bird crowded up against him.

She heard all that, with eyes staring off, as if looking for something far away. Finally she said, "John, you say it crowded up to him."

"It did that thing, as if it studied to get right inside him."

"Inside him!"

"That's right."

"Makes me think of something I heard somebody say about hoodoo folks," she said. "How the hoodoo folk sometimes put a stuff out, mostly in dark rooms. And it's part of them, but it takes the shape and mind of another person—once in a while, the shape and mind of an animal."

"Shoo," I said again, "now you mention it, I've heard the same thing. It might explain those Louisiana stories about werewolves."

"Shape and mind of an animal," she repeated herself. "Maybe the shape and mind of a bird. And they call it echo—no, ecto—ecto—"

"Ectoplasm," I remembered. "That's right. I've even seen

pictures they say were taken of such stuff. It seems to live—it'll yell, if you grab it or hit it or stab it."

"Could maybe—" she began, but a musical voice interrupted.

"He's been around here long enough," said Mr. Onselm.

He was back. With him were three men. Mr. Bristow, and a tall, gawky man with splay shoulders and a black-stubbled chin, and a soft, smooth-grizzled man with an old fancy vest over his white shirt.

Mr. Onselm acted like the leader of a posse. "Sam Heaver," he crooned at the soft, grizzled one, "can tramps loaf at your store?"

The soft old storekeeper looked dead and gloomy at me. "Better get going, son," he said, as if he'd memorized it.

I laid my guitar on the bench. "You men ail my stomach," I said, looking at them. "You let this half-born, half-bred hoodoo man sic you on me like hound dogs when I'm hurting nobody and nothing."

"Better go," he said again.

I faced Mr. Onselm, and he laughed like a sweetly played horn. "You," he said, "without a dime in your pocket! You can't do anything to anybody."

Without a dime...the Ugly Bird had seen me spend my silver money, the silver money that ailed Mr. Onselm.

"Take his guitar, Hobe," said Mr. Onselm, and the gawky man, clumsy but quick, grabbed the guitar from the bench and backed away to the door.

"That takes care of him," Mr. Onselm sort of purred, and he fairly jumped and grabbed Winnie by the wrist. He pulled her along toward the trail, and I heard her whimper.

"Stop him!" I bawled, but they stood and looked, scared and dumb. Mr. Onselm, still holding Winnie, faced me. He lifted his free hand, with the pink forefinger sticking out like the barrel of a pistol.

Just the look he gave me made me weary and dizzy. He was

going to hoodoo me, like he'd done the mules, like he'd done the woman who tried to hide her cake from him. I turned from him, sick and afraid, and I heard him giggle, thinking he'd won already. In the doorway stood the gawky man called Hobe, with the guitar.

I made a long jump at him and started to wrestle it away from him.

"Hang onto it, Hobe," I heard Mr. Onselm sort of choke out, and, from Mr. Bristow:

"There's the Ugly Bird!"

Its wings flapped like a storm in the air behind me. But I'd torn my guitar from Hobe's hands and turned on my heel.

A little way off, Mr. Onselm stood stiff and straight as a stone figure in front of a courthouse. He still held Winnie's wrist. Between them the Ugly Bird came swooping at me, its beak pointing for me like a stabbing bayonet.

I dug in my toes and smashed the guitar at it. Full-slam I struck its bulgy head above the beak and across the eyes, and I heard the polished wood of my music-maker crash to splinters.

And down went the Ugly Bird!

Down it went.

Quiet it lay.

Its great big wings stretched out on either side, without a flutter. Its beak was driven into the ground like a nail. It didn't kick or flop or stir once.

But Mr. Onselm, standing where he stood holding Winnie, screamed out the way you might scream if something had clawed out all your insides with a single tearing grab.

He didn't move, I don't even know if his mouth came open. Winnie gave a pull with all her strength and tottered back, clear of him. And as if only his hold on her had kept him standing, Mr. Onselm slapped over and down on his face, his arms flung out like the Ugly Bird's wings, his face in the dirt like the Ugly Bird's face.

Still holding my broken guitar by the neck like a club, I ran to him and stooped. "Get up," I said, and took hold of what hair he had and lifted his face up.

One look was enough. From the war, I know a dead man when I see one. I let go his hair, and his face went back into the dirt as if it belonged there.

The others moved at last, tottering a few steps closer. And they didn't act like enemies now, for Mr. Onselm who had made them act so was down and dead.

Then Hobe gave a scared shout, and we looked that way.

The Ugly Bird all of a sudden looked rotten mushy, and was soaking, into the ground. To me, anyhow it looked shadowy and misty, and I could see through it. I wanted to move close, then I didn't want to. It was melting away like snow on top of a stove; only no wetness left behind.

It was gone, while we watched and wondered and felt bad all over.

Mr. Bristow knelt and turned Mr. Onselm over. On the dead face ran sick lines across, thin and purple, as though he'd been struck down by a blow of a toaster or a gridiron.

"The guitar strings," said Mr. Bristow. "The silver guitar strings. It finished him, like any hoodoo man."

That was it. Won't a silver bullet kill a witch, or a silver knife a witch's cat? And a silver key locks out ghosts, doesn't it?

"What was the word you said?" whispered Winnie to me.

"Ectoplasm," I told her. "Like his soul coming out—and getting struck dead outside his body."

More important was talk about what to do now. The men decided. They allowed to report to the county seat that Mr. Onselm's heart had stopped on him, which it had. They went over the tale three or four times to make sure they'd all tell it the same. They cheered up as they talked. You never saw gladder people to get rid of a neighbor.

"And, John," said Mr. Bristow, "we'd sure enough be proud if you stayed here. You took this curse off us."

Hobe wanted me to come live on his farm and help him work it on shares. Sam Heaver offered me all the money out of his old cash register. I thanked him and said no, sir, to Hobe I said thank you kindly, I'd better not. If they wanted their story to stick with the sheriff, they'd better forget that I'd been around when Mr. Onselm's heart stopped. All I was sorry for was my broken guitar.

But while we'd talked, Mr. Bristow was gone. He came back, with a guitar from his place, and he acted honored if I'd take it in place of mine. So I tightened my silver strings on it and tried a chord or two.

Winnie swore she'd pray for me by name each night of her life, and I told her that would sure see me safe from any assaults of the devil.

"Assaults of the devil, John!" she said, almost shrill in the voice, she was so earnest. "It's you who drove the devil from this valley."

The others all said they agreed on that.

"It was foretold about you in the Bible," said Winnie, her voice soft again. "There was a man sent from God, whose name was John."

But that was far too much for her to say, and I was that abashed, I said goodbye all around in a hurry. I strummed my new guitar as I walked away, until I got an old song back in my mind. I've heard tell that the song's written in an old-time book called *Percy's Frolics,* or *Relics,* or something:

> *Lady, I never loved witchcraft,*
> *Never dealt in privy wile,*
> *But evermore held the high way*
> *Of love and honor, free from guile....*

And though I couldn't bring myself to look back to the place I was leaving forever, I knew that Winnie watched me, and that she listened, listened, till she had to strain her ears to catch the last, faintest end of my song.

The Silken Swift

by THEODORE STURGEON

THERE'S A village by the Bogs, and in the village is a Great House. In the Great House lived a squire who had land and treasures and, for a daughter, Rita.

In the village lived Del, whose voice was a thunder in the inn when he drank there; whose corded, cabled body was golden-skinned, and whose hair flung challenges back to the sun.

Deep in the Bogs, which were brackish, there was a pool of purest water, shaded by willows and wide-wondering aspen, cupped by banks of a moss most marvellously blue. Here grew mandrake, and there were strange pipings in mid-summer. No one ever heard them but a quiet girl whose beauty was so very contained that none of it showed. Her name was Barbara.

There was a green evening, breathless with growth, when Del took his usual way down the lane beside the manor and saw a white shadow adrift inside the tall iron pickets. He stopped, and the shadow approached, and became Rita. "Slip around to the gate," she said, "and I'll open it for you."

She wore a gown like a cloud and a silver circlet round her

head. Night was caught in her hair, moonlight in her face, and in her great eyes, secrets swam.

Del said, "I have no business with the squire."

"He's gone," she said. "I've sent the servants away. Come to the gate."

"I need no gate." He leaped and caught the top bar of the fence, and in a continuous fluid motion went high and across and down beside her. She looked at his arms, one, the other; then up at his hair. She pressed her small hands tight together and made a little laugh, and then she was gone through the tailored trees, lightly, swiftly, not looking back. He followed, one step for three of hers, keeping pace with a new pounding in the sides of his neck. They crossed a flower bed and a wide marble terrace. There was an open door, and when he passed through it he stopped, for she was nowhere in sight. Then the door clicked shut behind him and he whirled. She was there, her back to the panel, laughing up at him in the dimness. He thought she would come to him then, but instead she twisted by, close, her eyes on his. She smelt of violets and sandalwood. He followed her into the great hall, quite dark but full of the subdued lights of polished wood, cloisonné, tooled leather and gold-threaded tapestry. She flung open another door, and they were in a small room with a carpet made of rosy silences, and a candle-lit table. Two places were set, each with five different crystal glasses and old silver as prodigally used as the iron pickets outside. Six teakwood steps rose to a great oval window. "The moon," she said, "will rise for us there."

She motioned him to a chair and crossed to a sideboard, where there was a rack of decanters—ruby wine and white; one with a strange brown bead; pink, and amber. She took down the first and poured. Then she lifted the silver domes from the salvers on the table, and a magic of fragrance filled the air. There were smoking sweets and savories, rare seafood and slivers of fowl, and morsels of strange meat wrapped in flower petals, spitted with foreign fruits and tiny soft seashells.

All about were spices, each like a separate voice in the distant murmur of a crowd: saffron and sesame, cumin and marjoram and mace.

And all the while Del watched her in wonder, seeing how the candles left the moonlight on her face, and how completely she trusted her hands, which did such deftness without supervision—so composed she was, for all the silent secret laughter that tugged at her lips, for all the bright dark mysteries that swirled and swam within her.

They ate, and the oval window yellowed and darkened while the candlelight grew bright. She poured another wine, and another, and with the courses of the meal they were as May to the crocus and as frost to the apple.

Del knew it was alchemy and he yielded to it without questions. That which was purposely over-sweet would be piquantly cut; this induced thirst would, with exquisite timing, be quenched. He knew she was watching him; he knew she was aware of the heat in his cheeks and the tingle at his fingertips. His wonder grew, but he was not afraid.

In all this time she spoke hardly a word; but at last the feast was over and they rose. She touched a silken rope on the wall, and panelling slid aside. The table rolled silently into some ingenious recess and the panel returned. The waved him to an L-shaped couch in one corner, and as he sat close to her, she turned and took down the lute which hung on the wall behind her. He had his moment of confusion; his arms were ready for her, but not for the instrument as well. Her eyes sparkled, but her composure was unshaken.

Now she spoke, while her fingers strolled and danced on the lute, and her words marched and wandered in and about the music. She had a thousand voices, so that he wondered which of them was truly hers. Sometimes she sang; sometimes it was a wordless crooning. She seemed at times remote from him, puzzled at the turn the music was taking, and at other times she seemed to hear the pulsing roar in his eardrums, and she played laughing syncopations to it. She sang words which he almost understood:

Bee to blossom, honey dew,
Claw to mouse, and rain to tree,
Moon to midnight, I to you;
Sun to starlight, you to me...

and she sang something wordless:

Ake ya rundefle, rundefle fye,
Orel ya rundefle kown,
En yea, en yea ya bunderbee bye
En sor, en see, en sown.

which he also almost understood.

In still another voice she told him the story of a great hairy spider and a little pink girl who found it between the leaves of a half-open book; and at first he was all fright and pity for the girl, but then she went on to tell of what the spider suffered, with his home disrupted by this yawping giant, and so vividly did she tell of it that at the end he was laughing at himself and all but crying for the poor spider.

So the hours slipped by, and suddenly, between songs, she was in his arms; and in the instant she had twisted up and away from him, leaving him gasping. She said, in still a new voice, sober and low, "No, Del. We must wait for the moon."

His thighs ached and he realized that he had half-risen, arms out, hands clutching and feeling the extraordinary fabric of her gown though it was gone from them; and he sank back to the couch with an odd, faint sound that was wrong for the room. He flexed his fingers and, reluctantly, the sensation of white gossamer left them. At last he looked across at her and she laughed and leapt high lightly, and it was as if she stopped in midair to stretch for a moment before she alighted beside him, bent and kissed his mouth, and leapt away.

The roaring in his ears was greater, and at this it seemed

to acquire a tangible weight. His head bowed; he tucked his knuckles into the upper curve of his eye sockets and rested his elbows on his knees. He could hear the sweet susurrus of Rita's gown as she moved about the room; he could sense the violets and sandalwood. She was dancing, immersed in the joy of movement and of his nearness. She made her own music, humming, sometimes whispering to the melodies in her mind.

And at length he became aware that she had stopped; he could hear nothing, though he knew she was still near. Heavily he raised his head. She was in the center of the room, balanced like a huge white moth, her eyes quite dark now with their secrets quiet. She was staring at the window, poised, waiting.

He followed her gaze. The big oval was black no longer, but dusted over with silver light. Del rose slowly. The dust was a mist, a loom, and then, at one edge, there was a shard of the moon itself creeping and growing.

Because Del stopped breathing, he could hear her breathe; it was rapid and so deep it faintly strummed her versatile vocal cords.

"Rita..."

Without answering she ran to the sideboard and filled two small glasses. She gave him one, then, "Wait," she breathed, "oh, wait!"

Spellbound, he waited while the white stain crept across the window. He understood suddenly that he must be still until the great oval was completely filled with direct moonlight, and this helped him, because it set a foreseeable limit to his waiting; and it hurt him, because nothing in life, he thought, had ever moved so slowly. He had a moment of rebellion, in which he damned himself for falling in with her complex pacing; but with it he realized that now the darker silver was wasting away, now it was a finger's breadth, and now a thread, and now, and *now*—.

She made a brittle feline cry and sprang up the dark steps to the window. So bright was the light that her body was a jet cameo against it. So delicately wrought was her gown that he could see the epaulettes of silver light the moon gave her. She was so beautiful his eyes stung.

"Drink," she whispered. "Drink with me, darling, darling..."

For an instant he did not understand her at all, and only gradually did he become aware of the little glass he held. He raised it toward her and drank. And of all the twists and titillations of taste he had had this night, this was the most startling; for it had no taste at all, almost no substance, and a temperature almost exactly that of blood. He looked stupidly down at the glass and back up at the girl. He thought that she had turned about and was watching him, though he could not be sure, since her silhouette was the same.

And then he had his second of unbearable shock, for the light went out.

The moon was gone, the window, the room. Rita was gone.

For a stunned instant he stood tautly, stretching his eyes wide. He made a sound that was not a word. He dropped the glass and pressed his palms to his eyes, feeling them blink, feeling the stiff silk of his lashes against them. Then he snatched the hands away, and it was still dark, and more than dark; this was not a blackness. This was like trying to see with an elbow or with a tongue; it was not black, it was *Nothingness.*

He fell to his knees.

Rita laughed.

An odd, alert part of his mind seized on the laugh and understood it, and horror and fury spread through his whole being; for this was the laugh which had been tugging at her lips all evening, and it was a hard, cruel, self-assured laugh. And at the same time, because of the anger or in spite of it, desire exploded whitely within him. He moved toward the sound, groping, mouthing. There was a quick, faint series of rustling sounds from the steps, and then a light, strong web fell around him. He struck out at it, and recognized it for the unforgettable thing it was—her robe. He caught at it, ripped it, stamped upon it. He heard her bare feet run lightly down and past him, and lunged, and caught nothing. He stood, gasping painfully.

She laughed again.

"I'm blind," he said hoarsely. "Rita, I'm blind!"

"I know," she said coolly, close beside him. And again she laughed.

"What have you done to me?"

"I've watched you be a dirty animal of a man," she said.

He grunted and lunged again. His knees struck something—a chair, a cabinet—and he fell heavily. He thought he touched her foot.

"Here, lover, here!" she taunted.

He fumbled about for the thing which had tripped him, found it, used it to help him upright again. He peered uselessly about.

"Here, lover!"

He leaped, and crashed into the door jamb: cheekbone, collarbone, hip-bone, ankle were one straight blaze of pain. He clung to the polished wood.

After a time he said, in agony, "Why?"

"No man has ever touched me and none ever will," she sang. Her breath was on his cheek. He reached and touched nothing, and then he heard her leap from her perch on a statue's pedestal by the door, where she had stood high and leaned over to speak.

No pain, no blindness, not even the understanding that it was her witch's brew working in him could quell the wild desire he felt at her nearness. Nothing could tame the fury that shook him as she laughed. He staggered after her, bellowing.

She danced around him, laughing. Once she pushed him into a clattering rack of fire-irons. Once she caught his elbow from behind and spun him. And once, incredibly, she sprang past him and, in midair, kissed him again on the mouth.

He descended into Hell, surrounded by the small, sure patter of bare feet and sweet cool laughter. He rushed and crashed, he crouched and bled and whimpered like a hound. His roaring and blundering took an echo, and that must have been the great hall. Then there were walls that seemed more than unyielding; they struck back. And there were panels to lean against, gasping, which became opening doors as he leaned. And always the black nothingness, the writhing temptation of the pat-pat of firm flesh on smooth stones, and the ravening fury.

It was cooler, and there was no echo. He became aware of the whisper of the wind through trees. The balcony, he thought; and then, right in his ear, so that he felt her warm breath, "Come, lover..." and he sprang. He sprang and missed, and instead of sprawling on the terrace, there was nothing, and nothing, and nothing, and then, when he least expected it, a shower of cruel thumps as he rolled down the marble steps.

He must have had a shred of consciousness left, for he was vaguely aware of the approach of her bare feet, and of the small, cautious hand that touched his shoulder and moved to his mouth, and then his chest. Then it was withdrawn, and either she laughed or the sound was still in his mind.

Deep in the Bogs, which were brackish, there was a pool of purest water, shaded by willows and wide-wondering aspens, cupped by banks of a moss most marvellously blue. Here grew mandrake, and there were strange pipings in mid-summer. No one ever heard them but a quiet girl whose beauty was so very contained that none of it showed. Her name was Barbara.

No one noticed Barbara, no one lived with her, no one cared. And Barbara's life was very full, for she was born to receive. Others are born wishing to receive, so they wear bright masks and make attractive sounds like cicadas and operettas, so others will be forced, one way or another, to give to them. But Barbara's receptors were wide open, and always had been, so that she needed no substitute for sunlight through a tulip petal, or the sound of morning glories climbing, or the tangy sweet smell of formic acid which is the only death cry possible to an ant, or any other of the thousand things overlooked by folk who can only wish to receive. Barbara had a garden and an orchard, and took things in to market when she cared to, and the rest of the time she spent in taking what was given. Weeds grew in her garden, but since they were welcomed, they grew only where they could keep the watermelons from being sunburned. The rabbits were welcome, so they kept to the two rows of carrots, the one of lettuce, and the one of tomato vines which were planted for them, and they left the rest alone. Goldenrod shot up beside the bean hills to lend a hand upward, and the birds ate only the figs and peaches from the waviest top branches, and in return patrolled the lower ones for caterpillars and egg-laying flies. And if a fruit stayed green for two weeks longer until Barbara had time to go to market, or if a mole could channel moisture to the roots of the corn, why it was the least they could do.

For a brace of years Barbara had wandered more and more, impelled by a thing she could not name—if indeed she was aware of it at all. She knew only that over-the-rise was a strange and friendly place, and that it was a fine thing on arriving there to find another rise to go over. It may very well be that she now needed someone to love, for loving is a most receiving thing, as anyone can attest who has been loved without returning it. It is the one who is loved who must give and give. And she found her love, not in her wandering, but at the market. The shape of her love, his colors and sounds, were so much with her that when she saw him first it was without surprise; and thereafter, for a very long while, it was quite enough that he lived. He gave to her by being alive, by setting the air athrum with his mighty voice, by his stride, which was, for a man afoot, the exact analog of what the horseman calls a "perfect seat."

After seeing him, of course, she received twice and twice again as much as ever before. A tree was straight and tall for the magnificent sake of being straight and tall, but wasn't straightness a part of him, and being tall? The oriole gave more now than song, and the hawk more than walking the wind, for had they not hearts like his, warm blood and his same striving to keep it so for tomorrow? And more and more, over-the-rise was the place for her, for only there could there be more and still more things like him.

But when she found the pure pool in the brackish Bogs, there was no more over-the-rise for her. It was a place without hardness or hate, where the aspens trembled only for wonder, and where all contentment was rewarded. Every single rabbit there was *the* champion nose-twinkler, and every waterbird could stand on one leg the longest, and proud of it. Shelf-fungi hung to the willow-trunks, making that certain, single purple of which the sunset is incapable, and a tanager and a cardinal gravely granted one another his definition of "red."

Here Barbara brought a heart light with happiness, large with love, and set it down on the blue moss. And since the loving heart can receive more than anything else, so it is most needed, and Barbara took the best bird songs, and the richest colors, and the deepest peace, and all the other things which are most worth giving. The chipmunks brought her nuts when she was hungry and the prettiest stones when she was not. A green snake explained to her, in pantomime, how a river of jewels may flow uphill, and three mad otters described how a bundle of joy may slip and slide down and down and be all the more joyful for it. And there was the magic moment when a midge hovered, and then a honeybee, and then a bumblebee, and at last a hummingbird; and there they hung, playing a chord in A sharp minor.

Then one day the pool fell silent, and Barbara learned why the water was pure.

The aspens stopped trembling.

The rabbits all came out of the thicket and clustered on the blue bank, backs straight, ears up, and all their noses as still as coral.

The waterbirds stepped backwards, like courtiers, and stopped on the brink with their heads turned sidewise, one eye closed, the better to see with the other.

The chipmunks respectfully emptied their cheek pouches, scrubbed their paws together and tucked them out of sight; then stood still as tent pegs.

The pressure of growth around the pool ceased: the very grass waited.

The last sound of all to be heard—and by then it was very quiet—was the soft *whick!* of an owl's eyelids as it awoke to watch.

He came like a cloud, the earth cupping itself to take each of his golden hooves. He stopped on the bank and lowered his head, and for a brief moment his eyes met Barbara's, and she looked into a second universe of wisdom and compassion. Then there was the arch of the magnificent neck, the blinding flash of his golden horn.

And he drank, and he was gone. Everyone knows the water is pure, where the unicorn drinks.

How long had he been there? How long gone? Did time wait too, like the grass?

"And couldn't he stay?" she wept. "Couldn't he stay?"

To have seen the unicorn is a sad thing; one might never see him more. But then—to have seen the unicorn!

She began to make a song.

It was late when Barbara came in from the Bogs, so late the moon was bleached with cold and fleeing to the horizon. She struck the highroad just below the Great House and turned to pass it and go out to her garden house.

Near the locked main gate an animal was barking. A sick animal, a big animal...

Barbara could see in the dark better than most, and soon saw the creature clinging to the gate, climbing, uttering that coughing moan as it went. At the top it slipped, fell outward, dangled; then there was a ripping sound, and it fell heavily to the ground and lay still and quiet.

She ran to it, and it began to make the sound again. It was a man, and he was weeping.

It was her love, her love, who was tall and straight and so very alive—her love, battered and bleeding, puffy, broken, his clothes torn, crying.

Now of all times was the time for a lover to receive, to take from the loved one his pain, his trouble, his fear. "Oh, hush, hush," she whispered, her hands touching his bruised face like swift feathers. "It's all over now. It's all over."

She turned him over on his back and knelt to bring him up sitting. She lifted one of his thick arms around her shoulder. He was very heavy, but she was very strong. When he was upright, gasping weakly, she looked up and down the road in the waning moonlight. Nothing, no one. The great House was dark. Across the road, though, was a meadow with high hedgerows which might break the wind a little.

"Come, my love, my dear love," she whispered. He trembled violently.

All but carrying him, she got him across the road, over the shallow ditch, and through a gap in the hedge. She almost fell with him there. She gritted her teeth and set him down gently. She let him lean against the hedge, and then ran and swept up great armfuls of sweet broom. She made a tight springy bundle of it and set it on the ground beside him, and put a corner of her cloak over it, and gently lowered his head until it was pillowed. She folded the rest of the cloak about him. He was very cold.

There was no water near, and she dared not leave him. With her kerchief she cleaned some of the blood from his face. He was still very cold. He said, "You devil. You rotten little devil."

"Shh." She crept in beside him and cradled his head. "You'll be warm in a minute."

"Stand still," he growled. "Keep running away."

"I won't run away," she whispered. "Oh, my darling, you've been hurt, so hurt. I won't leave you. I promise I won't leave you."

He lay very still. He made the growling sound again.

"I'll tell you a lovely thing," she said softly. "Listen to me, think about the lovely thing," she crooned.

"There's a place in the bog, a pool of pure water, where the trees live beautifully, willow and aspen and birch, where everything is peaceful, my darling, and the flowers grow without tearing their petals. The moss is blue and the water is like diamonds."

"You tell me stories in a thousand voices," he muttered.

"Shh. Listen, my darling. This isn't a story, it's a real place. Four miles north and a little west, and you can see the trees from the ridge with the two dwarf oaks. And I know why the water is pure!" she cried gladly. "I know why!"

He said nothing. He took a deep breath and it hurt him, for he shuddered painfully.

"The unicorn drinks there," she whispered. "I *saw* him!"

Still he said nothing. She said, "I made a song about it. Listen, this is the song I made:

And He—suddenly gleamed! My dazzled eyes
Coming from outer sunshine to this green
And secret gloaming, met without surprise
The vision. Only after, when the sheen
And Splendor of his going fled away,
I knew amazement, wonder and despair,
That he should come—and pass—and would not stay,
The Silken-swift—the gloriously Fair!
That he should come—and pass—and would not stay,
So that, forever after, I must go,
Take the long road that mounts against the day,
Travelling in the hope that I shall know
Again that lifted moment, high and sweet,
Somewhere—on purple moor or windy hill—
Remembering still his wild and delicate feet,
The magic and the dream—remembering still!

His breathing was more regular. She said, "I truly *saw* him!"

"I'm blind," he said, "Blind, I'm blind."

"Oh, my dear..."

He fumbled for her hand, found it. For a long moment he held it. Then, slowly, he brought up his other hand and with them both he felt her hand, turned it about, squeezed it. Suddenly he grunted, half sitting. "You're here."

"Of course, darling. Of course I'm here."

"Why?" he shouted. "Why? *Why?* Why all of this? Why blind me?" He sat up, mouthing, and put his great hand on her throat. "Why do all that if..." The words ran together into an animal noise. Wine and witchery, anger and agony boiled in his veins.

Once she cried out.

Once she sobbed.

"Now," he said, "You'll catch no unicorns. Get away from me." He cuffed her.

"You're mad. You're sick," she cried.

"Get away," he said ominously.

Terrified, she rose. He took the cloak and hurled it after her. It almost toppled her as she ran away, crying silently.

After a long time, from behind the hedge, the sick, coughing sobs began again.

Three weeks later Rita was in the market when a hard hand took her upper arm and pressed her into the angle of a cottage wall. She did not start. She flashed her eyes upward and recognized him, and then said composedly, "Don't touch me."

"I need you to tell me something," he said. "And tell me you *will!*" His voice was as hard as his hand.

"I'll tell you anything you like," she said. "But don't touch me."

He hesitated, then released her. She turned to him casually. "What is it?" Her gaze darted across his face and its almost-healed scars. The small smile tugged at one corner of her mouth.

His eyes were slits. "I have to know this: why did you make

up all that...prettiness, that food, that poison...just for me? You could have had me for less."

She smiled. "Just for you? It was your turn, that's all."

He was genuinely surprised. "It's happened before?"

She nodded. "Whenever it's the full of the moon—and the squire's away."

"You're lying!"

"You forget yourself!" she said sharply. Then, smiling. "It is the truth, though."

"I'd've heard talk—"

"Would you now? And tell me—how many of your friends know about your humiliating adventure?"

He hung his head.

She nodded. "You see? They go away until they're healed, and they come back and say nothing. And they always will."

"You're a devil...why do you do it? Why?"

"I told you," she said openly. "I'm a woman and I act like a woman in my own way. No man will ever touch me, though. I am virgin and shall remain so."

"You're *what?*" he roared.

She held up a restraining, ladylike glove. "Please," she said, pained.

"Listen," he said, quietly now, but with such intensity that for once she stepped back a pace. He closed his eyes, thinking hard. "You told me—the pool, the pool of the unicorn, and a song, wait. 'The Silken-swift, the gloriously Fair...' Remember? And then I—I saw to it that *you'd* never catch a unicorn!"

She shook her head, complete candor in her face. "I like that, 'The Silken-swift.' Pretty. But believe me—no! That isn't mine."

He put his face close to hers, and though it was barely a whisper, it came out like bullets. "Liar! Liar! I couldn't forget. I was sick, I was hurt, I was poisoned, but I know what I did!" He turned on his heel and strode away.

She put the thumb of her glove against her upper teeth for a second, then ran after him. "Del!"

He stopped but, rudely, would not turn. She rounded him, faced him. "I'll not have you believing that of me—it's the one thing I have left," she said tremulously.

He made no attempt to conceal his surprise. She controlled her expression with a visible effort, and said, "Please. Tell me a little more—just about the pool, the song, whatever it was."

"You don't remember?"

"I don't *know!*" she flashed. She was deeply agitated.

He said with mock patience. "You told me of a unicorn pool out on the Bogs. You said you had seen *him* drink there. You made a song about it. And then I—"

"Where? Where was this?"

"You forget so soon?"

"Where? Where did it happen?"

"In the meadow, across the road from your gate, where you followed me," he said. "Where my sight came back to me, when the sun came up."

She looked at him blankly, and slowly her face changed. First the imprisoned smile struggling to be free, and then—she was herself again, and she laughed. She laughed a great ringing peal of the laughter that had plagued him so, and she did not stop until he put one hand behind his back, then the other, and she saw his shoulders swell with the effort to keep from striking her dead.

"You animal!" she said, goodhumoredly. "Do you know what you've done? Oh, you…you *animal!*" She glanced around to see that there were no ears to hear her. "I left you at the foot of the terrace steps," she told him. Her eyes sparkled. "Inside the gates, you understand? And you…"

"Don't laugh," he said quietly.

She did not laugh. "That was someone else out there. Who, I can't imagine. But it wasn't I."

He paled. "You followed me out."

"On my soul I did not," she said soberly. Then she quelled another laugh.

"That can't be," he said. "I couldn't have…"

"But you were blind, blind and crazy, Del-my-lover!"

"Squire's daughter, take care," he hissed. Then he pulled his big hand through his hair. "It can't be. It's three weeks; I'd have been accused..."

"There are those who wouldn't," she smiled. "Or—perhaps she will, in time."

"There has never been a woman so foul," he said evenly, looking her straight in the eye. "You're lying—you know you're lying."

"What must I do to prove it—aside from that which I'll have no man do?"

His lip curled. "Catch the unicorn," he said.

"If I did, you'd believe I was virgin?"

"I must," he admitted. He turned away, then said, over his shoulder, "But—*you?*"

She watched him thoughtfully until he left the marketplace. Her eyes sparkled; then she walked briskly to the goldsmith's, where she ordered a bridle of woven gold.

If the unicorn pool lay in the Bogs nearby, Rita reasoned, someone who was familiar with that brackish wasteland must know of it. And when she made a list in her mind of those few who travelled the Bogs, she knew whom to ask. With that, the other deduction came readily. Her laughter drew stares as she moved through the marketplace.

By the vegetable stall she stopped. The girl looked up patiently.

Rita stood swinging one expensive glove against the other wrist, half-smiling. "So you're the one." She studied the plain, inward-turning, peaceful face until Barbara had to turn her eyes away. Rita said, without further preamble, "I want you to show me the unicorn pool in two weeks."

Barbara looked up again, and now it was Rita who dropped her eyes. Rita said, "I can have someone else find it, of course. If you'd rather not." She spoke very clearly, and people turned to listen. They looked from Barbara to Rita and back again, and they waited.

"I don't mind," said Barbara faintly. As soon as Rita had left, smiling, she packed up her things and went silently back to her house.

The goldsmith, of course, made no secret of such an extraordinary commission; and that, plus the gossips who had overheard Rita talking to Barbara, made the expedition into a cavalcade. The whole village turned out to see; the boys kept firmly in check so that Rita might lead the way; the young bloods ranged behind her (some a little less carefree than they might be) and others snickering behind their hands. Behind them the girls, one or two a little pale, others eager as cats to see the squire's daughter fail, and perhaps even... but then, only she had the golden bridle.

She carried it casually, but casualness could not hide it, for it was not wrapped, and it swung and blazed in the sun. She wore a flowing white robe, trimmed a little short so that she might negotiate the rough bogland; she had on a golden girdle and little gold sandals, and a gold chain bound her head and hair like a coronet.

Barbara walked quietly a little behind Rita, closed in with her own thoughts. Not once did she look at Del, who strode somberly by himself.

Rita halted a moment and let Barbara catch up, then walked beside her. "Tell me," she said quietly, "why did you come? It needn't have been you."

"I'm his friend." Barbara said. She quickly touched the bridle with her finger. "The unicorn."

"Oh," said Rita. "The unicorn." She looked archly at the other girl. "You wouldn't betray all your friends, would you?"

Barbara looked at her thoughtfully, without anger. "If—when you catch the unicorn," she said carefully, "what will you do with him?"

"What an amazing question! I shall keep him, of course!"

"I thought I might persuade you to let him go."

Rita smiled, and hung the bridle on her other arm. "You could never do that."

"I know," said Barbara. "But I thought I might, so that's why I came." And before Rita could answer, she dropped behind again.

The last ridge, the one which overlooked the unicorn pool, saw a series of gasps as the ranks of villagers topped it, one after the other, and saw what lay below; and it was indeed beautiful.

Surprisingly, it was Del who took it upon himself to call out, in his great voice, "Everyone wait here!" And everyone did; the top of the ridge filled slowly, from one side to the other, with craning, murmuring people. And then Del bounded after Rita and Barbara.

Barbara said, "I'll stop here."

"Wait," said Rita, imperiously. Of Del she demanded, "What are you coming for?"

"To see fair play," he growled. "The little I know of witchcraft makes me like none of it."

"Very well," she said calmly. Then she smiled her very own smile. "Since you insist, I'd rather enjoy Barbara's company too."

Barbara hesitated. "Come, he won't hurt you, girl," said Rita. "He doesn't know you exist."

"Oh," said Barbara, wonderingly.

Del said gruffly, "I do so. She has the vegetable stall."

Rita smiled at Barbara, the secrets bright in her eyes. Barbara said nothing, but came with them.

"You should go back, you know," Rita said silkily to Del, when she could. "Haven't you been humiliated enough yet?"

He did not answer.

She said, "Stubborn animal! Do you think I'd have come this far if I weren't sure?"

"Yes," said Del, "I think perhaps you would."

They reached the blue moss. Rita shuffled it about with her feet and then sank gracefully down to it. Barbara stood alone in the shadows of the willow grove. Del thumped gently at an aspen with his fist. Rita, smiling, arranged the bridle to cast, and laid it across her lap.

The rabbits stayed hid. There was an uneasiness about the grove. Barbara sank to her knees, and put out her hand. A chipmunk ran to nestle in it.

This time there was a difference. This time it was not the slow silencing of living things that warned of his approach, but a sudden babble from the people on the ridge.

Rita gathered her legs under her like a sprinter, and held the bridle poised. Her eyes were round and bright, and the tip of her tongue showed between her white teeth. Barbara was a statue. Del put his back against his tree, and became as still as Barbara.

Then from the ridge came a single, simultaneous intake of breath, and silence. One knew without looking that some stared speechless, that some buried their faces or threw an arm over their eyes.

He came.

He came slowly this time, his golden hooves choosing his paces like so many embroidery needles. He held his splendid head high. He regarded the three on the bank gravely, and then turned to look at the ridge for a moment. At last he turned, and came round the pond by the willow grove. Just on the blue moss, he stopped to look down into the pond. It seemed that he drew one deep clear breath. He bent his head then, and drank, and lifted his head to shake away the shining drops.

He turned toward the three spellbound humans and looked at them each in turn. And it was not Rita he went to, at last, nor Barbara. He came to Del, and he drank of Del's eyes with his own just as he had partaken of the pool—deeply and at leisure. The beauty and wisdom were there, and the compassion, and what looked like a bright white point of anger. Del knew that the creature had read everything then, and that he knew all three of them in ways unknown to human beings.

There was a majestic sadness in the way he turned then, and dropped his shining head, and stepped daintily to Rita. She sighed, and rose up a little, lifting the bridle. The unicorn lowered his horn to receive it—

—and tossed his head, tore the bridle out of her grasp, sent the golden thing high in the air. It turned there in the sun, and fell into the pond.

And the instant it touched the water, the pond was a bog and the birds rose mourning from the trees. The unicorn looked up at them, and shook himself. Then he trotted to Barbara and knelt, and put his smooth, stainless head in her lap.

Barbara's hands stayed on the ground by her sides. Her gaze roved over the warm white beauty, up to the tip of the golden horn and back.

The scream was frightening. Rita's hands were up like claws, and she had bitten her tongue; there was blood on her mouth. She screamed again. She threw herself off the now withered moss toward the unicorn and Barbara. "She can't be!" Rita shrieked. She collided with Del's broad right hand. "It's wrong, I tell you, she, you, I..."

"I'm satisfied," said Del, low in his throat. "Keep away, squire's daughter."

She recoiled from him, made as if to try to circle him. He stepped forward. She ground her chin into one shoulder, then the other, in a gesture of sheer frustration, turned suddenly and ran toward the ridge. "It's mine, it's mine, "she screamed. "I tell you it can't be hers, don't you understand? I never once, I never did, but she, but she—"

She slowed and stopped, then, and fell silent at the sound that rose from the ridge. It began like the first patter of rain on oak leaves, and it gathered voice until it was a rumble and then a roar. She stood looking up, her face working, the sound washing over her. She shrank from it.

It was laughter.

She turned once, a pleading just beginning to form on her

face. Del regarded her stonily. She faced the ridge then, and squared her shoulders, and walked up the hill, to go into the laughter, to go through it, to have it follow her all the way home and all the days of her life.

Del turned to Barbara just as she bent over the beautiful head. She said, "Silken-swift...go free."

The unicorn raised its head and looked up at Del. Del's mouth opened. He took a clumsy step forward, stopped again. "*You!*"

Barbara's face was set. "You weren't to know," she choked. "You weren't ever to know...I was so glad you were blind, because I thought you'd never know."

He fell on his knees beside her. And when he did, the unicorn touched her face with his satin nose, and all the girl's pent-up beauty flooded outward. The unicorn rose from his kneeling, and whickered softly. Del looked at her, and only the unicorn was more beautiful. He put out his hand to the shining neck, and for a moment felt the incredible silk of the mane flowing across his fingers. The unicorn reared then, and wheeled, and in a great leap was across the bog, and in two more was on the crest of the farther ridge. He paused there briefly, with the sun on him, and then was gone.

Barbara said, "For us, he lost his pool, his beautiful pool."

And Del said, "He will get another. He must." With difficulty he added, "He couldn't be...punished...for being so gloriously Fair."

The Golem

by AVRAM DAVIDSON

THE GRAY-FACED person came along the street where old Mr. and Mrs. Gumbeiner lived. It was afternoon, it was autumn, the sun was warm and soothing to their ancient bones. Anyone who attended the movies in the twenties or the early thirties has seen that street a thousand times. Past these bungalows with their half-double roofs Edmund Lowe walked arm-in-arm with Leatrice Joy and Harold Lloyd was chased by Chinamen waving hatchets. Under these squamous palm trees Laurel kicked Hardy and Woolsey beat Wheeler upon the head with a codfish. Across these pocket-handkerchief-sized lawns the juveniles of the Our Gang Comedies pursued one another and were pursued by angry fat men in golf knickers. On this same street—or perhaps on some other one of five hundred streets exactly like it.

Mrs. Gumbeiner indicated the gray-faced person to her husband.

"You think maybe he's got something the matter?" she asked. "He walks kind of funny, to me."

"Walks like a *golem,*" Mr. Gumbeiner said indifferently.

The old woman was nettled.

"Oh, I don't know," she said. "*I* think he walks like your cousin Mendel."

The old man pursed his mouth angrily and chewed on his pipestem. The gray-faced person turned up the concrete path, walked up the steps to the porch, sat down in a chair. Old Mr. Gumbeiner ignored him. His wife stared at the stranger.

"Man comes in without a hello, goodbye, or howareyou, sits himself down and right away he's at home.... The chair is comfortable?" she asked. "Would you like maybe a glass tea?"

She turned to her husband.

"Say something, Gumbeiner!" she demanded. "What are you, made of wood?"

The old man smiled a slow, wicked, triumphant smile.

"Why should *I* say anything?" he asked the air. "Who am I? Nothing, that's who."

The stranger spoke. His voice was harsh and monotonous.

"When you learn who—or, rather, what—I am, the flesh will melt from your bones in terror." He bared porcelain teeth.

"Never mind about my bones!" the old woman cried. "You've got a lot of nerve talking about my bones!"

"You will quake with fear," said the stranger. Old Mrs. Gumbeiner said that she hoped he would live so long. She turned to her husband once again.

"Gumbeiner, when are you going to mow the lawn?"

"All mankind—" the stranger began.

"*Shah!* I'm talking to my husband.... He talks *eppis* kind of funny, Gumbeiner, no?"

"Probably a foreigner," Mr. Gumbeiner said, complacently.

"You think so?" Mrs. Gumbeiner glanced fleetingly at the stranger. "He's got a very bad color in his face, *nebbich,* I suppose he came to California for his health."

"Disease, pain, sorrow, love, grief—all are nought to—"

Mr. Gumbeiner cut in on the stranger's statement.

"Gall bladder," the old man said. "Guinzburg down at the *shule* looked exactly the same before his operation. Two professors they had in for him, and a private nurse day and night."

"I am not a human being!" the stranger said loudly.

"Three thousand seven hundred fifty dollars it cost his son, Guinzburg told me. 'For you, Poppa, nothing is too expensive—only get well,' the son told him."

"I am not a human being!"

"Ai, is that a son for you!" the old woman said, rocking her head. "A heart of gold, pure gold." She looked at the stranger. "All right, all right, I heard you the first time. Gumbeiner! I asked you a question. When are you going to cut the lawn?"

"On Wednesday, *odder* maybe Thursday, comes the Japaneser to the neighborhood. To cut lawns is *his* profession. *My* profession is to be a glazier—retired."

"Between me and all mankind is an inevitable hatred," the stranger said. "When I tell you what I am, the flesh will melt—"

"You said, you said already," Mr. Gumbeiner interrupted.

"In Chicago where the winters were as cold and bitter as the Czar of Russia's heart," the old woman intoned, "you had strength to carry the frames with the glass together day in and day out. But in California with the golden sun to mow the lawn when your wife asks, for this you have no strength. Do I call in the Japaneser to cook for you supper?"

"Thirty years Professor Allardyce spent perfecting his theories. Electronics, neuronics—"

"Listen, how educated he talks," Mr. Gumbeiner said, admiringly. "Maybe he goes to the University here?"

"If he goes to the University, maybe he knows Bud?" his wife suggested.

"Probably they're in the same class and he came to see him about the homework, no?"

"Certainly he must be in the same class. How many classes are there? Five *in ganzen:* Bud showed me on his program card." She counted off on her fingers. "Television Appreciation and Criticism, Small Boat Building, Social Adjustment,

The American Dance.... The American Dance—*nu,* Gumbeiner—"

"Contemporary Ceramics," her husband said, relishing the syllables. "A fine boy, Bud. A pleasure to have him for a boardner."

"After thirty years spent in these studies," the stranger, who had continued to speak unnoticed, went on, "he turned from the theoretical to the pragmatic. In ten years' time he had made the most titanic discovery in history: he made mankind, *all* mankind, superfluous; he made *me.*"

"What did Tillie write in her last letter?" asked the old man.

The old woman shrugged.

"What should she write? The same thing. Sidney was home from the Army, Naomi has a new boy friend—"

"He made ME!"

"Listen, Mr. Whatever-your-name-is," the old woman said, "maybe where you came from is different, but in *this* country you don't interrupt people the while they're talking.... Hey. Listen—what do you mean, he *made* you? What kind of talk is that?"

The stranger bared all his teeth again, exposing the too-pink gums.

"In his library, to which I had a more complete access after his sudden and as yet undiscovered death from entirely natural causes, I found a complete collection of stories about androids, from Shelley's *Frankenstein* through Capek's *R.U.R.* to Asimov's—"

"Frankenstein?" said the old man, with interest. "There used to be a Frankenstein who had the soda-*wasser* place on Halstead Street—a Litvack, *nebbich.*"

"What are you talking?" Mrs. Gumbeiner demanded. "His name was Franken*thal,* and it wasn't on Halstead, it was on Roosevelt."

"—clearly shown that all mankind has an instinctive antipathy towards androids and there will be an inevitable struggle between them—"

"Of course, of course!" Old Mr. Gumbeiner clicked his teeth against his pipe. "I am always wrong, you are always right. How could you stand to be married to such a stupid person all this time?"

"I don't know," the old woman said. "Sometimes I wonder, myself. I think it must be his good looks." She began to laugh. Old Mr. Gumbeiner blinked, then began to smile, then took his wife's hand.

"Foolish old woman," the stranger said. "Why do you laugh? Do you not know I have come to destroy you?"

"What?" old Mr. Gumbeiner shouted. "Close your mouth, you!" He darted from his chair and struck the stranger with the flat of his hand. The stranger's head struck against the porch pillar and bounced back.

"When you talk to my wife, talk respectable, you hear?"

Old Mrs. Gumbeiner, cheeks very pink, pushed her husband back to his chair. Then she leaned forward and examined the stranger's head. She clicked her tongue as she pulled aside a flap of gray, skinlike material.

"Gumbeiner, look! He's all springs and wires inside!"

"I *told* you he was a *golem,* but no, you wouldn't listen," the old man said.

"You said he *walked* like a *golem.*"

"How could he walk like a *golem* unless he *was* one?"

"All right, all right.... You broke him, so now fix him."

"My grandfather, his light shines from Paradise, told me that when MoHaRaL—Moreyne Ha-Rav Löw—his memory for a blessing made the *golem* in Prague, three hundred? four hundred years ago? he wrote on his forehead the Holy Name."

Smiling reminiscently, the old woman continued, "And the *golem* cut the rabbi's wood and brought his water and guarded the ghetto."

"And one time only he disobeyed the Rabbi Löw, and Rabbi Löw erased the *Shem Ha-Mephorash* from the *golem's* forehead and the *golem* fell down like a dead one. And they put him up in the attic of the *shule* and he's still there today if the Communisten haven't sent him to Moscow.... This is not just a story," he said.

"*Avadda* not!" said the old woman.

"I myself have seen both the *shule and* the rabbi's grave," her husband said, conclusively.

"But I think this must be a different kind of *golem*, Gumbeiner. See, on his forehead; nothing written."

"What's the matter, there's a law I can't write something there? Where is that lump clay Bud brought us from his class?"

The old man washed his hands, adjusted his little black skullcap, and slowly and carefully wrote four Hebrew letters on the gray forehead.

"Ezra the Scribe himself couldn't do better," the old woman said, admiringly. "Nothing happens," she observed, looking at the lifeless figure sprawled in the chair.

"Well, after all, am I Rabbi Löw?" her husband asked, deprecatingly. "No," he answered. He leaned over and examined the exposed mechanism. "This spring goes here... this wire comes with this one...." The figure moved. "But this one goes where? And this one?"

"Let be," said his wife. The figure sat up slowly and rolled its eyes loosely.

"Listen, Reb *Golem*," the old man said, wagging his finger. "Pay attention to what I say—you understand?"

"Understand...."

"If you want to stay here, you got to do like Mr. Gumbeiner says."

"Do-like—Mr.-Gumbeiner-says...."

"*That's* the way I like to hear a *golem* talk. Malka, give here the mirror from the pocketbook. Look, you see your face? You see on the forehead, what's written? If you don't do like Mr. Gumbeiner says, he'll wipe out what's written and you'll be no more alive."

"No-more-alive...."

"*That's* right. Now, listen. Under the porch you'll find a lawnmower. Take it. And cut the lawn. Then come back. Go."

"Go. . . ." The figure shambled down the stairs. Presently the sound of the lawnmower whirred through the quiet air in the street just like the street where Jackie Cooper shed huge tears on Wallace Beery's shirt and Chester Conklin rolled his eyes at Marie Dressler.

"So what will you write to Tillie?" old Mr. Gumbeiner asked.

"What should I write?" old Mrs. Gumbeiner shrugged. "I'll write that the weather is lovely out here and that we are both, Blessed be the Name, in good health."

The old man nodded his head slowly, and they sat together on the front porch in the warm afternoon sun.

That Hell-Bound Train

by ROBERT BLOCH

WHEN MARTIN was a little boy, his Daddy was a Railroad Man. Daddy never rode the high iron, but he walked the tracks for the CB&Q, and he was proud of his job. And every night when he got drunk, he sang this old song about *That Hell-Bound Train.*

Martin didn't quite remember any of the words, but he couldn't forget the way his Daddy sang them out. And when Daddy made the mistake of getting drunk in the afternoon and got squeezed between a Pennsy tank-car and an AT&SF gondola, Martin sort of wondered why the Brotherhood didn't sing the song at his funeral.

After that, things didn't go so good for Martin, but somehow he always recalled Daddy's song. When Mom up and ran off with a traveling salesman from Keokuk (Daddy must have turned over in his grave, knowing she'd done such a thing, and with a *passenger,* too!) Martin hummed the tune to himself every night in the Orphan Home. And after Martin himself ran away, he used to whistle the song softly at night in the jungles, after the other bindlestiffs were asleep.

Martin was on the road for four-five years before he realized he wasn't getting anyplace. Of course he'd tried his hand at a lot of things—picking fruit in Oregon, washing dishes in a Montana hash-house, stealing hub-caps in Denver and tires in Oklahoma City—but by the time he'd put in six months on the chain-gang down in Alabama he knew he had no future drifting around this way on his own.

So he tried to get on the railroad like his Daddy had and they told him that times were bad.

But Martin couldn't keep away from the railroads. Wherever he traveled, he rode the rods; he'd rather hop a freight heading north in sub-zero weather than lift his thumb to hitch a ride with a Cadillac headed for Florida. Whenever he managed to get hold of a can of Sterno, he'd sit there under a nice warm culvert, think about the old days, and often as not he'd hum the song about *That Hell-Bound Train.* That was the train the drunks and the sinners rode—the gambling men and the drifters, the big-time spenders, the skirt-chasers, and all the jolly crew. It would be really fine to take a trip in such good company, but Martin didn't like to think of what happened when that train finally pulled into the Depot Way Down Yonder. He didn't figure on spending eternity stoking boilers in Hell, without even a Company Union to protect him. Still, it would be a lovely ride. If there was *such* a thing as a Hell-Bound Train. Which, of course, there wasn't.

At least Martin didn't *think* there was, until that evening when he found himself walking the tracks heading south, just outside of Appleton Junction. The night was cold and dark, the way November nights are in the Fox River Valley, and he knew he'd have to work his way down to New Orleans for the winter, or maybe even Texas. Somehow he didn't much feel like going, even though he'd heard tell that a lot of those Texas automobiles had solid gold hub-caps.

No sir, he just wasn't cut out for petty larceny. It was worse than a sin—it was unprofitable, too. Bad enough to do the Devil's work, but then to get such miserable pay on top of it! Maybe he'd better let the Salvation Army convert him.

Martin trudged along humming Daddy's song, waiting for a rattler to pull out of the Junction behind him. He'd have to catch it—there was nothing else for him to do.

But the first train to come along came from the other direction, roaring towards him along the track from the south.

Martin peered ahead, but his eyes couldn't match his ears, and so far all he could recognize was the sound. It *was* a train, though; he felt the steel shudder and sing beneath his feet.

And yet, how could it be? The next station south was Neenah-Menasha, and there was nothing due out of there for hours.

The clouds were thick overhead, and the field-mists rolled like a cold fog in a November midnight. Even so, Martin should have been able to see the headlight as the train rushed on. But there was only the whistle, screaming out of the black throat of the night. Martin could recognize the equipment of just about any locomotive ever built, but he'd never heard a whistle that sounded like this one. It wasn't signalling; it was screaming like a lost soul.

He stepped to one side, for the train was almost on top of him now. And suddenly there it was, looming along the tracks and grinding to a stop in less time than he'd believed possible. The wheels hadn't been oiled, because they screamed too, screamed like the damned. But the train slid to a halt and the screams died away into a series of low, groaning sounds, and Martin looked up and saw that this was a passenger train. It was big and black, without a single light shining in the engine cab or any of the long string of cars; Martin couldn't read any lettering on the sides, but he was pretty sure this train didn't belong on the Northwestern Road.

He was even more sure when he saw the man clamber down out of the forward car. There was something wrong about the way he walked, as though one of his feet dragged, and about the lantern he carried. The lantern was dark, and the man held it up to his mouth and blew, and instantly it glowed redly. You don't have to be a member of the Railway Brotherhood to know that this is a mighty peculiar way of lighting a lantern.

As the figure approached, Martin recognized the conductor's cap perched on his head, and this made him feel a little better for a moment—until he noticed that it was worn a bit too high, as though there might be something sticking up on the forehead underneath it.

Still, Martin knew his manners, and when the man smiled at him, he said, "Good evening, Mr. Conductor."

"Good evening, Martin."

"How did you know my name?"

The man shrugged. "How did you know I was the Conductor?"

"You *are,* aren't you?"

"To you, yes. Although other people, in other walks of life, may recognize me in different roles. For instance, you ought to see what I look like to the folks out in Hollywood." The man grinned. "I travel a great deal," he explained.

"What brings you here?" Martin asked.

"Why, you ought to know the answer to that, Martin. I came because you needed me. Tonight, I suddenly realized you were backsliding. Thinking of joining the Salvation Army, weren't you?"

"Well—" Martin hesitated.

"Don't be ashamed. To err is human, as somebody-or-other once said. *Reader's Digest,* wasn't it? Never mind. The point is, I felt you needed me. So I switched over and came your way."

"What for?"

"Why, to offer you a ride, of course. Isn't it better to travel comfortably by train than to march along the cold streets behind a Salvation Army band? Hard on the feet, they tell me, and even harder on the eardrums."

"I'm not sure I'd care to ride your train, sir," Martin said. "Considering where I'm likely to end up."

"Ah, yes. The old argument." The Conductor sighed. "I suppose you'd prefer some sort of bargain, is that it?"

"Exactly," Martin answered.

"Well, I'm afraid I'm all through with that sort of thing. There's no shortage of prospective passengers any more. Why should I offer you any special inducements?"

"You must want me, or else you wouldn't have bothered to go out of your way to find me."

The Conductor sighed again. "There you have a point. Pride was always my besetting weakness, I admit. And somehow I'd hate to lose you to the competition, after thinking of you as my own all these years." He hesitated. "Yes, I'm prepared to deal with you on your own terms, if you insist."

"The terms?" Martin asked.

"Standard proposition. Anything you want."

"Ah," said Martin.

"But I warn you in advance, there'll be no tricks. I'll grant you any wish you can name—but in return, you must promise to ride the train when the time comes."

"Suppose it never comes?"

"It will."

"Suppose I've got the kind of a wish that will keep me off forever?"

"There is no such wish."

"Don't be too sure."

"Let me worry about that," the Conductor told him. "No matter what you have in mind, I warn you that I'll collect in the end. And there'll be none of this last-minute hocus-pocus, either. No last-hour repentances, no blonde *frauleins* or fancy lawyers showing up to get you off. I offer a clean deal. That is to say, you'll get what you want, and I'll get what I want."

"I've heard you trick people. They say you're worse than a used-car salesman."

"Now, wait a minute—"

"I apologize," Martin said, hastily. "But it *is* supposed to be a fact that you can't be trusted."

"I admit it. On the other hand, you seem to think you have found a way out."

"A sure-fire proposition."

"Sure-fire? Very funny!" The man began to chuckle, then halted. "But we waste valuable time, Martin. Let's get down to cases. What do you want from me?"

Martin took a deep breath. "I want to be able to stop Time."

"Right now?"

"No. Not yet. And not for everybody. I realize that would be impossible, of course. But I want to be able to stop Time for myself. Just once, in the future. Whenever I get to a point where I know I'm happy and contented, that's where I'd like to stop. So I can just keep on being happy forever."

"That's quite a proposition," the Conductor mused. "I've got to admit I've never heard anything just like it before—and believe me, I've listened to some lulus in my day." He grinned at Martin. "You've really been thinking about this, haven't you?"

"For years," Martin admitted. Then he coughed. "Well, what do you say?"

"It's not impossible, in terms of your own *subjective* time-sense," the Conductor murmured. "Yes, I think it could be arranged."

"But I mean *really* to stop. Nor for me just to *imagine* it."

"I understand. And it can be done."

"Then you'll agree?"

"Why not? I promised you, didn't I? Give me your hand."

Martin hesitated. "Will it hurt very much? I mean, I don't like the sight of blood, and—"

"Nonsense! You've been listening to a lot of poppycock. We already have made our bargain, my boy. I merely intend to put something into your hand. The ways and means of fulfilling your wish. After all, there's no telling at just what moment you may decide to exercise the agreement, and I can't drop everything and come running. So it's better if you can regulate matters for yourself."

"You're going to give me a Time-stopper?"

"That's the general idea. As soon as I can decide what would be practical." The Conductor hesitated. "Ah, the very thing! Here, take my watch."

He pulled it out of his vest-pocket; a railroad watch in a silver case. He opened the back and made a delicate adjustment; Martin tried to see just exactly what he was doing, but the fingers moved in a blinding blur.

"There we are," the Conductor smiled. "It's all set, now. When you finally decide where you'd like to call a halt, merely turn the stem in reverse and unwind the watch until it stops. When it stops, Time stops, for you. Simple enough?" And the Conductor dropped the watch into Martin's hand.

The young man closed his fingers tightly around the case. "That's all there is to it, eh?"

"Absolutely. But remember—you can stop the watch only once. So you'd better make sure that you're satisfied with the moment you choose to prolong. I caution you in all fairness; make very certain of your choice."

"I will." Martin grinned. "And since you've been so fair about it, I'll be fair, too. There's one thing you seem to have forgotten. It doesn't really matter *what* moment I choose. Because once I stop Time for myself, that means I stay where I am forever. I'll never have to get any older. And if I don't get any older, I'll never die. And if I never die, then I'll never have to take a ride on your train."

The Conductor turned away. His shoulders shook convulsively, and he may have been crying. "And you said *I* was worse than a used-car salesman," he gasped, in a strangled voice.

Then he wandered off into the fog, and the train-whistle gave an impatient shriek, and all at once it was moving swiftly down the track, rumbling out of sight in the darkness.

Martin stood there, blinking down at the silver watch in

his hand. If it wasn't that he could actually see it and feel it there, and if he couldn't smell that peculiar odor, he might have thought he'd imagined the whole thing from start to finish—train, Conductor, bargain, and all.

But he had the watch, and he could recognize the scent left by the train as it departed, even though there aren't many locomotives around that use sulphur and brimstone as fuel.

And he had no doubts about his bargain. That's what came of thinking things through to a logical conclusion. Some fools would have settled for wealth, or power, or Kim Novak. Daddy might have sold out for a fifth of whiskey.

Martin knew that he'd made a better deal. Better? It was foolproof. All he needed to do now was choose his moment.

He put the watch in his pocket and started back down the railroad track. He hadn't really had a destination in mind before, but he did now. He was going to find a moment of happiness....

Now young Martin wasn't altogether a ninny. He realized perfectly well that happiness is a relative thing; there are conditions and degrees of contentment, and they vary with one's lot in life. As a hobo, he was often satisfied with a warm handout, a double-length bench in the park, or a can of Sterno made in 1957 (a vintage year). Many a time he had reached a state of momentary bliss through such simple agencies, but he was aware that there were better things. Martin determined to seek them out.

Within two days he was in the great city of Chicago. Quite naturally, he drifted over to West Madison Street, and there he took steps to elevate his role in life. He became a city bum, a panhandler, a moocher. Within a week he had risen to the point where happiness was a meal in a regular one-arm luncheon joint, a two-bit flop on a real army cot in a real flophouse, and a full fifth of muscatel.

There was a night, after enjoying all three of these luxuries to the full, when Martin thought of unwinding his watch at the pinnacle of intoxication. But he also thought of the faces of the honest johns he'd braced for a handout today. Sure, they were squares, but they were prosperous. They wore good clothes, held good jobs, drove nice cars. And for them, happiness was even more ecstatic—they ate dinner in fine hotels, they slept on innerspring mattresses, they drank blended whiskey.

Square or no, they had something there. Martin fingered his watch, put aside the temptation to hock it for another bottle of muscatel, and went to sleep determined to get himself a job and improve his happiness-quotient.

When he awoke he had a hangover, but the determination was still with him. Before the month was out Martin was working for a general contractor over on the South Side, at one of the big rehabilitation projects. He hated the grind, but the pay was good, and pretty soon he got himself a one-room apartment out on Blue Island Avenue. He was accustomed to eating in decent restaurants now, and he bought himself a comfortable bed, and every Saturday night he went down to the corner tavern. It was all very pleasant, but—

The foreman liked his work and promised him a raise in a month. If he waited around, the raise would mean that he could afford a secondhand car. With a car, he could even start picking up a girl for a date now and then. Other fellows on the job did, and they seemed pretty happy.

So Martin kept on working, and the raise came through and the car came through and pretty soon a couple of girls came through.

The first time it happened, he wanted to unwind his watch immediately. Until he got to thinking about what some of the older men always said. There was a guy named Charlie, for example, who worked alongside him on the hoist. "When you're young and don't know the score, maybe you get a kick out of running around with those pigs. But after a while, you want something better. A nice girl of your own. That's the ticket."

Martin felt he owed it to himself to find out. If he didn't like it better, he could always go back to what he had.

Almost six months went by before Martin met Lillian Gillis. By that time he'd had another promotion and was working inside, in the office. They made him go to night school to learn how to do simple bookkeeping, but it meant another fifteen bucks extra a week, and it was nicer working indoors.

And Lillian *was* a lot of fun. When she told him she'd marry him, Martin was almost sure that the time was now. Except that she was sort of—well, she was a *nice* girl, and she said they'd have to wait until they were married. Of course, Martin couldn't expect to marry her until he had a little more money saved up, and another raise would help, too.

That took a year. Martin was patient, because he knew it was going to be worth it. Every time he had any doubts, he took out his watch and looked at it. But he never showed it to Lillian, or anybody else. Most of the other men wore expensive wristwatches and the old silver railroad watch looked just a little cheap.

Martin smiled as he gazed at the stem. Just a few twists and he'd have something none of these other poor working slobs would ever have. Permanent satisfaction, with his blushing bride—

Only getting married turned out to be just the beginning. Sure, it was wonderful, but Lillian told him how much better things would be if they could move into a new place and fix it up. Martin wanted decent furniture, a TV set, a nice car.

So he started taking night courses and got a promotion to the front office. With the baby coming, he wanted to stick around and see his son arrive. And when it came, he realized he'd have to wait until it got a little older, started to walk and talk and develop a personality of its own.

About this time the company sent him out on the road as a troubleshooter on some of those other jobs, and now he *was* eating at those good hotels, living high on the hog and the expense-account. More than once he was tempted to unwind his watch. This was the good life....Of course, it would be even better if he just didn't have to *work*. Sooner or later, if he could cut in on one of the company deals, he could make a pile and retire. Then everything would be ideal.

It happened, but it took time. Martin's son was going to high school before he really got up there into the chips. Martin got a strong hunch that it was now or never, because he wasn't exactly a kid any more.

But right about then he met Sherry Westcott, and she didn't seem to think he was middle-aged at all, in spite of the way he was losing hair and adding stomach. She taught him that a *toupee* would cover the bald spot and a cummerbund could cover the potgut. In fact, she taught him quite a lot and he so enjoyed learning that he actually took out his watch and prepared to unwind it.

Unfortunately, he chose the very moment that the private detectives broke down the door of the hotel room, and then there was a long stretch of time when Martin was so busy fighting the divorce action that he couldn't honestly say he was enjoying any given moment.

When he made the final settlement with Lil he was broke again, and Sherry didn't seem to think he was so young, after all. So he squared his shoulders and went back to work.

He made his pile, eventually, but it took longer this time, and there wasn't much chance to have fun along the way. The fancy dames in the fancy cocktail lounges didn't seem to interest him any more, and neither did the liquor. Besides, the Doc had warned him off that.

But there were other pleasures for a rich man to investigate. Travel, for instance—and not riding the rods from one hick burg to another, either. Martin went around the world by plane and luxury liner. For a while it seemed as though he would find his moment after all, visiting the Taj Mahal by moonlight. Martin pulled out the battered old watchcase, and got ready to unwind it. Nobody else was there to watch him—

And that's why he hesitated. Sure, this was an enjoyable

moment, but he was alone. Lil and the kid were gone, Sherry was gone, and somehow he'd never had time to make any friends. Maybe if he found new congenial people, he'd have the ultimate happiness. That must be the answer—it wasn't just money or power or sex or seeing beautiful things. The real satisfaction lay in friendship.

So on the boat trip home, Martin tried to strike up a few acquaintances at the ship's bar. But all these people were much younger, and Martin had nothing in common with them. Also they wanted to dance and drink, and Martin wasn't in condition to appreciate such pastimes. Nevertheless, he tried.

Perhaps that's why he had the little accident the day before they docked in San Francisco. "Little accident" was the ship's doctor's way of describing it, but Martin noticed he looked very grave when he told him to stay in bed, and he'd called an ambulance to meet the liner at the dock and take the patient right to the hospital.

At the hospital, all the expensive treatment and the expensive smiles and the expensive words didn't fool Martin any. He was an old man with a bad heart, and they thought he was going to die.

But he could fool them. He still had the watch. He found it in his coat when he put on his clothes and sneaked out of the hospital.

He didn't have to die. He could cheat death with a single gesture—and he intended to do it as a free man, out there under a free sky.

That was the real secret of happiness. He understood it now. Not even friendship meant as much as freedom. This was the best thing of all—to be free of friends or family or the furies of the flesh.

Martin walked slowly beside the embankment under the night sky. Come to think of it, he was just about back where he'd started, so many years ago. But the moment was good, good enough to prolong forever. Once a bum, always a bum.

He smiled as he thought about it, and then the smile twisted sharply and suddenly, like the pain twisting sharply and suddenly in his chest. The world began to spin and he fell down on the side of the embankment.

He couldn't see very well, but he was still conscious, and he knew what had happened. Another stroke, and a bad one. Maybe this was it. Except that he wouldn't be a fool any longer. He wouldn't wait to see what was still around the corner.

Right now was his chance to use his power and save his life. And he was going to do it. He could still move, nothing could stop him.

He groped in his pocket and pulled out the old silver watch, fumbling with the stem. A few twists and he'd cheat death, he'd never have to ride that Hell-Bound Train. He could go on forever.

Forever.

Martin had never really considered the word before. To go on forever—but *how?* Did he *want* to go on forever, like this; a sick old man, lying helplessly here in the grass?

No. He couldn't do it. He wouldn't do it. And suddenly he wanted very much to cry, because he knew that somewhere along the line he'd outsmarted himself. And now it was too late. His eyes dimmed, there was a roaring in his ears...

He recognized the roaring, of course, and he wasn't at all surprised to see the train come rushing out of the fog up there on the embankment. He wasn't surprised when it stopped, either, or when the Conductor climbed off and walked slowly towards him.

The Conductor hadn't changed a bit. Even his grin was still the same.

"Hello, Martin," he said. "All aboard."

"I know," Martin whispered. "But you'll have to carry me. I can't walk. I'm not even really talking any more, am I?"

"Yes you are," the Conductor said. "I can hear you fine. And you can walk, too." He leaned down and placed his hand on Martin's chest. There was a moment of icy numbness, and then, sure enough, Martin could walk after all.

He got up and followed the Conductor along the slope, moving to the side of the train.

"In here?" he asked.

"No, the next car," the Conductor murmured. "I guess you're entitled to ride Pullman. After all, you're quite a successful man. You've tasted the joys of wealth and position and prestige. You've known the pleasures of marriage and fatherhood. You've sampled the delights of dining and drinking and debauchery, too, and you traveled high, wide and handsome. So let's not have any last-minute recriminations."

"All right," Martin sighed. "I can't blame you for my mistakes. On the other hand, you can't take credit for what happened, either. I worked for everything I got. I did it all on my own. I didn't even need your watch."

"So you didn't." the Conductor said, smiling. "But would you mind giving it back to me now?"

"Need it for the next sucker, eh?" Martin muttered.

"Perhaps."

Something about the way he said it made Martin look up. He tried to see the Conductor's eyes, but the brim of his cap cast a shadow. So Martin looked down at the watch instead.

"Tell me something," he said, softly. "If I give you the watch, what will you do with it?"

"Why, throw it into the ditch," the Conductor told him. "That's all I'll do with it." And he held out his hand.

"What if somebody comes along and finds it? And twists the stem backwards, and stops Time?"

"Nobody would do that," the Conductor murmured. "Even if they knew."

"You mean, it was all a trick? This is only an ordinary, cheap watch?"

"I didn't say that," whispered the Conductor. "I only said that no one has ever twisted the stem backwards. They've all been like you, Martin—looking ahead to find that perfect happiness. Waiting for the moment that never comes."

The Conductor held out his hand again.

Martin sighed and shook his head. "You cheated me after all."

"You cheated yourself, Martin. And now you're going to ride that Hell-Bound Train."

He pushed Martin up the steps and into the car ahead. As he entered, the train began to move and the whistle screamed. And Martin stood there in the swaying Pullman, gazing down the aisle at the other passengers. He could see them sitting there, and somehow it didn't seem strange at all.

Here they were; the drunks and the sinners, the gambling men and the grifters, the big-time spenders, the skirt-chasers, and all the jolly crew. They knew where they were going, of course, but they didn't seem to give a damn. The blinds were drawn on the windows, yet it was light inside, and they were all living it up—singing and passing the bottle and roaring with laughter, throwing the dice and telling their jokes and bragging their big brags, just the way Daddy used to sing about them in the old song.

"Mighty nice traveling companions," Martin said. "Why, I've never seen such a pleasant bunch of people. I mean, they seem to be really enjoying themselves!"

The Conductor shrugged. "I'm afraid things won't be quite so jazzy when we pull into that Depot Way Down Yonder."

For the third time, he held out his hand. "Now, before you sit down, if you'll just give me that watch. A bargain's a bargain—"

Martin smiled. "A bargain's a bargain," he echoed. "I agreed to ride your train if I could stop Time when I found the right moment of happiness. And I think I'm about as happy right here as I've ever been."

Very slowly, Martin took hold of the silver watch-stem.

"No!" gasped the Conductor. "No!"

But the watch-stem turned.

"Do you realize what you've done?" the Conductor yelled. "Now we'll never reach the Depot! We'll just go on riding, all of us—forever!"

Martin grinned. "I know," he said. "But the fun is in the trip, not the destination. You taught me that. And I'm looking forward to a wonderful trip. Look, maybe I can even help. If you were to find me another one of those caps, now, and let me keep this watch—"

And that's the way it finally worked out. Wearing his cap and carrying his battered old silver watch, there's no happier person in or out of this world—now and forever—than Martin. Martin, the new Brakeman on That Hell-Bound Train.

Kings in Darkness

by MICHAEL MOORCOCK

Three Kings in Darkness lie,
Gutheran of Org, and I,
Under a bleak and sunless sky—
The third Beneath the Hill.
—Song of Veerkad

IT WAS Elric, Lord of the lost and sundered Empire of Melnibone, who rode like a fanged wolf from a trap—all slavering madness and mirth. He rode from Nadsokor, City of Beggars, and there was hate in his wake. The citizens had judged him rightly for what he was—a nigromancer of superlative powers. Now they hounded him and also the grotesque little man who rode laughing at Elric's side; Moonglum the Outlander, from Elwher and the unmapped East.

The flames of brands devoured the velvet of the night as the yelling, ragged throng pushed their bony nags in pursuit of the pair.

Starvelings and tattered jackals that they were, there was strength in their gaudy numbers and long knives and bone bows glinted in the brandlight. They were too strong for a couple of men to fight, too few to represent serious danger in a hunt, so Elric and Moonglum had chosen to leave the city without dispute and now sped towards the full and rising moon which stabbed its sickly beams through the darkness to show them the disturbing waters of the Varkalk River and a chance of escape from the incensed mob.

They had half a mind to stand and face the mob, since the Varkalk was their only alternative. But they knew well what the beggars would do to them, whereas they were uncertain what would become of them once they had entered the river. The horses reached the sloping banks of the Varkalk and reared, with hooves lashing.

Cursing, the two men spurred the steeds and forced them down towards the water. Into the river the horses plunged, snorting and spluttering. Into the river which led a roaring course towards the hell-spawned Forest of Troos which lay within the borders of Org, country of necromancy and rotting, ancient evil.

Elric blew water away from his mouth and coughed. "They'll not follow us to Troos, I think," he shouted at his companion.

Moonglum said nothing. He only grinned, showing his white teeth and the unhidden fear in his eyes. The horses swam strongly with the current and behind them the ragged mob shrieked in frustrated blood-lust while some of their number laughed and jeered.

"Let the forest do our work for us!"

Elric laughed back at them, wildly, as the horses swam on down the dark , straight river, wide and deep, towards a sun-starved morning, cold and spiky with ice. Scattered, slim-peaked crags loomed on either side of the flat plain, through which the river ran swiftly. Green-tinted masses of jutting blacks and browns spread color through the rocks and the grass was waving on the plain as if for some purpose. Through the dawnlight, the beggar crew chased along the banks, but eventually gave up their quarry to return, shuddering, to Nadsokor.

When they had gone, Elric and Moonglum made their mounts swim toward the banks and climb them, stumbling, to the top where rocks and grass had already given way to sparse forest land which rose starkly on all sides, staining the earth with somber shades. The foliage waved jerkily, as if alive—sentient.

It was a forest of malignantly erupting blooms, blood-colored and sickly-mottled. A forest of bending, sinuously smooth trunks, black and shiny; a forest of spiked leaves of murky purples and gleaming greens—certainly an unhealthy place if judged only by the odor of rotting vegetation which was almost unbearable, impinging as it did upon the fastidious nostrils of Elric and Moonglum.

Moonglum wrinkled his nose and jerked his head in the direction they had come. "Back now?" he inquired. "We can avoid Troos and cut swiftly across a corner of Org to be in Bakshaan in just over a day. What say you, Elric?"

Elric frowned. "I don't doubt they'd welcome us in Bakshaan with the same warmth we received in Nadsokor. They'll not have forgotten the destruction we wrought there—and the wealth we acquired from their merchants. No, I have a fancy to explore the forest a little. I have heard tales of Org and its unnatural forest and should like to investigate the truth of them. My blade and sorcery will protect us, if necessary."

Moonglum sighed. "Elric—this once, let us not court the danger."

Elric smiled icily. His scarlet eyes blazed out of his dead white skin with peculiar intensity. "Danger? It can bring only death."

"Death is not to my liking, just yet," Moonglum said. "The fleshpots of Bakshaan, or if you prefer—Jadmar—on the other hand..."

But Elric was already urging his horse onward, heading for the forest. Moonglum sighed and followed.

Soon dark blossoms hid most of the sky, which was dark enough, and they could see only a little way in all directions. The rest of the forest seemed vast and sprawling; they could sense this, though sight of most of it was lost in the depressing gloom.

Moonglum recognized the forest from descriptions he had heard from mad-eyed travelers who drank purposefully in the shadows of Nadsokor's taverns.

"This is the forest of Troos, sure enough," he said to Elric. "It's told of how the Doomed Folk released tremendous forces upon the earth and caused terrible changes among men, beasts and vegetation. This forest is the last they created, and the last to perish. They must have resented the planet giving them birth."

"A child will always hate its parents at certain times," Elric said impassively.

"Children of whom to be extremely wary, I should think," Moonglum retorted. "Some say that when they were at the peak of their power, they had no Gods to frighten them."

"A daring people, indeed," Elric replied, with a faint smile. "They have my respect. But their lack of Gods and fear was probably our downfall, if not theirs. Now fear and the Gods are back and that, at least, is comforting."

Moonglum puzzled over this for a short time, and then, eventually, said nothing.

He was beginning to feel uneasy.

The place was full of malicious rustlings and whispers, though no living animal inhabited it, as far as they could tell. There was a discomforting absence of birds, rodents or insects and, though they normally had no love for such creatures, they would have appreciated their company in the disconcerting forest.

In a quavering voice, Moonglum began to sing a song in the hope that it would keep his spirits up, and his thoughts off the lurking forest.

A grin and a word is my trade;
From these, my profit is made.
Though my body's not tall and my courage is small,
My frame will take longer to fade.

So singing, with his natural amiability returning, Moonglum rode after the man he regarded as a friend—a friend who possessed something akin to mastery over the little man, though neither admitted it.

Elric smiled at Moonglum's song. "To sing of one's own lack of size and absence of courage is not an action designed to ward off one's enemies, Moonglum."

"But this way I offer no provocation," Moonglum replied glibly. "If I sing of my shortcomings, I am safe. If I were to boast of my talents, then someone might consider this to be a challenge and decide to teach me a lesson."

"True," Elric assented gravely, "and well spoken."

He began pointing at certain blossoms and leaves, remarking upon their alien tint and texture, referring to them in words which Moonglum could not understand, though he knew the words to be part of a sorcerer's vocabulary. The albino seemed to be untroubled by the fears which beset the Eastlander, but often, Moonglum knew, appearances with Elric could hide the opposite of what they indicated.

They stopped for a short break while Elric sifted through some of the samples he had torn from trees and plants. He carefully placed his prizes in his belt-pouch but would say nothing of why he did so to Moonglum.

"Come," he said, "Troos mysteries await us."

But then a new voice, a woman's said softly from the gloom: "Save the excursion for another day, strangers."

Elric reined his horse, one hand at *Stormbringer*'s hilt. The voice had had an unusual effect upon him. It had been low, deep and had, for a moment, sent the pulse in his throat throbbing. Incredibly, he sensed that he was suddenly standing on one of Fate's roads, but where the road would take him, he did not know. Quickly, he controlled his mind and then his body and looked towards the shadows from where the voice had come.

"You are very kind to offer us advice, madame," he said sternly. "Come, show yourself and give explanation..."

She rode out then, very slowly, on a black-coated gelding that pranced with a power she could barely restrain. Moonglum drew an appreciative breath for although heavy featured, she was incredibly beautiful. Her face and bearing was patrician, her eyes were gray-green, combining enigma and innocence. She was very young. For all her obvious womanhood and beauty, Moonglum aged her at seventeen or little more.

Elric frowned: "Do you ride alone?"

"I do now," she replied, trying to hide her obvious astonishment at the albino's weird lack of coloring. "I need aid—protection. Men who will escort me safely to Karlaak. There, they will be paid."

"Karlaak, by the Weeping Waste? It lies the other side of Ilmoira, a hundred leagues away and a week's traveling at speed." Elric did not wait for her to reply to this statement. "We are not hirelings, madame. We are noblemen in our own lands."

"Then you are bound by the vows of chivalry, sir, and cannot refuse my request."

Elric laughed shortly. "Chivalry, madame? We come not from the upstart nations of the South with their strange codes and rules of behavior. We are nobles of older stock whose actions are governed by our own desires. You would not ask what you do, if you knew our names."

She wetted her full lips with her tongue and said almost timidly: "You are...?"

"Elric of Melnibone, madame, called Elric Womanslayer in the West and this is Moonglum of Elwher; he has no conscience."

She gasped. "I have heard of you. There are stories—legends—the white-faced reaver, the hell-driven sorcerer with a blade that drinks the souls of men..."

"Aye, that's true. And however magnified they are with the retelling, they cannot hint, those tales, at the darker truths which lie in their origin. Now, madame, do you still seek our aid?" Elric's voice was gentle, without menace, as he saw that she was very much afraid, although she had managed to control the signs of fear and her lips were tight with determination.

"I have no choice. I am at your mercy. My father, the Senior Senator of Karlaak, is very rich. Karlaak is called the City of the Jade Towers, as you will know, and such rare jades and ambers we have. Many could be yours."

"Be careful, madame, lest you anger me," warned Elric, although Moonglum's bright eyes lighted with avarice. "We are not nags to be hired or goods to be bought. Beside which," he smiled disdainfully, "I am from crumbling Imrryr, the Dreaming City, from the Isle of the Dragon, hub of Ancient Melnibone, and I know what beauty really is. Your baubles cannot tempt one who has looked upon the milky Heart of Arioch, upon the blinding iridescence that throbs from the Ruby Throne, of the langorous and unnameable colors in the Actorios stone of the Ring of Kings. These are more than jewels, madame—they contain the life-stuff of the universe."

"I apologize, Lord Elric, and to you Sir Moonglum."

Elric laughed, almost with affection. "We are grim clowns, lady, but the Gods of Luck aided our escape from Nadsokor and we owe them a debt. We'll escort you to Karlaak, City of the Jade Towers, and explore the Forest of Troos another time."

Her thanks was tempered with a wary look in her eyes.

"And now we have made introductions," said Elric, "perhaps you would be good enough to give your name and tell us your story."

"I am Zarozinia from Karlaak, a daughter of the Voashoon, the most powerful clan in South Eastern Ilmoira. We have kinsmen in the trading cities on the coasts of Pikarayd and I went with two cousins and my uncle to visit them."

"A perilous journey, Lady Zarozinia."

"Aye and there are not only natural dangers, sir. Two weeks ago we made our goodbyes and began the journey home. Safely we crossed the Straits of Vilmir and there employed men-at-arms, forming a strong caravan to journey through Vilmir and so to Ilmoira. We skirted Nadsokor since we had heard that the City of Beggars is inhospitable to honest travelers..."

Here, Elric smiled: "And sometimes to dishonest travelers, as we can appreciate."

Again the expression on her face showed that she had some difficulty in equating his obvious good humor with his evil reputation. "Having skirted Nadsokor," she continued, "we came this way and reached the borders of Org wherein, of course, Troos lies. Very warily we traveled, knowing dark Org's reputation, along the fringes of the forest. And then we were ambushed and our hired men-at-arms deserted us."

"Ambushed, eh?" broke in Moonglum. "By whom, madame, did you know?"

"By their unsavory looks and squat shapes they seemed native Orgians. They fell upon the caravan and my uncle and cousins fought bravely but were slain. One of my cousins slapped the rump of my gelding and sent it galloping so that I could not control it. I heard—terrible screams—mad, giggling shouts—and when I at last brought my horse to a halt, I was lost. Later I heard you approach and waited in fear for you to pass, thinking you also were Orgians, but when I heard your accents and some of your speech, I thought that you might help me."

"And help you we shall, madame," said Moonglum bowing

gallantly from the saddle. "And I am indebted to you for convincing Lord Elric here of your need. But for you, we should be deep in this awful forest by now and experiencing strange terrors no doubt. I offer my sorrow for your dead kinfolk and assure you that you will be protected from now onward by more than swords and brave hearts, for sorcery can be called up if needs be."

"Let's hope there'll be no need," frowned Elric.

"You talk blithely of sorcery, friend Moonglum—you who hate me to use the art."

Moonglum grinned.

"I was consoling the young lady, Elric. And I've had occasion to be grateful for your horrid powers, I'll admit. Now I suggest that we make camp for the night and so refreshed be on our way at dawn."

"I'll agree to that," said Elric, glancing almost with embarrassment at the girl. Again he felt the pulse in his throat begin to throb and this time he had more difficulty in controlling it.

The girl also seemed fascinated by the albino. There was an attraction between them which might be strong enough to throw both their destinies along wildly different paths than any they had guessed.

Night came again quickly, for the days were short in those parts. While Moonglum tended the fire, nervously peering around him, Zarozinia, her richly embroidered cloth-of-gold gown shimmering in the firelight, walked gracefully to where Elric sat sorting the herbs he had collected. She glanced at him cautiously and then seeing that he was absorbed, stared at him with open curiosity.

He looked up and smiled faintly, his eyes for once unprotected, his strange face frank and pleasant. "Some of these are healing herbs," he said, "and others are used in summoning spirits. Yet others give unnatural strength to the imbiber and some turn men mad. They will be useful to me."

She sat down beside him, her thick-fingered hands pushing

her black hair back. Her full breasts lifted and fell rapidly.

"Are you really the terrible evil-bringer of the legends, Lord Elric? I find it hard to credit."

"I have brought evil to many places," he said, "but usually there has already been evil to match mine. I seek no excuses, for I know what I am and I know what I have done. I have slain malignant sorcerers and destroyed oppressors, but I have also been responsible for slaying fine men, and a woman, my cousin, whom I loved, I killed—or my sword did."

"And you are master of your sword."

"Yes—perhaps. I often wonder. Without it, I am helpless." He put his hand around *Stormbringer's* hilt. "I should be grateful to it." Once again his red eyes seemed to become deeper, protecting some bitter emotion which was rooted at the core of his soul.

"I'm sorry if I revived unpleasant recollection..."

"Do not feel sorry, Lady Zarozinia. The pain is within me—you did not put it there. In fact I'd say you relieve it greatly by your presence."

Half-startled, she glanced at him and smiled. "I am no wanton, sir," she said, "but..."

He got up quickly.

"Moonglum, is the fire going well?"

"Aye, Elric. She'll stay in for the night." Moonglum cocked his head on one side. It was unlike Elric to make such empty queries, but Elric said nothing further so the Eastlander shrugged, turned away to check his gear.

Since he could think of little else to say, Elric turned and said quietly, urgently: "I'm a killer and a thief, not fit to..."

"Lord Elric, I am..."

"You are infatuated by a legend, that is all."

"No! If you feel what I feel, then you'll know it's more."

"You are young."

"Old enough."

"Beware. I must fulfil my destiny."

"Your destiny?"

"It is no destiny at all, but an awful thing called doom. And I have no pity at all except when I see something in my own soul. Then I have pity—and I pity. But I hate to look and this is part of the doom which drives me. Not Fate, nor the Stars, nor Men, nor Demons, nor Gods. Look at me, Zarozinia—it is Elric, poor white chosen plaything of the Gods of Time—Elric of Melnibone who causes his own gradual and terrible destruction."

"It is suicide!"

"Aye. Suicide of a dreadful sinning kind, for I drive myself to slow death. And those who go with me suffer also."

"You speak falsely, Lord Elric—from guilt-madness."

"Because I am guilty, Lady."

"And does Sir Moonglum go to doom with you?"

"He is unlike others—he is indestructible in his own self-assurance."

"I am confident, also, Lord Elric."

"But your confidence is that of youth, it is different."

"Need I lose it with my youth?"

"You have strength. You are as strong as we are. I'll grant you that."

She opened her arms, rising. "Then be reconciled, Elric of Melnibone."

And he was. He seized her greedily, kissed her with a deeper need than that of passion. For the first time, Cymoril of Imrryr was forgotten as they dropped to the soft turf, oblivious of Moonglum who polished away at his curved sword with wry jealousy.

They all slept and the fire waned.

Elric, in his joy, had forgotten, or not heeded, that he had a watch to take and Moonglum, who had no source of strength but himself, stayed awake for as long as he could but sleep overcame him.

In the shadows of the awful trees, figures moved with shambling caution.

The misshapen men of Org began to creep inward towards the sleepers.

Then Elric opened his eyes, aroused by instinct, stared at Zarozinia's peaceful face beside him, moved his eyes without turning his head and saw the danger. He rolled over, grasped *Stormbringer* and tugged the runeblade from its sheath. The sword hummed as if in anger at being awakened.

"Moonglum! Danger!" Elric bellowed in fear, for he had more to protect than his own life. The little man's head jerked up. His curved saber was already across his knees and he jumped to his feet, ran towards Elric as the Orgians closed in.

"I apologize," he said.

"My fault, I..."

And then the Orgians were at them. Elric and Moonglum stood over the girl as she came awake, saw the situation and did not scream. Instead she looked around for a weapon but found none. She remained still, where she was, the only thing to do.

Smelling like offal, the gibbering Orgians, some dozen of them, slashed at Elric and Moonglum with heavy blades like cleavers, long and dangerous.

Stormbringer whined and smote through a cleaver, cut into an Orgian's neck and beheaded him. Blood gurgled from the corpse as it slumped back across the fire. Moonglum ducked beneath a howling cleaver, lost his balance, fell, slashed at his opponent's legs and hamstrung him so that he collapsed shrieking. Moonglum stayed on the ground and lunged upwards, taking another in the heart. Then he sprang to his feet and stood shoulder to shoulder with Elric while Zarozinia got up behind them.

"The horses," grunted Elric. "If it's safe, try to get them."

There were still seven Orgians standing and Moonglum groaned as a cleaver sliced flesh from his left arm, retaliated, pierced the man's throat, turned slightly and sheared off another's face. They pressed forward, taking the attack to the incensed Orgians. His left hand covered with his own blood, Moonglum painfully pulled his long poniard from its sheath and held it with his thumb along the handle, blocked an opponent's swing, closed in and killed him with a ripping upward thrust of the dagger, the action of which caused his wound to pound with agony.

Elric held his great runesword in both hands and swung it in a semicircle, hacking down the howling misshapen things. Zarozinia darted towards the horses, leaped on to her own and led the other two towards the fighting men. Elric smote at another and got into his saddle, thanking his own forethought to leave the equipment on the horses in case of danger. Moonglum quickly joined him and they thundered out of the clearing.

"The saddlebags," Moonglum called in greater agony than that created by his wound. "We've left the saddlebags!"

"What of it? Don't press your luck, my friend."

"But all our treasure's in them!"

Elric laughed, partly in relief, partly from real humor. "We'll retrieve them, friend, never fear."

"I know you, Elric. You've no value for the realities."

But even Moonglum was laughing as they left the enraged Orgians behind them and slowed to a canter.

Elric reached and hugged Zarozinia. "You have the courage of your noble clan in your veins," he said.

"Thank you," she replied, pleased with the compliment, "but we cannot match such swordmanship as that displayed by you and Moonglum. It was fantastic."

"Thank the blade," he said shortly.

"No. I will thank you. I think you place too much reliance upon that hell weapon, however powerful it is."

"I need it."

"For what?"

"For my own strength and, now, to give strength to you."

"I'm no vampire," she smiled, "and need no such fearful strength as that supplies."

"Then be assured that I do," he told her gravely. "You would not love me if the blade did not give me what I need. I am like a spineless sea-thing without it."

"I do not believe that, but will not dispute with you now."

They rode for a while without speaking.

Later, they stopped, dismounted and Zarozinia put herbs that Elric had given her upon Moonglum's wounded arm and began to bind it.

Elric was thinking deeply. The forest rustled with macabre, sensuous sounds. "We're in the heart of Troos," he said, "and our intention to skirt the forest has been forestalled. I have it in mind to call on the King of Org and so round off our visit."

Moonglum laughed. "Shall we send our swords along first? And bind our own hands?" His pain was already eased by the herbs which were having quick effect.

"I mean it. We owe, all of us, much to the Orgians. They slew Zarozinia's uncle and cousins, they wounded you and they now have our treasure. We have many reasons for asking the King for recompense. Also, they seem stupid and should be easy to trick."

"Aye. The king will pay us back for our lack of common-sense by tearing our limbs off."

"I'm in earnest. I think we should go."

"I'll agree that I'd like our wealth returned to us. But we cannot risk the lady's safety, Elric."

"I am to be Elric's wife, Moonglum. Therefore if he visits the King of Org, I shall come too."

Moonglum lifted an eyebrow. "A quick courtship."

"She speaks the truth, however. We shall all go to Org—and sorcery will protect us from the King's uncalled for wrath."

"And still you wish for death and vengeance, Elric," shrugged Moonglum, mounting. "Well, it's all the same to me since your roads, whatever else, are profitable ones. You may be the Lord of Bad Luck by your own reckoning, but you bring good luck to me, I'll say that."

"No more courting death," smiled Elric, "but we'll have some revenge, I hope."

"Dawn will be with us soon," Moonglum said. "The Orgian citadel lies six hours ride from here by my working, South-South-East by the Ancient Star, if the map I memorized in Nadsokor was correct."

"You have an instinct for direction that never fails, Moonglum. Every caravan should have such a man as you."

"We base an entire philosophy on the stars in Elwher," Moonglum replied. "We regard them as the master plan for everything that happens on earth. As they revolve around the planet they see all things, past, present and future. They are our Gods."

"Predictable Gods, at least," said Elric and they rode off towards Org with light hearts considering the enormity of their risk.

Little was known of the tiny kingdom of Org save that the Forest of Troos lay within its boundaries and to that, other nations felt, it was welcome. The people were unpleasant to look upon, for the most part, and their bodies were stunted and strangely altered. Legend had it that they were the descendants of the Doomed Folk who had wrought such destruction upon the earth an entire Time Cycle before. Their rulers, it was said, were shaped like normal men insofar as their outward bodily appearance went, but their minds were warped more horribly than the limbs of their subjects.

The inhabitants were few and were generally scattered, ruled by their king from his citadel which was also called Org.

It was for this citadel that Elric and his companions rode

and, as they did so, Elric explained how he planned to protect them all from the Orgians.

In the forest he had found a particular leaf which, when used with certain invocations (which were harmless in that the invoker was in little danger of being harmed by the spirits he marshalled) would invest that person, and anyone else to whom he gave the drug distilled from the leaf, temporary invulnerability.

The spell somehow reknitted the skin and flesh structure so that it could withstand any edge and almost any blow. Elric explained, in a rare garrulous mood, how the drug and spell combined to achieve the effect, but his archaicisms and esoteric words meant little to the other two.

They stopped an hour's ride from where Moonglum expected to find the citadel so that Elric could prepare the drug and invoke the spell.

He worked swiftly over a small fire, using an alchemist's pestle and mortar, mixing the shredded leaf with a little water. As the brew bubbled on the fire, he drew peculiar runes on the ground, some of which were twisted into such alien forms that they seemed to disappear into a different dimension and reappear beyond it.

Bone and blood and flesh and sinew,
Spell and spirit bind anew;
Potent potion work the life charm,
Keep its takers safe from harm.

So Elric chanted as a small pink cloud formed in the air over the fire, wavered, reformed into a spiral shape which curled downwards into the bowl. The brew spluttered and then was still. The albino sorcerer said: "An old boyhood spell, so simple that I'd near forgotten it. The leaf for the potion grows only in Troos and therefore it is rarely possible to perform."

The brew, which had been liquid, had now solidified and Elric broke it into small pellets. "Too much," he warned, "taken at one time is poison, and yet the effect can last for several hours. Not always, though, but we must accept that small risk." He handed both of them a pellet which they received dubiously. "Swallow them just before we reach the citadel," he told them, "or in the event of the Orgians finding us first."

Then they mounted and rode on again.

Some miles to the Southeast of Troos, a blind man sang a grim song in his sleep and so woke himself...

They reached the brooding citadel of Org at dusk. Gutteral, drooling voices shouted at them from the battlements of the square-cut ancient dwelling place of the Kings of Org. The thick rock oozed moisture and was corroded by lichen and sickly, mottled moss. The only entrance large enough for a mounted man to pass through was reached by a path almost a foot deep in evil-smelling black mud.

"What's your business at the Royal Court of Gutheran the Mighty?"

They could not see who asked the question.

"We seek hospitality and an audience with your liege," called Moonglum cheerfully, successfully hiding his nervousness. "We bring important news to Org."

A twisted face peered down from the battlements. "Enter strangers and be welcome," it said unwelcomingly.

The heavy wooden drawgate shifted upward to allow them entrance and the horses pushed their way slowly through the mud and so into the courtyard of the citadel.

Overhead, the gray sky was a racing field of black tattered clouds which streamed towards the horizon as if to escape the horrid boundaries of Org and the disgusting Forest of Troos.

The courtyard was covered, though not so deeply, with the same foul mud as had impaired their progress to the citadel. It was full of heavy, unmoving shadow. On Elric's right, a flight of steps went up to an arched entrance which was hung, partially, with the same unhealthy lichen he had seen on the outer walls and, also, in the Forest of Troos.

Through this archway, brushing at the lichen with a pale, beringed hand, a tall man came and stood on the top step, regarding the visitors through heavy lidded eyes. He was, in contrast to the other Orgians, handsome with a massive, leonine head and long hair as white as Elric's; although the hair on the head of this great, solid man was somewhat dirty, tangled, unbrushed. He was dressed in a heavy jerkin of quilted, embossed leather, a yellow kilt which reached to his ankles and he carried a wide-bladed dagger, naked in his belt. He was older than Elric, aged between forty and fifty and his powerful, if somewhat decadent, face was seamed and pockmarked.

He stared at them in silence and did not welcome them; instead he signed to one of the battlement guards who caused the drawgate to be lowered. It came down with a crash, blocking off their way of escape.

"Kill the men and keep the woman," said the massive man in a low monotone. Elric had heard dead men speak in that manner.

As planned, Elric and Moonglum stood either side of Zarozinia and remained where they were, arms folded.

Puzzled, shambling Orgians came warily at them, their loose trousers dragging in the mud, their hands hidden by the long shapeless sleeves of their filthy garments. They swung their cleavers. Elric felt a faint shock as the blade thudded on to his arm, but that was all. Moonglum's experience was similar.

The Orgians fell back, amazement and confusion on their bestial faces.

The tall man's eyes widened. He put one ring-covered hand on his thick lips, chewing at a nail.

"Our swords have no effect upon them, King! They do not cut and they do not bleed. What are these folk?"

Elric laughed theatrically. "We are not common folk, little

human, be assured. We are the messengers of the Gods and come to your King with a message from our great masters. Do not worry, we shall not harm you since we are in no danger of being harmed. Stand aside and make us welcome."

Elric could see that King Gutheran was puzzled and not absolutely taken in by his words. Elric cursed to himself. He had measured the Orgian's intelligence by those he had seen. This king, mad or not, was much more intelligent, was going to be harder to deceive. He led the way up the steps towards glowering Gutheran.

"Greetings, King Gutheran. The Gods have, at last, returned to Org and wish you to know this."

"Org has had no Gods to worship for an eternity," said Gutheran hollowly, turning back into the citadel. "Why should we accept them now?"

"You are impertinent, King."

"And you are audacious. How do I know you come from the Gods?" He walked ahead of them, leading them through the low-roofed halls.

"You saw that the swords of your subjects had no effect upon us."

"True. I'll take that incident as proof for the moment. I suppose there must be a banquet in your—honor—I shall order it. Be welcome, messengers." His words were ungracious but it was virtually impossible to detect anything from Gutheran's tone, since the man's voice stayed at the same pitch.

Elric pushed his heavy riding cloak back from his shoulders and said lightly: "We shall mention your kindness to our masters."

The Court was a place of gloomy halls and false laughter and although Elric put many questions to Gutheran, the king would not answer them, or did so by means of ambiguous phrases which meant nothing. They were not given chambers wherein they could refresh themselves but instead stood about for several hours in the main hall of the citadel and Gutheran, while he was with them and not giving orders for the banquet, sat slumped on his throne and chewed at his nails, ignoring them.

"Pleasant hospitality," whispered Moonglum.

"Elric—how long will the effects of the drug last?" Zarozinia had remained close to him. He put his arm around her shoulders. "I do not know. Not much longer. But it has served its purpose. I doubt if they will try to attack us a second time. However, beware of other attempts, subtler ones, upon our lives."

The main hall, which had a higher roof than the others and was completely surrounded by a gallery which ran around it well above the floor, fairly close to the roof, was chilly and unwarmed. No fires burned in the several hearths, which were open and let into the floor, and the walls dripped moisture and were undecorated; damp, solid stone, timeworn and gaunt. There were not even rushes upon the floor which was strewn with old bones and pieces of decaying food.

"Hardly house-proud, are they?" commented Moonglum looking around him with distaste and glancing at brooding Gutheran who was seemingly oblivious of their presence.

A servitor shambled into the hall and whispered a few words to the king. He nodded and arose, leaving the Great Hall.

Soon men came in, carrying benches and tables and began to place them about the hall.

The banquet was, at last, due to commence. And the air had menace in it.

The three visitors sat together on the right of the King who had donned a richly jeweled chain of kingship, while his son and several pale-faced female members of the Royal line sat on the left, unspeaking even among themselves.

Prince Hurd, a sullen-faced youth who seemed to bear a resentment against his father, picked at the unappetizing food which was served them all.

He drank heavily of the wine which had little flavor but

was strong, fiery stuff and this seemed to warm the company a little.

"And what do the Gods want of us poor Orgians?" Hurd said, staring hard at Zarozinia with more than friendly interest.

Elric answered: "They ask nothing of you but your recognition. In return they will, on occasions, help you."

"That is all?" Hurd laughed. "That is more than those from the Hill can offer, eh, father?"

Gutheran turned his great head slowly to regard his son.

"Yes," he murmured, and the word seemed to carry warning.

Moonglum said: "The Hill—what is that?"

He got no reply. Instead a high-pitched laugh came from the entrance to the Great Hall. A thin, gaunt man stood there staring ahead with a fixed gaze. His features though emaciated, strongly resembled Gutheran's. He carried a stringed instrument and plucked at the gut so that it wailed and moaned with melancholy insistence.

Hurd said savagely: "Look, father, 'tis blind Veerkad, the minstrel, your brother. Shall he sing for us?"

"Sing?"

"Shall he sing his songs, father?"

Gutheran's mouth trembled and twisted and he said after a moment: "He may entertain our guests with an heroic ballad if he wishes, but..."

"But certain other songs he shall not sing..." Hurd grinned maliciously. He seemed to be tormenting his father deliberately in some way which Elric could not guess. Hurd shouted at the blind man: "Come Uncle Veerkad—sing!"

"There are strangers present," said Veerkad hollowly above the wail of his own music. "Strangers in Org?"

Hurd giggled and drank more wine. Gutheran scowled and continued to tremble, gnawing at his nails.

Elric called: "We'd appreciate a song, minstrel."

"Then you'll have the song of the Three Kings in Darkness, strangers, and hear the ghastly story of the Kings of Org."

"No!" shouted Gutheran, leaping from his place, but Veerkad was already singing:

Three Kings in darkness lie,
Gutheran of Org, and I,
Under a bleak and sunless sky—
The third beneath the Hill.
When shall the third arise?
Only when another dies...

"Stop!" Gutheran got up in an obviously insane rage and stumbled across the table, trembling in terror, his face blanched, striking at the blind man, his brother. Two blows and the minstrel fell, slumping to the floor and not moving. "Take him out! Do not let him enter again." The king shrieked and foam flecked his lips.

Hurd, sober for a moment, jumped across the table, scattering dishes and cups and took his father's arm.

"Be calm, father. I have a new plan for our entertainment."

"You! You seek my throne. 'Twas you who goaded Veerkad to sing his dreadful song. You know I cannot listen without..." He stared at the door. "One day the legend shall be realized and the Hill-King shall come. Then shall I, you and Org perish."

"Father," Hurd was smiling horribly, "let the female visitor dance for us a dance of the Gods."

"What?"

"Let the woman dance for us, father."

Elric heard him. By now the drug must have worn off. He could not afford to show his hand by offering his companions further doses. He got to this feet.

"What sacrilege do you speak, Prince?"

"We have given you entertainment. It is the custom in Org for our visitors to give us entertainment also."

The hall was electric with menace. Elric regretted his plan to trick the Orgians, now. But there was nothing he could do. He had intended to exact tribute from them in the name of the Gods, but obviously these mad men feared more immediate and tangible dangers than any the Gods might represent.

He had made a mistake, put the lives of his friends in danger as well as his own, What should he do? Zarozinia murmured: "I have learned dances in Ilmiora where all ladies are taught the art. Let me dance for them. It might placate them and bedazzle them to make our work easier."

"Arioch knows our work is hard enough now. I was a fool to have conceived this plan. Very well, Zarozinia, dance for them, but with caution." He shouted at Hurd: "Our companion will dance for you, to show you the beauty that the Gods create. Then you must pay the tribute, for our masters grow impatient."

"The tribute?" Gutheran looked up. "You mentioned nothing of tribute."

"Your recognition of the Gods must take the form of precious stones and metals, King Gutheran. I thought you to understand that."

"You seem more like common thieves than uncommon messengers, my friends. We are poor in Org and have nothing to give away to charlatans."

"Beware of your words, King!" Elric's clear voice echoed warningly through the hall.

"We'll see the dance and then judge the truth of what you've told us."

Elric seated himself, grasped Zarozinia's hand beneath the table as she arose, giving her comfort.

She walked gracefully and confidently into the center of the hall and there began to dance. Elric, who loved her, was amazed at her splendid grace and artistry. She danced the old, beautiful dances of Ilmiora, entrancing even the thick-skulled Orgians and, as she danced, a great golden Guest Cup was brought in.

Hurd leaned across his father and said to Elric: "The Guest Cup, Lord. It is our custom that our guests drink from it in friendship."

Elric nodded, annoyed at being disturbed in his watching of the wonderful dance, his eyes fixed on Zarozinia as she postured and glided. There was silence in the hall.

Hurd handed him the cup and absently he put it to his lips, seeing this Zarozinia danced on to the table and began to weave along it to where Elric sat. As he took the first sip, Zarozinia cried out and, with her foot, knocked the cup from his hand. The wine splashed on to Gutheran and Hurd who half rose, startled. "It was drugged, Elric. They drugged it!"

Hurd lashed at her with his hand, striking her across the face. She fell from the table and lay moaning slightly on the filthy floor. "Bitch! Would the messengers of the Gods be harmed by a little drugged wine?"

Enraged, Elric pushed aside Gutheran and struck savagely at Hurd so that the young man's mouth gushed blood. But the drug was already having effect. Gutheran shouted something and Moonglum drew his saber, glancing upward. Elric was swaying, his senses were jumbled and the scene had an unreal quality. He saw servants grasp Zarozinia but could not see how Moonglum was faring. He felt sick and dizzy, could hardly control his limbs.

Summoning up his last remaining strength, Elric clubbed Hurd down with one tremendous blow. Then he collapsed into unconsciousness.

There was the cold clutch of chains about his wrists and a thin drizzle was falling directly on to his face which stung where Hurd's nails had ripped it.

He looked about him. He was chained between two stone menhirs upon an obvious burial barrow of gigantic size. It was night and a pale moon hovered in the heavens above him. He looked down at the group of men below. Hurd and Gutheran were among them. They grinned at him mockingly.

"Farewell, messenger. You will serve us a good purpose and placate the Ones from the Hill!" Hurd called as he and the others scurried back toward the citadel which lay, silhouetted, a short distance away.

Where was he? What had happened to Zarozinia—and Moonglum? Why had he been chained thus upon—realisation and remembrance came—*the Hill!*

He shuddered, helpless in the strong chains which held him. Desperately he began to tug at them, bu' 'hey would not yield. He searched his brain for a plan, but he was confused by torment and worry for his friends' safety. He heard a dreadful scuttling sound from below and saw a ghastly white shape dart into the gloom. Wildly he struggled in the rattling iron which held him.

In the Great Hall of the citadel, a riotous celebration was now reaching the state of an ecstatic orgy. Gutheran and Hurd were totally drunk, laughing insanely at their victory.

Outside the Hall, Veerkad listened and hated. Particularly he hated his brother, the man who had deposed and blinded him to prevent his study of sorcery by means of which he had planned to raise the King from Beneath the Hill.

"The time has come, at last," he whispered to himself and stopped a passing servant.

"Tell me—where is the girl kept?"

"In Gutheran's chamber, master."

Veerkad released the man and began to grope his way through the gloomy corridors up twisting steps, until he reached the room he sought. Here he produced a key, one of many he'd had made without Gutheran's knowing, and unlocked the door.

Zarozinia saw the blind man enter and could do nothing. She was gagged and bound with her own dress and still dazed from the blow Hurd had given her. They had told her of Elric's fate, but Moonglum had so far escaped them, guards hunted him even now in the stinking corridors of Org.

"I've come to take you to your companion, lady," smiled blind Veerkad, grasping her roughly with strength that his insanity had given him, picked her up and fumbled his way towards the door. He knew the passages of Org perfectly, for he had been born and grown up among them.

But two men were in the corridor outside Gutheran's chambers. One of them was Hurd, Prince of Org, who resented his father's appropriation of the girl and desired her for himself. He saw Veerkad bearing the girl away and stood silent while his uncle passed.

The other man was Moonglum, who observed what was happening from the shadows where he had hidden from the searching guards. As Hurd followed Veerkad, on cautious feet, Moonglum followed him.

Veerkad went out of the citadel by a small side door and carried his living burden toward the looming Burial Hill.

All about the foot of the monstrous barrow swarmed the leprous-white ghouls who sensed the presence of Elric, the Orgian's sacrifice to them.

Now Elric understood.

These were the things the Orgians feared more than the Gods. These were the living-dead ancestors of those who now reveled in the Great Hall. Perhaps these were actually the Doomed Folk. Was that their doom? Never to rest? Never to die? Just to degenerate into mindless ghouls? Elric shuddered.

Now desperation brought back his memory.

He cried to Arioch, the Demon God of Melnibone, and his voice was in agonized wail to the brooding sky and the pulsing earth.

"Arioch! Destroy the stones. Save your servant! Arioch—master—aid me!"

It was not enough. The ghouls gathered together and began to scuttle, gibbering up the barrow toward the helpless albino.

"Arioch! These are the things that would forsake your memory! Aid me to destroy them!"

The earth trembled and the sky became overcast, hiding the moon but not the white-faced, bloodless ghouls who were now almost upon him.

And then a ball of fire formed in the sky above him and the very sky seemed to shake and sway around it. Then, with a roaring crash two bolts of lightening slashed down, pulverizing the stones and releasing Elric.

He got to his feet, knowing that Arioch would demand his price, as the first ghouls reached him.

He did not retreat, but in his rage and desperation leapt among them, smashing and flailing with the lengths of chain. The ghouls fell back and fled, gibbering in fear and anger, down the hill and into the barrow.

Elric could now see that there was a gaping entrance to the barrow below him; black against the blackness. Breathing heavily, he found that his belt pouch had been left him. From it he took a length of slim, gold wire and began frantically to pick at the locks of the manacles.

Veerkad chuckled to himself and Zarozinia hearing him was almost mad with terror. He kept drooling the words into her ear: "When shall the third arise? Only when another dies. When that other's blood flows red—we'll hear the footfalls of the dead. You and I, we shall resurrect him and such vengeance will be wreck upon my cursed brother. Your blood, my dear, it will be that released him." He felt that the ghouls were gone and judged them placated by their feast. "Your lover has been useful to me," he laughed as he began to enter the barrow. The smell of death almost overpowered the girl as the blind madman bore her downward into the heart of the Hill.

Hurd, sobered after his walk in the colder air, was horrified when he saw where Veerkad was going; the barrow, the Hill of the King, was the most feared spot in the land of Org. Hurd paused before the black entrance and turned to run. Then, suddenly, he saw the form of Elric, looming huge and bloody, descending the barrow slope, cutting off his escape.

With a wild yell he fled into the Hill passage.

Elric had not previously noticed the Prince, but the yell startled him and he tried to see who had given it but was too late. He began to run down the steep incline toward the entrance of the barrow. Another figure came scampering out of the darkness.

"Elric! Thank the stars and all the Gods of earth! You live!"

"Thank Arioch, Moonglum. Where's Zarozinia?"

"In there—the mad minstrel took her with him and Hurd followed. They are all insane, these kings and princes, I see no sense to their actions."

"I have an idea that the minstrel means Zarozinia no good. Quickly, we must follow."

"By the stars, the stench of death! I have breathed nothing like it—not even at the great battle of the Eshmir Valley where the armies of Elwher met those of Tararn Gashtek, Lord of the Mounted Hordes, and half a million corpses strewed the valley from end to end."

"If you've no stomach..."

"I wish I had none. It would not be so bad. Come..."

They rushed into the passage, led by the far away sounds of Veerkad's maniacal laughter and the somewhat nearer movements of a fear-maddened Hurd who was now trapped between two enemies and yet more afraid of a third.

Hurd blundered along in the blackness, sobbing to himself in his terror.

In the weirdly phosphorescent Central Tomb, surrounded by the mummified corpses of his ancestors, Veerkad chanted the resurrection ritual before the great coffin of the Hill-King—

a giant thing, half as tall again as Veerkad who was tall enough. Veerkad was forgetful for his own safety and thinking only of vengeance upon his brother Gutheran. He held a long dagger over Zarozinia who lay huddled and terrified upon the ground near the coffin.

The spilling of Zarozinia's blood would be the culmination of the ritual and then—

Then Hell would, quite literally, be let loose. Or so Veerkad planned. He finished his chanting and raised the knife just as Hurd came screeching into the Central Tomb with his own sword drawn. Veerkad swung round, his blind face working in thwarted rage.

Savagely, without stopping for a moment, Hurd ran his sword into Veerkad's body, plunging the blade in up to the hilt so that its bloody point appeared sticking from his back. But the other, in his groaning death spasms, locked his hands about the Prince's throat. Locked them immovably.

Somehow, the two men retained a semblance of life and, struggling with each other in a macabre death-dance, swayed about the glowing chamber. The coffin of the Hill-King began to tremble and shake slightly, the movement hardly perceptible.

So Elric and Moonglum found Veerkad and Hurd. Seeing that both were near dead, Elric raced across the Central Tomb to where Zarozinia lay, unconscious, mercifully, from her ordeal. Elric picked her up and made to return.

He glanced at the throbbing coffin.

"Quickly, Moonglum. That blind fool has invoked the dead, I can tell. Hurry, my friend, before the hosts of Hell are upon us."

Moonglum gasped and followed Elric as he ran back towards the cleaner air of night.

"Where to now, Elric?"

"We'll have to risk going back to the citadel. Our horses are there and our goods. We need the horses to take us quickly away, for I fear there's going to be a terrible bloodletting soon if my instinct is right."

"There should not be too much opposition, Elric. They were all drunk when I left. That was how I managed to evade them so easily. By now, if they continued drinking as heavily as when last I saw them, they'll be unable to move at all."

"Then let's make haste."

They left the Hill behind them and began to run towards the citadel.

Moonglum had spoken truth. Everyone was lying about the Great Hall in drunken sleep. Open fires had been lit in the hearths and they blazed, sending shadows skipping around the Hall. Elric said softly:

"Moonglum, go with Zarozinia to the stables and prepare our horses. I will settle our debt with Gutheran first." He pointed. "See, they have heaped their booty upon the table, gloating in their apparent victory."

Stormbringer lay upon a pile of burst sacks and saddle-bags which contained the loot stolen from Zarozinia's uncle and cousins and from Elric and Moonglum.

Zarozinia, now conscious but confused, left with Moonglum to locate the stables and Elric picked his way towards the table, across the sprawled shapes of drunken Orgians, around the blazing fires and caught up, thankfully, his hell-forged runeblade.

Then he leaped over the table and was about to grasp Gutheran, who still had his fabulously gemmed chain of kingship around his neck, when the great doors of the Hall crashed open and a howling blast of icy air sent the torches dancing and leaping. Elric turned, Gutheran forgotten, and his eyes widened.

Framed in the doorway stood the King from Beneath the Hill.

* * *

The long-dead monarch had been raised by Veerkad whose own blood had completed the work of resurrection. He stood in rotting robes, his fleshless bones covered by tight, tattered skin. His heart did not beat, for he had none; he drew no breath, for his lungs had been eaten by the creatures which feasted on such things. But, horribly, he lived...

The King from the Hill. He had been the last great ruler of the Doomed Folk who had, in their fury, destroyed half the earth and created the Forest of Troos. Behind the dead King crowded the ghastly hosts who had been buried with him in a legendary past.

The massacre began!

What secret vengeance was being reaped, Elric could only guess at—but whatever the reason, the danger was still very real.

Elric pulled out *Stormbringer* as the awakened horde vented their anger upon the living. The Hall became filled with the shrieking, horrified screams of the unfortunate Orgians. Elric remained, half-paralyzed in his horror, beside the throne. Aroused, Gutheran woke up and saw the King from the Hill and his host. He screamed, almost thankfully:

"At last I can rest!"

And fell dying in a seizure, robbing Elric of his vengeance.

Veerkad's grim song echoed in Elric's memory. The Three Kings in Darkness—Gutheran, Veerkad, and the King from Beneath the Hill. Now only the last lived—and he had been dead for millenia.

The King's cold, dead eyes roved the Hall and saw Gutheran sprawled upon his throne, the ancient chain of office still about his throat. Elric wrenched it off the body and backed away as the King from Beneath the Hill advanced. And then his back was against a pillar and there were feasting ghouls everywhere else.

The dead King came nearer and then, with a whistling moan which came from the depths of his decaying body, launched himself at Elric who found himself fighting desperately against the Hill-King's clawing, abnormal strength, cutting at flesh that neither bled nor suffered pain. Even the sorcerous rune-blade could do nothing against this horror that had no soul to take and no blood to let.

Frantically, Elric slashed and hacked at the Hill-King but ragged nails raked his flesh and teeth snapped at his throat. And above everything came the almost overpowering stench of death as the ghouls, packing the Great Hall with their horrible shapes, feasted on the living and the dead.

Then Elric heard Moonglum's voice calling and saw him upon the gallery which ran around the Hall. He held a great oil jar.

"Lure him close to the central fire, Elric. There may be a way to vanquish him. Quickly man, or you're finished!"

In a frantic burst of energy, the Melnibonean forced the giant king toward the flames. Around them, the ghouls fed off the remains of their victims, some of whom still lived, their screams calling hopelessly over the sound of carnage.

The Hill-King now stood, unfeeling, with his back to the leaping central fire. He still slashed at Elric. Moonglum hurled the jar.

It shattered upon the stone hearth, spraying the King with blazing oil. He staggered, and Elric struck with his full power, the man and the blade combining to push the Hill-King backward. Down went the King into the flames and the flames began to devour him.

A dreadful, lost howling came from the burning giant as he perished.

Flames licked everywhere throughout the Great Hall and soon the place was like Hell itself, an inferno of licking fire through which the ghouls ran about, still feasting, unaware of their destruction. The way to the door was blocked.

Elric stared around him and saw no way of escape—save one.

Sheathing *Stormbringer,* he ran a few paces and leaped upwards, just grasping the rail of the gallery as flames engulfed the spot where he had been standing.

Moonglum reached down and helped him to clamber across the rail.

"I'm disappointed, Elric," he grinned, "you forgot to bring the treasure."

Elric showed him what he grasped in his left hand—the jewel-encrusted chain of kingship.

"This bauble is some reward for our hardships," he smiled, holding up the glittering chain. "I stole nothing, by Arioch! There are no kings left in Org to wear it! Come let's join Zarozinia and get our horses."

They ran from the gallery as masonry began to crash downwards into the Great Hall.

They rode fast away from the halls of Org and looking back saw great fissures appear in the walls and heard the roar of destruction as the flames consumed everything that had been Org. They destroyed the seat of the monarchy, the remains of the Three Kings in Darkness, the present and the past. Nothing would be left of Org save an empty burial mound and two corpses, locked together, lying where their ancestors had lain for centuries in the Central Tomb. They destroyed the last link with the previous Time Cycle and cleansed the earth of an ancient evil. Only the dreadful Forest of Troos remained to mark the coming and the passing of the legendary Doomed Folk.

And the Forest of Troos was a warning.

Weary and yet relieved, the three saw the outlines of Troos in the distance, behind the blazing funeral pyre.

And yet, in his happiness, Elric had a fresh problem on his mind now that danger was past.

"Why do you frown now, love?" asked Zarozinia.

"Because I think you spoke the truth. Remember you said I placed too much reliance on my runeblade here?"

"Yes—and I said I would not dispute with you."

"Agreed. But I have a feeling that you were partially right. On the burial mound and in it I did not have *Stormbringer* with me—and yet I fought and won, because I feared for your safety." His voice was quiet. "Perhaps, in time, I can keep my strength by means of certain herbs I found in Troos and dispense with the blade forever?"

Moonglum shouted with laughter hearing these words.

"Elric—I never thought I'd witness this. You daring to think of dispensing with that foul weapon of yours. I don't know if you ever shall, but the thought is comforting."

"It is, my friend, it is." He leaned in his saddle and grasped Zarozinia's shoulders, pulling her dangerously toward him as they galloped without slackening speed. And as they rode he kissed her, heedless of their pace.

"A new beginning!" he shouted above the wind. "A new beginning, my love!"

And then they all rode laughing toward Karlaak by the Weeping Waste, to present themselves, to enrich themselves, and to attend the strangest wedding the Northern Lands had ever witnessed. For it would be more than a marriage between the awful evil-bringer of legends and a senator's youthful daughter—it would be a marriage between the dark wisdom of the Ancient World and the bright hope of the New.

And who could tell what such a combination would bring about?

The earth would soon know, for Elric of Melnibone was the maker of legends, and there were legends yet to make!

Pretty Maggie Moneyeyes

by HARLAN ELLISON

WITH AN eight hole-card and a queen showing, with the dealer showing a four up, Kostner decided to let the house do the work. So he stood, and the dealer turned up. Six.

The dealer looked like something out of a 1935 George Raft film: Arctic diamond-chip eyes, manicured fingers long as a brain surgeon's, straight black hair slicked flat away from the pale forehead. He did not look up as he peeled them off. A three. Another three. Bam. A five. Bam. Twenty-one, and Kostner saw his last thirty dollars—six five-dollar chips—scraped on the edge of the cards, into the dealer's chip racks. Busted. Flat. Down and out in Las Vegas, Nevada. Playground of the Western World.

He slid off the comfortable stool-chair and turned his back on the blackjack table. The action was already starting again, like waves closing over a drowned man. He had been there, was gone, and no one had noticed. No one had seen a man blow the last tie with salvation. Kostner now had his choice:

he could bum his way into Los Angeles and try to find something that resembled a new life...or he could go blow his brains out through the back of his head.

Neither choice showed much light or sense.

He thrust his hands deep into the pockets of his worn and dirty chinos, and started away down the line of slot machines clanging and rattling on the other side of the aisle between blackjack tables.

He stopped. He felt something in his pocket. Beside him, but all-engrossed, a fiftyish matron in electric lavender capris, high heels and Ship'n' Shore blouse was working two slots, loading and pulling one while waiting for the other to clock down. She was dumping quarters in a seemingly inexhaustible supply from a Dixie cup held in her left hand. There was a surrealistic presence to the woman. She was almost automated, not a flicker of expression on her face, the eyes fixed and unwavering. Only when the gong rang, someone down the line had pulled a jackpot, did she look up. And at that moment Kostner knew what was wrong and immoral and deadly about Vegas, about legalized gambling, about setting the traps all baited and open in front of the average human. The woman's face was gray with hatred, envy, lust and dedication to the game—in that timeless instant when she heard another drugged soul down the line winning a minuscule jackpot. A jackpot that would only lull the player with words like *luck* and *ahead of the game.* The jackpot lure: the sparkling, bobbling many-colored wiggler in a sea of poor fish.

The thing in Kostner's pocket was a silver dollar.

He brought it out and looked at it.

The eagle was hysterical.

But Kostner pulled to an abrupt halt, only one half-footstep from the sign indicating the limits of Tap City. He was still with it. What the high-rollers called the edge, the *vigerish,* the fine hole-card. One buck. One cartwheel. Pulled out of the pocket not half as deep as the pit into which Kostner had just been about to plunge.

What the hell, he thought, and turned to the row of slot machines.

He had thought they'd all been pulled out of service, the silver dollar slots. A shortage of coinage, said the United States Mint. But right there, side by side with the nickel and quarter bandits, was one cartwheel machine. Two thousand dollar jackpot. Kostner grinned foolishly. If you're gonna go out, go out like a champ.

He thumbed the silver dollar into the coin slot and grabbed the heavy, oiled handle. Shining cast aluminum and pressed steel. Big black plastic ball, angled for arm ease, pull it all day and you won't get weary.

Without a prayer in the universe, Kostner pulled the handle.

She had been born in Tucson, mother full-blooded Cherokee, father a bindlestiff on his way through. Mother had been working a truckers' stop, father had popped for spencer steak and sides. Mother had just gotten over a bad scene, indeterminate origins, unsatisfactory culminations. Mother had popped for bed. And sides. Margaret Annie Jessie had come nine months later; black of hair, fair of face, and born into a life of poverty. Twenty-three years later, a determined product of Miss Clairol and Berlitz, a dream-image formed by Vogue *and intimate association with the rat race, Margaret Annie Jessie had become a contraction.*

Maggie.

Long legs, trim and coltish; hips a trifle large, the kind that promote that *specific thought in men, about getting their hands around it; belly flat, isometrics; waist cut to the bone, a waist that works in any style from dirndl to disco-slacks; no breasts—all nipple, but no breast, like an expensive whore (the way O'Hara pinned it)—and no padding...forget the cans, baby, there's other, more important action; smooth, Michelangelo-sculpted neck, a pillar, proud; and all that face.*

Outthrust chin, perhaps a tot too much belligerence, but if you'd walloped as many gropers, you too, sweetheart; nar-

row mouth, petulant lower lip, nice to chew on, a lower lip as though filled with honey, bursting, ready for things to happen; a nose that threw the right sort of shadow, flaring nostrils, the acceptable words—aquiline, patrician, classic, allathat; cheekbones as stark and promontory as a spit of land after ten years of open ocean; cheekbones holding darkness like narrow shadows, sooty beneath the taut-fleshed bone-structure; amazing cheekbones, the whole face, really; an ancient kingdom's uptilted eyes, the touch of the Cherokee, eyes that looked out at you, as you looked in at them, like someone peering out of the keyhole as you peered in; actually, dirty eyes, they said you can get it.

Blonde hair, a great deal of it, wound and rolled and smoothed and flowing, in the old style, the pageboy thing men always admire; no tight little cap of slicked plastic; no ratted and teased Anapurna of bizarre coiffure; no ironed-flat discothèque hair like number 3 flat noodles. Hair, the way a man wants it, so he can dig his hands in at the base of the neck and pull all that face very close.

An operable woman, a working mechanism, a rigged and sudden machinery of softness and motivation.

Twenty-three, and determined as hell never to abide in that vale of poverty her mother had called purgatory for her entire life; snuffed out in a grease fire in the last trailer, somewhere in Arizona, thank God no more pleas for a little money from babygirl Maggie hustling drinks in a Los Angeles topless joint. (There ought to be some *remorse in there somewhere, for a Mommy gone where all the good grease-fire victims go. Look around, you'll find it.)*

Maggie.

Genetic freak. Mommy's Cherokee uptilted eye-shape, and Polack quickscrewing Daddy WithoutaName's blue as innocence color.

Blue-eyed Maggie, dyed blonde, alla that face, alla that leg, fifty bucks a night can get it and it sounds *like it's having a climax.*

Irish-innocent blue-eyed-innocent French-legged-innocent Maggie. Polack. Cherokee. Irish. All-woman and going on the market for this month's rent on the stucco pad, eighty bucks' worth of groceries, a couple month's worth for a Mustang, three appointments with the specialist in Beverly Hills about that shortness of breath after a night on the hustle bump the sticky thigh the disco lurch the gotcha sweat: woman minutes. Increments under the meat; perspiration purchases, yeah it does.

Maggie, Maggie, Maggie, pretty Maggie Moneyeyes, who came from Tucson and trailers and rheumatic fever and a surge to live that was all kaleidoscope frenzy of clawing scrabbling no-nonsense. If it took lying on one's back and making sounds like a panther in the desert, then one did it, because nothing, but nothing *was as bad as being dirt-poor, itchy-skinned, soiled-underwear, scufftoed, hairy and ashamed lousy with the no-gots. Nothing!*

Maggie. Hooker. Hustler. Grabber. Swinger. If there's a buck in it, there's rhythm and the onomatopoeia is Maggie Maggie Maggie.

She who puts out. For a price, whatever that might be.

Maggie was dating Nuncio. He was Sicilian. He had dark eyes and an alligator-grain wallet with slip-in pockets for credit cards. He was a spender, a sport, a highroller. They went to Vegas.

Maggie and the Sicilian. Her blue eys and his slip-in pockets. But mostly her blue eyes.

The spinning reels behind the three long glass windows blurred, and Kostner knew there wasn't a chance. Two thousand dollar jackpot. Round and round, whirring. Three bells or two bells and a jackpot bar, get 18; three plums or two plums and a jackpot bar, get 14; three oranges or two oranges and a jac—

Ten, five, two bucks for a single cherry cluster in first position. Something...I'm drowning...something...

The whirring...

Round and round...

As something happened that was not considered in the pit-boss manual.

The reels whipped and snapped to a stop, clank clank clank, tight in place.

Three bars looked up at Kostner. But they did not say JACK-POT. They were three bars from which stared three blue eyes. Very blue, very immediate, very JACKPOT!!

Twenty silver dollars clattered into the payoff trough at the bottom of the machine. An orange light popped on in the casino cashier's cage, bright orange on the jackpot board. And the gong began clanging overhead.

The Slot Machine Floor Manager nodded once to the Pit Boss, who pursed his lips and started toward the seedy-looking man still standing with his hand on the slot's handle.

The token payment—twenty silver dollars—lay untouched in the payoff trough. The balance of the jackpot—one thousand nine hundred and eighty dollars—would be paid manually by the casino cashier. And Kostner stood, dumbly, as the three blue eyes stared up at him.

There was a moment of idiotic disorientation, as Kostner stared back at the three blue eyes; a moment in which the slot machine's mechanisms registered to themselves; and the gong was clanging furiously.

All through the hotel's casino people turned from their games to stare. At the roulette tables the white-on-white players from Detroit and Cleveland pulled their watery eyes away from the clattering ball and stared down the line for a second, at the ratty-looking guy in front of the slot machine. From where they sat, they could not tell it was a two grand pot, and their rheumy eyes went back into billows of cigar smoke, and that little ball.

The blackjack hustlers turned momentarily, screwing around in their seats, and smiled. They were closer to the slot-players in temperament, but they knew the slots were a dodge to keep the old ladies busy, while the players worked toward their endless twenty-ones.

And the old dealer, who could no longer cut it at the fast-action boards, who had been put out to pasture by a grateful management, standing at the Wheel of Fortune near the entrance to the casino, even he paused in his zombie-murmuring ("Annnnother winner onna Wheel of Forchun!") to no one at all, and looked toward Kostner and that incredible gong-clanging. Then, in a moment, still with no players, he called *another* nonexistent winner.

Kostner heard the gong from far away. It had to mean he had won two thousand dollars, but that was impossible. He checked the payoff chart on the face of the machine. Three bars labeled JACKPOT meant JACKPOT. Two thousand dollars.

But these three bars did not say JACKPOT. They were three gray bars, rectangular in shape, with a blue eye directly in the center of each bar.

Blue eyes?

Somewhere, a connection was made, and electricity, a billion volts of electricity, were shot through Kostner. His hair stood on end, his fingertips bled raw, his eyes turned to jelly, and every fiber in his musculature became radioactive. Somewhere, out there, in a place that was not this *place, Kostner had been inextricably bound to—to someone.* Blue eyes?

The gong had faded out of his head, the constant noise level of the casino, chips chittering, people mumbling, dealers calling plays, it had all gone, and he was embedded in silence.

Tied to that someone else, out there somewhere, through those three blue eyes.

Then in an instant, it had passed, and he was alone again, as though released by a giant hand, the breath crushed out of him. He staggered up against the slot machine.

"You all right, fellah?"

A hand gripped him by the arm, steadied him. The gong was still clanging overhead somewhere, and he was breathless from a journey he had just taken. His eys focused and he found himself looking at the stocky Pit Boss who had been on duty while he had been playing blackjack.

"Yeah...I'm okay, just a little dizzy is all."

"Sounds like you got yourself a big jackpot, fellah." The Pit Boss grinned; it was a leathery grin; something composed of stretched muscles and conditioned reflexes, totally mirthless.

"Yeah...great..." Kostner tried to grin back. But he was still shaking from that electical absorption that had kidnaped him.

"Let me check it out," the Pit Boss was saying, edging around Kostner, and staring at the face of the slot machine. "Yeah, three jackpot bars, all right. You're a winner."

Then it dawned on Kostner! Two thousand dollars! He looked down at the slot machine and saw—

Three bars with the word JACKPOT on them. No blue eyes, just words that meant money. Kostner looked around frantically, was he losing his mind? *From somewhere, not in the casino, he heard a tinkle of rhodium-plated laughter.*

He scooped up the twenty silver dollars. The Pit Boss dropped another cartwheel into the Chief, and pulled the jackpot off. Then the Pit Boss walked him to the rear of the casino, talking to him in a muted, extremely polite tone of voice. At the cashier's window, the Pit Boss nodded to a weary-looking man at a huge Rolodex cardfile, checking credit ratings.

"Barney, jackpot on the cartwheel Chief; slot five-oh-oh-one-five." He grinned at Kostner, who tried to smile back. It was difficult. He felt stunned.

The cashier checked a payoff book for the correct amount to be drawn and leaned over the counter toward Kostner. "Check or cash, sir?"

Kostner felt buoyancy coming back to him. "Is the casino's check good?" They all three laughed at that. "A check's fine,"

Kostner said. The check was drawn, and the Check-Riter punched out the little bumps that said two thousand. "The twenty cartwheels are a gift," the cashier said, sliding the check through to Kostner.

He held it, looked at it, and still found it difficult to believe. Two grand, back on the golden road.

As he walked back through the casino with the Pit Boss, the stocky man asked pleasantly, "Well, what are you going to do with it?" Kostner had to think a moment. He didn't have any plans. But then the sudden realization came to him: "I'm going to play that slot machine again." The Pit Boss smiled: a congenital sucker. He would put all twenty of those silver dollars back into the Chief, and then turn to the other games. Blackjack, roulette, faro, baccarat...in a few hours he would have redeposited the two grand with the hotel Casino. It always happened.

He walked Kostner back to the slot machine, and patted him on the shoulder. "Lotsa luck, fellah."

As he turned away, Kostner slipped a silver dollar into the machine, and pulled the handle.

The Pit Boss had taken only five steps when he heard the incredible sound of the reels clicking to a stop, the clash of twenty token silver dollars hitting the payoff trough, and that goddamned gong went out of its mind again.

She had known that sonofabitch Nuncio was a perverted swine. A walking filth. A dungheap between his ears. Some kind of monster in nylon undershorts. There weren't many kinds of games Maggie hadn't played, but what that Sicilian de Sade wanted to do was outright vomity!

She nearly fainted when he suggested it. Her heart—which the Beverly Hills specialist had said she should not tax—began whumping frantically. "You pig!" she screamed. "You filthy dirty ugly pig you, Nuncio you pig!" She had bounded out of the bed and started to throw on clothes. She didn't even bother with a brassiere, pulling the poorboy sweater on over her thin breasts, still crimson with the touches and love-bites Nuncio had showered on them.

He sat up in the bed, a pathetic-looking little man, gray hair at the temples and no hair atall on top, and his eyes were moist. He was porcine, was indeed the swine she called him, but he was helpless before her. He was in love with his hooker, with the tart whom he was supporting. It had been the first time for the swine Nuncio, and he was helpless. Back in Detroit, had it been a floozy, a bimbo, a chippy broad, he would have gotten out of the double bed and rapped her around pretty good. But this Maggie, she tied him in knots. He had suggested... that, *what they should do together... because he was so consumed with her. But* she *was furious with* him. *It wasn't* that *bizarre an idea!*

"Gimme a chanct'a talk t'ya, honey... Maggie..."

"You filthy pig, Nuncio! Give me some money, I'm going down to the casino, and I don't want to see your filthy pig face for the rest of the day, remember that!"

And she had gone in his wallet and pants, and taken eight hundred and sixteen dollars, while he watched. He was helpless before her. She was something stolen from a world he knew only as "class" and she could do what she wanted with him.

Genetic freak Maggie, blue-eyed posing mannequin Maggie, pretty Maggie Moneyeyes, who was one-half Cherokee and one-half a buncha other things, had absorbed her lessons well. She was the very model of a "class broad."

"Not for the rest of the day, do you understand?" She stared at him till he nodded; then she went downstairs, furious, to fret and gamble and wonder about nothing but years of herself.

Men stared after her as she walked. She carried herself like a challenge, the way a squire carried a pennon, the way a prize bitch carried herself in the judge's ring. Born to the blue. The wonders of mimicry and desire.

Maggie had no lust for gambling, none whatever. She merely wanted to taste the fury of her relationship with the swine Sicilian, her need for solidity in a life built on the edge of the slide area, the senselessness of being here in Las Vegas when she could be back in Beverly Hills. She grew angrier and more ill at the thought of Nuncio upstairs in the room, taking another shower. She bathed three times a day. But it was different with him. He knew she resented his smell; he had the soft odor of wet fur sometimes, and she had told him about it. Now he bathed constantly, and hated it. He was a foreigner to the bath. His life had been marked by various kinds of filths, and baths for him now were more of an obscenity than dirt could ever have been. For her, bathing was different. It was a necessity. She had to keep the patina of the world off her, had to remain clean and smooth and white. A presentation, not an object of flesh and hair. A chromium instrument, something never pitted by rust and corrosion.

When she was touched by them, by any one of them, by the men, by all the Nuncios, they left little pitholes of bloody rust on her white, permanent flesh; cobwebs, sooty stains. She had *to bathe. Often.*

She strolled down between the tables and the slots, carrying eight hundred and sixteen dollars. Eight one hundred dollar bills and sixteen dollars in ones.

At the change booth she got cartwheels for the sixteen ones. The Chief waited. It was her baby. She played it to infuriate the Sicilian. He had told her to play the nickel slots, the quarter or dime slots, but she always infuriated him by blowing fifty or a hundred dollars in ten minutes, one coin after another, in the big Chief.

She faced the machine squarely, and put in the first silver dollar. She pulled the handle that swine Nuncio. Another dollar, pulled the handle how long does this go on? The reels cycled and spun and whirled and whipped in a clattering blurringspinning metalhumming overandoverandover as Maggie blue-eyed Maggie hated and hated and thought of hate and all the days and nights of swine behind her and ahead of her and if only she had all the money in this room in this casino in this hotel in this town right now this very instant just an instant thisinstant it would be enough to whirring and humming and spinning and overandoverandoverand over and she would be free free free and all the world would never touch her body again the swine would never touch her white flesh again and then suddenly as dollarafterdollarafterdollar went aroundaroundaround hummmmming in reels of cherries and bells and bars and plums and oranges there was suddenly painpainpain a SHARP pain! pain!pain! in her chest, her heart, her center, a needle, a lancet, a burning, a pillar of flame that was purest pure purer PAIN!

Maggie, pretty Maggie Moneyeyes, who wanted all that money in that cartwheel Chief slot machine, Maggie who had come from filth and rheumatic fever, who had come all the way to three baths a day and a specialist in Very Expensive Beverly Hills, that *Maggie suddenly had a seizure, a flutter, a slam of a coronary thrombosis and fell instantly dead on the floor of the casino. Dead.*

One instant she had been holding the handle of the slot machine, willing her entire being, all that hatred for all the swine she had ever rolled with, willing every fiber of every cell of every chromosome into that machine, wanting to suck out every silver vapor within its belly, and the next *instant—so close they might have been the same—her heart exploded and killed her and she slipped to the floor. . . still touching the Chief.*

On the floor.
Dead.
Struck dead.
Liar. All the lies that were her life.
Dead on a floor.

[A moment out of time ■ lights whirling and spinning in a cotton candy universe ■ down a bottomless funnel roundly sectioned like a goat's horn ■ a cornucopia that rose up cuculiform smooth and slick as a worm belly ■ endless nights that pealed ebony funeral bells ■ out of fog ■ out of weightlessness ■ suddenly total cellular knowledge ■ memory running backward ■ gibbering spastic blindness ■ a soundless owl of frenzy trapped in a cave of prisms ■ sand endlessly draining down ■ billows of forever ■ edges of the world as they splintered ■ foam rising drowning from inside ■ the smell of rust ■ rough green corners that burn ■ memory the gibbering spastic blind memory ■ seven rushing vacuums of nothing ■ yellow ■ pinpoints cast in amber straining and elongating running like live wax ■ chill fevers ■ overhead the odor of stop ■ this is the stopover before hell or heaven ■ this is limbo ■ trapped and doomed alone in a mist-eaten nowhere ■ a soundless screaming a soundless whirring a soundless spinning spinning spinning ■ spinning ■ spinning ■ spinning ■ spinningggggggg]

> Maggie had wanted all the silver in the machine. She had died, willing herself into the machine. Now looking out from within, from inside the limbo that had become her own purgatory, Maggie was trapped, in the oiled and anodized interior of the silver dollar slot machine. The prison of her final desires, where she had wanted to be, completely trapped in that last instant of life between life/death. Maggie, gone inside; all soul now; trapped for eternity in the cage soul of the soulless machine. Limbo. Trapped.

"I hope you don't mind if I call over one of the slot men," the Slot Machine Floor Manager was saying, from a far distance. He was in his late fifties, a velvet-voiced man whose eyes held nothing of light and certainly nothing of kindness. He had stopped the Pit Boss as the stocky man had turned in mid-step to return to Kostner and the jackpotted machine; he had taken the walk himself. "We have to make sure, you know how it is: somebody didn't fool the slot, you know, maybe it's outta whack or something, you know."

He lifted his left hand and there was a clicker in it, the kind children use at Halloween. He clicked half a dozen times, like a rabid cricket, and there was a scurrying in the pit between the tables.

Kostner was only faintly aware of what was happening. Instead of being totally awake, feeling the surge of adrenaline through his veins, the feeling any gambler gets when he is ahead of the game, a kind of desperate urgency when he has hit it for a boodle, he was numb, partaking of the action around him only as much as a drinking glass involves itself in the alcoholic's drunken binge.

All color and sound had been leached out of him.

A tired-looking, resigned-weary man wearing a gray porter's jacket, as gray as his hair, as gray as his indoor skin, came to them, carrying a leather wrap-up of tools. The slot repairman studied the machine, turning the pressed steel body around on its stand, studying the back. He used a key on the back door and for an instant Kostner had a view of gears, springs, armatures and the clock that ran the slot mechanism. The repairman nodded silently over it, closed and relocked it, turned it around again and studied the face of the machine.

"Nobody's been spooning it," he said, and went away.

Kostner stared at the Floor Manager.

"Gaffing. That's what he meant. Spooning's another word for it. Some guys use a little piece of plastic, or a wire, shove it down through the escalator, it kicks the machine. Nobody thought that's what happened here, but you know, we have to make sure, two grand is a big payoff, and twice... well, you know, I'm sure you'll understand. If a guy was doing it with a boomerang—"

Kostner raised an eyebrow.

"—uh, yeah, a boomerang, it's another way to spoon the machine. But we just wanted to make a little check, and now everybody's satisfied, so if you'll just come back to the casino cashier with me—"

And they paid him off again.

So he went back to the slot machine, and stood before it for a long time, staring at it. The change girls and the dealers going off-duty; the little old ladies with their canvas work gloves worn to avoid calluses when pulling the slot handles, the men's room attendant on his way up front to get more matchbooks, the floral tourists, the idle observers, the hard drinkers, the sweepers, the busboys, the gamblers with poached-egg eyes who had been up all night, the showgirls with massive breasts and diminutive sugar daddies, all of them conjectured mentally about the beat-up walker who was staring at the silver dollar Chief. He did not move, merely stared at the machine...and they wondered.

The machine was staring back at Kostner.

Three blue eyes.

The electric current had sparked through him again, as the machine had clocked down and the eyes turned up a second time, as he had *won* a second time. But this time he knew there was something more than luck involved, for no one else had seen those three blue eyes.

So now he stood before the machine, waiting. It spoke to him. Inside his skull, where no one had ever lived but himself, now someone else moved and spoke to him. A girl. A beautiful girl. Her name was Maggie, and she spoke to him.

I've been waiting for you. A long time, I've been waiting for you, Kostner. Why do you think you hit the jackpot? Because I've been waiting for you, and I want you. You'll win all the jackpots. Because I want you, I need you. Love me, I'm Maggie, I'm so alone, love me.

Kostner had been staring at the slot machine for a very long time, and his weary brown eyes had seemed to be locked to the blue eyes on the jackpot bars. But he knew no one else could see the blue eyes, and no one else could hear the voice, and no one else knew about Maggie.

He was the universe to her. Everything to her.

He thumbed in another silver dollar, and the Pit Boss watched, the slot machine repairman watched, the Slot Machine Floor Manager watched, three change girls watched, and a pack of unidentified players watched, some from their seats.

The reels whirled, the handle snapped back, and in a second they flipped down to a halt, twenty silver dollars tokened themselves into the payoff trough and a woman at one of the crap tables belched a fragment of hysterical laughter.

And the gong went insane again.

The Floor Manager came over and said, very softly, "Mr. Kostner, it'll take us about fifteen minutes to pull this machine and check it out. I'm sure you understand." As two slot repairmen came out of the back, hauled the Chief off its stand, and took it into the repair room at the rear of the casino.

While they waited, the Floor Manager regaled Kostner with stories of spooners who had used intricate magnets inside their clothes, of boomerang men who had attached their plastic implements under their sleeves so they could be extended on spring-loaded clips, of cheaters who had come equipped with tiny electric drills in their hands and wires that slipped into the tiny drilled holes. And he kept saying he knew Kostner would understand.

But Kostner knew the Floor Manager would not understand.

When they brought the Chief back, one of the repairmen nodded assuredly. "Nothing wrong with it. Works perfectly. Nobody's been boomin' it."

But the blue eyes were gone on the jackpot bars.

Kostner knew they would return.

They paid him off again.

He returned and played again. And again. And again. They put a "spotter" on him. He won again. And again. And again. The crowd had grown to massive proportions. Word had spread like the silent communications of the telegraph vine, up and down the Strip, all the way to downtown Vegas and the sidewalk casinos where they played night and day every day of the year, and the crowd surged in a tide toward the hotel, and the casino, and the seedy-looking walker with his weary brown eyes. The crowd moved to him inexorably, drawn like lemmings by the odor of the luck that rose from him like musky electrical cracklings. And he won. Again and again. Thirty-eight thousand dollars. And the three blue eyes continued to stare up at him. Her lover was winning. Maggie and her Moneyeyes.

Finally, the casino decided to speak to Kostner. They pulled the Chief for fifteen minutes, for a supplemental check by experts from the slot machine company in downtown Vegas, and while they were checking it, they asked Kostner to come to the main office of the hotel.

The owner was there. His face seemed faintly familiar to Kostner. Had he seen it on television? The newspapers?

"Mr. Kostner, my name is Jules Hartshorn."

"I'm pleased to meet you."

"Quite a string of luck you're having out there."

"It's been a long time coming."

"You realize, this sort of luck is impossible."

"I'm compelled to believe it, Mr. Hartshorn."

"Um. As am I. It's happening to my casino. But we're thoroughly convinced of one of two possibilities, Mr. Kostner: one, either the machine is inoperable in a way we can't detect; or two, you are the cleverest spooner we've ever had in here."

"I'm not cheating."

"As you can see, Mr. Kostner, I'm smiling. The reason I'm smiling is at your naïveté in believing I would take your word for it. I'm perfectly happy to nod politely and say of course you aren't cheating. But no one can win thirty-eight thousand dollars on nineteen straight jackpots off one slot machine; it doesn't even have mathematical odds against its happening, Mr. Kostner. It's on a cosmic scale of improbability with three dark planets crashing into our sun within the next twenty minutes. It's on a par with the Pentagon, the Forbidden City and the Kremlin all three pushing the red button at the same microsecond. It's an impossibility, Mr. Kostner. An impossibility that's happening to me."

"I'm sorry."

"Not really."

"No, not really. I can use the money."

"For what, exactly, Mr. Kostner?"

"I hadn't thought about it, really."

"I see. Well, Mr. Kostner, let's look at it this way. I can't stop you from playing, and if you continue to win, I'll be required to pay off. And no stubble-chinned thugs will be waiting in an alley to jackroll you and take the money. The checks will be honored. The best I can hope for, Mr. Kostner, is the attendant publicity. Right now, every high-roller in Vegas is in that casino, waiting for you to drop cartwheels into that machine. It won't make up for what I'm losing, if you continue the way you've been; but it'll help. Every sucker in town likes to rub up next to luck. All I ask is that you cooperate a little."

"The least I can do, considering your generosity."

"An attempt at humor."

"I'm sorry. What is it you'd like me to do?"

"Get about ten hours' sleep."

"While you pull the slot and have it worked over thoroughly?"

"Yes."

"If I wanted to keep winning, that might be a pretty stupid move on my part. You might change the thigamajig inside so I couldn't win if I put back every dollar of that thirty-eight grand."

"We're licensed by the state of Nevada, Mr. Kostner."

"I come from a good family, too, and take a look at me. I'm a bum with thirty-eight thousand dollars in my pocket."

"Nothing will be done to that slot machine, Kostner."

"Then why pull it for ten hours?"

"To work it over thoroughly in the shop. If something as undetectable as metal fatigue or a worn escalator tooth or—we want to make sure this doesn't happen with other machines. And the extra time will get the word around town; we can use the crowd. Some of those tourists will stick to our fingers, and it'll help defray the expense of having you break the bank at this casino—on a slot machine."

"I have to take your word."

"This hotel will be in business long after you're gone, Kostner."

"Not if I keep winning."

Hartshorn's smile was a stricture. "A good point."

"So it isn't much of an argument."

"It's the only one I have. If you want to get back out on that floor, I can't stop you."

"No Mafia hoods ventilate me later?"

"I beg your pardon?"

"I said: no Maf—"

"You have a picturesque manner of speaking. In point of fact, I haven't the faintest idea what you're talking about."

"I'm sure you haven't."

"You've got to stop reading *The National Enquirer.* This is a legally run business. I'm merely asking a favor."

"Okay, Mr. Hartshorn, I've been three days without any sleep. Ten hours will do me a world of good."

"I'll have the desk clerk find you a quiet room on the top floor. And thank you, Mr. Kostner."

"Think nothing of it."

"I'm afraid that will be impossible."

"A lot of impossible things are happening lately."

He turned to go, as Hartshorn lit a cigarette.

"Oh, by the way, Mr. Kostner?"

Kostner stopped and half-turned. "Yes?"

His eyes were getting difficult to focus. There was a ringing in his ears. Hartshorn seemed to waver at the edge of his vision like heat lightning across a prairie. Like memories of things Kostner had come across the country to forget. Like the whimpering and pleading that kept tugging at the cells of his brain. The voice of Maggie. Still back in there, saying...things...

They'll try to keep you from me.

All he could think about was the ten hours of sleep he had

been promised. Suddenly it was more important than the money, than forgetting, than anything. Hartshorn was talking, was saying things, but Kostner could not hear him. It was as if he had turned off the sound and saw only the silent rubbery movement of Hartshorn's lips. He shook his head trying to clear it.

There were half a dozen Hartshorns all melting into and out of one another. And the voice of Maggie.

I'm warm here, and alone. I could be good to you, if you can come to me. Please come, please hurry.

"Mr. Kostner?"

Hartshorn's voice came draining down through exhaustion as thick as velvet flocking. Kostner tried to focus again. His extremely weary brown eyes began to track.

"Did you know about that slot machine?" Hartshorn was saying. "A peculiar thing happened with it about six weeks ago."

"What was that?"

"A girl died playing it. She had a heart attack, a seizure while she was pulling the handle, and died right out there on the floor."

Kostner was silent for a moment. He wanted desperately to ask Hartshorn what color the dead girl's eyes had been, but he was afraid the owner would say blue.

He paused with his hand on the office door. "Seems as though you've had nothing but a streak of bad luck on that machine."

Hartshorn smiled an enigmatic smile. "It might not change for a while, either."

Kostner felt his jaw muscles tighten. "Meaning I might die, too, and wouldn't *that* be bad luck."

Hartshorn's smile became hieroglyphic, permanent, stamped on him forever. "Sleep tight, Mr. Kostner."

In a dream, she came to him. Long, smooth thighs and soft golden down on her arms; blue eyes deep as the past, misted with a fine scintillance like lavender spiderwebs; taut body that was the only body Woman had ever had, from the very first. Maggie came to him.

Hello, I've been traveling a long time.

"Who are you?" Kostner asked, wonderingly. He was standing on a chilly plain, or was it a plateau? The wind curled around them both, or was it only around him? She was exquisite, and he saw her clearly, or was it through a mist? Her voice was deep and resonant, or was it light and warm as night-blooming jasmine?

I'm Maggie. I love you. I've waited for you.

"You have blue eyes."

Yes. *With love.*

"You're very beautiful."

Thank you. *With female amusement.*

"But why me? Why let it happen to me? Are you the girl who—are you the one that was sick—the one who—?"

I'm Maggie. And you, I picked you, because you need me. You've needed someone for a long long time.

Then it unrolled for Kostner. The past unrolled and he saw who he was. He saw himself alone. Always alone. As a child, born to kind and warm parents who hadn't the vaguest notion of who he was, what he wanted to be, where his talents lay. So he had run off, when he was in his teens, and alone always alone on the road. For years and months and days and hours, with no one. Casual friendships, based on food, or sex, or artificial similarities. But no one to whom he could cleave, and cling, and belong. It was that way till Susie, and with her he had found light. He had discovered the scents and aromas of a spring that was eternally one day away. He had laughed, really laughed, and known with her it would at last be all right. So he had poured all of himself into her, giving her everything; all his hopes, his secret thoughts, his tender dreams; and she had taken them, taken him, all of him, and he had known for the first time what it was to have a place to live, to have a home in someone's heart. It was all the silly and gentle things he laughed at in other people, but for him it was breathing deeply of wonder.

He had stayed with her for a long time, and had supported her, supported her son from the first marriage; the marriage Susie never talked about. And then one day, he *had come back, as Susie had always known he would. He was a dark creature of ruthless habits and vicious nature, but she had been his woman, all along, and Kostner realized he had been used as a stop-gap, as a bill-payer till her wandering terror came home to nest. Then she had asked him to leave. Broke, and tapped out in all the silent inner ways a man can be drained, he had left, without even a fight, for all the fight had been leached out of him. He had left, and wandered west, and finally come to Las Vegas, where he had hit bottom. And found Maggie. In a dream, with blue eyes, he had found Maggie.*

I want you to belong to me. I love you. *Her truth was vibrant in Kostner's mind. She was his, at last someone who was special, was his.*

"Can I trust you? I've never been able to trust anyone before. Women, never. But I need someone. I really need someone."

It's me, always. Forever. You can trust me.

And she came to him, fully. Her body was a declaration of truth and trust such as no other Kostner had ever known before. She met him on a windswept plain of thought, and he made love to her more completely than he had known any passion before. She joined with him, entered him, mingled with his blood and his thought and his frustration, and he came away clean, filled with glory.

"Yes, I can trust you, I want you, I'm yours," he whispered to her, when they lay side by side in a dream nowhere of mist and soundlessness. "I'm yours."

She smiled, a woman's smile of belief in her man; a smile of trust and deliverance. And Kostner woke up.

* * *

The Chief was back on its stand, and the crowd had been penned back by velvet ropes. Several people had played the machine, but there had been no jackpots.

Now Kostner came into the casino, and the "spotters" got themselves ready. While Kostner had slept, they had gone through his clothes, searching for wires, for gaffs, for spoons or boomerangs. Nothing.

Now he walked straight to the Chief, and stared at it.

Hartshorn was there. "You look tired," he said gently to Kostner, studying the man's weary brown eyes.

"I am, a little." Kostner tried a smile; it didn't work. "I had a funny dream."

"Oh?"

"Yeah...about a girl..." He let it die off.

Hartshorn's smile was understanding. Pitying, empathic and understanding. "There are lots of girls in this town. You shouldn't have any trouble finding one with your winnings."

Kostner nodded, and slipped his first silver dollar into the slot. He pulled the handle. The reels spun with a ferocity Kostner had not heard before and suddenly everything went whipping slantwise as he felt a wrenching of pure flame in his stomach, as his head was snapped on its spindly neck, as the lining behind his eyes was burned out. There was a terrible shriek, of tortured metal, of an express train ripping the air with its passage, of a hundred small animals being gutted and torn to shreds, of incredible pain, of night winds that tore the tops off mountains of lava. And a keening whine of a voice that wailed and wailed and wailed as it went away from there in blinding light—

Free! Free! Heaven or Hell it doesn't matter! Free!

The sound of a soul released from an eternal prison, a genie freed from a dark bottle. And in that instant of damp soundless nothingness, Kostner saw the reels snap and clock down for the final time:

One, two, three. Blue eyes.

But he would never cash his checks.

The crowd screamed through one voice as he fell sidewise and lay on his face. The final loneliness...

The Chief was pulled. Bad luck. Too many gamblers resented its very presence in the casino. So it was pulled. And returned to the company, with explicit instructions it was to be melted down to slag. And not till it was in the hands of the ladle foreman, who was ready to dump it into the slag furnace, did anyone remark on the final tally the Chief had clocked.

"Look at that, ain't that weird," said the ladle foreman to his bucket man. He pointed to the three glass windows.

"Never saw jackpot bars like that before," the bucket man agreed. "Three eyes. Must be an old machine."

"Yeah, some of these old games go way back," the foreman said, hoisting the slot machine onto the conveyor track leading to the slag furnace.

"Three eyes, huh. How about that. Three brown eyes." And he threw the knife-switch that sent the Chief down the track, to puddle in the roaring inferno of the furnace.

Three brown *eyes.*

Three brown eyes that looked very very weary. That looked very very trapped. That looked very very betrayed. Some of these old games go way back.

Gonna Roll the Bones

by FRITZ LEIBER

SUDDENLY JOE Slattermill knew for sure he'd have to get out quick or else blow his top and knock out with the shrapnel of his skull the props and patches holding up his decaying home, that was like a house of big wooden and plaster and wallpaper cards except for the huge fireplace and ovens and chimney across the kitchen from him.

Those were stone-solid enough, though. The fireplace was chin-high, at least twice that long, and filled from end to end with roaring flames. Above were the square doors of the ovens in a row—his Wife baked for part of their living. Above the ovens was the wall-long mantelpiece, too high for his Mother to reach or Mr. Guts to jump any more, set with all sorts of ancestral curios, but any of them that weren't stone or glass or china had been so dried and darkened by decades of heat that they looked like nothing but shrunken human heads and black golf balls. At one end were clustered his Wife's square gin bottles. Above the mantelpiece hung one old chromo, so high and so darkened by soot and grease that you couldn't tell whether the swirls and fat cigar shape were a whaleback steamer ploughing through a hurricane or a spaceship plunging through a storm of light-driven dust motes.

As soon as Joe curled his toes inside his boots, his Mother knew what he was up to. "Going bumming," she mumbled with conviction. "Pants pockets full of cartwheels of house money, too, to spend on sin." And she went back to munching the long shreds she stripped fumblingly with her right hand off the turkey carcass set close to the terrible heat, her left hand ready to fend off Mr. Guts, who stared at her yellow-eyed, gaunt-flanked, with long mangy tail a-twitch. In her dirty dress, streaky as the turkey's sides, Joe's Mother looked like a bent brown bag and her fingers were lumpy twigs.

Joe's Wife knew as soon or sooner, for she smiled thin-eyed at him over her shoulder from where she towered at the centermost oven. Before she closed its door, Joe glimpsed that she was baking two long, flat, narrow, fluted loaves and one high, round-domed one. She was thin as death and disease in her violet wrapper. Without looking, she reached out a yard-long, skinny arm for the nearest gin bottle and downed a warm slug and smiled again. And without a word spoken, Joe knew she'd said, "You're going out and gamble and get drunk and lay a floozy and come home and beat me and go to jail for it," and he had a flash of the last time he'd been in the dark gritty cell and she'd come by moonlight, which showed the green and yellow lumps on her narrow skull where he'd hit her, to whisper to him through the tiny window in the back and slip him a half pint through the bars.

And Joe knew for certain that this time it would be that bad and worse, but just the same he heaved up himself and his heavy, muffledly clanking pockets and shuffled straight to the door, muttering, "Guess I'll roll the bones, up the pike a stretch and back," swinging his bent, knobbly-elbowed arms like paddlewheels to make a little joke about his words.

When he'd stepped outside, he held the door open a hand's breadth behind him for several seconds. When he finally closed it, a feeling of deep misery struck him. Earlier years, Mr. Guts would have come streaking along to seek fights and females on the roofs and fences, but now the big tom was content to stay home and hiss by the fire and snatch for turkey and dodge a broom, quarreling and comforting with two house-bound women. Nothing had followed Joe to the door but his Mother's chomping and her gasping breaths and the clink of the gin bottle going back on the mantel and the creaking of the floor boards under his feet.

The night was up-side-down deep among the frosty stars. A few of them seemed to move, like the white-hot jets of spaceships. Down below it looked as if the whole town of Ironmine had blown or buttoned out the light and gone to sleep, leaving the streets and spaces to the equally unseen breezes and ghosts. But Joe was still in the hemisphere of the musty dry odor of the worm-eaten carpentry behind him, and as he felt and heard the dry grass of the lawn brush his calves, it occurred to him that something deep down inside him had for years been planning things so that he and the House and his Wife and Mother and Mr. Guts would all come to an end together. Why the kitchen heat hadn't touched off the tindery place ages ago was a physical miracle.

Hunching his shoulders, Joe stepped out, not up the pike, but down the dirt road that led past Cypress Hollow Cemetery to Night Town.

The breezes were gentle, but unusually restless and variable tonight, like leprechaun squalls. Beyond the drunken, white-washed cemetery fence dim in the starlight, they rustled the scraggly trees of Cypress Hollow and made it seem they were stroking their beards of Spanish moss. Joe sensed that the ghosts were just as restless as the breezes, uncertain where and whom to haunt, or whether to take the night off, drifting together in sorrowfully lecherous companionship. While among the trees the red-green vampire lights pulsed faintly and irregularly, like sick fireflies or a plague-stricken space fleet. The feeling of deep misery stuck with Joe and deepened and he was tempted to turn aside and curl up in any convenient tomb or around some half-toppled head board and cheat his Wife and the other two behind him out of a shared doom. He thought: Gonna roll the bones, gonna roll 'em up and go to sleep. But while he was deciding, he got past the sagged-open gate and the rest of the delirious fence and Shantyville too.

At first Night Town seem dead as the rest of Ironmine, but then he noticed a faint glow, sick as the vampire lights but more feverish, and with it a jumping music, tiny at first as a jazz for jitterbugging ants. He stepped along the springy sidewalk, wistfully remembering the days when the spring was all in his own legs and he'd bound into a fight like a bobcat or a Martian sand-spider. God, it had been years now since he had fought a real fight, or felt *the power.* Gradually the midget music got raucous as a bunny-hug for grizzly bears and loud as a polka for elephants, while the glow became a riot of gas flares and flambeaux and corpse-blue mercury tubes and jiggling pink neon ones that all jeered at the stars where the spaceships roved. Next thing, he was facing a three-story false front flaring everywhere like a devil's elbow, with a pale blue topping of St. Elmo's fire. There were wide swinging doors in the center of it, spilling light above and below. Above the doorway, golden calcium light scrawled over and over again, with wild curlicues and flourishes, "The Boneyard," while a fiendish red kept printing out, "Gambling."

So the new place they'd all been talking about for so long had opened at last! For the first time that night, Joe Slattermill felt a stirring of real life in him and the faintest caress of excitement.

Gonna roll the bones, he thought.

He dusted off his blue-green work clothes with big, careless swipes and slapped his pockets to hear the clank. Then he threw back his shoulders and grinned his lips sneeringly and pushed through the swinging doors as if giving a foe the straight-armed heel of his palm.

Inside, The Boneyard seemed to cover the area of a township and the bar looked as long as the railroad tracks. Round pools of light on the green poker tables alternated with hourglass shapes of exciting gloom, through which drink girls and change-girls moved like white-legged witches. By the jazz-stand in the distance, belly dancers made *their* white hourglass shapes. The gamblers were thick and hunched down as mushrooms, all bald from agonizing over the fall of a card or a die or the dive of an ivory ball, while the Scarlet Women were like fields of poinsettia.

The calls of the croupiers and the slaps of dealt cards were as softly yet fatefully staccato as the rustle and beat of the jazz drums. Every tight-locked atom of the place was controlledly jumping. Even the dust motes jiggled tensely in the cones of light.

Joe's excitement climbed and he felt sift through him, like a breeze that heralds a gale, the faintest breath of a confidence which he knew could become a tornado. All thoughts of his House and Wife and Mother dropped out of his mind, while Mr. Guts remained only as a crazy young tom walking stiff-legged around the rim of his consciousness. Joe's own leg muscles twitched in sympathy and he felt them grow supplely strong.

He coolly and searchingly looked the place over, his hand going out like it didn't belong to him to separate a drink from a passing, gently bobbing tray. Finally his gaze settled on what he judged to be the Number One Crap Table. All the Big Mushrooms seemed to be there, bald as the rest but standing tall as toadstools. Then through a gap in them Joe saw on the other side of the table a figure still taller, but dressed in a long dark coat with collar turned up and a dark slouch hat pulled low, so that only a triangle of white face showed. A suspicion and a hope rose in Joe and he headed straight for the gap in the Big Mushrooms.

As he got nearer, the white-legged and shiny-topped drifters eddying out of his way, his suspicion received confirmation after confirmation and his hope budded and swelled. Back from one end of the table was the fattest man he'd ever seen, with a long cigar and a silver vest and a gold tie clasp at least eight inches wide that just said in thick script, "Mr. Bones." Back a little from the other end was the nakedest change-girl yet and the only one he'd seen whose tray, slung from her bare shoulders, and indenting her belly just below her breasts, was stacked with gold in gleaming little towers and with jet-black chips. While the dice-girl, skinnier and taller and longer armed than his Wife even, didn't seem to be wearing much but a pair of long white gloves. She was all right if you went for the type that isn't much more than pale skin over bones with breasts like china doorknobs.

Beside each gambler was a high round table for his chips. The one by the gap was empty. Snapping his fingers at the nearest silver change-girl, Joe traded all his greasy dollars for an equal number of pale chips and tweaked her left nipple for luck. She playfully snapped her teeth towards his fingers.

Not hurrying but not wasting any time, he advanced and carelessly dropped his modest stacks on the empty table and took his place in the gap. He noted that the second Big Mushroom on his right had the dice. His heart but no other part of him gave an extra jump. Then he steadily lifted his eyes and looked straight across the table.

The coat was a shimmering elegant pillar of black satin with jet buttons, the upturned collar of fine dull plush black as the darkest cellar, as was the slouch hat with down-turned brim and a band of only a thin braid of black horse-hair. The arms of the coat were long, lesser satin pillars, ending in slim, longfingered hands that moved swiftly when they did, but held each position of rest with a statue's poise.

Joe still couldn't see much of the face except for smooth lower forehead with never a bead or trickle of sweat—the eyebrows were like straight snippets of the hat's braid—and gaunt aristocratic cheeks and narrow but somewhat flat nose. The complexion of the face wasn't as white as Joe had first judged. There was a faint touch of brown in it, like ivory that's just begun to age, or Venusian soapstone. Another glance at the hands confirmed this.

Behind the man in black was a knot of just about the flashiest and nastiest customers, male or female, Joe had ever seen. He knew from one look that each bediamonded, pomaded bully had a belly gun beneath the flap of his flowered vest and a blackjack in his hip pocket, and each snake-eyed sporting girl a stiletto in her garter and a pearl-handled silver-plated derringer under the sequined silk in the hollow between her jutting breasts.

Yet at the same time Joe knew they were just trimmings. It was the man in black, their master, who was the deadly one, the kind of man you knew at a glance you couldn't touch and live. If without asking you merely laid a finger on his sleeve, no matter how lightly and respectfully, an ivory hand would move faster than thought and you'd be stabbed or shot. Or maybe just the touch would kill you, as if every black article of his clothing were charged from his ivory skin outwards with a high-voltage, high-amperage ivory electricity. Joe looked at the shadowed face again and decided he wouldn't care to try it.

For it was the eyes that were the most impressive feature. All great gamblers have dark-shadowed deep-set eyes. But this one's eyes were sunk so deep you couldn't even be sure you were getting a gleam of them. They were inscrutability incarnate. They were unfathomable. They were like black holes.

But all this didn't disappoint Joe one bit, though it did terrify him considerably. On the contrary, it made him exult. His first suspicion was completely confirmed and his hope spread into full flower.

This must be one of those really big gamblers who hit Ironmine only once a decade at most, come from the Big City on one of the river boats that ranged the watery dark like luxurious comets, spouting long thick tails of sparks from their sequoia-tall stacks with top foliage of curvy-snipped sheet iron.

Or like silver space-liners with dozens of jewel-flamed jets, their portholes atwinkle like ranks of marshaled asteroids.

For that matter, maybe some of those really big gamblers actually came from other planets where the nighttime pace was hotter and the sporting life a delirium of risk and delight.

Yes, this was the kind of man Joe had always yearned to pit his skill against. He felt *the power* begin to tingle in his rock-still fingers, just a little.

Joe lowered his gaze to the crap table. It was almost as wide as a man is tall, at least twice as long, unusually deep, and lined with black, not green, felt, so that it looked like a giant's coffin. There was something familiar about its shape which he couldn't place. Its bottom, though not its sides or ends, had a twinkling iridescence, as if it had been lightly sprinkled with very tiny diamonds. As Joe lowered his gaze all the way and looked directly down, his eyes barely over the table, he got the crazy notion that it went down all the way through the world, so that the diamonds were the stars on the other side, visible despite the sunlight there, just as Joe was always able to see the stars by day up the shaft of the mine he worked in, and so that if a cleaned-out gambler, dizzy with defeat, toppled forward into it, he'd fall forever, towards the bottom-most bottom, be it Hell or some black galaxy. Joe's thoughts swirled and he felt the cold, hard-fingered clutch of fear at his crotch. Someone was crooning beside him, "Come on, Big Dick."

Then the dice, which had meanwhile passed to the Big Mushroom immediately on his right, came to rest near the table's center, contradicting and wiping out Joe's vision. But instantly there was another oddity to absorb him. The ivory dice were large and unusually roundcornered with dark red spots that gleamed like real rubies, but the spots were arranged in such a way that each face looked like a miniature skull. For instance, the seven thrown just now, by which the Big Mushroom to his right had lost his point, which had been ten, consisted of a two with the spots evenly spaced towards one side, like eyes, instead of towards opposite corners, and of a five with the same red eyespots but a central red nose and two spots close together below that to make teeth.

The long, skinny, white-gloved arm of the dice-girl snaked out like an albino cobra and scooped up the dice and whisked them on to the rim of the table right in front of Joe. He inhaled silently, picked up a single chip from his table and started to lay it beside the dice, then realized that wasn't the way things were done here, and put it back. He would have liked to examine the chip more closely, though. It was curiously lightweight and pale tan, about the color of cream with a shot of coffee in it, and it had embossed on its surface a symbol he could feel, though not see. He didn't know what the symbol was, that would have taken more feeling. Yet its touch had been very good, setting the power tingling full blast in his shooting hand.

Joe looked casually yet swiftly at the faces around the table, not missing the Big Gambler across from him, and said quietly, "Roll a penny," meaning of course one pale chip, or a dollar.

There was a hiss of indignation from all the Big Mushrooms and the moonface of big-bellied Mr. Bones grew purple as he started forward to summon his bouncers.

The Big Gambler raised a black-satined forearm and sculptured hand, palm down. Instantly Mr. Bones froze and the hissing stopped faster than that of a meteor prick in self-sealing space steel. Then in a whispery, cultured voice, without the faintest hint of derision, the man in black said, "Get on him, gamblers."

Here, Joe thought, was a final confirmation of his suspicion, had it been needed. The really great gamblers were always perfect gentlemen and generous to the poor.

With only the tiny, respectful hint of a guffaw, one of the Big Mushrooms called to Joe, "You're faded."

Joe picked up the ruby-featured dice.

Now ever since he had first caught two eggs on one plate, won all the marbles in Ironmine, and juggled six alphabet blocks so they finally fell in a row on the rug spelling "Mother,"

Joe Slattermill had been almost incredibly deft at precision throwing. In the mine he could carom a rock off a wall of ore to crack a rat's skull fifty feet away in the dark and he sometimes amused himself by tossing little fragments of rock back into the holes from which they had fallen, so that they stuck there, perfectly fitted in, for at least a second. Sometimes, by fast tossing, he could fit seven or eight fragments into the hole from which they had fallen, like putting together a puzzle block. If he could ever have got into space, Joe would undoubtedly have been able to pilot six Moon-skimmers at once and do figure eights through Saturn's rings blindfolded.

Now the only real difference between precision-tossing rocks or alphabet blocks and dice is that you have to bounce the latter off the end wall of a crap table, and that just made it a more interesting test of skill for Joe.

Rattling the dice now, he felt the power in his fingers and palm as never before.

He made a swift low roll, so that the bones ended up exactly in front of the white-gloved dice-girl. His natural seven was made up, as he'd intended, of a four and a three. In red-spot features they were like the five, except that both had only one tooth and the three no nose. Sort of baby-faced skulls. He had won a penny—that is, a dollar.

"Roll two cents," said Joe Slattermill.

This time, for variety, he made his natural with an eleven. The six was like the five, except it had three teeth, the best-looking skull of the lot.

"Roll a nickel less one."

Two Big Mushrooms divided that bet with a covert smirk at each other.

Now Joe rolled a three and an ace. His point was four. The ace, with its single spot off center towards a side, still somehow looked like a skull—maybe of a Lilliputian Cyclops.

He took a while making his point, once absentmindedly rolling three successive tens the hard way. He wanted to watch the dice-girl scoop up the cubes. Each time it seemed to him that her snake-swift fingers went under the dice while they were still flat on the felt. Finally he decided it couldn't be an illusion. Although the dice couldn't penetrate the felt, her white-gloved fingers somehow could, dipping in a flash through the black, diamond-sparkling material as if it weren't there.

Right away the thought of a crap-table-size hole through the earth came back to Joe. This would mean that the dice were rolling and lying on a perfectly transparent flat surface, impenetrable for them but nothing else. Or maybe it was only the dice-girl's hands that could penetrate the surface, which would turn into a mere fantasy Joe's earlier vision of a cleaned-out gambler taking the Big Dive down that dreadful shaft, which made the deepest mine a mere pin dent.

Joe decided he had to know which was true. Unless absolutely unavoidable, he didn't want to take the chance of being troubled by vertigo at some crucial stage of the game.

He made a few more meaningless throws, from time to time crooning for realism, "Come on, Little Joe." Finally he settled on his plan. When he did at last make his point—the hard way, with two twos—he caromed the dice off the far corner so that they landed exactly in front of him. Then, after a minimum pause for his throw to be seen by the table, he shot his left hand down under the cubes, just a flicker ahead of the dice-girl's strike, and snatched them up.

Wow! Joe had never had a harder time in his life making his face and manner conceal what his body felt, not even when the wasp had stung him on the neck just as he had been for the first time putting his hand under the skirt of his prudish, fickle, demanding Wife-to-be. His fingers and the back of his hand were in as much agony as if he'd stuck them into a blast furnace. No wonder the dice-girl wore white gloves. They must be asbestos. And a good thing he hadn't used his shooting hand, he thought as he ruefully watched the blisters rise.

He remembered he'd been taught in school what Twenty-Mile Mine also demonstrated; that the earth was fearfully hot under its crust. The crap-table-size hole must pipe up that heat, so that any gambler taking the Big Dive would fry before he'd fallen a furlong and come out less than a cinder in China.

As if his blistered hand weren't bad enough, the Big Mushrooms were all hissing at him again and Mr. Bones had purpled once more and was opening his melon-size mouth to shout for his bouncers.

Once again a lift of the Big Gambler's hand saved Joe. The whispery, gentle voice called, "Tell him, Mr. Bones."

The latter roared towards Joe, "No gambler may pick up the dice he or any other gambler has shot. Only my dice-girl may do that. Rule of the house!"

Joe snapped Mr. Bones the barest nod. He said coolly, "Rolling a dime less two," and when that still peewee bet was covered, he shot Phoebe for his point and then fooled around for quite a while, throwing anything but a five or a seven, until the throbbing in his left hand should fade and all his nerves feel rock-solid again. There had never been the slightest alteration in the power in his right hand; he felt that strong as ever, or stronger.

Midway of this interlude, the Big Gambler bowed slightly but respectfully towards Joe, hooding unfathomable eye sockets, before turning around to take a long black cigarette from his prettiest and evilest-looking sporting girl. Courtesy in the smallest matters, Joe thought, another mark of the master devotee of games of chance. The Big Gambler sure had himself a flash crew, all right, though in idly looking them over again as he rolled, Joe noted one bummer towards the back who didn't fit in—a raggedly elegant chap with the elflocked hair and staring eyes and TB-spotted cheeks of a poet.

As he watched the smoke trickling up from under the black slouch hat, he decided the either the lights across the table had dimmed or else the Big Gambler's complexion was yet a shade darker than he'd thought at first. Or it might even be—wild fantasy—that the Big Gambler's skin was slowly darkening tonight, like a meerschaum pipe being smoked a mile a second. That was almost funny to think of—there was enough heat in this place, all right, to darken meerschaum, as Joe knew from sad experience, but so far as he was aware it was all under the table.

None of Joe's thoughts, either familiar or admiring, about the Big Gambler decreased in the slightest degree his certainty of the supreme menace of the man in black and his conviction that it would be death to touch him. And if any doubts had stirred in Joe's mind, they would have been squelched by the chilling incident which next occurred.

The Big Gambler had just taken into his arms his prettiest-evilest sporting girl and was running an aristocratic hand across her haunch with perfect gentility, when the poet chap, green-eyed from jealousy and lovesickness, came leaping forward like a wildcat and aimed a long gleaming dagger at the black satin back.

Joe couldn't see how the blow could miss, but without taking his genteel right hand off the sporting girl's plush rear end, the Big Gambler shot out his left arm like a steel spring straightening. Joe couldn't tell whether he stabbed the poet chap in the throat, or judo-chopped him there, or gave him the Martian double-finger, or just touched him, but anyhow the fellow stopped as dead as if he'd been shot by a silent elephant gun or an invisible ray pistol and he slammed down on the floor. A couple of darkies came running up to drag off the body and nobody paid the least attention, such episodes apparently being taken for granted at The Boneyard.

It gave Joe quite a turn and he almost shot Phoebe before he intended to.

But by now the waves of pain had stopped running up his left arm and his nerves were like metal-wrapped new guitar strings, so three rolls later he shot a five, making his point, and set in to clean out the table.

He rolled nine successive naturals, seven sevens and two elevens, pyramiding his first wager of a single chip to a stake of over four thousand dollars. None of the Big Mushrooms had dropped out yet, but some of them were beginning to look worried and a couple were sweating. The Big Gambler still hadn't covered any part of Joe's bets, but he seemed to be following the play with interest from the cavernous depths of his eye sockets.

Then Joe got a devilish thought. Nobody could beat him tonight, he knew, but if he held on to the dice until the table was cleaned out, he'd never get a chance to see the Big Gambler exercise *his* skill, and he was truly curious about that. Besides, he thought, he ought to return courtesy for courtesy and have a crack at being a gentleman himself.

"Pulling out forty-one dollars less a nickel," he announced. "Rolling a penny."

This time there wasn't any hissing and Mr. Bones's moon-face didn't cloud over. But Joe was conscious that the Big Gambler was staring at him disappointedly, or sorrowfully, or maybe just speculatively.

Joe immediately crapped out by throwing boxcars, rather pleased to see the two best-looking tiny skulls grinning ruby-toothed side by side, and the dice passed to the Big Mushroom on his left.

"Knew when his streak was over," he heard another Big Mushroom mutter with grudging admiration.

The play worked rather rapidly around the table, nobody getting very hot and the stakes never more than medium high. "Shoot a fin." "Rolling a sawbuck." "An Andrew Jackson." "Rolling thirty bucks." Now and then Joe covered part of a bet, winning more than he lost. He had over seven thousand dollars, real money, before the bones got around to the Big Gambler.

That one held the dice for a long moment on his statue-steady palm while he looked at them reflectively, though not the hint of a furrow appeared in his almost brownish forehead down which never a bead of sweat trickled. He murmured, "Rolling a double sawbuck," and when he had been faded, he closed his fingers, lightly rattled the cubes—the sound was like big seeds inside a small gourd only half dry—and negligently cast the dice towards the end of the table.

It was a throw like none Joe had ever seen before at any crap table. The dice travelled flat through the air without turning over, struck the exact juncture of the table's end and bottom, and stopped there dead, showing a natural seven.

Joe was distinctly disappointed. On one of his own throws he was used to calculating something like, "Launch three-up, five north, two and a half rolls in the air, hit on the six-five-three corner, three-quarter roll and a one-quarter side-twist right, hit end on the one-two edge, one-half reverse roll and three-quarter side-twist left, land on five face, roll over twice, come up two," and that would be for just one of the dice, and a really commonplace throw, without extra bounces.

By comparison, the technique of the Big Gambler had been ridiculously, abysmally, horrifyingly simple. Joe could have duplicated it with the greatest ease, of course. It was no more than an elementary form of his old pastime of throwing fallen rocks back into their holes. But Joe had never once thought of pulling such a babyish trick at the crap table. It would make the whole thing too easy and destroy the beauty of the game.

Another reason Joe had never used the trick was that he'd never dreamed he'd be able to get away with it. By all the rules he'd ever heard of, it was a most questionable throw. There was the possibility that one or the other die hadn't completely reached the end of the table, or lay a wee bit cocked against the end. Besides, he reminded himself, weren't both dice supposed to rebound off the end, if only for a fraction of an inch?

However, as far as Joe's very sharp eyes could see, both dice lay perfectly flat and sprang up against the end wall. Moreover, everyone else at the table seemed to accept the throw, the dice-girl had scooped up the cubes, and the Big Mushrooms who had faded the man in black were paying off. As far as the rebound business went, well, The Boneyard appeared to put a slightly different interpretation on that rule, and Joe believed in never questioning House Rules except in dire extremity—

both his Mother and Wife had long since taught him it was the least troublesome way.

Besides, there hadn't been any of his own money riding on that roll.

In a voice like wind through Cypress Hollow or on Mars, the Big Gambler announced, "Roll a century." It was the biggest bet yet tonight, ten thousand dollars, and the way the Big Gambler said it made it seem something more than that. A hush fell on The Boneyard, they put the mutes on the jazz horns, the croupiers' calls became more confidential, the cards fell softlier, even the roulette balls seemed to be trying to make less noise as they rattled into their cells. The crowd around the Number One Crap Table quietly thickened. The Big Gambler's flash boys and girls formed a double semicircle around him, ensuring him lots of elbow room.

That century bet, Joe realized, was thirty bucks more than his own entire pile. Three or four of the Big Mushrooms had to signal each other before they'd agreed how to fade it.

The Big Gambler shot another natural seven with exactly the same flat, stop-dead throw.

He bet another century and did it again.

And again.

And again.

Joe was getting mighty concerned and pretty indignant too. It seemed unjust that the Big Gambler should be winning such huge bets with such machinelike, utterly unromantic rolls. Why, you couldn't even call them rolls, the dice never turned over an iota, in the air or after. It was the sort of thing you'd expect from a robot, and a very dully programmed robot at that. Joe hadn't risked any of his own chips fading the Big Gambler, of course, but if things went on like this he'd have to. Two of the Big Mushrooms had already retired sweatingly from the table, confessing defeat, and no one had taken their places. Pretty soon there'd be a bet the remaining Big Mushrooms couldn't entirely cover between them, and then he'd have to risk some of his own chips or else pull put of the game himself—and he couldn't do that, not with the power surging in his right hand like chained lightning.

Joe waited and waited for someone else to question one of the Big Gambler's shots, but no one did. He realized that, despite his efforts to look imperturbable, his face was slowly reddening.

With a little lift of his left hand, the Big Gambler stopped the dice-girl as she was about to snatch at the cubes. The eyes that were like black wells directed themselves at Joe, who forced himself to look back into them steadily. He still couldn't catch the faintest gleam in them. All at once he felt the lightest touch-on-neck of a dreadful suspicion.

With the utmost civility and amiability, the Big Gambler whispered, "I believe that the fine shooter across from me has doubts about the validity of my last throw, though he is too much of a gentleman to voice them. Lottie, the card test."

The wraith-tall, ivory dice-girl plucked a playing card from below the table and with a venomous flash of her little white teeth spun it low across the table through the air at Joe. He caught the whirling pasteboard and examined it briefly. It was the thinnest, stiffest, flattest, shiniest playing card Joe had ever handled. It was also the Joker, if that meant anything. He spun it back lazily into her hand and she slid it very gently, letting it descend by its own weight, down the end wall against which the two dice lay. It came to rest in the tiny hollow their rounded edges made against the black felt. She deftly moved it about without force, demonstrating that there was no space between either of the cubes and the table's end at any point.

"Satisfied?" the Big Gambler asked. Rather against his will Joe nodded. The Big Gambler bowed to him. The dice-girl smirked her short, thin lips and drew herself up, flaunting her white china-doorknob breasts at Joe.

Casually, almost with an air of boredom, the Big Gambler

returned to his routine of shooting a century and making a natural seven. The Big Mushrooms wilted fast and one by one tottered away from the table. A particularly pink-faced Toadstool was brought extra cash by a gasping runner, but it was no help, he only lost the additional centuries. While the stacks of pale and black chips beside the Big Gambler grew skyscraper-tall.

Joe got more and more furious and frightened. He watched like a hawk or spy satellite the dice nesting against the end wall, but never could spot justification for calling for another card test, or nerve himself to question the House Rules at this late date. It was maddening, in fact insanitizing, to know that if only he could get the cubes once more he could shoot circles around that black pillar of sporting aristocracy. He damned himself a googolplex of ways for the idiotic, conceited, suicidal impulse that had led him to let go of the bones when he'd had them.

To make matters worse, the Big Gambler had taken to gazing steadily at Joe with those eyes like coal mines. Now he made three rolls running without even glancing at the dice or the end wall, as far as Joe could tell. Why, he was getting as bad as Joe's Wife or Mother—watching, watching, watching Joe.

But the constant staring of those eyes that were not eyes was mostly throwing a terrific scare into him. Supernatural terror added itself to his certainty of the dead lines of the Big Gambler. Just who, Joe kept asking himself, had he got into a game with tonight? There was curiosity and there was dread—a dreadful curiosity as strong as his desire to get the bones and win. His hair rose and he was all over goose bumps, though the power was still pulsing in his hand like a braked locomotive or a rocket wanting to lift from the pad.

At the same time the Big Gambler stayed just that—a black satin-coated, slouch-hatted elegance, suave, courtly, lethal. In fact, almost the worst thing about the spot Joe found himself in was that, after admiring the Big Gambler's perfect sportsmanship all night, he must now be disenchanted by his machinelike throwing and try to catch him out on any technicality he could.

The remorseless mowing down of the Big Mushrooms went on. The empty spaces outnumbered the Toadstools. Soon there were only three left.

The Boneyard had grown still as Cypress Hollow or the Moon. The jazz had stopped and the gay laughter and the shuffle of feet and the squeak of goosed girls and the clink of drinks and coins. Everybody seemed to be gathered around the Number One Crap Table, rank on silent rank.

Joe was racked by watchfulness, sense of injustice, selfcontempt, wild hopes, curiosity and dread. Especially the last two.

The complexion of the Big Gambler, as much as you could see of it, continued to darken. For one wild moment Joe found himself wondering if he'd got into a game with a nigger, maybe a witchcraft-drenched Voodoo Man whose white makeup was wearing off.

Pretty soon there came a century wager which the two remaining Big Mushrooms couldn't fade between them. Joe had to make up a sawbuck from his miserably tiny pile or get out of the game. After a moment's agonizing hesitation, he did the former.

And lost his ten.

The two Big Mushrooms reeled back into the hushed crowd.

Pit-black eyes bored into Joe. A whisper: "Rolling your pile."

Joe felt well up in him the shameful impulse to confess himself licked and run home. At least his six thousand dollars would make a hit with his Wife and Ma.

But he just couldn't bear to think of the crowd's laughter, or the thought of living with himself knowing that he'd had a final chance, however slim, to challenge the Big Gambler and passed it up.

He nodded.

The Big Gambler shot. Joe leaned out over and down the table, forgetting his vertigo, as he followed the throw with eagle or space-telescope eyes.

"Satisfied?"

Joe knew he ought to say, "Yes," and slink off with head held as high as he could manage. It was the gentlemanly thing to do. But then he reminded himself that he wasn't a gentleman, but just a dirty, working-stiff miner with a talent for precision hurling.

He also knew that it was probably very dangerous for him to say anything but, "Yes," surrounded as he was by enemies and strangers. But then he asked himself what right had he, a miserable, mortal, homebound failure, to worry about danger.

Besides, one of the ruby-grinning dice looked just the tiniest hair out of line with the other.

It was the biggest effort yet of Joe's life, but he swallowed and managed to say, "No. Lottie, the card test."

The dice-girl fairly snarled and reared up and back as if she were going to spit in his eyes, and Joe had a feeling her spit was cobra venom. But the Big Gambler lifted a finger at her in reproof and she skimmed the card at Joe, yet so low and viciously that it disappeared under the black felt for an instant before flying up into Joe's hand.

It was hot to the touch and singed a pale brown all over, though otherwise unimpaired. Joe gulped and spun it back high.

Sneering poisoned daggers at him, Lottie let it glide down the end wall...and after a moment's hesitation, it slithered behind the die Joe had suspected.

A bow and then the whisper: "You have sharp eyes, sir. Undoubtedly that die failed to reach the wall. My sincerest apologies and...your dice, sir."

Seeing the cubes sitting on the black rim in front of him almost gave Joe apoplexy. All the feelings racking him, including his curiosity, rose to an almost unbelievable pitch of intensity, and when he'd said, "Rolling my pile," and the Big Gambler had replied, "You're faded," he yielded to an uncontrollable impulse and cast the two dice straight at the Big Gambler's ungleaming, midnight eyes.

They went right through into the Big Gambler's skull and bounced around inside there, rattling like big seeds in a big gourd not quite yet dry.

Throwing out a hand, palm back, to either side, to indicate that none of his boys or girls or anyone else must make a reprisal on Joe, the Big Gambler dryly gargled the two cubical bones, then spat them out so that they landed in the center of the table, the one die flat, the other leaning against it.

"Cocked dice, sir," he whispered as graciously as if no indignity whatever had been done him. "Roll again."

Joe shook the dice reflectively, getting over the shock. After a little bit he decided that though he could now guess the Big Gambler's real name, he'd still give him a run for his money.

A little corner of Joe's mind wondered how a live skeleton hung together. Did the bones still have gristle and thews, were they wired, was it done with force-fields, or was each bone a calcium magnet clinging to the next?—this tying in somehow with the generation of the deadly ivory electricity.

In the great hush of The Boneyard, someone cleared his throat, a Scarlet Woman tittered hysterically, a coin fell from the nakedest change-girl's tray with a golden clink and rolled musically across the floor.

"Silence," the Big Gambler commanded and in a movement almost too fast to follow whipped a hand inside the bosom of his coat and out to the crap table's rim in front of him. A short-barrelled silver revolver lay softly gleaming there. "Next creature, from the humblest nigger night-girl to you, Mr. Bones, who utters a sound while my worthy opponent rolls, gets a bullet in the head."

Joe gave him a courtly bow back, it felt funny, and then decided to start his run with a natural seven made up of an ace and a six. He rolled and this time the Big Gambler, judging from the movements of his skull, closely followed the course of the cubes with his eyes that weren't there.

The dice landed, rolled over, and lay still. Incredulously, Joe realized that for the first time in his crap-shooting life he'd made a mistake. Or else there was a power in the Big Gambler's gaze greater than that in his own right hand. The six cube had come down okay, but the ace had taken an extra half roll and come down six too.

"End of the game," Mr. Bones boomed sepulchrally.

The Big Gambler raised a brown skeletal hand. "Not necessarily," he whispered. His black eyepits aimed themselves at Joe like the mouths of siege guns. "Joe Slattermill, you still have something of value to wager, if you wish. Your life."

At that a giggling and a hysterical tittering and a guffawing and a braying and a shrieking burst uncontrollably out of the whole Boneyard. Mr. Bones summed up the sentiments when he bellowed over the rest of the racket. "Now what use or value is there in the life of a bummer like Joe Slattermill? Not two cents, ordinary money."

The Big Gambler laid a hand on the revolver gleaming before him and all the laughter died.

"I have a use for it," the Big Gambler whispered. "Joe Slattermill, on my part I will venture all my winnings of tonight, and throw in the world and everything in it for a side bet. You will wager your life, and on the side your soul. You to roll the dice. What's your pleasure?"

Joe Slattermill quailed, but then the drama of the situation took hold of him. He thought it over and realized he certainly wasn't going to give up being stage center in a spectacle like this to go home broke to his Wife and Mother and decaying House and the dispirited Mr. Guts. Maybe, he told himself encouragingly, there wasn't a power in the Big Gambler's gaze, maybe Joe had just made his one and only crap-shooting error. Besides, he was more inclined to accept Mr. Bones's assessment of the value of his life than the Big Gambler's.

"It's a bet," he said.

"Lottie, give him the dice."

Joe concentrated his mind as never before, the power tingled triumphantly in his hand, and he made his throw.

The dice never hit the felt. They went swooping down, then up, in a crazy curve far out over the end of the table, and then came streaking back like tiny red-glinting meteors towards the face of the Big Gambler, where they suddenly nested and hung in his black eye sockets, each with the single red gleam of an ace showing.

Snake eyes.

The whisper, as those red-glinting dice-eyes stared mockingly at him: "Joe Slattermill, you've crapped out."

Using thumb and middle finger—or bone rather—of either hand, the Big Gambler removed the dice from his eye sockets and dropped them in Lottie's white-gloved hand.

"Yes, you've crapped out, Joe Slattermill," he went on tranquilly. "And now you can shoot yourself"—he touched the silver gun—"or cut your throat"—he whipped a gold-handled bowie knife out of his coat and laid it beside the revolver—"or poison yourself"—the two weapons were joined by a small black bottle with white skull and crossbones on it—"or Miss Flossie here can kiss you to death." He drew forward beside him his prettiest, evilest-looking sporting girl. She preened herself and flounced her short violet skirt and gave Joe a provocative, hungry look, lifting her carmine upper lip to show her long white canines.

"Or else," the Big Gambler added, nodding significantly towards the black-bottomed crap table, "you can take the Big Dive."

Joe said evenly, "I'll take the Big Dive."

He put his right foot on his empty chip table, his left on the black rim, fell forward...and suddenly kicking off from the rim, launched himself in a tiger spring straight across the crap table at the Big Gambler's throat, solacing himself with the thought that certainly the poet chap hadn't seemed to suffer long.

As he flashed across the exact center of the table he got an instant photograph of what really lay below, but his brain had no time to develop that snapshot, for the next instant he was ploughing into the Big Gambler.

Stiffened brown palm edge caught him in the temple with a lightning-like judo chop...and the brown fingers or bones flew all apart like puff paste. Joe's left hand went through the Big Gambler's chest as if there were nothing there but black satin coat, while his right hand, straight-armedly clawing at the slouch-hatted skull, crunched it to pieces. Next instant Joe was sprawled on the floor with some black clothes and brown fragments.

He was on his feet in a flash and snatching at the Big Gambler's tall stacks. He had time for one left-handed grab. He couldn't see any gold or silver or any black chips, so he stuffed his left pants pocket with a handful of the pale chips and ran.

Then the whole population of The Boneyard was on him and after him. Teeth, knives and brass knuckles flashed. He was punched, clawed, kicked, tripped and stamped on with spike heels. A gold-plated trumpet with a bloodshot-eyed black face behind it bopped him on the head. He got a white flash of the golden dice-girl and made a grab for her, but she got away. Someone tried to mash a lighted cigar in his eye. Lottie, writhing and flailing like a white boa constrictor, almost got a simultaneous stranglehold and scissors on him. From a squat wide-mouth bottle Flossie, snarling like a feline fiend, threw what smelled like acid past his face. Mr. Bones peppered shots around him from the silver revolver. He was stabbed at, gouged, rabbit-punched, scragmauled, slugged, kneed, bitten, bear-hugged, butted, beaten and had his toes trampled.

But somehow none of the blows or grabs had much real force. It was like fighting ghosts. In the end it turned out that the whole population of The Boneyard, working together, had just a little more strength than Joe. He felt himself being lifted by a multitude of hands and pitched out through the swinging doors so that he thudded down on his rear end on the board sidewalk. Even that didn't hurt much. It was more like a kick of encouragement.

He took a deep breath and felt himself over and worked his bones. He didn't seem to have suffered any serious damage. He stood up and looked around. The Boneyard was dark and silent as the grave, or the planet Pluto, or all the rest of Ironmine. As his eyes got accustomed to the starlight and occasional roving spaceship-gleam, he saw a padlocked sheet-iron door where the swinging ones had been.

He found he was chewing on something crusty that he'd somehow carried in his right hand all the way through the final fracas. Mighty tasty, like the bread his Wife baked for best cutomers. At that instant his brain developed the photograph it had taken when he had glanced down as he flashed across the center of the crap table. It was a thin wall of flames moving sideways across the table and just beyond the flames the faces of his Wife, Mother, and Mr. Guts, all looking very surprised. He realized that what he was chewing was a fragment of the Big Gambler's skull, and he remembered the shape of the three loaves his Wife had started to bake when he left the House. And he understood the magic she'd made to let him get a little ways away and feel half a man, and then come diving home with his fingers burned.

He spat out what was in his mouth and pegged the rest of the bit of giant-popover skull across the street.

He fished in his left pocket. Most of the pale poker chips had been mashed in the fight, but he found a whole one and explored its surface with his fingertips. The symbol embossed on it was a cross. He lifted it to his lips and took a bite. It tasted delicate, but delicious. He ate it and felt his strength revive. He patted his bulging left pocket. At least he'd started out well provisioned.

Then he turned and headed straight for home, but he took the long way, around the world.

The Ones Who Walk Away from Omelas

by URSULA K. LE GUIN

WITH A clamor of bells that set the swallows soaring, the Festival of Summer came to the city Omelas, bright-towered by the sea. The rigging of the boats in harbor sparkled with flags. In the streets between houses with red roofs and painted walls, between old moss-grown gardens and under avenues of trees, past great parks and public buildings, processions moved. Some were decorous: old people in long stiff robes of mauve and gray, grave master workmen, quiet, merry women carrying their babies and chatting as they walked. In other streets the music beat faster, a shimmering of gong and tambourine, and the people went dancing, the procession was a dance. Children dodged in and out, their high calls rising like the swallows' crossing flights over the music and the singing. All the processions wound towards the north side of the city, where on the great water-meadow called the Green Fields boys and girls, naked in the bright air, with mud-stained feet and ankles and long, lithe arms, exercised their restive horses before the race. The horses wore no gear at all but a halter without bit. Their manes were braided with streamers of silver, gold, and green. They flared their nostrils and pranced and boasted to one another; they were vastly excited, the horse being the only animal who has adopted our ceremonies as his own. Far off to the north and west the mountains stood up half encircling Omelas on her bay. The air of morning was so clear that the snow still crowning the Eighteen Peaks burned with white-gold fire across the miles of sunlit air, under the dark blue of the sky. There was just enough wind to make the banners that marked the racecourse snap and flutter now and then. In the silence of the broad green meadows one could hear the music winding through the city streets, farther and nearer and ever approaching, a cheerful faint sweetness of the air that from time to time trembled and gathered together and broke out into the great joyous clanging of the bells.

Joyous! How is one to tell about joy! How describe the citizens of Omelas?

They were not simple folk, you see, though they were happy. But we do not say the words of cheer much any more. All smiles have become archaic. Given a description such as this one tends to make certain assumptions. Given a description such as this one tends to look next for the King, mounted on a splendid stallion and surrounded by his noble knights, or perhaps in a golden litter borne by great-muscled slaves. They were not barbarians. I do not know the rules and laws of their society, but I suspect that they were singularly few. As they did without monarchy and slavery, so they also got on without the stock exchange, the advertisement, the secret police, and the bomb. Yet I repeat that these were not simple folk, not dulcet shepherds, noble savages, bland utopians. They were not less complex than us. The trouble is that we have a bad habit, encouraged by pedants and sophisticates, of considering happiness as something rather stupid. Only pain is intellectual, only evil interesting. This is the treason of the artist: a refusal to admit the banality of evil and the terrible boredom of pain. If you can't lick 'em, join 'em. If it hurts, repeat it. But to praise despair is to condemn delight, to embrace violence is to lose hold of everything else. We have almost lost hold; we can no longer describe a happy man, nor make any celebration of joy. How can I tell you about the people of Omelas? They were not naïve and happy children—though their children were, in fact, happy. They were mature, intelligent, passionate adults whose lives were not wretched. O miracle! but I wish I could describe it better. I wish I could convince you. Omelas sounds in my words like a city in a fairy tale, long ago and far away, once upon a time. Perhaps it would be best if you imagined it as your own fancy bids, assuming it will rise to the occasion, for certainly I cannot suit you all. For instance, how about technology? I think that there would be no cars or helicopters in and above the streets; this follows from the fact that the people of Omelas are happy people. Happiness is based on a just discrimination of what is necessary, what is neither necessary nor destructive, and what is destructive. In the middle category, however—that of the unnecessary but undestructive, that of comfort, luxury, exuberance, etc.—they could perfectly well have central heating, subway trains, washing machines, and all kinds of marvelous devices not yet invented here, floating light-sources, fuelless power, a cure for the common cold. Or they could have none of that: it doesn't matter. As you like it. I incline to think that people from towns up and down the coast have been coming in to Omelas during the last days before the Festival on very fast little trains and double-decked trams, and that the train station of Omelas is actually the handsomest building in town, though plainer than the magnificent Farmers' Market. But even granted trains, I fear that Omelas so far strikes some of you as goody-goody. Smiles, bells, parades, horses, bleh. If so, please add an orgy. If an orgy would help, don't hesitate. Let us not, however, have temples from which issue beautiful nude priests and priestesses already half in ecstasy and ready to copulate with any man or woman, lover or stranger, who desires union with the deep godhead of the blood, although that was my first idea. But really it would be better not to have any temples in Omelas—at least, not manned temples. Religion yes, clergy no. Surely the beautiful nudes can just wander about, offering themselves like divine soufflés to the hunger of the needy and the rapture of the flesh. Let them join the processions. Let tambourines be struck above the copulations, and the glory of desire be proclaimed upon the gongs, and (a not unimportant point) let the offspring of these delightful rituals be beloved and looked after by all. One thing I know there is none of in Omelas is guilt. But what else should there be? I thought at first there were no drugs, but that is puritanical. For those who like it, the faint insistent sweetness of *drooz* may perfume the ways of the city, *drooz* which first brings a great lightness and brilliance to the mind and limbs, and then after some hours a dreamy languor, and wonderful visions at last of the very arcana and inmost secrets of the Universe, as well as exciting the pleasure of sex beyond all belief; and it is not habit-forming. For more modest tastes I think there ought to be beer. What else, what else belongs in the joyous city? The sense of victory, surely, the celebration of courage. But as we did without clergy, let us do without soldiers. The joy built upon successful slaughter is not the right kind of joy; it will not do; it is fearful and it is trivial. A boundless and generous contentment, a magnanimous triumph felt not against some outer enemy but in communion with the finest and fairest in the souls of all men everywhere and the splendor of the world's summer: this what swells the hearts of the people of Omelas, and the victory they celebrate is that of life. I really don't think many of them need to take *drooz*.

Most of the processions have reached the Green Fields by now. A marvelous smell of cooking goes forth from the red and blue tents of the provisioners. The faces of small children are amiably sticky; in the benign gray beard of a man a couple of crumbs of rich pastry are entangled. The youths and girls have mounted their horses and are beginning to group around the starting line of the course. An old woman, small, fat, and laughing, is passing out flowers from a basket, and tall young men wear her flowers in their shining hair. A child of nine or ten sits at the edge of the crowd, alone, playing on a wooden flute. People pause to listen, and they smile, but they do not speak to him, for he never ceases playing and never sees them, his dark eyes wholly rapt in the sweet, thin magic of the tune.

He finishes, and slowly lowers his hands holding the wooden flute.

As if that little private silence were the signal, all at once a trumpet sounds from the pavilion near the starting line: imperious, melancholy, piercing. The horses rear on their slender legs, and some of them neigh in answer. Sober-faced, the young riders stroke the horses' necks and soothe them, whispering, "Quiet, quiet, there my beauty, my hope...." They begin to form in rank along the starting line. The crowds along the racecourse are like a field of grass and flowers in the wind. The Festival of Summer has begun.

Do you believe? Do you accept the festival, the city, the joy? No? Then let me describe one more thing.

In a basement under one of the beautiful public buildings of Omelas, or perhaps in the cellar of one of its spacious private homes, there is a room. It has one locked door, and no window. A little light seeps in dustily between cracks in the boards, secondhand from a cobwebbed window somewhere across the cellar. In one corner of the little room a couple of mops, with stiff, clotted, foul-smelling heads, stand near a rusty bucket. The floor is dirt, a little damp to the touch, as cellar dirt usually is. The room is about three paces long and two wide: a mere broom closet or disused tool room. In the room a child is sitting. It could be a boy or a girl. It looks about six, but actually is nearly ten. It is feebleminded. Perhaps it was born defective, or perhaps it has become imbecile through fear, malnutrition, and neglect. It picks its nose and occasionally fumbles vaguely with its toes or genitals, as it sits hunched in the corner farthest from the bucket and the two mops. It is afraid of the mops. It finds them horrible. It shuts its eyes, but it knows the mops are still standing there; and the door is locked; and nobody will come. The door is always locked; and nobody ever comes, except that sometimes—the child has no understanding of time or interval—sometimes the door rattles terribly and opens, and a person, or several people, are there. One of them may come in and kick the child to make it stand up. The others never come close, but peer in at it with frightened, disgusted eyes. The food bowl and the water jug are hastily filled, the door is locked, the eyes disappear. The people at the door never say anything, but the child, who has not always lived in the tool room, and can remember sunlight and its mother's voice, sometimes speaks. "I will be good," it says. "Please let me out. I will be good!" They never answer. The child used to scream for help at night, and cry a good deal, but now it only makes a kind of whining, "Eh-haa, eh-haa," and it speaks less and less often. It is so thin there are no calves to its legs; its belly protrudes; it lives on a half-bowl of corn meal and grease a day. It is naked. Its buttocks and thighs are a mass of festered sores, as it sits in its own excrement continually.

They all know it is there, all the people of Omelas. Some of them have come to see it, others are content merely to know it is there. They all know that it has to be there. Some of them understand why, and some do not, but they all understand that their happiness, the beauty of their city, the tenderness of their friendships, the health of their children, the wisdom of their scholars, the skill of their makers, even the abundance of their harvest and the kindly weathers of their skies, depend wholly on this child's abominable misery.

This is usually explained to children when they are between eight and twelve, whenever they seem capable of understanding; and most of those who come to see the child are young people, though often enough an adult comes, or comes back, to see the child. No matter how well the matter has been explained to them, these young spectators are always shocked and sickened at the sight. They feel disgust, which they had thought themselves superior to. They feel anger, outrage, impotence, despite all the explanations. They would like to do something for the child. But there is nothing they can do. If the child were brought up into the sunlight out of that vile place, if it were cleaned and fed and comforted, that would be a good thing, indeed; but if it were done, in that day and hour all the prosperity and beauty and delight of Omelas would wither and be destroyed. Those are the terms. To exchange all the goodness and grace of every life in Omelas for that single, small improvement: to throw away the happiness of thousands for the chance of the happiness of one: that would be to let guilt within the walls indeed.

The terms are strict and absolute; there may not even be a kind word spoken to the child.

Often the young people go home in tears, or in a tearless rage, when they have seen the child and faced this terrible paradox. They may brood over it for weeks or years. But as time goes on they begin to realize that even if the child could be released, it would not get much good of its freedom: a little vague pleasure of warmth and food, no doubt, but little more. It is too degraded and imbecile to know any real joy. It has been afraid too long ever to be free of fear. Its habits are too uncouth for it to respond to humane treatment. Indeed, after so long it would probably be wretched without walls about it to protect it, and darkness for its eyes, and its own excrement to sit in. Their tears at the bitter injustice dry when they begin to perceive the terrible justice of reality, and to accept it. Yet it is their tears and anger, the trying of their generosity and the acceptance of their helplessness, which are perhaps the true source of the splendor of their lives. Theirs is no vapid, irresponsible happiness. They know that they, like the child, are not free. They know compassion. It is the existence of the child, and their knowledge of its existence, that makes possible the nobility of their architecture, the poignancy of their music, the profundity of their science. It is because of the child that they are so gentle with children. They know that if the wretched ones were not there sniveling in the dark, the other one, the flute-player, could make no joyful music as the young riders line up in their beauty for the race in the sunlight of the first morning of summer.

Now do you believe in them? Are they not more credible? But there is one more thing to tell, and this is quite incredible.

At times one of the adolescent girls or boys who go to see the child does not go home to weep or rage, does not, in fact, go home at all. Sometimes also a man or woman much older falls silent for a day or two, and then leaves home. These people go out into the street, and walk down the street alone. They keep walking, and walk straight out of the city of Omelas, through the beautiful gates. They keep walking across the farmlands of Omelas. Each one goes alone, youth or girl, man or woman. Night falls; the traveler must pass down village streets, between the houses with yellow-lit windows, and on out into the darkness of the fields. Each alone, they go west or north, towards the mountains. They go on. They leave Omelas, they walk ahead into the darkness, and they do not come back. The place they go towards is a place even less imaginable to most of us than the city of happiness. I cannot describe it at all. It is possible that it does not exist. But they seem to know where they are going, the ones who walk away from Omelas.